The latest novel featuring Lieutenant Eve Dallas from #1 New York Times bestselling author J. D. Robb.

BROTHERHOOD IN DEATH

Sometimes "brotherhood" is just another word for "conspiracy" . . .

Just as Dennis Mira is about to confront his cousin Edward about selling the SoHo brownstone that belonged to their grandfather, he gets a shock: Edward is in front of him, bruised and bloody . . . and then everything goes black.

When Dennis comes to, Edward is gone. Luckily Dennis's wife is a top profiler for the NYPSD—and a close colleague of Lieutenant Eve Dallas. Now Eve is determined to uncover the secrets of Edward Mira and learn what enemies he may have made in his long career as a lawyer, judge, and senator. A badge and a billionaire husband can get you access to places others can't go, and Eve intends to shine some light on the dirty deals and dark motives behind the disappearance of a powerful man, the family discord over a multimillion-dollar piece of real estate . . . and a new case that no one saw coming.

"Robb is a virtuoso."   —*Seattle Post-Intelligencer*

Anthologies

SILENT NIGHT
(with Susan Plunkett, Dee Holmes, and Claire Cross)

OUT OF THIS WORLD
(with Laurell K. Hamilton, Susan Krinard, and Maggie Shayne)

REMEMBER WHEN
(with Nora Roberts)

BUMP IN THE NIGHT
(with Mary Blayney, Ruth Ryan Langan, and Mary Kay McComas)

DEAD OF NIGHT
(with Mary Blayney, Ruth Ryan Langan, and Mary Kay McComas)

THREE IN DEATH

SUITE 606
(with Mary Blayney, Ruth Ryan Langan, and Mary Kay McComas)

IN DEATH

THE LOST
(with Patricia Gaffney, Mary Blayney, and Ruth Ryan Langan)

THE OTHER SIDE
*(with Mary Blayney, Patricia Gaffney, Ruth Ryan Langan,
and Mary Kay McComas)*

TIME OF DEATH

THE UNQUIET
*(with Mary Blayney, Patricia Gaffney, Ruth Ryan Langan,
and Mary Kay McComas)*

MIRROR, MIRROR
*(with Mary Blayney, Elaine Fox, Mary Kay McComas,
and R. C. Ryan)*

DOWN THE RABBIT HOLE
*(with Mary Blayney, Elaine Fox, Mary Kay McComas,
and R. C. Ryan)*

BROTHERHOOD IN DEATH

J. D. Robb

BERKLEY BOOKS, NEW YORK

BERKLEY

An imprint of Penguin Random House LLC
375 Hudson Street, New York, New York 10014

BROTHERHOOD IN DEATH

A Berkley Book / published by arrangement with the author

ISBN: 9780425279007

PUBLISHING HISTORY
Berkley hardcover edition / February 2016
Berkley mass-market edition / August 2016

PRINTED IN THE UNITED STATES OF AMERICA

10 9 8 7 6 5 4 3 2 1

Cover art: *Yale University buildings* © f11photo/Shutterstock;
Lieutenant badge © Stephen Mulcahey/Shutterstock; *Chrysler building*
by GG Cornell; All other photos provided by George Cornell.
Cover design by George Cornell.

Penguin
Random
House

The Present is the living sum-total
of the whole Past.
—THOMAS CARLYLE

Justice is always violent to the party offending,
for every man is innocent in his own eyes.
—DANIEL DEFOE

Prologue

Loyalty to the dead had him traveling to SoHo in icy rain rather than heading home. At home he could have put up his feet—tired today, he admitted. He'd have enjoyed a cozy fire, a good book, and a small glass of whiskey while waiting for his wife to get home.

Instead, he sat in the back of a cab that smelled faintly of overripe peppers and someone's musky perfume as it skated along the nasty street toward what he feared would be an ugly confrontation.

He disliked ugly confrontations, wondered sometimes about people who, by all appearances, enjoyed them. Those who knew him would say he had a talent for evading or defusing them.

But this time, he expected to go head-to-head with his cousin Edward.

A pity, really, he thought as he watched the ice-tipped rain strike the cab windows. It hissed as it struck, he thought, like angry snakes.

Once, he and Edward had been close as brothers. Once they'd shared adventures and secrets and ambitions—lofty ones, of course. But time and divergent paths had separated them long ago.

He barely knew the man Edward had become, and understood him not at all. And sadly for him, liked Edward even less.

Regardless, they had shared the same paternal grandparents; their fathers were brothers. They were family. He hoped to use those blood ties, those shared experiences to bring their opposing views to some reasonable middle ground.

Then again, the man Edward had become rarely stood on middle ground. No, Edward staked a claim on his own ground and refused to move even an inch in any direction.

Otherwise, Edward would hardly have engaged a Realtor to sell their grandparents' lovely old brownstone.

Why, he wouldn't even have known about the Realtor, about the appointment made for a walk-through and assessment of the house if Edward's assistant to his assistant—or whatever title the girl owned—hadn't slipped up and mentioned it when he'd tried to contact Edward, arrange for a powwow.

He didn't have much of a temper—anger took such effort—but he was angry now. Angry enough he knew he could and would create a stink and a scene in front of the real estate person.

He had a half share of the property (as Edward had taken to calling it), and it couldn't be sold without his written consent.

He wouldn't give it, he wouldn't go against his grandfather's express wishes.

For a moment, in the back of the cab, he was transported to his grandfather's study, with all its warmth and rich colors, its bookcases full of books smelling of leather binding, wonderful old photos, and fascinating memorabilia.

He could feel the frailty of his grandfather's hand, once so big and strong, in his. Hear the waver of a voice that used to boom like cannon fire.

It's more than a house, more than a home. Though that's a precious thing. It has a history, has earned its place in the world. It's earned a legacy. I'm trusting you, you and Edward, to honor that history, and continue that legacy.

He would, he told himself as the cab finally pulled to the curb. At best, he would remind Edward of those wishes, that responsibility. At worst, he would find a way to buy out his cousin's interest.

If it was only property, only money, then money Edward would have.

He overtipped the driver—purposely because the weather was truly horrible. It might have been the generosity that prompted the driver to roll down the window and call out that he'd left his briefcase in the back of the cab.

"Thank you!" He hurried back to retrieve it. "So much on my mind."

Gripping the briefcase, he navigated the ice rink of a sidewalk, walked through the little iron gate and down the walkway—shoveled and treated, as he personally paid a neighborhood boy to see to it.

He climbed the short flight of steps as he had as a toddler, a young boy, a young man, and now an older one.

He might forget things—like his briefcase—but he remembered the passcode for the main door. Laid his palm on the plate, used his swipe card.

He opened the heavy front door, felt the change like a fresh stab in his heart.

No scent of the fresh flowers his grandmother would have arranged herself on the entrance table. No old dog to lumber into the foyer to greet him. Some of the furniture sat in other homes now—specific bequests—as some of the art graced other walls.

He was glad of that, as that was legacy, too.

Despite the fact he also paid a housekeeper—the daughter of his grandparents' longtime employee, Frankie—to tend the place once a week, he scented the disuse as well as lemon oil.

"Long enough," he muttered to himself as he set his briefcase down. "It's been empty long enough now."

He heard the sound of voices, and for a moment wondered if they, too, were just memories. Then he remembered his purpose—Edward and the Realtor. They were, he imagined, discussing square footage and location and market value.

And neither thinking, as he was, of family dinners around the big table, of blackberry tarts filched from the kitchen, of proudly presenting the woman he loved to his grandparents in the living room on a sunny Saturday afternoon.

He forced himself to push through the mists of time, start back toward the voices. Sentiment wouldn't sway Edward, he knew. If another reminder of a promise made to a man they'd both loved didn't do so, perhaps the reminder of the legalities would.

Failing all, there was money.

Still, he didn't want to sneak up on them like a thief so he called out his cousin's name.

The voices stilled, annoying him. Did they think they could hide from him? He continued back, clinging to the annoyance as a kind of weapon. And turning into the room he'd thought of in the cab, he saw Edward sitting in their grandfather's desk chair.

His cousin's eyes were wide—even the one swollen with a darkening bruise. Blood trickled in a thin line from the corner of his mouth, stained his teeth as he started to speak.

Annoyance forgotten in shock and concern, he stepped forward quickly.

"Edward."

Pain erupted, a flash of fire bursting in the back of his head. Helpless to stop his own fall, he pitched forward. Seconds before his temple struck the old oak floor and turned everything black, he heard Edward scream.

Chapter 1

After a long, tedious day—the first half spent in court, the second half with paperwork—Lieutenant Eve Dallas prepared to shut it all down.

At the moment all she wanted out of life was a quiet evening with her husband, her cat, and a glass—or two—of wine. Maybe a vid, she thought as she grabbed her coat, if Roarke hadn't brought too much work home.

Tonight—do the happy-time boogie—she was bringing home none of her own.

She could extend that wish list, she decided as she dug out the scarf her partner had made her for Christmas. Maybe a swim, and pool sex. She figured no matter how many deals Roarke needed to wheel, he could always be talked into pool sex.

She found the silly snowflake cap in another pocket of her long leather coat. Since the sky was heaving down ice, she tugged it on. She'd sent her partner home, had a couple of detectives out in the cold, working a hot. They'd contact her if they needed her.

She reminded herself she had another detective, newly

minted—whose induction ceremony was slated for the next morning.

But right now, on a particularly ugly January evening, she had nothing on her plate.

Spaghetti and meatballs, she decided. *That's* what she wanted on her plate. Maybe she'd beat Roarke home, and actually put that together for both of them. With wine, a couple candles. Right down in the pool area—no, she corrected as she started out. Maybe at the dining room table, like grown-ups, with a fire going.

She could program a couple of salads, use a couple of his half a zillion fancy plates.

And while the ice snapped and crackled outside, they'd—

"Eve."

She turned, spotted Mira—the department's shrink and top profiler—all but leaping off a glide and rushing toward her, pale blue coat flying open over her deep pink suit.

"You're still here. Thank God."

"Just leaving. What's the deal? What's wrong?"

"I'm not sure. I . . . Dennis—"

Instinctively Eve reached up to touch the snowflake hat, one Dennis Mira had snugged down on her head in his kind way on a snowy day in the last weeks of 2060.

"Is he hurt?"

"I don't think so." The normally unflappable Mira linked her fingers together to keep them still. "He wasn't clear, he was upset. His cousin—he said his cousin's hurt, and now is missing. He asked for you, specifically. I'm sorry to spring this on you, but—"

"Don't worry about it. Is he home—at your place?" She had already turned away, called for the elevator.

"No, he's at his grandparents'—what was their home—in SoHo."

"You're with me." She steered Mira into the elevator, crowded with cops going off shift. "I'll make sure you both get home. Who's his cousin?"

"Ah, Edward. Edward Mira. Former Senator Edward Mira."

"Didn't vote for him."

"Neither did I. I need a moment to gather my thoughts, and I want to let him know we're coming."

As Mira took out her 'link, Eve organized her own thoughts.

She didn't know or care much about politics, but she had a vague image of Senator Edward Mira. She'd never have put the bombastic, hard-line senator—sharp black eyebrows, close cropped black hair, hard and handsome face—on the same family tree as the sweet, slightly fuddled Dennis Mira.

But family made strange bedfellows.

Or was that politics?

Didn't matter.

When they reached her level in the garage, she pointed toward her slot, strode to the unremarkable-looking DLE her husband had designed for her. Mira hurried after her, hampered by spike-heeled boots and shorter legs.

Eve moved fast—sturdy boots and long legs—slid behind the wheel, a tall, leanly built woman with choppy brown hair currently under a watch cap with a sparkling snowflake emblem she, cop to the bone, wore because it had been an impromptu gift given by a man she had a helpless, harmless crush on.

"Address?" she asked when Mira, in her elegant winter coat and fashionable boots, got in beside her.

Eve plugged the address into the computer, pulled out of the slot. And bulleted out of the garage, hitting lights and siren.

"Oh, you don't have to . . . Thank you," Mira said when Eve merely flicked her a glance. "Thank you. He says he's fine, not to worry about him, but . . ."

"You are."

The DLE looked like your poky uncle's economy vehicle— and drove like a rocket. Eve swerved around vehicles whose drivers considered the sirens a casual suggestion. She hit vertical to leapfrog over others until Mira simply closed her eyes and hung on.

"Fill me in. Do you know why they were at the grandparents' house—who else would be there?"

"Their grandmother died about four years ago, and Bradley—Dennis's grandfather—just seemed to fade away. He lived about a year after her death, putting his affairs in order. Though knowing him, most of them already were. He left the house in equal shares to Dennis and Edward— the two oldest grandsons. That maxibus—"

Eve whipped the wheel, sent the DLE up. And took a corner as if in pursuit of a mass murderer. "Is behind us. Keep going."

"I can tell you Dennis and Edward have been at odds over the house. Dennis wants to keep it in the family, per Bradley's wishes. Edward wants to sell it."

"He can't sell it, I take it, unless Mr. Mira signs off."

"That's my understanding. I don't know why Dennis came down here today—he had a full day at the university, as one of his colleagues is ill and he's filling in. I should have asked him."

"It's okay." Eve double-parked, turning the quiet, tree-lined street into a battlefield of blasting horns. Ignoring them, she flipped up her On Duty light. "We'll ask him now."

But Mira was already out of the car, running in those treacherous heels across the slick sidewalk. Cursing, Eve bolted after her, grabbed her arm.

"You run in those things, I'm going to end up driving you to the ER. Nice place." She let Mira go as they went through the gate and onto cleared ground. "In this neighborhood, it's probably worth, what, five or six million?"

"I imagine. Dennis would know."

"He would?"

Mira managed a smile as she hurried up the steps. "It's important. He knows what's important. I don't remember the code." She pressed the buzzer, used the knocker.

When Dennis, disheveled gray hair, baggy pine-colored cardigan, opened the door, Mira grabbed his hands. "Dennis! You *are* hurt. Why didn't you tell me?" She took his chin, turned his head to study the raw bruise on his temple. "You angled this away so I wouldn't see it on the 'link."

"Now, Charlie. I'm all right. I didn't want to upset you.

Come in out of the cold now, both of you. Eve, thank you for coming. I'm worried about Edward. I've been all through the house. He's just not here."

"But he was?" Eve prompted.

"Oh, yes. In the study. He was hurt. A black eye, and his mouth was bleeding. I should show you the study."

When he turned, Mira let out a sound as much of frustration as distress. "Dennis, your head's bleeding." He hissed when she reached up to feel the knot. "You come in the living room and sit down, right now."

"Charlie, Edward—"

"You leave Edward to Eve," she said, pulling him into a big space that had either been decorated in a severely minimalist style, or several pieces of furniture had been removed. What remained appeared comfortably used and cheerful.

Mira took off her coat, tossed it carelessly aside, then dug into her enormous purse.

Eve got her first real clue why so many women carried handbags the size of water buffalos when Mira pulled a first aid kit out of hers.

"I'm going to clean up these lacerations, and ask Eve to drop us off at the nearest emergency room so you can have this X-rayed."

"Now, sweetie." He hissed again when Mira dabbed at the wound with an alcohol wipe, but managed to reach back and pat her leg. "I don't need X-rays or other doctors when I have you. I just have a bump on the head. I'm as lucid as I ever get."

Eve caught his smile, sly and sweet, when Mira laughed at that.

"No double vision, no dizziness or nausea," he assured her. "Maybe a little headache."

"If, after we get home and I give you a thorough exam—"

This time he turned around, wiggled his eyebrows, and grinned in a way that had Eve swallowing an embarrassed laugh of her own.

"Dennis." Mira sighed, and cupping his face in her hands, kissed him so softly, so tenderly, that Eve had to look away.

"Ah, maybe you could tell me where to find the study—where you last saw your cousin."

"I'll take you back."

"You're going to sit right here and behave until I'm finished," Mira told him. "It's straight back, Eve, and then on the left. Lots of wood, a big desk and chair, leather-bound books on shelves."

"I'll find it."

She could see where more art had been removed, more furniture—in fact, she found a room empty but for stacks of packing boxes. Yet she didn't see a single mote of dust, and caught the light scent of lemons as if someone had crushed their blossoms with the air.

She found the study, and at a glance decided nothing—or nothing much—had been taken out of this space.

Organized, attractive with its heavy wood trim, its sturdy masculine furniture and deep tones.

Burgundy and forest, she mused, taking a long look from the doorway. Family photos in black or silver frames, polished plaques from various charitable organizations.

The desk itself still held a coffee-colored leather blotter, matching accessories, and a slick little data and communication center.

Beside the fireplace with its thick mantel stood a bar—small, old, certainly valuable. On it sat two crystal decanters, half full of amber liquid, with silver labels. Whiskey. Brandy.

She moved from the wood floor to the rug stretched on it. The softly faded pattern told her it was likely old and valuable like the bar, like the crystal, like the pocket watch on display under a glass dome.

She saw no sign of struggle, no indication anything had been stolen. But when she crouched down, examined the space before the fringe of the rug brushed over wood, she saw a few drops of blood.

She circled the room slowly, carefully, touching nothing as yet. But she began to see . . . maybe.

She started back, paused at the doorway of the living

room to see Mira competently applying ointment to her husband's temple.

"Don't go in there yet," Eve said. "I'm just going out for my field kit."

"Oh, it's nasty out. Let me get that for you."

"I've got it," she said quickly when Dennis started to rise. "Just give me a minute."

She went back into the icy rain, got her field kit out of the trunk. As she went back she studied the neighboring houses, and pulled out her own 'link to send Roarke a quick text.

Got hung up. Will explain when I get home.

And considered she'd obeyed the Marriage Rules.

When she came back in, she set the kit down to take off her coat, scarf, hat. "Okay, let's take this by the numbers. Have you tried to contact your cousin?"

"Oh, yes. I did that right away. He didn't answer his 'link. I did try him at home as well, and reached his wife. I didn't want to alarm her," Dennis added, "so I didn't mention any of this. She told me he wasn't home, and would probably be running late. She may not know about his appointment here, but if she did, she wouldn't tell me."

"Appointment?"

"Oh, I am sorry. I haven't explained any of this." He gave Mira one of his absent smiles. "I tried to reach him earlier today, to see if the two of us could just . . . sit down and discuss our differences about the house. I got an assistant who seemed a little harried at the time. Otherwise she might not have mentioned he had an appointment here with a Realtor to assess the house for sale. It . . . Well, it set me right off. He shouldn't have done that behind my back."

Eve nodded, opened her kit to take out a can of Seal-It. "Pissed you off."

"Eve," Mira began, but Dennis patted her hand.

"Truth is best, Charlie. I was very upset. He wouldn't answer his personal 'link, so when I finished my last class,

I came here. Terrible traffic conditions. Something should be done."

"Yeah, I think that all the time. When did you get here, Mr. Mira?"

"Oh, I'm not at all sure. Let me see. I finished my last class . . . it must have been about four-thirty. My TA and a couple of students had questions, so that took a bit of time. Then I had to get my papers together, and it may have been five or so before I left. Then getting here." He added that sweet, vague smile, but his eyes, that dreamy green, held worry. "I couldn't really say exactly."

"Good enough," Eve told him, as clearly trying to determine the timing distressed him. "There's security on the house. Was it active?"

"It was. I have the passcode, and a swipe. My palm print is authorized."

"There's a cam."

"Yes!" The idea obviously delighted him. "Of course there is! It would show my arrival—and Edward. I never thought of it."

"Why don't we take a look at that first? Do you know where the security station is?"

"Yes, of course. I'll show you. Never thought of it," he said again, shaking his head as he rose. "If I'd just looked for myself, I'd have seen Edward coming and going. You relieve my mind, Eve."

"Mr. Mira, you were attacked."

He stopped, blinked. "I suppose I was. That's very upsetting. Who would have done that?"

"Let's see if we can find out."

He led her back, made a turn, then showed her a large, modern kitchen with some old-fashioned touches that suited the house.

It all looked . . . comfortable, and reminded her in some ways of the Miras' house uptown.

"There are viewing stations in several rooms," Dennis explained as he opened a door off the kitchen. "So my grandparents or the staff could see who was at the door. But this is the main hub."

He looked at it, gave everything a vague glance. "I'm afraid I'm not very good with complex electronics."

"Me, either." But she walked over to where she was damn sure a component should be. "But I can tell you somebody took the whole damn deal—the drive or whatever the hell it is, the discs."

"Oh dear."

"Yeah. Who else has access to the house?"

"Besides Edward and myself? The housekeeper—her mother worked for my grandparents for decades, and she's helped us out for several years. She would never—"

"Understood, but I'm going to want her name so I can talk to her."

"Is it all right if I make tea?" Dr. Mira asked.

"Sure, go ahead. Mr. Mira, I want you to walk me through exactly what happened. The cab dropped you off?"

"Yes. Right out front. I left my briefcase—so careless— but the driver called me back for it. I was angry and upset. I let myself in. It's a push-pull coming here. The memories are strong and good, but it's hard to know it's not the same, and can't be. I set my briefcase down, and I heard voices."

"More than one?" Eve prompted.

"Well . . . I think so. I expected to find Edward and the Realtor he'd engaged. I assumed they were talking. I called out to him. I didn't want to startle them. I started back, and when I got to the study, I saw him sitting in Granddad's desk chair. Black eye, the blood. He was frightened. I saw the fear, and I started forward to help him. I must have been struck from behind. It's never happened to me before, but I believe that's what happened."

"It knocked you out."

"The injuries are consistent with a strike from a heavy object, back of the skull." Mira brought Dennis a mug, wrapped his hands around it. "And with his right temple hitting the floor when he fell."

"I'm not questioning that, Dr. Mira."

"I know you're not." She sighed, then leaned into Dennis to gently kiss his bruised temple. "I know you're not."

"What did you do, Mr. Mira, when you came to?"

"I was disoriented, very confused initially. Edward wasn't there, and though we haven't been on the best of terms in a long time, he would never have left me on the floor that way. I called for him—I think—and I looked. I'm afraid I wandered around the house for a while, still a little confused, until it came to me something terrible had happened to Edward. I contacted Charlotte so she wouldn't worry, and asked her if you could come and look into it all."

He gave Eve a look with those soft, dreamy eyes that made her want to kiss his temple as Mira had. It mortified her.

"I realize now I should have simply contacted nine-one-one rather than bothering you."

"This isn't a bother. Are you up to taking a look at the study? Seeing if anything's missing or out of place?"

"Anything I can do."

When they walked back, she sealed her hands, her feet. "It's better if you don't touch anything. You've already been in there, and through the house, so sealing up's beside the point. But let's keep it to a minimum."

She paused at the doorway. "So your cousin was in the desk chair. Behind the desk."

"Yes, he was—oh, not behind it. The chair was in front of the desk." He frowned a moment. "Why would that be? But, yes, he was sitting in the chair, in front of the desk. On the rug."

"Okay." That jibed with her observations. "Hold it a minute."

She took what she needed from her kit, crouched down to take a swab of the blood from the floorboards, sealed it. Then meticulously swabbed an area of the rug.

She added drops of something from a small bottle to the swab, nodded. "Blood here. Somebody cleaned it up, but you don't get it all with a quick run of household cleaner."

She bent down, sniffed. "You can still smell it." She put

on microgoggles, peered close. "And if you're looking, you can see it, and the faint pattern where the chair rolled out and back, sat here with weight in it."

"Edward's weight."

"Looks that way. Another minute." She moved behind the desk, started an inch-by-inch exam of the chair.

"They missed some. Just a drop here." She swabbed again, carefully, leaving enough for the sweepers to take their own sample. "Was he restrained, Mr. Mira?"

"I . . ." He closed his eyes. "I don't think so. I don't think he was. I'm sorry. I'm not at all sure. I was so shocked."

"Okay. Black eye, bloody mouth. So someone assaulted him, put him in the chair, but out here, more in the center of the room. Scared him enough to keep him there. A stunner maybe, a knife, a weapon anyway, or the threat of more physical violence."

She circled the room again. "Voices. So they were talking. Wanted something from him, most likely. But before they can get it, or finish, you come in. You call out, so that gives them time to threaten him to keep it shut, to move out of sight. They don't stun you, if they have a stunner. You stun somebody, it takes a few seconds, and maybe you see them before you go down. Bash from behind. But they don't finish you off, or take you with them. You're not important in this. You're just an inconvenience. But they go to the trouble of cleaning up, putting the chair back behind the desk.

"Why?"

"It's fascinating, the science and art of what you do."

"What?"

"What you do," Dennis said, "it's a science, and an art. The observational skills are so polished, and—I think—innate. Sorry, my mind wandered." He smiled. "You asked why. I think I might understand that. If they knew Edward, they might know me. Some people would say, as my mind will wander, I simply fell and struck my head. And imagined the rest."

"Some people would be stupid," Eve said, making him smile. "Anything not here that should be, Mr. Mira, or out of place?"

"We've kept this almost exactly as he left it. My grand-father. Some of what's here comes to me, to my children, to others. But they were content to leave it like this for now. Everything's here. I don't think anything's been taken or moved."

"All right. You came to the doorway, saw him. You froze for a second—people do. You're focused on your cousin, and you move forward to help him."

She went to the doorway, paused, took a quick step in. Then scanned the shelves.

She picked up a stone bowl, brilliantly polished, frowned, set it down again. Tested the weight of an award plaque, dismissed it. Then she curled her fingers around the uplifted trunk of a large glass elephant in jubilant blues and greens. Had weight, she mused, and that handy grip.

"Dr. Mira?"

Mira moved forward, and like Eve examined the elephant. "Yes, yes, the legs. They're consistent with the wound."

As Eve got another swab, Mira turned to Dennis. "I will never, this is an oath, never complain about your hard head again."

"Cleaned it up, but we've got a little blood. Attacker steps back, side of the doorway. This is handy, heavy. You come in, *whack*, down you go. He, she, they—it's going to be they, one to deal with Edward, one to deal with you and the cleanup. So one of them gets rug cleaner, whatever, cleans things up, gets the hard drive, the discs. And they take him, leave you. I'm going to go through the house, make sure they didn't stuff him somewhere—sorry," she said immediately.

"No, don't be."

"I'm going to have sweepers come in, go over all this. I can contact Missing Persons, expedite there."

"Could you . . ."

"Will you take lead on this?" Understanding, Mira took Dennis's hand. "Both of us would feel easier if you remained in charge."

"Sure, I can clear that. Why don't you go back and sit down, let me get things rolling."

Eve bagged the elephant, contacted Crime Scene, ordered up some uniforms to canvass. Someone had walked in the house, most likely invited in by Edward Mira. She'd check on this Realtor. And someone had walked back out again, either carrying Edward's body or forcing him to leave with them.

They'd need transportation.

Not a burglary, she thought, and not a straight kidnapping, or why rough him up first? The chair in the middle of the room struck her as an interrogation.

Somebody wanted something from Edward Mira. Chances were he'd stay alive until they got it.

She went back to the living room. They'd turned on the fire, and sat together on a sofa, drinking tea.

Eve sat on the coffee table facing them, as it made a tighter connection.

"I need some information. The Realtor—name, contact?"

"I have no idea. I'm sorry. The assistant didn't mention it, and I was too upset to ask."

"Okay, I'll get that from his office. Where's his office?"

"He retired from Congress to create and head a political think tank," Mira told her. "He has an office in their headquarters, in the Chrysler Building."

"Prime real estate."

"Status is very important to Edward," Dennis said. "His organization, the Mira Institute, takes two floors, and owns a pied-à-terre in East Washington for Edward's use or when one of the other executives needs to be there."

"Need that address, too, and his home address. I'm going to talk to his wife when I leave here. How was their relationship?"

Dennis glanced at his wife, sighed.

"I'll take this. Mandy is a realist who enjoys the life she leads. She excelled on the campaign trail, continues to excel at fund-raisers and committees. The fact that Edward cheated, often? She considers that part of the whole, and not particularly important, as he's discreet. She's discreet as well, and uses the services of a licensed companion. Both their children are grown, of course, and while each play the game in public, neither have much affection for their parents or the choices their parents have made."

"The world's made up of all manner of parts, Charlie," Dennis murmured.

"I'm aware. My professional opinion is Mandy would do nothing to unbalance her world. She would never hurt Edward, and in her way, she's fond of him. In his way, he's both grateful for her contributions to his career, and proud of her standing socially."

"He'd have enemies."

"Oh, scores. Politically, as you'd expect."

"And personally?"

"He can and does charm—it's part of politics, again. He also believes himself right on whatever stand he takes, politically and personally, and that can cause friction. This house is an example," Mira continued. "Edward decided it needed to be sold, so to him, it will be."

"He's wrong," Dennis said quietly, "and it won't be. But that's not important right now. Someone hurt him, and there's been no mention of ransom." He looked at Eve now. "You haven't mentioned ransom."

"I'll talk to his wife about that. Mr. Mira, I want you to know I believe everything you've told me. And I don't believe, not for a second, you'd do anything to hurt your cousin. Or anyone."

"Thank you."

"But I have to ask what I'm going to ask, or I'm not doing my job. If I'm not doing my job, I'm not helping you."

"I understand. You need to ask me when I saw Edward last, how things were between us. If keeping this house in the family is so important to me, I might hire someone to frighten him."

He nodded, set his tea aside. "We saw each other over the holidays. For form, really, I'm sorry to say. Charlotte and I attended a cocktail party at his home. When was that, Charlie?"

"On the twenty-second of December. We only stayed

about an hour, as Edward tried to corner Dennis about selling the house."

"I didn't want to argue, so we left early. He sent me an e-mail shortly after the first of the year, outlining his reasons, again, and his plan of action."

"You didn't tell me that, Dennis."

"You get so angry with him." Dennis took Mira's hand again. "And there was nothing new in it. I don't like bringing that discord into our home. I answered him briefly that I didn't agree, and intended to keep my promise to our grandfather. When he responded immediately, I knew he was very angry. He would usually wait as if too busy to deal with such matters. But he responded right away, and said he would give me time to be reasonable, and warned he would be forced to take legal action if I insisted on clinging to sentiment. And . . . he claimed there had been no promise, that I—as I tend to do—had mixed things up."

"The hell with him!"

"Charlie—"

"The hell with him, that coldhearted bastard. I mean it, Dennis!" Outraged fury deepened her color, flashed in her eyes. "If you want to look at someone who'd have wanted to hurt him, look right here."

"Dr. Mira," Eve said coolly, "cut it out. I'm going to have EDD access those e-mails. That was your last communication?"

"Yes, it was. I didn't respond. It was a cruel thing to say, and it was a lie. We made a promise." Eve saw his baffled sorrow as clearly as Mira's outraged fury. "I didn't contact him again until today, but he didn't answer."

"All right." She couldn't help herself, and touched a hand to his knee. "You don't mix up anything that's important. I'll find the answers to all this. I promise."

She rose, grateful when the bell rang. "That's going to be for me. I'm going to put the sweepers on the study first, and I'm going through the house personally. I've got uniforms who'll knock on doors, see if any of the neighbors saw anything. I'm going to have a uniform take you home."

She pulled out her 'link. "Would you put all the names and contact data I asked for on here?"

"Charlie should. I'm terrible with electronics."

"So am I." She passed her 'link to Mira. "It's going to be okay."

Dennis rose. "You're such a smart woman. Such a good girl," he added to her baffled surprise. Then he kissed her cheek, sweetly, leaving a faint tickle from the stubble he'd probably missed when shaving. "Thank you."

Eve felt that tickle work its way into her heart as she went to answer the door.

Chapter 2

Eve saw them off, spoke with the uniforms, the sweepers, and decided to take the house top to bottom. But as she started up the stairs, she stopped, sat down on one.

And tagged Roarke.

She led with "I'm sorry."

"Don't be." His face filled the screen and, boy, what a face. It never failed to strike how some days the gods, the angels, the poets, the artists all got together to create something perfect. A beautifully carved mouth, wildly, impossibly blue eyes, sculpted cheekbones all framed by thick black silk.

"You've caught a case," he continued, with those mists of Ireland whispering in his voice to complete the perfection.

"Sort of. No body, which makes it different. Or none yet. Dennis Mira was attacked."

"What?" The just-for-her smile in his eyes vanished. "Is he hurt? What hospital? I'll meet you."

"He's okay. I just sent them home. He took a pretty good whack to the back of the head, then smacked his temple on the floor when he fell. Probably has a mild concussion, but Mira's on it."

"Where are you?"

"At his grandfather's house. Mr. Mira's grandfather. Or it was. It's half Mr. Mira's, half his cousin's—former Senator Edward Mira—who was also attacked, and is currently missing. I need to go through the house here to make sure he's not dead and stuffed in a closet, then I have to talk to some people on the way home. I don't know how long—"

"Give me the address there."

"Roarke, it's in SoHo. There's no need for you to come all the way down here on a night like this."

"You can give me the address or I can find it for myself. Either way, I'm on my way."

She gave him the address.

She'd gone through the top floor—both wings—before he got there. And could admit, seeing him and the go-cup of coffee he held out lifted her mood.

"I was going to make dinner."

Those wonderful lips curved, then brushed hers. "Were you now?"

"Hand to God. Nothing cooking at the shop, so I was heading out, figured I might beat you home, and set up wine and candles and spaghetti right in the dining room."

"I'll treasure the thought."

"Mira caught me. You don't see her seriously shaken often, and she was. Mr. Mira contacted her when he came to—took the bash downstairs in the study—and asked her to bring me."

"Of course he did. He's an intelligent man."

"I'll give you the background as I look for possibly dead Edward, but tell me first, Mr. Buys the Entire World and Its Satellites, if you were going to buy this place, what would you give for it?"

"I haven't done a full walk-through, but from what I've seen it's beautifully preserved and maintained. Likely built in the 1930s. Round about six thousand square feet, and in this neighborhood? I expect I'd offer about ten. If I were selling, I'd ask fifteen."

"That's million?"

"It is, yes."

"That's a big bunch of money."

"Do you fancy it? Does Dennis want to sell?"

"No—I mean, sure, it's a nice house, but we have one. I'm fine with one. And no, he doesn't want to sell, which is part of the deal here."

She filled him in as she searched, knew he'd take in every detail even when he stopped to admire a piece of furniture, some woodwork, or a ceiling medallion.

"I could get twenty, with the right buyer, and careful staging," he mused. "But back to the matter at hand. You know the senator's a complete burke—at least from my personal leanings."

"He's a complete burke from my perspective from what I got out of Mira, and what Mr. Mira didn't say. But it'll be nice to find him alive."

"Agreed."

With Roarke she walked back to the study. It smelled of sweeper dust and chemicals now.

"I knew Bradley Mira, a little."

"Get out."

"A very little," Roarke added. "And mostly by reputation. He was respected and admired. Have you run his background?"

"No, not immediately applicable."

"The prosecuting attorney for New York—before your time and mine. I believe there was some family money, and he made more. He became Judge Mira, and retired more than a decade ago—likely closer to two decades, if memory serves. He spent the last part of his life doing good works, as you see here from all the plaques displayed. An admirable man who, by all accounts, lived a good and productive life."

"Mr. Mira loved him, that comes through loud and clear. Twenty million?"

With those wild and canny blue eyes, Roarke scanned. "With the right buyer, yes."

"Half of that's big motivation to find the right buyer. I need to talk to this Realtor, which means I have to talk to whoever made the appointment for Edward Mira. But now, I want to talk to the housekeeper and the wife. Housekeeper's on the way to the wife."

"Why don't I drive, and you can run backgrounds?"

"It's a plan. Let me check on the canvass first."

Sila Robarts lived with her husband of twenty-seven years a few blocks away in the second-floor apartment of a converted townhome. She ran a cleaning company, Maid to Order, while her husband owned and operated We're Handy— a handyman business.

They'd raised two children, both of whom worked within the two companies, and had three grandchildren.

"They own the place." Eve nodded at the white brick townhouse after Roarke parked. "Use the first floor for their businesses, live on the second." She pressed the buzzer for the apartment at the front entrance.

A woman's voice, brisk and impatient, said, "Yes?"

"NYPSD, Mrs. Robarts. We need to speak with you."

"What the hell for? Let me see ID. Hold it up for the camera."

Eve held up her badge.

"What happened? Is one of my kids hurt?"

"No, ma'am. We just need to speak with you. Dennis Mira gave me your name and address."

"Mr. Dennis? Is he okay? What's this— Hell." The woman cut herself off, buzzed them in.

A hallway cut the first floor in half, with doors to the maid service and the handyman business on either side. Another door at the back was marked PRIVATE.

It, too, buzzed open.

They took the stairs up to the second floor, and a pair of double doors. One of them swung open.

"Are you sure Mr. Dennis is okay? Who are you?"

"NYPSD," Eve repeated, and once again offered her badge. "Lieutenant Dallas."

"Dallas? Dallas?" The woman had enormous eyes of bitter-chocolate brown and hair nearly the same color piled in a knot on top of her head. At the name, the eyes went big as planets. "Roarke? Dallas? I saw the vid, I listened to the book. Oh my sweet Jesus. Mel! Mel! Get out here. Something terrible's happened to the Miras."

"Mrs. Robarts, calm down. The Miras are fine."

"You're Homicide," Sila snapped, pulling at the neck of a sweatshirt bearing her company's logo. "You think I don't *know* that?" she demanded as footsteps pounded in from the rear of the apartment. "You work with Miss Charlotte."

"What happened to them?" The man who ran in moved fast for a big guy. He had to be two-fifty spread over about six foot two. An Arena Ball player's build. "Was there an accident?"

"I think they were murdered!"

"What? What?" The big guy grabbed his hysterical wife, and looked about to join her in the wailing parade. "Oh my God. My God! How—"

"Quiet!" Eve boomed it over the hysteria. "Both the Miras are fine, and probably sitting down eating dinner and maybe having a really big drink. Now everybody just calm the hell down, and sit the hell down!"

Tears rolled out of those bitter-chocolate eyes. "They're all right? You swear it?"

"If it'll stop the madness I'll sign an oath on it in my own blood."

"Okay, sorry." She swiped at her cheeks. "Sorry, Mel."

"What the hell, Sila?"

"It's Dallas and Roarke."

"Dallas and . . . somebody's dead."

"A lot of people are dead," Eve pointed out. "But none of them are Charlotte and/or Dennis Mira."

"I got scared, that's all." Sila sniffled. "I got so scared. They're family."

"Then understand they're mine, too."

"Mr. Dennis speaks highly of you. He came by when I was cleaning the big house, and listening to the book. The Icove book. I asked if he knew you, seeing as you worked with Miss Charlotte, and he said he did, and you were good, caring people. And courageous. I just love that man."

"Okay." Eve could relate. "He's okay."

"I'm going to get you a glass of wine," Mel said to his wife. "I can get you some wine," he added to Eve and Roarke.

"Thanks, but on duty."

"I'm not," Roarke said cheerfully, "and I'd love a glass of wine."

"I can get you something else, Miss Dallas. Coffee, tea maybe. Got Pepsi."

"Pepsi?" Sila narrowed her still damp eyes. "Melville Robarts, you said you were cutting that out."

The big man hunched his shoulders like a small boy caught swiping cookies. "Maybe there's a stray tube or two around."

"I'll take it," Eve said to settle the matter. "It's Lieutenant. You work for Dennis Mira, clean his grandfather's house."

"Yeah, that's right. Look, let's sit down, like you said."

Sila moved off into the living area, a comfortable space and so clean it nearly sparkled, sank into a high-backed chair of bold blue.

"My mama did for Judge Mira and Miss Gwen almost as long as I can remember. When I got old enough, I'd help out sometimes. Miss Gwen, she passed. So sudden, too, and the judge, he just lost his heart, and he passed some months after. My mama still misses them. So do I."

"Me, too." Mel came in with a tray holding three glasses of red wine and one of iced Pepsi. "I did work for them around the house when they needed. That's how I first met Sila—we were sixteen. Is there trouble, Miss—Lieutenant Dallas?"

"There's trouble. Mr. Mira is fine," she said again, "but he was attacked earlier this evening, in his grandfather's house."

"Attacked? In the house?" Once again those dark eyes narrowed. "The senator went at him, didn't he? Couldn't push Mr. Dennis around with words, so he went at him. *Senator* Edward Mira. He's Mr. Dennis's cousin, though you wouldn't know they shared blood. Different as wet to dry."

"Why would you think Edward Mira would attack Mr. Mira?"

"Because that man wants his own way, in everything. Nothing but a bully, and always was, if you ask me. I don't think much of him or his snooty wife. They have nice kids, though. Good people, and the kids' kids are as sweet as cherry pie. Did you arrest him?"

"No. He didn't attack Mr. Mira, and was, in fact, attacked himself. And he's missing."

"I don't understand."

"Mr. Mira walked in on the attack and was knocked unconscious. When he came to, Edward Mira was gone, as were the attackers."

Sila took a gulp of wine, breathed out hard. "I'm sorry for what I said about him—it's the truth, but I'm sorry. Was someone trying to rob them? They've got really good security on that house. I never worried a minute about being there alone or with Mama or my girl."

"When were you there last?"

"Just today, from about seven-thirty to about two-thirty. My daughter and I cleaned there today, and my mama came, too. She can't clean like she used to, but she loves that house. We went over bright an' early, gave it top to bottom—that's once a month rotation. I swear to you, we set the alarms and the locks when we finished up."

"Did anyone come to the door?"

"No, ma'am."

"Have you noticed anyone, today or otherwise, who shouldn't be in the neighborhood? You know what I mean."

"Yes, I do, and no, I haven't. It's a nice neighborhood. A few retired folks like the judge, and professionals, mostly. Doctors and lawyers and the like. Mr. Dennis came by every few weeks, just to say hello and spend some time in the house."

"How about the senator?"

Her nose wrinkled. "More lately, with dollar signs in his eyes."

"Sila."

"I can't help it. He took some of the furniture—had it taken," she corrected, "but Mr. Dennis said it was left to him and it was all right. I didn't tell Mr. Dennis how I overheard the senator talking on his 'link about appraisals for the pieces he took. It would have hurt Mr. Dennis's feelings to know what his grandparents loved was being sold to strangers."

Eve asked more questions, digging into what she already sensed was fallow ground. When they rose to leave, Sila touched her arm.

"I want to contact Mr. Dennis, just want to hear his voice. I don't think I can settle down until I do. Is that all right?"

"Sure." Eve hesitated. "Give this about a week, but if you get a chance, maybe you could go back over there, clean the study. Crime Scene leaves dust."

"You can bet I will."

Eve brooded on their way uptown, then turned to Roarke.

"Selling furniture, wanting to sell the house. Some people are just greedy, but maybe you can take a good look at his finances. It could be gambling debts, blackmail over an affair. Maybe he doesn't just want to sell. Maybe he needs to sell."

"Permission to wiggle my fingers in someone else's finances is always delightful. Permission in this case, a veritable treat."

"You really don't like him."

"Not in the least."

"Could he force Mr. Mira to sell?"

Smoothly, Roarke maneuvered around a mini, fishtailing on the slick streets. "I don't know the particulars, but if they own equal shares, I think it would be a considerable battle. Dennis could buy Edward out."

"Sure, if he has ten million lying around gathering dust."

"Ten million doesn't gather dust, it—if used well—makes more millions. We could easily lend him what he'd need. Family," Roarke added when Eve stared at him.

She took his hand. "I really was going to do the dinner

thing. And I was thinking about a swim with pool sex, and maybe a vid."

He gave her a slow, easy grin. "All that?"

"I was working out the details. I'm really sorry I didn't get a chance to pull it off."

"We're young yet."

Roarke pulled the DLE to the curb in front of a gleaming silver building. Eve smirked when the doorman, who looked like a formal polar bear in white livery with gold braiding, hustled through the icy rain to scowl at them.

"You own this place?"

"No. Why don't we go in, see if we want to."

"I get to intimidate the doorman," she said before they got out. "Do *not* bribe him."

"And spoil your fun? What do you take me for?"

She got out, planted her feet as the doorman curled his lip.

"You can't park that heap here."

"I just did."

"Now you're just going to move it. This space is reserved for pickups, drop-offs. For cabs, limos, and vehicles that aren't an embarrassment to the vehicle industry."

She flipped out her badge. "This is an official NYPSD vehicle, and it works for me. It stays where I put it."

"Look, look, I'm all in support for the boys—and girls—in blue, but I can't have junkers like that sitting out here."

"Don't judge a book by its title."

"What?"

"Cover," Roarke supplied. "It's cover, darling."

"Whatever. It stays . . ." She scanned his name tag. "Eugene. Have you seen Senator Mira tonight?"

"No, haven't seen him and I've been on the door since four. Look, look, pull that thing around the corner, into the garage. I'll buzz 'em, and you won't have to pay."

"Some might consider that attempting to bribe a police officer. I'm going to let it pass. How about Mrs. Mira?"

"Her social secretary left about twenty minutes ago, so as far as I know Mrs. Mira's up there. What's the beef here?"

"I'm going to have one with you if you don't clear us up to the Mira apartment, and now. It's been a long day, pal, and now I'm wet and cold. I can make your life a living hell should I choose to do so."

"Cops," he mumbled under his breath and lumbered back to the doors. He stomped over to the lobby comp.

"Mrs. Mira or one of her people have to clear you. They bought a private elevator, and if I try to send you up without clearance, that trips an alarm. And it's my job. You can make my life a living hell, but, sister, you've got nothing on my wife. I lose my job, she'll make me wish I was in hell."

"That's *Lieutenant* Sister—and let them know the NYPSD needs to speak with Mrs. Mira."

He tapped something on the screen, then put on an earpiece for privacy. "Yo, Hank, it's Eugene on the door. I got the NYPSD down here needing to speak with the boss. Uh-huh. Yeah, that's next. Got it."

He turned to Eve. "Need to scan that for verification, and Mrs. Mira's security is informing her you want to come up."

"Scan away."

Once he verified, he went back to the screen and Hank. "Dallas, Lieutenant Eve, verified. All right. Security wants to know what you want to talk to Mrs. Mira about."

"I'll discuss that with Mrs. Mira, in order to respect her privacy."

"She said— Okay, you heard her. I got it."

He turned away from the screen to gesture to the last elevator in a line of three. "That's the private. I'm going to send you straight up. Security will meet you."

"Dandy." Eve strolled to the elevator with Roarke, waited for the doors to open.

They did so with barely a whisper. The car had soft gold walls, a bench padded with royal blue on each side, and a small table holding a vase of white roses on the back wall.

"Who does that?" Eve wondered. "Who puts flowers in an elevator?"

Roarke continued to work on his PPC. "They purchased the entire top floor—that's four units and terraces—eight years ago."

"The whole top floor."

"Indeed they did, to the tune of twelve-point-three million. You did say to have a go at their finances."

"I figured that for when we're home."

"The anticipation was too much for my fragile willpower. Oh, the car has ears and eyes as well, but I took the liberty of jamming both when we got in."

"You do keep busy."

"Idle hands are the devil's workshop."

"Why? They're idle when you're sleeping—does he set up shop then? Are we all supposed to stay awake using our hands so the devil doesn't make stuff? What if you broke your hand? Is he doing his workshop thing while you're waiting to have it fixed?"

Roarke contemplated the pale gold ceiling. "Such a simple, if moralistic, phrase now thoroughly destroyed."

"I keep busy, too." Pleased with herself, she strode off when the doors whispered open.

A big, built black guy, who looked as if he should grace the cover of some men's fashion mag, stepped forward in the wide entrance foyer. There were more white roses, more benches, subdued lighting—and double doors, firmly closed.

"Lieutenant, sir," he said to them with a faint British accent. "I'll need to stow and secure your weapons as well as any electronic devices before I let you in to see Mrs. Mira."

"Not a single, solitary chance in hell."

"Then I'm afraid, without a warrant, this is as far as you go."

"All right. I'll assume Mrs. Mira isn't concerned about her husband being attacked and possibly kidnapped this evening. Any change there, she can contact me at Central tomorrow. I'm going off duty. Let's go eat spaghetti," she said to Roarke and turned back to the elevator.

"Just a minute. Are you claiming Mr. Mira's been attacked?"

"With meatballs," Eve added. "And a nice glass of wine."

"Sounds absolutely perfect to me. In front of the fire?" Roarke added. "It's a night for a fire in the hearth."

"Lieutenant Dallas!"

She glanced back over her shoulder. "Are you talking to me?"

"Has Senator Mira been injured?"

"Look, *Hank*, I'm here to speak with Mandy Mira on official police business. She either agrees to the access or she doesn't. Stop wasting my time."

"Please wait here. I need a minute."

"That's what you've got. Sixty seconds. From right now." She lifted her arm, deliberately consulting her wrist unit as Hank opened the doors, slipped inside.

Then she drew a deep breath. "Why are people so bitchy to cops?"

"I can't imagine, but now I actively crave spaghetti."

"We'll get there." She turned around as the doors opened again on the thirty second mark.

"If you'll come in, Mrs. Mira will be right with you."

"Fine. She's got about twenty-five seconds left."

"Lieutenant," he began, looking relieved when he was interrupted by the quick click of heels.

Mandy Mira was a tall, impressive-looking woman with a statuesque figure and a gilded swing of hair. It fascinated Eve that one side stopped at the ear while the other curved at her chin.

Eyes, coldly blue under a sweep of deep brown eyebrows, managed to convey annoyance and boredom.

"What is this nonsense? I'm not accustomed to having the police at my door, and don't appreciate you using some wild fabrication of an attack to worm your way in."

"Have you spoken to your husband in the last couple hours, Mrs. Mira?"

"That's none of your business."

"Okay, sorry for the worming in." Eve turned to go.

"I demand to know what this is about!"

"This is about investigating a reported attack on Edward Mira and the fact that he subsequently went missing."

"That's ridiculous."

"Then you can contact him right now, prove that, and we'll be out of your hair with sincere apologies for the interruption to your evening."

"Hank!" She actually snapped her fingers. "Contact Senator Mira."

"Ma'am, I've attempted to do so, on all numbers. I can't reach him."

"Give me that thing." She snatched Hank's 'link out of his hand, strode off with it on sky-high, sky-blue heels.

"Wow, she must be a joy to work for," Eve commented.

She stuck her hands in her pockets, took a measure of the living space.

A lot of chilly blues, selected, Eve deduced, because they matched Mandy Mira's eyes. And everything slick and sleek and shiny.

Just as well they hadn't been asked to sit, as every chair looked like an ass-bruiser.

Another huge display of white roses sitting on a glossy white piano—and white drapes framing the wall of glass leading to a terrace. By the time she'd gotten to the portrait of the senator and his wife over the unlit fireplace, Mandy's outrage shot back at her.

"What do you mean you don't *know*? You're paid to know. If you want to continue to be paid, you'll contact Senator Mira *now*. Is that understood?"

She stormed back, shoved the 'link at Hank. "The senator is currently incommunicado, which should be no concern of yours. However, I want an explanation. Why are you here, suggesting something has happened to him?"

"Are you aware your husband had an appointment today with a Realtor regarding his grandfather's home?"

"I am."

"Do you have the name and contact of said Realtor?"

"I have no interest whatsoever in that property or its disposition."

"I take that as a no. Your husband's cousin Dennis Mira—"

"Oh, for God's sake." Mandy waved that away as if it were a vaguely unpleasant odor. "If Dennis contacted you, he's wasted your time as well as mine. He's a foolish and befuddled little man, and one strangely attached to that property. I'd say he arranged all this to complicate the sale, but that's far too much complex thinking for Dennis."

Roarke laid a hand on Eve's arm, squeezed lightly. He spoke before she could so she only imagined—vividly—plowing her fist into Mandy Mira's face.

"Dennis Mira was assaulted seconds after he tried to rush to the aid of your injured husband. If you'd stop interrupting," Roarke continued in a tone cold enough to freeze the balls Eve imagined Mandy sported under her white silk lounging pants, "the lieutenant could give you the details."

"And who are you?"

"Roarke, and at the moment, Lieutenant Dallas's civilian consultant."

Those cold eyes narrowed. "Of course. Yes, of course. I know who you are—both of you. Riffraff. And here, no doubt, at the instigation of Dennis and Charlotte Mira. You can go back and tell them I'm not interested in their pitiful ploys, and my husband will do whatever he chooses to do with that ridiculous old house and everything in it. If you come here again trying to stir up trouble, I'll have something to say about it to the governor—and we'll see how long Charlotte continues her embarrassing association with the police. Hank, put these people out. Now."

Eve leaned forward, just a little. "You can kiss my ass."

Color flooded Mandy's face. "How *dare* you. You can be sure I'll contact your superior and report your behavior."

"That would be Whitney, Commander Jack. Cop Central." Eve took out her badge. "Make a note of the name and number. I cleaned up some of your husband's blood in that ridiculous old house today—you think about that. You think about that and the fact that you can't find him. And you remember Dennis Mira ended up unconscious on the floor, shedding some of his own blood because he tried to help. And you—"

"Eve," Roarke murmured.

"No, bullshit, not done. And you think about the fact a cop came to your door to inform you, to gather information in the investigation of your husband's whereabouts, and you stonewalled. As a cop I'm now looking right at you, right straight at you as my chief suspect.

"You got anything hiding in your closets, sister? I guarantee I'll find it."

Astonished outrage stripped Mandy Mira's face of color. "Get them out. Get them out of my house."

She stalked off as Eve turned back to the entrance foyer. Hank closed the doors behind them.

"Lieutenant? Sir? I want to apologize for—"

"You got your job, I've got mine."

"Are you certain Senator Mira was injured, and is missing?"

"Yes." The change in tone had her glancing back at him. "Do you know who he was set to meet at the brownstone today?"

"I don't, but I'll try to find out. I do know he was due home more than an hour ago. I should be home myself, but Mrs. Mira insisted I stay until he got home."

"Is that usual?"

"It's not unusual. If I find out anything that can help, I'll contact you at Central. Just FYI—she will contact the governor and your commanding officer."

"She can contact God as far as I'm concerned."

When the elevator doors shut, Roarke slid his hand down to take hers. He could all but feel the rage vibrating off her skin.

"I'll be Riff," he said.

"What?"

"I'll be Riff, which leaves you with Raff."

He saw the momentary confusion on her face, then the quick glint—a reluctant humor—in her eyes. "Why do you get Riff? Because it's first?"

"Because I like the sound of it. I think it suits me. You're more a Raff, definitely. My Raff."

"That's Lieutenant Raff."

"As you like."

"You're trying to calm me down so I don't bust up the elevator."

"It's a by-product of calming myself. I don't often have an urge to strike a woman—it's just against my nature. But I had a powerful one up there."

"When I mentally punched her, blood exploded out of her nose."

"Well then, that will have to do us both. And yet . . ." He brought her fingers to his lips. "We'll go home and work into all hours trying to find the breathtakingly rude bitch's husband."

"He has to be a dick. Nobody would stay married to that unless he was a dick. But yeah, we'll work on it."

He kept her hand in his as they crossed the lobby. "Maybe he faked an abduction to escape her."

"It would be hard to blame him, except he's a dick."

She contacted Mira as Roarke drove home, let her know she'd notified Mandy Mira.

"How did she take it?"

"She claims it's bullshit you and Mr. Mira cooked up, insulted me, Roarke, both of you, and intends to contact the governor and Whitney to report me. I told her to kiss my ass."

"I'll take care of it."

"Hey, no. I don't want you to—"

"I'll take care of it, Eve. I insist. Expect an apology."

"I don't want her to—"

"Don't argue with me on this."

Eve started to do just that, but saw the fatigue, the strain. "Okay, fine. How's Mr. Mira?"

"He's all right. No worrying symptoms. I'll keep an eye on him tonight, but I truly believe he's fine. Worried about Edward, of course."

"Let him know we're working on it, and I'll be in touch if and when."

She clicked off before Mira could thank her again, and considered investigative approaches as they turned through the gates, and toward home.

Lights gleamed welcome in the dozens and dozens of windows, glowing against the dignified stone, even in the fanciful turrets.

She considered coming home to such a wonder after an endless day her personal miracle.

They got out opposite sides of the car, circled around.

"How long did it take you to design the house—the whole elegant fortress with a touch of castle?"

"Oh, I spent years building it in my head as a boy. Every time I went to bed hungry or bruised, it got bigger."

Since his childhood had been as much a nightmare as her own, it surprised her he'd restrained himself to just huge.

"I pulled it in a bit," he said, taking her hand again as they approached the door. "Eliminated the guard towers, the moat, and accepted that the catapults of my fancy had no practical purpose."

"I don't know. Catapults would be pretty frosty."

When they stepped inside, she saw the first thing she'd have loaded into one: Roarke's majordomo.

Summerset stood in his habitual black suit—the living corpse who haunted the house. The fat cat gave one of Summerset's bony legs a rub, then jogged over to twine through Eve's, Roarke's, in a kind of pudgy feline ballet.

Eve waited a beat for the expected sneering remark on how late they'd come home, or some other insult. But he only said:

"Mr. Mira?"

"He's right enough," Roarke said, shrugging out of his coat. "Eve's just spoken with Dr. Mira."

"I'm glad to hear it. If there's anything I can do, you've only to let me know."

He drifted away in that nearly silent way of his, leaving Eve frowning after him.

"After a day like this, I don't even get to take a shot at him?"

"You told a former senator's wife to kiss your ass." He slipped off Eve's coat. "Be satisfied with that."

"That was a professional kiss my ass."

Roarke gave Galahad a quick rub before starting up the steps. "There's always tomorrow."

Since that would have to be good enough, Eve went up with him, and the cat thumped up the steps behind them.

"Dinner first," he insisted. "We'll have it in the bedroom with the fire, and the wine."

She could live with that. After, she'd set up a board in her office, do some runs, harangue the detective in Missing Persons she'd alerted. Roarke could check finances, which would entertain him. She could—

"I'll deal with the fire and the wine," Roarke said. "You deal with the pasta."

"Right. Okay. I'm going to contact his two kids, just see if they have any information. I can hit this brain trust of his in the morning if nothing's turned up."

"You mean a body. You think like a murder cop, don't you?"

"I am a murder cop. A body, because if this was kidnapping, a straight deal, there'd have been a demand for ransom. If someone just hauled him off to get something out of him, maybe they let him go after."

"But why?"

She programmed the spaghetti, added the herbed breadsticks they both liked. "Yeah, why? Unless it's some deal where he'd have to keep it zipped or be in worse. I don't know enough about him yet to get a solid handle. Instinct says we'll find the body, but that's maybe knee-jerk."

"His wife doesn't love him."

The cop she'd been would have reached that conclusion, but the cop she'd become, the one who knew love, was certain of it. "Not even in the general vicinity of love. But she's territorial, protective of their status. I don't see her setting this up. Maybe I find something that swings it that way. Mira said he played around, but the wife didn't care. Maybe she started to care for some reason—threat of divorce and loss of status."

She brought plates with generous portions to the table in the sitting area of the bedroom. Now the fire crackled, and Roarke poured deep red wine into glasses.

And the cat watched avidly.

"Summerset would've fed him, right?" Eve said.

"Oh, of course."

"Crap." She went back to the AutoChef, programmed a small dish of salmon. "He'll give us the beady eye while we eat otherwise," she claimed when Roarke lifted an eyebrow.

When Galahad pounced like a starving thing on the fish, she went back to sit, picked up the wine.

"This was supposed to happen hours ago." She took a deep drink.

"And still, here we are. It's a nice thing, however delayed, to share a meal in front of the fire on an ugly winter's night."

She twirled spaghetti around her fork, sampled. "It seriously doesn't suck. The Realtor." She twirled up another bite. "I need the Realtor. Either he—or she—is in on it, or got called off. In on it is most probable."

She forked off a bite of meatball. "It's not about selling the house." She shook her head. "Mr. Mira's the wedge there. Maybe it's politics, maybe it's personal. Maybe he owes somebody a bunch of money. But they got him into that house—meaning they knew about that house—where they assumed they'd have plenty of time and privacy. Mr. Mira screwed that up."

"So while Dennis is unconscious, they spirit Edward Mira away. And that requires a vehicle."

"Yeah, so it's most likely, having that handy, he/she/they planned to haul him off all along. Tune him up some first. Goes back to why it sounds personal. Or it's about money, which is pretty personal to a lot of people. Still . . ."

"If it were money, he's pushing to sell a valuable property, which would cover all but the most insane of debts."

"Exactly. So again, if it's money, the sensible thing is to go after the obstacle, and that's Mr. Mira. But they don't. Odds are on personal."

"Someone he judged, sentenced," Roarke suggested. "A relation or loved one of someone he sentenced. Someone he twisted the wrong way while in Congress, or someone he passed over for a position." Roarke lifted a shoulder. "A man who's had those careers makes enemies."

"A man who cats around makes them, too. A woman he dumped, the husband or lover of someone he had an affair with. A lot of ground on personal."

Nodding, Roarke twirled some pasta of his own. "Why not just finish him where he sat?"

"Yeah, yeah, yeah." She continued to eat while it stewed around in her brain. "That's why I figured kidnapping at first. But it's been hours, and no ransom demand. So . . . Wanted more time to play with him—which again leans toward getting information or just making him suffer more."

"The attack came at Dennis from behind."

She nodded, sampled the wine again. "Took some care he didn't see the attacker. Now, cold-blooded? Why not give him another whack or two, take him out, and use the violence to scare the piss out of Edward. But, no. He wasn't on the agenda."

"Which tells you there *is* an agenda."

"Take a look at this." She shifted in her chair. "The attacker walks in the house with him. That says to me, he doesn't know this person, not as a threat. Or does, again, not as a threat. The Realtor ploy—or the attacker is a Realtor, and that helped set the trap. Without the vic around to tell us, or his body to tell us, we don't know if the attacker stunned him, lured him, forced him into the study. And we don't know why they chose that spot—whether it's significant—for the tuning up. Mr. Mira doesn't think his cousin was restrained in the chair, and I didn't see any signs of it on scene. So I think at least two people. One to hold a weapon on the vic, the other to smack him around."

"If he owed money, which I hope to find out, they might

have been a couple of spine-crackers. But the ploy to get him to that location seems a bit sophisticated and unnecessary."

"Exactly. And why then take him instead of just breaking his legs? Maybe there will be a ransom demand, but without one, I don't think this is about money. Not in the usual sense. We need to cross it off, but I don't feel that."

"Sex follows next."

"Yeah. Sex makes people crazy. Mean, vindictive, violent."

"Promise?" he said and made her choke on her wine.

"Such a pervert."

"Card-carrying. But you're talking the nonentertaining and nonconsensual crazy. And I agree. But . . ." He tore a breadstick in half, offered her a share. "If beating him to death over an affair, or a thwarted affair, why take him?"

"Mr. Mira."

Roarke nodded. "The unexpected, perhaps some panic. But not enough to rush the beating. Take him elsewhere."

"That's the one I like. Shit, what do we do now? Let's get out of here—take him with us." She gestured with the breadstick, bit in. "Five gets you ten we find the body within the next twenty-four."

"I feel, even for us, such a bet would be in poor taste."

"Yeah." As she ate, she wondered who'd come up with the concept of a ball of meat, and if they'd been properly compensated. "Anyway, I'm going to approach it as a murder—let Missing Persons handle it as a missing. But if a body turns up, I'll have a jump on it. It'll be hard on Mr. Mira, even though he and his cousin weren't what you'd call friendly."

"Family's often a different kettle, isn't it?"

"Yeah, it is, and I guess the whole cousin thing can get unwieldy. Still, when you hear McNab or Peabody talk about their cousins—then there's your whole Irish cousins thing—there's a lot of ties, a lot of . . . liking. But with this cousin and his fuckhead of a wife, it's not just a lack of liking or ignoring of ties, it's . . ."

"Contempt," Roarke said, and she jabbed her fork at him in agreement.

"That's the exact word. And anybody who has contempt for somebody like Mr. Mira has to be an asshole."

"So you are expecting the dead body of an asshole within the next twenty-four."

She nodded, ate one last bite. "Yeah. Doesn't mean we don't do the job. We should add that as like an addendum to the banner the bullpen made. You know, 'No matter your race, creed, blah blah, we protect and serve, because you could get dead.' We should put one of those . . ."

She squiggled a shape with a finger in the air, making him smile because he understood her so easily. "Asterisk."

"Yeah, that thing. And add: 'Even if you're an asshole.'"

"Past tense might be more applicable, being Homicide. 'Even if you *were* an asshole.'"

"Hmm. Good point. And I'd better get started. You'll take the financials."

"With considerable delight."

They walked out together. "I'm going to send Peabody a report, bring her up to speed. I'll copy Mira on it. It shook her up. You don't see her shaken very often, but it really shook her, seeing he'd been hurt."

"Love makes us vulnerable."

"He soothed her. He's got this way. I know he was upset, and he took a hell of a knock, so he *was* hurt, but he soothed her."

"And love makes us strong. That's its wonder."

"I don't know if many people are born kind. Like it's just part of their DNA. I think Mr. Mira was. So I really wish I'd punched the Mandy-Bitch."

"You have your visual of exploding blood." Roarke patted her shoulder. "Let that be enough."

"It'll have to be."

They split off, her to her office, Roarke toward his that adjoined it. The cat opted to stick with Eve, and trotted directly to her sleep chair, leaped up, circled, circled, circled, and collapsed as if he'd run a marathon.

She went to her desk first, sat, and saw from her incomings the sweepers had taken her rush-it order to heart.

The blood on the desk chair was Edward Mira's. Floor-boards, Dennis Mira. The only prints in the study, entrance-way, doors, belonged to: Dennis and Edward Mira; Sila Robarts; Frankie Trent, Sila's mother; and Dara Robarts, Sila's daughter—the housekeepers.

So the suspects sealed up, she concluded. They'd had a plan.

She began to construct a report, with the sweepers' early results attached. Then deciding it best to also copy her com-mander, cleaned it up a little. She considered whatever hit she'd take over the "kiss my ass" comment worth it.

With the book already begun with the reports, her notes, she set up her board. Pretty thin so far, she thought, circling in and studying Edward Mira's ID shot. But still ahead of the game when the body showed up.

She started back to her desk intending to start deeper runs on all connected parties, and Roarke stepped in.

"That fast?" she commented.

"Initially. I can tell you the senator could very much use a large influx of cash."

"Gambling?"

"Not particularly, no. Lifestyle. And the Mira Institute isn't yet self-sustaining. He pumped a lot of money into it, and it continues to drain his resources. Basically, they spend a great deal. Security, entertaining, travel. They have the penthouse here in the city, another home in East Hampton, a pied-à-terre in East Washington. And memberships at very exclusive coun-try clubs in each location. The Institute also rents a suite at my Palace Hotel, as well as carrying a substantial payroll, and very high operating expenses."

He wandered over, helped himself to the coffee she had on her desk. "He's made some poorly considered invest-ments in the last two or three years, and that's depleted some of the income. There has been sporadic income from the sale of some antiques and collectibles."

"From the grandfather's estate."

"Yes, indeed. But they'll have to begin to cut a few cor-ners, or sell off one of their properties, unless they have a serious increase in cash flow. This includes his two buried accounts, and her one."

"You found three secret accounts already?" When he merely sipped her coffee, studied her over the rim, she shook her head. "Of course you did. Illegal accounts?"

"Questionable, and for a man in his position politically, unethical. The sale of the house would absolutely give him some breathing room."

"But nothing that looks like he owed somebody who'd send the spine-crackers?"

"I'll look deeper, but what I've already gone through paints a fairly clear picture. These are people accustomed to a certain lifestyle—and status—unwilling to pull back on expenses to keep their financial ship comfortably afloat. For instance, she spends between ten and twelve thousand a month on salon and spa visits. Not including twice a year body and face work, which triples that amount. He isn't far behind her in that area."

"Jesus, that's, what, in the land of a quarter of a mil annually for vanity."

"That's the geography. And this is nothing, really, up against what he's invested and continues to invest in the Institute. He put in twenty million of his own to launch it, and though he receives around a million annually from it, he pumps that, and a bit more, back in to keep it running. I can tell you that in the last eighteen months to two years, money has become a serious issue for him."

"Okay, he needs to sell—that's his motive. We need to find out who gets his share of said potential sale on his death. Wife and/or kids, most likely."

She circled the board again. "The wife doesn't want to give up the lifestyle. Would she have him killed over it?" Pausing, Eve studied the ID shot. "Wouldn't surprise me. She's got the chops for it. He probably has death insurance. He kicks, she's not only the grieving widow, but she'd be pretty well set."

She stuck her hands in her pockets, rocked back on her heels. Shook her head. "But the method's all wrong for it.

Even if she hired somebody. Here's a bunch of money. Beat up my husband, kill him—and do it in this location because maybe she figures Dennis would agree to sell under those conditions."

"My cousin's grieving wife, he was killed here. Selling it will help us all heal. Yes." Considering, Roarke offered her the rest of the coffee. "I could see it. Convoluted as it is."

"Too convoluted. Plus, if they're hired hits, be done with it. You don't haul him off."

"You're back to personal."

"Yeah, I am. He doesn't owe anybody, no signs he's paying or extorting blackmail?"

"Not that I've found, no."

"So, it's about the money for him, but it's not about money for whoever has him. Sex."

Roarke wrapped his arms around her waist. "Delighted."

"Not us, ace. Money, politics, women—those appear to be his main deals. Money just isn't playing. Politics—he's not a senator anymore, but there's that brain trust. I'll look into that, but if he's fueling it to keep it running, how much influence does it, or he, have . . . politically? So it comes down to sex. The suite at your hotel. I bet it makes a nice love nest."

"We do try to keep such things well-feathered."

"Ha. I bet you could tug a line and get me some names of lovebirds Senator Hound Dog might have roosted with. That doesn't sound right," she realized with a frown. "I've lost the colorful metaphor."

"But it held long enough. I can tug a line, of course. And if he used it to entertain, I'll have names or at least faces for you. Give me a few minutes."

She went back for more coffee, then sat down to do the runs.

It didn't surprise her when Roarke finished his task before she did.

"Five women in the past year. I've sent you their names. All multiple visits, on a weekly basis, most lasting between six and eight weeks. I want a brandy."

"Five, in a year. And he's nearly seventy."

"Medical science, and we salute it, has made that issue moot." He opened the wall slot, took out a decanter. "I've sent them to you in order of appearance. I can also tell you: While the senator uses the suite on the average of once a week for personal purposes, he generally stays the night. The lady of the moment rarely does."

She generated ID shots, added them to the board. "All but two legally married. And the latest is twenty-five. I mean, humping Jesus, he has more than forty years on her. It's just wrong."

When Roarke just swirled and sipped brandy, she narrowed her eyes. "He's old enough to be her grandfather."

"I don't like the man—less now than I did before—but I can't help but admire his . . . stamina."

"That's dick-thinking."

"Well . . ." Roarke glanced down at his own. "It does have opinions."

Muttering to herself, she got up to circle the board. "They're all lookers, I'll give him that. And not one of them within fifteen years of his age. This Lauren Canford's his oldest pick at forty-two. Married, two kids, a lobbyist. That's a political thing. And the baby of the bunch, Charity Downing, twenty-five, single, an artist who works at Eclectia—a gallery in SoHo. Asha Coppola, on her second marriage, works for a nonprofit—age thirty-one. Allyson Byson, third marriage—is that optimism or insanity? Anyway, third marriage at age thirty-four, no occupation. And Carlee MacKensie, twenty-eight, single, freelance writer.

"I'll take a look at them, and their spouses."

"I've some work of my own unless you need something more."

"No, go ahead. Thanks."

He gave her until midnight and, as expected, found her starting to droop over the work.

"That's a big enough jump on things for one night."

She didn't argue, knew she had to let it simmer and settle.

And if she was wrong, Edward Mira might limp home before morning.

But she wasn't wrong.

"Did you know Mr. Mira and his cousin both went to Yale? The senator was a year ahead of him—would've been two but Mr. Mira graduated early. And he came out of Yale with that Latin deal—the magnum thing."

"Magna cum laude."

"Yeah, that. And the Phi Beta deal, too. Graduated third in his class. The senator graduated like seventy-whatever in his. Mr. Mira has all these letters after his name. Don't know what half of them are, and he served as class president his senior year, was the valedictorian. The senator did more than okay, but on an academic level, Mr. Mira kicked his ass."

"I imagine that didn't sit well with the future senator."

"I'm thinking not. Anyway, the Urbans were just starting to rumble, and Mr. Mira was a frigging captain of the campus peace patrol. The campus was far enough out of the city, so reasonably safe, but there was trouble, and demonstrations, and regular bomb threats."

In the bedroom, she sat to take off her boots. "The senator got his law degree, and took a job with a law firm in Sunnyside— away from the conflict. Mr. Mira came back to New York, got his master's from Columbia. He got the doctorate from there, too, so they're *both* Dr. Mira. He and Mira cohabbed for like a year."

She shook her head as she undressed. "I never figured them for cohabs, you know? And looking into that stuff felt weird. Voyeuristic, but still. And they're both starting out their careers and their life together in a city shaking from the Urbans. They got married at the grandparents' house. There was this whole story I dug up. I shouldn't have been taking time to look at stuff like that, but . . ."

"It's lovely."

"Yeah. And it shows another reason why the house matters so much to him." She pulled on a sleep shirt, crawled into bed. "The senator and Mandy tied it up at the Palace—before your time—in a big, splashy deal."

She turned to him when he slid into bed with her. "You could've had a big, splashy deal when we tied it up. Why didn't you?"

"You wouldn't have liked it." He wrapped around her, drawing her in where he liked her best. "And for myself, I wanted our lives to begin where it mattered most. Home. I wanted that memory to be here—like the painting you had done for me. Of the two of us, under the arbor on our wedding day."

She let out a sigh. "Maybe we'll make it there."

"Make it where?"

But she'd already dropped away into sleep, and didn't answer.

Chapter 3

She hovered just under the surface of sleep with strange little dreams winding through, braiding together, then fading off like ribbons of smoke.

Despite the misty parade of dreams, more odd than disturbing, she felt warm and secure and content.

So when Roarke shifted away, she edged over, holding on to that warmth, that security, that contentment.

His lips brushed her brow as he started to untangle himself from her.

She said, "Uh-uh."

"Sleep," he murmured, and would have lifted her arm away but she tightened her hold.

"Too early. Still dark. Stay."

"I've a holo conference in—"

She just didn't care, and angling her head found his mouth in the dark.

She wanted not just the arousal, but the intimacy of the quiet, the silky splendor of unity before the world woke and pulled them both back into the bright and the hard.

Just him—she wanted just him—in the big bed under the sky window before dawn crept in cold.

So she drew him with her into the soft and the sweet.

He heard her sigh with the kiss that built a shimmering bridge between night and day, one that poured love into him like liquid gold. And she shifted over him, laying heart to heart, mouth to mouth, body to body.

The long lines of her enchanted him: smooth skin, firm muscle. His hands roamed, slid under the thin shirt she slept in, glided up the lean length. He thought he could be content, his world complete, if a moment just like this spun into forever.

Then she rose up, tugged her shirt up and away, and took him in.

Pleasure leaped, one hot, hard bound, then settled into soft beats, like a pulse, a proof of life. They were shadows in the dark, cocooned in its secrets, bathed in its silence, enspelled by each other. She rocked him, rocked herself, toward bliss with slow, undulating movements that gripped his heart, ruled his body.

He rose up to her, his hands lost in her hair, his mouth locked on hers, and his heart—all its chambers—flooded with love. They took each other now into the slow burn of sensations kindled by that steady flame of love, beat by beat until the pulse was all.

Joined, they rose and they fell together.

Again she sighed, still wound around him, her cheek pressed to his. "Okay," she said, sighing again. "Okay."

When he lay back with her, she was limp as melted wax and just as warm. He brushed his hand over her hair, over her cheek, made her smile.

"I think we'll make it."

"Didn't we just?"

Still smiling, she jabbed a finger in his belly. "Not that—though that was really nice. I guess my brain keeps circling around the Miras. You weren't there with them at the crime scene. It was . . . it's the way they look at each other, and touch. A couple times I had to look away because it felt like

I was intruding. They've been married for decades, but when you see them like that . . . like last night? You know why."

She closed her eyes. "I want that. I never thought I did or could or would, but I want that. I want to be with you for decades and have you still look at me the way he looks at her."

"You're the love of my life. And always will be."

"Maybe you could tell me that in like thirty years."

"That's a promise. And now, love of my life, go back to sleep."

She frowned when he rolled out of bed. "It's the middle of the night."

"It's near to half five now."

"Some people, who aren't you, consider that the middle of the night."

"It's the middle of the day in Europe, and I've a holo conference very shortly."

While he went to shower, she half dozed, but found her mind wouldn't shut down again. She barely heard him come out, dress—the man moved like a shadow.

Which probably factored into his success as a thief back in the day.

Alone, she lay another few minutes, then gave it up.

"Lights twenty-five percent."

When they came on, she nearly jolted. The cat was sprawled at the foot of the bed, giving her the beady eye.

"Christ, you're as bad as Roarke, skulking around."

She figured the early morning sex had annoyed the cat, but it had set her up just fine. She programmed coffee, started fueling her brain as she went into the shower.

Since she beat Roarke to the AutoChef, she programmed breakfast for both of them—nothing like waffles on a cold January morning to her mind—and left them under their warming domes while she dressed.

She sat down with coffee, her PPC, and got a jump on her workday.

"Now, here's a lovely sight on a bitter winter's day."

She glanced over, decided he was a pretty good sight

himself in his ruler-of-the-business-world suit. "Finished buying Europe already?"

"Not buying today—so far—just a bit of engineering and tech advancing through the R&D stage. And well advancing."

He sat, poured coffee from the pot on the table, then uncovered the breakfast plates. "Waffles, is it?"

"It should almost always be. I'm having Peabody meet me at the Mira Institute at eight sharp. I want to get a sense of the place, what Edward Mira had going there. We should have time to grab an interview with a couple of his skirts before we have to head back. Trueheart's getting his shield at oh-ten hundred."

"I hate to miss that, particularly since you'll be in uniform." He watched her drown her waffles in butter and syrup.

So did Galahad, who began a stealthy inch-by-inch bellying forward until Roarke cocked an eyebrow at him. The cat rolled onto his back, batting busily at the air.

"I'll be stripping off the uniform as soon as the ceremony's over."

"I *really* hate to miss that."

"Ha ha. We'll hit the rest of the skirts, then talk to his offspring. Maybe they'll have more to say than his wife."

"I assume you've already checked, and he hasn't shown up. Alive or dead."

"Not so far. I'll check in again later with Missing Persons, and have Peabody keep up a running check with hospitals. Got a BOLO on him, and an alert."

She stuffed in more waffles, and thought if every day started off with sex and waffles, people would maybe be less inclined to kill each other.

Or maybe not.

"If he shows up dead, I'll get tagged," she added. "Meanwhile, I'm having the locals check his other residences, just in case. I expect the lab to confirm the elephant this morning."

"That's not a phrase you hear often."

"Heavy object used to whack Mr. Mira. Fancy elephant statue. I dreamed it came to life and started rampaging through that brownstone. It's only about this big." She stopped eating long enough to hold up her hands. "But still, elephant."

"There are times I envy the creativity of your dream life."

"I think I stunned it before it got out and tore up the neighborhood, but it's vague, and it sort of rolled into another one."

"The elephant rolled into another elephant?"

"No, the dream—well, sort of the elephant. I had it in Interview. You know like: You're looking at attempted murder, Mr. Phant, but if you cooperate I can see about dealing that down to simple assault."

He laughed hard enough to have Galahad making another try for waffles. Roarke just waved the cat away. "Is it a wonder I adore you? 'Mr. Phant.' "

"Yeah, it seems funny now, but I was pretty serious. I think the damn elephant's the only tangible thing I've got here, and it was nothing more than handy. It doesn't apply."

"It was used to hurt someone who matters a great deal to you."

"Yeah, I guess. I'm going to try to swing by there sometime today, depending on how things go." Since they were there, she plucked a fat blackberry out of the little bowl, frowned. "Am I supposed to take something? Like, I don't know, flowers or something?"

"I wouldn't think it's necessary, but flowers or a small token? Never wrong."

"Okay, well, we'll see how it goes." She polished off the waffles. "I'm going to review a couple things, check in with Mira, and get going."

"Let me know if the senator shows up, one way or the other, would you?"

"Sure."

"I'll be seeing Nadine later today," he said when Eve rose to strap on her weapon harness, toss a jacket over it. "She's got where she wants to be down to a warehouse space prime for conversion and a triplex on the Upper West Side."

"Triplex—a penthouse kind of thing, slick building, fully secured, lots of amenities?"

"It is, yes."

"Tell her to take the triplex. She might think a warehouse is frosty, and how she can renovate it, make it slick and sleek, but the process would make her crazy. Plus, when? She's got her gigs at Channel Seventy-five, the book thing, blah blah."

She glanced back at him. "Both of them yours?"

"They are—she eliminated several other locations and properties, then asked me to suggest two of mine. And asked if I'd take her through both today. She's been having nightmares and wants to get out of her apartment."

"Told her not to open the damn door," Eve muttered. "Triplex, done." She walked back, leaned over, and kissed him. "Later."

He tugged her back for another kiss. "Take care of my cop."

"I gotta, since you've got something to tell me about thirty years from now. Triplex," she repeated as she started out. "Tell her to stop fucking around and do it."

She'd assumed she'd left in plenty of time—even early—but traffic snarled and stalled the entire way. She reached the Chrysler Building, wondering why more people didn't work from home and leave the streets to those who really needed them. She hunted up parking, then traveled two blocks on foot.

Roarke had been correct about the bitter morning. The sky was a bowl of hard, pale blue, and the air was just as hard and pale. She stuffed her hands in the pockets of her coat, searching for warmth, and found gloves.

New gloves, with some sort of lining that felt like a warm cloud. It wouldn't take her long to lose them, she thought, but for the moment, they were welcome.

She started to tag Peabody to get an ETA, then spotted her partner at the crosswalk.

There was no mistaking that pink coat in a sea of blacks, grays, and dark blues. Add the multicolored hat on the short flip of dark hair, the mile of scarf—in bleeding blues today—and she could've spotted Peabody six blocks off.

She waited while her partner joined the river surge across the street.

"How's Mr. Mira?" Peabody asked immediately. "Did you check this morning?"

"Not yet. I don't want to bother them if they're sleeping."

"Yeah, but if he has a concussion—"

"Mira will haul him to the hospital if he needs it. He looked okay yesterday by the time I sent them home."

"I hate that somebody hurt him."

"They could've done worse—be glad they didn't."

She turned toward the entrance of the grand Deco building.

"I never put it together he was related to Senator Mira. I mean, could they be less alike?"

Eve frowned as she pushed through the door. "You know Edward Mira?"

"Yes. I mean, not personally. Politically. Free-Ager," Peabody reminded her. "I pretty much disagree with everything he's for, but . . ."

Peabody trailed off, gaping and neck-craning like a tourist. "I've never been in here. It's abso mag!"

"Stop gawking." Eve added an elbow jab. "Be a fricking cop."

It impressed, sure, with its three-story entrance, the golden-red marble walls, the glow of the golden floors and palatial pillars.

But cops didn't gawk.

Eve left Peabody trailing behind her—likely still gawking—and approached one of the info screens.

Welcome. Please state your desired destination.

"The Mira Institute."

The image of the iconic building on screen morphed into the logo for the Institute.

The Mira Institute occupies floors thirty and thirty-one, with its main lobby on floor thirty. Please state the party or department you wish to visit, and you will be directed.

"The main lobby works."

Please see the guard at the security station for screening and admittance. Enjoy your visit and the rest of your day.

Even as Eve turned, two uniformed guards stepped in front of her.

"Keep your hands visible. You need to come with us."

Already been screened, she thought, and their weapons had alerted security.

"We're NYPSD. I'm going to reach for my badge. Got that?"

She kept her moves slow just in case one of them had a jumpy stunner finger, took out her badge.

The man she showed it to took it, ran it with a pocket scanner. "Lieutenant," he said, handing it back. "We'll need to see yours, too," he added to Peabody.

Once satisfied, he nodded and his companion stepped away, murmured into a lapel mic.

"You're clear. Take the east bank of elevators to thirty. I'll alert them. Otherwise, you'll be stopped when you get off. They have secondary security on thirty."

"Appreciate it."

They crossed the lobby, joined a small, chatty group getting on the elevator. She smelled coffee in someone's go-cup, so sweet it nearly made her teeth ache, and someone else's overly floral perfume. Two women chirped like mynah birds about hitting the inventory sales downtown on their lunch break, while some guy in a Russian cossack hat droned on into his pocket 'link about a nine o'clock staff meeting.

Eve decided if she was forced to always work in an office, she'd just jump out the nearest window and be done with it.

The mynah birds got off on twenty. Coffee-flavored sugar on twenty-three. Drenched in flowers glided off on spike-heeled boots and a swish of black coat on twenty-seven.

They got off on thirty with the droner.

Reception centered around an S-shaped counter backed by a floor-to-ceiling logo in sober and serious block letters. The waiting area faced the wide window, tinted to cut the glare. Black gel sofas ranged alongside a trio of gold scoop chairs with controls in their wide backs for music, refreshment, privacy settings, and communication. A life-size portrait of Edward Mira peered down righteously from the far wall.

A woman manned the first wide curve of the counter. She wore a black suit with thin silver piping and triangular shoulders sharp enough to slice bread. She worked busily at a muscular computer, but paused to flash a welcoming smile.

"Lieutenant Dallas, Detective Peabody. Security notified me of your arrival. How can I help you today?"

"We need to speak to whoever's in charge."

"Of what?"

Eve pointed at the enormous logo. "Of this."

"I'm afraid Senator Mira isn't in. If you'd tell me the nature of your visit, I should be able to direct you to the appropriate party."

"The second in command."

The faintest flicker of annoyance ran through the polite mask. "Perhaps Ms. MacDonald or Mr. Book could assist you. If you'd care to take a seat, I'll see if either are available."

"They'll want to be." Rather than moving to the waiting area, Eve simply stood where she was.

"One moment."

The woman tapped a control on the arm of her chair. It glided along the S, stopped at the far curve. She tapped her earpiece, turned one of her lethally clad shoulders.

"It feels like nobody here knows the founder's missing."

Eve glanced toward the portrait. "The detective on the missing angle's started the ball rolling. I'd say it hasn't rolled this far yet."

"But wouldn't his wife—"

"You had to be there," Eve said as the receptionist glided back.

"Ms. MacDonald will see you. If you'll just take the elevator to three-one, someone will escort you to her office."

Eve stepped in, requested the floor. Then shook her head when Peabody pulled out her PPC. "I ran the top dogs last night. MacDonald, Tressa, forty-three. Divorce times two. One offspring, male. Law degree, Harvard with a side of poli-sci. Clerked for Judge Mira back in the day, served as his chief of staff during the senator years."

"That's a lot without notes."

"I figure the senator did her along the way, and she deserves a close look."

If the entrance to thirty had been slickly professional, the thirty-first floor hit palatial.

Yeah, Eve thought, this was top-dog territory with its thick red rugs over white marble. Three people worked at the single curve of red counter, and lush potted trees flanked the window wall. Seating ran to slate-gray leather arranged in conversational groupings. Currently the gigantic wall screen split to show six of the twenty-four/seven media broadcasts.

It wouldn't be long, Eve thought, before those broadcasts included stories on former Senator Mira—alive or dead.

As they started for the counter, a beefy man with a neck thick as a boar's came through double, frosted doors.

He looked like a brawler wearing a ten-thousand-dollar suit.

"Lieutenant Dallas, Detective Peabody. I'm Aiden Bannion, Ms. MacDonald's admin. I'll take you to her office."

She'd never seen anyone who looked less like an admin, but followed him through the doors and into an open office area where workstations were separated by willpower rather than structure.

She smelled coffee and someone's take-out breakfast while voices clashed, 'links jangled, keyboards clattered.

If you took away the fancy floors and colors, the fashionable wardrobe and footwear, it wasn't much different from her own bullpen.

They wound through, past offices with doors firmly closed, and to the corner office with the double doors signaling its rank.

As these were open, he stepped straight in.

"Lieutenant Dallas and Detective Peabody."

"Thanks, Aiden—two seconds." She tapped her earpiece. "I'm back. If you take care of your end on that, I'll take care of mine. By end of day. That's great. We'll talk later. Bye now."

She rose as she signed off, a small, slender woman in a soft gray suit with a little frill of white over the cleavage. She wore her hair, flaming, fiery red, in curls that spilled to her shoulders.

She came around the desk, assessing Eve with dark green eyes.

"Tressa MacDonald." She held out a hand, shook Eve's, then Peabody's with a brisk, firm grip. "Someone's hurt or worse. I know who you are," she explained in a voice as brisk and firm as her handshake. "I know your reputation. You're Homicide. If someone's dead, would you tell me quickly?"

"There's been no homicide or death I know of at this time."

Tressa let out a short breath. "All right, that's a relief. Please, sit. Can I offer you coffee? Aiden's assistant makes a killer latte."

"I'd love one," Peabody said before Eve could deny them both.

"That's two lattes. Lieutenant?"

"Just coffee. Straight coffee. Black."

"Thanks, Aiden." Tressa gestured to her sitting area, taking the sofa in nearly the same shade as her eyes while Eve and Peabody sat in deep blue chairs. "What's this about?"

"Yesterday at approximately five P.M. Edward Mira was assaulted—"

"What?" Tressa's spine snapped straight. "Where is he? How seriously was he hurt?"

"I can't tell you because he's missing."

"What do you mean 'missing'? I don't—" She stopped herself, shook her head. "I'm sorry. I know better. One second." She looked away, drew a breath, then another, slower. "Please, tell me what you know."

"Were you aware that Senator Mira had an appointment yesterday with a real estate agent regarding the sale of a property he owns with his cousin Dennis Mira?"

"No." She rubbed two fingers over the space between her eyes. "No, I wasn't aware."

"Do you know the name of the Realtor he worked with?"

"He'd worked with Silas Greenbaum—Greenbaum Realty—until recently."

"Until recently?"

"Yes." She glanced over as Aiden brought in the coffee, with a dish of thin cookies, on a tray. "Thanks, Aiden. Do you know what Realtor the senator was using?"

"No, I don't, not since he severed ties with Greenbaum."

"Check with Liddy, would you? See who he had an appointment with regarding the Spring Street property yesterday."

"Of course."

"And close the door please, Aiden. You believe whoever he met assaulted him?"

"He was assaulted in the house. His cousin Dennis Mira entered the property, followed the sound of voices to the study. He saw Edward Mira, injured, started in to assist him, and was himself attacked from behind."

"Dennis?" Her fingers lifted to the white frill at her bodice. "Is he all right?"

"You know Dennis Mira?"

"Yes, very well. You can't possibly think he had anything to do . . . Of course you don't." Now she pushed at her hair. "You work with his wife, you know him. And from everything I know about you, the two of you, you're not idiots, so you know Dennis would never hurt anyone. I'm sorry to keep interrupting. I can't sit."

She rose, began to pace. "I'll handle it better on my feet."

Since Eve generally felt the same, she nodded. "When

Dennis Mira regained consciousness, the senator was gone. Unless he's shown up since we came in here, he hasn't been seen since."

"Kidnapping? But no demand for ransom? You've spoken with Mandy, surely. If there was a ransom demand it would go to her, or come through here."

"Yes, I've spoken with her. She wasn't able to offer any information."

"He has a house in the Hamptons, and an apartment in East Washington. But you've checked."

"I have."

After a brief knock, Aiden opened the door. "The senator didn't give Liddy a name, just told her he had an outside appointment. A four-thirty with a new Realtor. He left shortly after four. Vinnie drove him to the Spring Street property. The senator told him not to wait, he had transportation from there. Liddy doesn't have any information about a new Realtor."

"Thank you, Aiden. Would you tell Wyatt to put aside whatever he's doing and come in here?"

"Right away."

When he left, Tressa squared her shoulders, came back to sit, picked up her latte. "You'll need to know where I was yesterday. Four-thirty?"

"Let's make it from four to six P.M."

"I was in meetings here until about a quarter to five. Wyatt, Aiden, and several others can verify. I had drinks scheduled for five with Marcella Candine at Bistro on Lex. We were there until shortly after six. I took a cab from there to my mother's. It was my sister's birthday, and we had a dinner party. Family dinner."

Wyatt Book didn't knock. He simply strode in, an imposing man twenty years Tressa's senior with a shock of hair in an improbable inky black. His crisp suit mirrored the color, as did his eyes. They flicked off Tressa, zeroed in on Eve.

"What's this about?"

"Edward's missing."

" 'Missing'? Don't be ridiculous."

"Have you seen or spoken with him since yesterday afternoon?" Eve asked.

"No, but that hardly means he's missing, and he certainly won't appreciate having the police hound him or blather gossip to the media."

Eve started to rise, but Tressa beat her to it. "Wyatt, sit down, be quiet for a minute. Edward was attacked in his grandfather's brownstone, and now he's missing."

"'Attacked'? Absurd. Where was Vinnie?"

"Edward dismissed him. He went there to meet someone, supposedly a new Realtor. Dennis Mira was also attacked."

"Ha." The mild concern faded into mild amusement. "The two of them probably finally took swings at each other."

"Now who's being ridiculous and absurd."

"For God's sake." Irritation flashed over his face as he pulled out his 'link. "I'm sending a nine-one-one to his private number, which he won't appreciate, either. But it will stop this malarkey." But he frowned. "It's not going through, even to v-mail."

"Which tells me whoever has him is smart enough to destroy his 'link," Eve put in. "Who's the new Realtor?"

"I have no idea, and that's more malarkey. He'll go back to Silas once they both cool down."

"They had an altercation?"

"Edward fired him a couple weeks ago because Silas refused to list or show the property."

"Which Silas can't do," Tressa continued, "as Edward doesn't own the property outright."

"I'm aware. Does Senator Mira have any enemies?"

Wyatt let out a derisive snort, plopped down on the couch. "Whose coffee is this?"

"Go ahead," Eve told him. "I haven't touched it."

"He's a lawyer who became a judge who became a senator." Wyatt gulped down coffee. "He made an enemy every time he woke up in the morning."

"There have been threats," Tressa said more frankly. "As long as I've known him. Anything serious was investigated. But that's certainly eased off since he retired from Congress."

"Anyone stick out?" Eve waited a beat. "Any of the women he's been involved with? Someone he severed ties with there, or a spouse who didn't appreciate the relationship."

"I stay out of Edward's personal life," Tressa said coolly, but Wyatt leaned forward.

"We can't have any talk of extramarital affairs and dalliances leaked to the media."

"I'm not interested in gossip, Mr. Book. I'm interested in finding Senator Mira. Investigating his personal life is part of the job, nothing more or less."

"I'm warning you—"

"You want to be careful about warning me when it comes to doing my job. Who's he seeing now?"

"She's an artist." Tressa stopped Wyatt's protest with a hot look. "Finding Edward's more important than pretenses. She's young. I don't know her name. I really do try to stay out of it. Aiden can find out."

"It's okay. I've got that one already. And, surprise, there's been no media bulletin. Detective Hanson will follow up." Eve got to her feet. "He's leading the missing persons investigation. If you have any more information, you can contact him or me."

"Is there anything we can do in the meantime?"

"Find out the name of the Realtor," Eve suggested. "Thanks for your time."

Chapter 4

They wound their way out.

"You don't want a look at his appointment book, his calendar?" Peabody asked.

"The place is thick with lawyers. We're not getting a look at anything without a warrant. Once it's murder, I'll get one. Hanson has to run his angle from here—so send him the name of the driver and the former Realtor. We'll talk to the list of women, his son and daughter," she began, checking the time. "Later. This took longer than I planned."

"We're heading in? We're not going to miss Trueheart?"

"We're heading in."

"Yay!"

"Hold the yay. Impressions, observations, conclusions," Eve said as they rode down.

"The whole place is big on status, and that sort of thing usually comes from the top. I thought places like this—political think tanks, activists, and the like—would be lower key, even a little sweaty. I didn't get any vibe from either of them, or Aiden, at least not this time around. MacDonald seemed genuinely worried. Book, not so much."

"Why do you think that is?"

"I'd say Book doesn't care as much about the senator, not personally. What? You don't think that's it?"

"Might be, part of it anyway. I figure Book thinks the senator's off snuggled up with the young artist or some other sidepiece. That plays for him more than any kind of abduction."

For sentiment as much as warmth Eve pulled on the snow-flake hat as they crossed the lobby. "MacDonald had a strong point. Back when he was a judge, then a senator, he likely had a serious enemies list. He was a hard-liner on the bench and in Congress and kept himself in the spotlight pushing agendas. He still goes on those political talk shows and sort of raves about anything he disagrees with. Government spending's high on the list and he goes off on a lot of social programs. During his last term he went hard after professional parenthood, had all these figures on what it would save the government to gut the law, and how his wife was honored to be a stay-at-home mother when their children came along, and never took a dime of government money for it."

"Did anyone point out his wife was rolling in it, and I bet my ass and yours had a staff?"

"Yeah, that sort of thing, and the fact that the Professional Parent Act is about as popular as they get, is why his numbers tanked. The pundits figure he opted not to run because he couldn't win."

"The pundits."

Peabody shrugged, all but buried her chin in the folds of her scarf. "Sometimes I watch when I'm crafting. McNab doesn't mind because if they have someone like Senator Horseshit on there, or Congresswoman Vidali—you know about her?"

"I don't, and don't want to."

"Well, she's such a liar, and a hypocrite. I *hate* when people like that start in on how God wants them to whatever, like they have some secret handshake with God the rest of us don't know about. It gets me pretty worked up. Then we have hot sex."

Eve's eye wanted to twitch, but she willed it away. "You and Vidali."

Peabody snickered. "Oh yeah, we're all over each other. But seriously, mostly I'd like to punch her. I'll think: Man, I'd like to punch you right in your lying face. So I jump McNab instead. It works for us."

Eve thought of the scarf she was wearing, and wondered how many times Peabody had jumped McNab during the making thereof. She decided never to think about it again. Ever.

She got in the car, shot into a skinny gap in traffic, and let horns blast in her wake.

"We'll take ten after the ceremony, then it's back in street clothes. I want to talk to the artist first."

"In her twenties, right? That's just icky—and I'm not an age bigot."

"What do the pundits say?"

"Not much on screen. Maybe it's an unspoken rule or something. But if you go on some political blogs and websites, there's a lot of chatter about his diddling. Not just him, but this is about him, so . . . I haven't read anything about the artist. Yet."

"Why don't you dig into that area? The diddling area. Maybe there's chatter about somebody not on my list, or smoke about bitter breakups. You dig up anything, you copy me and Hanson."

"On it, over it, and through it. In fact . . ." Peabody pulled out her PPC. "I'll get started on it now."

Eve drove the rest of the way in silence, broken only by the occasional angry mutter from her partner.

She took a quick scan when she turned into Homicide. Carmichael hustled in from the locker room, in full dress blues. Trueheart and his trainer, now partner, were either still sprucing up or already headed down for the induction. Both Santiago and Jenkinson sat at their desks, one on a 'link, the other on a comp.

Santiago obviously still had some time on the bet he'd lost to Carmichael, as he had the cowboy hat perched on his head. And Jenkinson had managed to find yet another eye-burning tie. This one had puke-green and piss-yellow stripes.

Saying nothing, she circled a finger in the air in a wind-it-up signal, then took five in her office to grab coffee and write up brief notes.

She made it to the locker room after Peabody and found her partner in her uniform pants, bra, undertank, and tears.

"What? What is it? Don't do that."

"My pants are loose."

"Well, Christ, tighten your belt."

At Eve's impatient order, a fresh tear spilled. "They're loose in the waist, and even a little baggy in the butt. I lost some weight. I actually lost some weight. I know how this uniform fit the last time I wore it. And now it's just a little bit loose."

"Okay, great, woo! Now pull it together."

"I've really been trying, especially the last few weeks. I've been hitting the gym three times a week. I stopped weighing myself," she said as Eve pulled out her own uniform. "Because the number just wouldn't budge and it's so damn discouraging. You don't know what it's like."

Though undressing in front of anyone but Roarke made her uncomfortable, Eve started to strip. "Maybe I don't, exactly. But I was skinny. I don't mean thin or lean, I mean skinny. And weak. I had to work to build myself up some, to build some muscle, get strong. So I know what it's like to look in the mirror and not really like what's looking back."

"I never thought of it like that."

"You lose weight, tone up, you do it to get fit and strong, not to hit a number. Anybody with a brain knows that."

"I do know that. I still want the number, but I know that. I've been working on my hand-to-hand, too."

"Good." Eve pulled on her own uniform pants, decided they fit the way they always did.

"But . . . does my ass look smaller?"

"Jesus, Peabody."

"Come on, be a pal. Does it?"

Eve pulled on her uniform jacket, narrowed her eyes in a long, hard study. "I can barely see it."

On a watery laugh, Peabody did a little shuffle dance. "Thanks. You've got to wear your medals."

"Yeah, yeah."

"Want me to help you pin them on? All that weight."

"Bite me. And next time I'm getting dressed in my office."

Smiling, Peabody buttoned her jacket. "I'm proud to wear the uniform today. I mean, I always was, but especially today."

"Because your pants are loose."

"Well, that, but mostly for Trueheart. I'm proud to wear it for Trueheart."

Eve took out the box that held her medals and thought, Yes. For Trueheart.

She caught Baxter—who'd traded his usually snappy suit for dress blues—already seated in the front row.

"Cutting it close, LT."

"I've got time. You need to switch with me, stand up there with Trueheart."

Baxter got to his feet. "I appreciate the offer, sincerely. But he deserves his lieutenant. I'm going to sit here, front row center—saved you a spot, Peabody—and bask. His mom's right over there, and his girl. You should say something to her. Them."

"I will, after."

She went around the back, through a river of blue, and spotted Commander Whitney standing aside in conversation with Chief Tibble.

She started toward Trueheart, who was looking young, a little pale, and daisy fresh, but Whitney signaled her over.

"Commander. Chief Tibble. It's a good day."

"It is." Whitney scanned the lineup, a broad-shouldered man beside Tibble's longer length.

"It's good you could be here, Chief. It means a lot to the men and women being promoted."

"And to me. Before we get to that, to acknowledging them, I'd like the status on Senator Mira."

"Detective Peabody and I just got back from interviews at his institute. As far as we can ascertain no one there knew he was missing. He didn't give the name of the individual he arranged to meet at the property in SoHo to his admin, and dismissed his driver on arrival there. I've reached out to Detective Hanson in Missing Persons, and he should be following up at the Institute by now. Peabody and I will begin questioning certain women the senator had relationships with over the past year. I have information he took them, regularly, to the Institute's suite at the Palace Hotel."

Tibble's jaw tightened as he shook his head. "The media's going to tear into that like lions on an antelope. Not our problem. No ransom demands as yet?"

"Not to my knowledge."

"I don't have to tell you to dot all the *i*'s. This will hit the media soon, one way or the other. They'll rip through him, but they'll spotlight the department and the investigation."

"Understood, sir."

"For now, we'll honor our officers. I've heard good things about your boy, Lieutenant."

"My boy, sir?"

Tibble smiled, deepening the lines fanning out from his eyes. "Trueheart. You did well there."

"Detective Baxter trained him. He did well."

"I'll make sure to tell him so. Excuse me."

When Tibble moved off, Whitney turned to Eve, his dark, wide face sober. "It isn't prudent or professional to tell a former senator's wife to kiss your ass."

"No, sir. I apologize for any difficulty my lapse caused you and the department."

"My wife told her to shove it."

"I'm sorry, what?"

Though his tone remained quiet and serious, humor, bright and unmistakable, fired up in his eyes. "Anna served on a couple of charity committees with Mandy Mira. In general, my wife's anger is shown in cold disdain."

"I'm aware," Eve said before she could stop herself, but Whitney only chuckled.

"However, Mandy Mira flipped the switch, and among other unkind suggestions, Anna told her to shove it. She won't serve on any committee or function with the senator's wife any longer. She was delighted when she overheard my conversation with Mandy Mira last night, and enjoyed talking to our own Mira about the incident when Charlotte contacted me about it. Officially, I can't condone your behavior."

"No, sir."

"Consider yourself reprimanded." His face settled back into commanding lines. "Now, let's give some good cops their moment, and get back to work."

Eve stood on the stage with other ranking officers and those being promoted. She stood at parade rest through the speeches—mercifully brief—from Tibble, from Whitney. A scan of the audience showed every single member of her division in attendance, and, though she wondered who the hell was manning the ship, it made her proud to know every one of them—detectives, uniforms—took the time to be there for Trueheart.

She picked out Feeney, McNab, Mira, who like Trueheart looked a little pale, and to her surprise, Morris. As each officer's name was called he or she stepped up to Whitney for the presentation, a few personal words from the commander, the photo op.

She could pick out family members by their glistening eyes during the applause.

"Troy Trueheart, Detective, third grade."

Applause broke out hard and fast, and she managed to keep her face sober—even through the whistles and foot stomping from her division. She watched him cross the stage, a little flushed rather than pale now, and accept his gold shield.

"Lieutenant Dallas saw your potential," Whitney said

quietly to Trueheart. "Detective Baxter nurtured it. But it's what you are that's earned this shield. Congratulations, Detective."

"Thank you, sir. Thank you, Commander. I won't disappoint them, or you."

He held his new shield up for the photo op, and did the right thing to her mind by looking straight at Baxter before he shifted his gaze to his mother and his sweetheart.

Then he turned to take his place at the back of the stage and sent Eve a grin that was Christmas morning, the Fourth of July, and New Year's Eve all in one.

At the end, the newly promoted officers filed off the stage to more applause, and Eve wondered if the echoes of it would help offset some of the crap they'd have thrown at them daily on the job.

She went back, intending to work her way around, spend five or ten minutes to speak to whoever she had to speak to, then duck out, change, and get back on the street.

But Trueheart waited for her.

"Lieutenant."

"Let's see it." She held out a hand, wiggled her fingers so he gave her his shield. "Nice. Keep it shiny, Detective Trueheart." She gave it back to him.

"Yes, sir, I will. I just wanted to thank you. I wouldn't be here, I wouldn't have this if it wasn't for you."

"You got yourself here, with some good training from Baxter."

"Sir, I hate starting my first day as detective correcting my LT, but I might still be walking the beat in Sidewalk City if you hadn't taken a chance on me. And if you hadn't put me with Baxter. Seeing I could do it, well, that's why you're the LT."

"You've got a point. Congratulations, Detective." She held out a hand.

He took it, swallowed hard. "I know you don't really like this, but . . ." He pulled her in, wrapped his arms around her in a fierce hug.

"Hey. Okay." She gave his back a pat, considering the moment, and nudged him away with her other hand, considering dignity.

"I wanted to get that done back here, before we were out there with a lot of people. Where you really wouldn't like it."

"That's good thinking. Go see your mother."

"Yes, sir!"

When she went out, Trueheart was wrapped around his mother with his girl—What was her name?—beaming at them and most of the division surrounding them.

She cut away to grab a minute with Mira.

"How's Mr. Mira doing?"

"He insisted I come, and our daughter's with him, so . . . He's fine, really. He actually planned to go to the university today, but I put my foot down. He needs another day."

"You didn't get much sleep."

"No, no, I didn't. I have a lot of people I care about who put their lives on the line every day. It's part of working with the police. I've lost some, and seen others injured. You live with it, cope with it. But Dennis . . . he lives a quiet life, and I wasn't prepared to have him hurt like this."

She stopped, drew a breath. "Well. I spoke with the governor."

"Seriously?"

"Mandy's not the only one with connections," Mira said, and now her voice was brisk and cool. "He understands the situation and circumstances, and since he knows her . . . suffice it to say there'll be no blowback from that quarter."

"Okay."

"I also spoke with Mandy."

"You keep busy."

"We detest each other, but I know how to read her, and how to push buttons. She hasn't heard from him, there's been no contact from whoever took him. She's more angry than worried. If it wasn't for Dennis I'd advise you to toss this case aside, but—"

"Look, I'm going to keep working this, but Hanson's in a position to get warrants so he's likely to get deeper than I can. But we're on it, and I'll be in touch. I've got to say something to Trueheart's mother, then Peabody and I are going to have a talk with his current sidepiece."

Mira laid a hand on Eve's arm. "He won't thank you for that, even if information you gather helps save his life."

"Good thing I'm not in it for the thanks."

She walked up to Trueheart's mother, had to resign herself to another hug, this one a little on the weepy side.

"Thank you, Lieutenant. Troy's wanted this since he was a boy, and you helped him reach that dream. Last night I asked him what he wanted now, now that he'd made detective. He told me he wanted to be as good a cop as you are."

"Mrs. Trueheart—"

"Pauline, please, it's Pauline. I'm glad you set the bar high. I don't want him to settle for less. I want you to know he'll be proud every day when he picks up his shield, and I'll be proud of him."

Eve wanted escape, wanted the work, but found herself speaking. "He's smart, and he's observant, and has a way of working through a problem thoughtfully. His looks don't hurt. He looks handsome and homespun," Eve explained. "And some people mistake that for him being a soft touch, easy to dupe. He's not. And he's got a shiny code of honor you should be proud of because I figure you're the one who put it in him."

"Thank you for that, thank you very much for that." Her voice broke, her eyes welling up. "Sorry. Emotional day." She gave Eve's hand a squeeze, then hurried away.

"That was really good stuff to say to her." Peabody stepped up beside her.

"She started crying again."

"It's a mom thing."

"Let's get the hell out of here and go do the cop thing."

"There's cake."

"Your pants are loose, Peabody."

"Damn it." As she rushed after Eve, Peabody glanced back at the refreshment table. "Having loose pants means I could eat a little cake."

"Having loose pants means you can get out of them quicker so we can get back in the field."

"Somebody said it was buttercream frosting." But with a heavy sigh, Peabody got in the elevator.

Back in her street clothes, Eve took a few minutes in her office to connect with Hanson. Still no communication from Senator Mira, or his probable abductor. Hanson and his partner would interview Vinnie, the driver, and had already spoken to Silas Greenbaum. They'd work their way through the Mira Institute while Eve and Peabody took on the list of women.

By the time she came out Jenkinson and his tie were back at his desk, Santiago at his, and some of the uniforms had trickled in.

"Is anyone actually working today?"

"We're on it, Dallas." Knowing her sharp eye, Jenkinson hastily brushed cake crumbs from his shirt. "It was a good thing."

"Yeah, it was a good thing. You know what else is good? Catching murdering bastards."

"I like that even better than buttercream frosting," Santiago said, earning a glare from Peabody.

"You guys are just mean."

"Then catch me some murdering bastards," Eve advised. "Peabody, with me."

"You on a hot one, Dallas?"

She glanced back at Jenkinson as she strode toward the door. "I'll let you know when I know. Don't even think about whining over buttercream frosting," Eve warned, and Peabody settled into a pout as she got on the elevator.

"We'll hit the baby skirt at the gallery where she works. We're going by the crime scene first. I want another look around, and you haven't seen it firsthand."

"Mira said Mr. Mira was okay, but she looked really stressed. She hardly ever looks stressed."

"She'll deal."

Eve considered herself lucky that the elevator only

stopped five times on the descent, and no more than a dozen people filed on, filed off.

"We'll make a circuit with the known sidepieces," Eve said as they got in the car. "Say he's still seeing the artist, but she's starting to make noises. Oh, Senator Granddaddy—"

"Eeww."

"Yeah, well. She's all, If you get a divorce we could be together all the time. And he's, Now, now, Sweet Baby Sidepiece—"

"Ick, ick, mega ick!"

"Can't ditch my marriage: appearances, finances, blah blah. How about some ice cream!"

"This is really turning my stomach, so I don't even want any buttercream frosting. Thanks."

"You're welcome. Or she's got a former, more age-appropriate but poor boyfriend—maybe even current—and they figure they'll pound and intimidate a nice fat chunk of the change out of him. Maybe start off the blackmail with a black eye. Then Mr. Mira walks in, and panic changes their plans."

"I like it."

"Or, the next up the line gets steamed, stews, and thinks how he's dumped her more mature ass for this baby slut. Now he must pay. Also requires a partner."

"To pose as the Realtor to get him in the house."

"Then it's, Surprise, you horny bastard, we're going to tune you up." She paused at a light. "I've got problems with all those scenarios, but they're a launch point."

She played with all the problems as she drove, then shot out another launch point. "MacDonald's alibied tight. Hanson will follow up, but her alibi's going to hold. So maybe if she's been a sidepiece, or there's another issue, she hires somebody to deal with him. We'll look at her finances, but we're not looking at a pro. Still, a lawyer's bound to know some shady types, especially a political lawyer."

She studied the neighborhood as she approached the brownstone. "Quiet, established, upper end. The canvass got nothing, but then most people would be at work, or occupied. Who stares out the window checking for activity on the street or around their neighbors on a crappy day? That's just luck, and it bothers me. It's just luck getting an injured man out of the house, into a vehicle without anybody seeing anything."

"Lucky that it was crappy, gloomy daylight and not broad."

"Yeah, nobody can plan that."

Eve got out, took another minute to study the house, its position.

"It's really beautiful," Peabody commented. "Old, but in a dignified, ageless sort of way. I can see why Mr. Mira wants to keep it."

"It's more what's inside—I don't mean the stuff. It's what he remembers, what he felt, the pictures in his head. And he promised, that's the big one. If Edward Mira knew him at all, he'd know Mr. Mira wasn't about to break his promise."

"Wait! What if this is all a ploy to get him to do that?" Running with it, Peabody loosened her scarf as they walked through the little gate. "He stages it all, and it's Mr. Mira who'll be contacted after he's worried half to death."

"Sign off on the sale of the house or your cousin gets it? Why would anyone buy that?"

"You said the senator needed money, right? So the fake kidnapper claims he owes him a bundle. Now sell the house so I get paid or I kill him until he's dead."

Eve frowned, worked it around. "That's actually a launching point, no shakier than . . . Seal's compromised."

She held up a hand to stop Peabody, studied the police seal she'd affixed herself. "Somebody got through it and went in. Recorders on."

Without another word they both drew their weapons.

Eve stepped to the door, glanced at Peabody, nodded.

They went through, high and low, right and left.

Eve straightened, kept her weapon at the ready as she looked up.

Edward Mira hung from the crystal chandelier. His face was blackened from bruising, his throat gouged and smeared with dried blood. And he was naked but for a computer-generated sign that covered his torso.

JUSTICE IS SERVED

"Well, fuck."

"I guess it wasn't a ploy."

"If it was, it sure went wrong. Let's clear the house, Peabody, and call this in."

Chapter 5

They cleared the house, every step on record. While Peabody called it in, Eve located the mechanism for lowering the chandelier. Something she only knew about because she'd seen them work in her own foyer.

"You can clean it and stuff without hauling in a ladder," she told Peabody.

"Handy. Man, they messed him up good before they hanged him."

"I'd say he was alive when they hauled him up there. Gouges on the neck likely self-inflicted. Skin and blood under his nails is likely his. ME will determine that and COD."

As Peabody had brought in their field kits, Eve opened hers. While they sealed up, she studied the body. "Beat his face, his genitals, stripped him naked. That says personal, really pissed, and probably sexual."

"Sure doesn't read trying to score a bunch of money. One of the women he diddled with, but like you said before, getting him in and out? Probably had to have a partner."

Eve got out tools and gauges, first verified his identity for the record with the Identi-pad.

"Victim is Mira, Edward James, age sixty-eight. Severe facial contusions and lacerations. Looks like both cheekbones are broken as well as some teeth." She put on micro-goggles. "Check TOD, Peabody. I don't think these were caused by fists," she said as she peered closer. "Maybe a sap, likely weighted. Same with the genitals, but there's some . . . almost like punctures in the groin area."

"TOD oh-three-thirty-six."

"So, worked on him for a while. Bruising on the wrists, look at the pattern." Rigor mortis had yet to pass, so she used her own wrists to demonstrate, holding them up and together, palms facing. "Looks like he was restrained, hung up, see the pattern? Restrained by the wrists, hoisted up. No sign of bruising on the ankles. Kicked him in the balls, repeatedly. Those shallow punctures? I'm betting shoes with those ridiculous pointed toes."

"That says female killer."

"I've seen plenty of those stupid shoes on guys' feet, but, yeah, this reads female to me. And sexual motives. Going to kick your balls till they fall off, you fucker. That's what it says to me.

"And they sodomized him."

Peabody's shoulders hunched up. "What?"

"You didn't look at him from the back. His anus is torn, bloody. They used something to sodomize him. It's very sexually motivated. It's personal, and it's planned out. Bringing him back here where they probably intended to do it all in the first place."

"But Mr. Mira came in."

"They had a place to take him, and the transportation. Maybe that was always backup, maybe they always intended to haul him off, haul him back, and hang him."

She sat back on her heels. "I bet they waited to hoist him up, waited until he was coming to, waited until he could be aware, could know and feel. Then they pushed that button, let him struggle as he went up, watched him choke, watched him tear at his own throat. You don't go this personal and not want him to feel death, not want to watch it happen."

"But do you go that vicious over ending an affair? Do you think someone could be that pissed about being dumped?"

"Sure. Of course, that means she's batshit crazy, but there's no lack of batshit crazy in the world. It would have to mean whoever helped her is equally batshit."

Eve got to her feet, closed her eyes a moment to help herself see it.

"Okay. Yesterday they conned the vic into coming here, talking about selling the house he couldn't sell without Mr. Mira's approval, which he wasn't going to get. He lets them in. Maybe the batshit crazy ex—if so—has hid the crazy and hooks him up with this Realtor. Or maybe she comes as a surprise at his door. One way or the other, they get him back to the study."

She moved around the body, a few paces down the foyer.

"No restraints—or Mr. Mira doesn't think so, ME will verify—so they have a weapon on him. One holds it on him, the other smacks him around. Mr. Mira comes in, calls out, walks down. They don't use the weapon on him, are careful to keep out of sight until they can knock him out."

She paced as she worked it through because there were variables. The pictures changed depending on how she juggled them in.

Dissatisfied, she started again.

"Back up, consider the timing. When the vic first arrived, when Mr. Mira came in. There's a solid gap of time."

"You said they'd started on the vic. That Mr. Mira saw he was injured."

"Yeah, but . . . They walked around with the vic some first. Black eye, bloody lip when this is your endgame? They'd barely gotten started, so they walked around, didn't force him back to the study, that was just part of the tour, the place they jumped him."

To satisfy herself, Peabody walked back, glancing in rooms, stopped at the study. And she could see it, too.

"So if he knew one of them, and he had to because it's really personal, he wasn't worried about it."

"Exactly. She didn't pose a threat to him. Fast-forward to

Mr. Mira unconscious on the study floor. Completely batshit finishes him off, so not completely batshit. They decide to get the vic out, take him somewhere they can work on him. One of them knows enough to take the security hard drive."

Following, Peabody walked back. "Not completely batshit, and not in total panic mode."

"That's right. They have an agenda, a plan, and they hold it together, follow through."

"How do they get him out? Counting on the weather to mask the abduction, okay," Peabody continued. "But how do they get him to go with them?"

"Maybe they stun him—light stun, just enough to unbalance him. Or drug him. Morris will look for it. They get him into a vehicle. Then they've got to do it all again on the other end. Get him out of the vehicle and into wherever they're going to torture him.

"He's going to have to tell us some of it. Whether he was stunned, tranq'd, just intimidated in and out, out and in. Morris will find some of the answers."

She looked around. "I don't think it was about this house. The house was their ploy, and they used it to get him where they could take him. Hanging him here, they wanted him found, but they wanted some *impact*."

" 'Justice is served,' " Peabody read. "Could be someone he sent up, or about someone he didn't. And the woman, you know, vamped him into a relationship to get close to him, to get intel, to become someone who didn't worry him."

"Maybe so, and we'll have to dig there. If it's about someone he sent up, or didn't, it was about rape. On some level it's about rape."

"Because they raped him."

"Somebody does this to another human being and calls it justice? It's about vengeance, and vengeance this sexual is about sex. So rape's going to be a factor. At least that's how it reads for me right now."

She glanced over at the knock on the door. "Probably the sweepers or the dead wagon. Go ahead, let them in. And let's get the uniforms started on a canvass. Anybody who saw a vehicle near the house, noticed lights on last night, with another hit on yesterday between sixteen and eighteen hundred, just to cover it."

She looked back down at Edward Mira. She doubted very much if she'd have liked him in life. But in death, he was hers.

She pulled out her 'link, walked back toward the study as the morgue team filed in. After blowing out a breath, she contacted Mira.

"Eve." Mira barely blinked, and gave Eve no chance to speak at all. "Edward's dead."

"I'm sorry."

"No, please. Tell me where you are, what happened."

"In the house on Spring, and I'm sorry about that, too. I can't officially determine COD. Morris will—"

"Eve."

Hell, Eve thought. "His face and genitals were severely beaten. He was sodomized."

"Ah, dear God."

"Ligature marks on his wrists are consistent, to my eye, with him being restrained vertically—arms over his head. I believe he was likely still alive before he was hanged from the ceiling light in the entrance foyer. He had a comp-generated sign around his neck reading 'Justice Is Served.'"

"All right." With her eyes closed, Mira rubbed her fingers over the middle of her forehead. "It's very personal, sexual—"

"I'm not asking for a profile, Dr. Mira, not right now. Take a minute. I'm not sure what you want to tell Mr. Mira."

Mira opened her eyes. "I'll tell him what you tell me. Of course."

"Okay. I'm going to need to talk to him again. I'm sorry."

"Don't apologize." There was a snap in the words. Mira held up a hand, visibly regrouped. "Don't apologize," she said again, calmly now. "Both Dennis and I want you to do everything you have to do, everything you can do to find who did this. Do you want him to come to Central?"

"No, don't do that. I'll go to him. I have to inform next

of kin, then I'll go by and talk to him before I go in. Officially, I'm not going to be able to consult with you on this."

"Of course not, the conflict of interest. I'm not thinking straight yet."

"But unofficially I'm going to want your help with the profile. Later," she added. "Go home. You're going to want to be with him when I interview him. I'm going to contact Whitney, go by the victim's residence and speak to his wife. That'll give you time to go home, to tell Mr. Mira before I get there."

"Yes, you're right. I'll leave here in a few minutes."

"One last thing. I'm going to leak this to Nadine Furst."

"Oh," Mira said, on a kind of sigh.

"The media's going to know about this fast. I'm going to leak it to her so she can get out in front of it. You're going to want to screen any incomings, because once this hits, the media's going to try to talk to you and Mr. Mira. You need a statement."

"I know what to do. I'll take care of that end. Please do what you have to do."

"I'll speak to you within ninety minutes."

Eve turned, saw Peabody in the doorway.

"Sweepers are here, uniforms are canvassing. The morgue wagon's on its way. I flagged him for Morris."

"That covers it. The sweepers will go through the house, but there's nothing relevant that's not in the entranceway. For now, we're finished here. Let's go break it to the vic's wife."

"I hate that part."

"We all do. You're probably going to hate this time more than usual."

She contacted Whitney before she left the crime scene.

"Tibble was right about the media, particularly given the sexual implications of the murder."

"Yes, sir. I'm going to contact Nadine Furst. I'd rather have someone I know and trust, someone who knows the Miras, take the media lead on this. Whatever comes after, what goes out first will be fair."

"Do it. I'll speak with Tibble and with our media liaison. And dot those *i*'s, Dallas, right down the line."

"Let's move," she told Peabody when Whitney clicked off. "I'll contact Nadine on the way."

The minute she slid behind the wheel, Eve used the in-dash to contact Nadine.

The reporter, looking on-camera ready as usual, greeted her with a brilliant smile. "Dallas. I happen to be with your delicious husband in what may be my new triplex penthouse. I was just wishing he came with it, then it would be a done deal."

"Get your own, and put on your media hat."

The humor dropped out of Nadine's foxy green eyes, turning them sharp. "What do you have?"

"Less than an hour ago Peabody and I discovered the body of former Senator Edward Mira in the former residence of the senator's grandparents."

"Shit, damn, fuck. Let me get my recorder."

"Just listen. The victim had been brutally beaten, then hanged. He'd also been sodomized."

"Christ, this story's going to burn."

"Yesterday at approximately five-twenty-five P.M., accord-ing to the log of the Rapid Cab used for transportation, the senator's cousin Dennis Mira—no, go with Professor Mira, he's one of those—entered the residence, and was attacked and rendered unconscious after seeing the senator injured and trying to go to his assistance. Professor Mira contacted the NYPSD. Since that time, investigators have attempted to locate the senator, who they believe was held against his will in another location before being brought back to the residence. The chief medical examiner is working to determine the time and cause of death. The primary investigator has no comment at this time, but the department intends to issue a statement once details are confirmed."

"God, when you drop one on me, you drop it big-time."

"I'm on my way to notify next of kin. You can't air that until Peabody gives you the green."

"All right. How's Dennis? Is he all right?"

Eve let out a breath. Friendships didn't come easily to her, but when they did, they came solid.

"There are two reasons I'm giving you the jump. You'll wait for the green, and you asked about Mr. Mira. He's okay. He got banged up a little, but he's okay."

"And now it's my job to ask if you have any leads, any suspects."

"No, because I'm still doing my job. Since you're with Roarke, tell him I okayed it for him to fill you in on the details of the grandfather's estate, the brownstone. That's going to come out anyway, and I'd rather you played it at the opening. What I don't want is even a whiff that Mr. Mira is a suspect, even a person of interest. He's a witness and a victim himself. That's it."

"You should know me better."

"I do, that's why I contacted you before I notified next of kin. Peabody will give you the green as soon as we do. I've got to go."

"So do I now."

They both clicked off, and Eve scowled at the traffic.

"How are you going to handle Mr. Mira?"

Eve's scowl deepened. "What do you mean, 'handle'?"

"Look, first off, I know he didn't have anything to do with this. I'm talking about the whole dotting the *i*'s thing. He was the last person to see the vic alive, and he and the vic had a strained relationship at least partially due to the house the vic's body was hanged in. So I know how we'd handle it if we didn't know and love Mr. Mira. But . . ."

"We'll dot the fucking *i*'s, Peabody."

"I don't want to throw off the rhythm."

"You won't."

By the time she pulled up in front of the shiny spear of the building, Eve was primed for trouble. A different doorman wore the polar bear suit and instantly jogged her way. Eve slammed out of the car, shot up her badge.

"We're the police, and here on police business. That's a police vehicle and it stays just where it is. You give me any lip over that, my partner here is going to arrest you for obstruction of justice and interfering in a police investigation, and arrange to have you hauled down to Central."

He had a deep brown face against the snow white of the livery, and that face went carefully blank. "I didn't say a word."

"That's smart. You need to clear us up to Edward and Mandy Mira's apartment."

Now he winced. "It just would be. Look, I have to follow procedure. You're doing your job, right? I've got to do mine. I need to clear it with the Miras' personal security."

"Then do that."

He walked toward the building, and had the grace—or the training—to hold the door open for them. "If you'll give me a minute."

He went to the same system used the night before, tapped in a code. "Hank, it's Jonah on the door. There are a couple of cops here who—"

Eve nudged Jonah aside. "Hank, Lieutenant Dallas. Don't screw around. You need to clear me and my partner up there, asap."

"It could be my ass this time. She put you on the banned list."

"She needs to talk to me. If she won't let me up, she'll end up hearing what I have to tell her on a media bulletin. Clear me up, tell her that."

"Hell, it's a crap job anyway. You're clear. Jonah, they're clear."

"Copy that."

"I know the way," Eve told him, and walked to the elevator she'd used before.

"Fancy," Peabody said when they stepped on.

"Eyes and ears," Eve said.

"Really?" Humming to herself, Peabody looked around the car, sniffed the roses. "You get to use the new dojo much?"

"I've managed a couple times a week. I'm learning to be a bear, a rooster, a crane, a tiger, a dragon. It's like the animal kingdom. But somehow it ends up being frosty by the time I'm done."

"I could like being a dragon," Peabody speculated, and the doors opened.

Hank gave them a pained look.

"She's going to have the senator give me the what for when he gets back. You get three minutes, then she's contacting the governor again."

"I think she's not going to do either of those things. Open up, Hank."

He shook his head, but opened the doors.

Mandy stood, arms crossed, chin up, eyes filled with contempt.

"This is harassment. I'll be contacting the governor and our lawyers in precisely three minutes ten seconds.

"Mrs. Mira, I regret to inform you that your husband's dead. We're sorry for your loss."

Color hoisted like red flags on her cheeks. "What are you talking about? How dare you come here and say such a thing to me!"

"His body was found hanging from the entrance chandelier in the house on Spring Street. Visible evidence of physical violence was obvious. His body has been transported to the chief medical examiner, who will determine cause of death."

Mandy lost the red flags, and all of her color—every shade of it. But her voice remained full and furious. "You're a liar."

"I am the primary investigator into your husband's death, and as such have come here to inform you thereof. We understand this is a difficult time for you, but we have some questions. The answers may help us find the person or persons who murdered your husband."

"Get out, get out of my house. You're lying. You're lying to upset me."

"You know I'm not."

When she swayed, Hank rushed over, took her by the arm. "Mrs. Mira, ma'am, you need to sit down. You sit down, and I'm going to get you some water."

"You're lying." But this time her voice trembled.

Eve didn't sit, but stepped over to her. The woman didn't weep, but sat pale as ice. The shock in her eyes struck as genuine.

"My partner and I entered the house on Spring approximately sixty minutes ago and discovered your husband's body. I'm a murder cop, Mrs. Mira, a ranked officer. I don't lie about murder. Can you tell me if you know anyone who would want to kill him?"

"No one would do this. No one would dare."

"Someone did this, Mrs. Mira. Someone dared. They hurt him, are you hearing me? They made sure he felt pain before they ended it. Who wanted to cause him pain?"

"I don't know. Go away."

Peabody made an attempt, her voice soothing, sympathetic. "Is there anyone we can contact for you, Mrs. Mira? Family, a friend?"

"I don't want your help. Get out. Get out or I'll have you thrown out!"

Hank rushed back with a glass of water. She grabbed it and flung it across the room. "All of you, get out!"

"You can reach me at Central if you have any questions or want to make a statement." Eve turned, walked to the door. She glanced back once, saw that Mandy continued to sit, hands gripped together, eyes shocked but dry.

"You're leaving?" Eve asked Hank as he came out with them, shut the doors.

"I'll stick for now, in case. I don't know what to say. Can I contact her son, her daughter?"

"Go ahead. Make sure you give them my name." She stepped back on the elevator with Peabody. "Good luck, Hank."

"She's scary." Despite eyes and ears, Peabody blurted it out. "I know people react in all kinds of ways to death notifications, but she's scary."

"She is what she is, and we did what we came to do."

Eve's head throbbed, a dull but steady beat as she drove toward the Miras' home. Again, she'd do what she had to do—and didn't expect anyone to call her a liar or throw a glass. Maybe that's what made this one harder.

She found street parking just over a block from the pretty townhome. When they got out, started to walk, she stuck her hands in her pockets and found the gloves she'd forgotten about.

At least she hadn't lost them yet.

"Give Nadine the green." Rolling her shoulders, she started up the short steps to the front door.

She rang the bell, focused on her approach, the basic procedure. The woman who opened it had Mira's coloring, Mr. Mira's lankier build. Gillian, Eve remembered, the Wiccan daughter who lived in . . . yeah, New Orleans.

"Dallas. Hi, Peabody."

"Hey, Gillian. I didn't know you were in town."

"I came in last night. I had a feeling, something off, and contacted my mother. So here I am."

"It's nice to see you, even given."

Gillian smiled at Peabody, stepped back. "The same for you. Mom and Dad are in the living room. This is hard on him, so don't you be."

"We were figuring on hauling him down to Central in restraints where we keep the saps and rubber hoses."

Gillian just gave Eve a cool stare with her mother's eyes. "Let me take your coats."

She did her hostess duty, then led them in.

They'd lit a fire, and the Miras sat together on the sofa in the pretty room much as they had at the crime scene. He looked tired, Eve thought, and felt a pang of guilt knowing she would add to the strain.

"Cops in the house," Gillian said, but lightly, before she walked over to sit on the arm of the sofa by her father.

United front.

"We're sorry, Mr. Mira," Eve began, "for your loss."

"Thank you. Edward and I . . . our relationship wasn't what it had been, but I remember the boy he was. The boys we were together. It was a hard death?"

He looked at her with those kind green eyes. She wanted

to lie to him, give him that much. But she couldn't spare him. "Yes, it was."

"It's odd, even with Charlotte's work, and knowing what people can and will do to people, you never expect it to happen to one of your own. Despite our differences, Edward was my family. You've spoken to Mandy?"

"We were just there."

"She won't answer her 'link," Mira explained. "Dennis is concerned about her."

"She . . ." How to put it? Eve wondered.

"Her personal security was contacting her children," Peabody put in.

"That's good." He patted Gillian's knee. "They're a comfort. I know she's a difficult woman. You're too polite to say."

"I'm not all that polite," Eve said, making him laugh, just a little.

"I'll bet you haven't had lunch."

The segue threw Eve off balance. "We aren't really—"

"You have to eat. I'm going to make sandwiches."

"Mr. Mira, I'm sorry, but we need to ask you some questions. I need to interview you, on the record. I need to read you your rights."

"You're not treating him like a suspect." Gillian shoved off the arm of the sofa, an arrow yanked from the quiver.

"Gillian, I explained this to you." Mira rubbed Dennis's thigh, rose. "It's procedure, and has to be done."

"I don't care about procedure."

"I have to," Eve said, then looked at Dennis. "I'm sorry. I have to."

"Of course you do. But you also need to eat. We can do this in the kitchen while I make sandwiches."

"Dad, I made soup, remember?"

"That's right, of course, that's right." He got to his feet in his baggy green cardigan and tousled hair. "Gilly makes wonderful soup. It's potato leek, isn't it?"

"Chicken and rice."

"That's right. Potato leek was last time. Soup's a comfort," he said to Eve. "We could all use it."

Eve couldn't say no, just couldn't make herself draw the hard line with him. So she ended up in the big kitchen with the comfort of soup scenting the air, sitting across from him in the breakfast nook with the winter sun eking pale through the windows.

"You eat a bit first, both of you," he said when Gillian set bowls in front of them. "Charlie tells me that nice young policeman was promoted today."

"Trueheart. He got his detective's shield."

"Good for him. He's a nice young man. Bright, I take it?"

"He is. He's a good cop." She ate because it was there. "It's nice soup."

"It really is." Peabody glanced at Gillian. "The sage really makes it. My granny always uses sage in hers."

"You like to cook?"

"Bake mostly, when I have time. It's relaxing."

Eve let the small talk circle around her. She should cut it off. She shouldn't be cozied up here in the kitchen with soup and conversation. She should—

Dennis reached over, patted her hand. "You mustn't worry. You mustn't worry about doing your job. I want to help you find whoever gave Edward a hard death."

"Mr. Mira, you're not a suspect. Nobody thinks you had anything to do with this. But we have to go through this, and some of the questions I have to ask are going to be pointed, they're going to feel hard and intimidating. I'm sorry."

"There's no need to be sorry. You go ahead—but finish your soup first." He shifted to Peabody. "And how is your young man? I like him quite a lot. He's so colorful."

"Yeah, he is. He's great."

Eve finished her soup, caught Mira's eye and the quiet gratitude in it. So maybe it had been the right thing, just to give Mr. Mira time to settle.

"I'm going to make hot chocolate," Dennis announced. "You like my hot chocolate," he said to Eve.

"Who wouldn't, but—"

"You and Delia— You like hot chocolate?"

"It's a big weakness of mine, and now I know why I didn't get any cake earlier."

"It's better than cake." He winked at her, tugging hard on Eve's heart. "You and Delia come sit at the counter while I make it. It'll keep my hands busy while you interview me. And, Charlie, you and Gillian sit right there. Gilly, you behave."

"Maybe."

He chuckled as he rose.

They'd do it his way, Eve decided and got up to switch to a stool at the big kitchen counter while Dennis hunted in cupboards.

"You make it from scratch?" Peabody's eyes went shiny as he found a big bar of chocolate, a canister of sugar. "It's a real treat to watch somebody make hot chocolate from scratch."

Eve sent Peabody a look to remind her they weren't there for a treat.

As Dennis put an actual pan on an actual cooktop, Eve reminded herself of the same.

"Record on."

Chapter 6

Eve entered their names, the case file, into the record. Recited the Revised Miranda.

"Do you understand your rights and obligations, Professor Mira?"

He gave her a vague smile at the use of his title, put a pot on top of the pot of water—What was that about?—began to add chocolate. "Yes, I do, thank you."

"Edward Mira was your cousin."

"Yes, first cousin, on my father's side."

He chose a small metal bowl, put it in the freezer.

Eve wondered if she should point out his mistake, but decided to push forward with the interview. "Would you relate, for the record, what happened yesterday, with your arrival at the property at 2314 Spring Street?"

He took them through it, the weather, the cab ride, made her wish she'd warned him not to elaborate as he stated on record he was angry with his cousin. When he said he'd heard voices, Eve interrupted.

"Can you tell me how many voices?"

"Oh." He frowned, looked sweetly bewildered. "I'm

not sure, not at all sure, but at least two, as it was a kind
of conversation—I should say it *felt* like hearing a kind of
conversation. I couldn't hear the words, and I'm afraid I was
distracted. But they stopped talking when I called out for
Edward. I'm sure of that. I called out, as I didn't want to startle
anyone."

"At least two voices. You couldn't make out the words,
but could you tell if they were male or female?"

"That's an excellent question." And one he looked a
bit startled by. "I assumed one was Edward's, but I wasn't
paying attention. I often don't. I have a little trick Charlie
taught me that helps me remember when I haven't paid
enough attention. It seems I'm too often thinking of something else."

He closed his eyes, took some quiet breaths. "I'm walking
into the house. It's warm after the bitter wind. I smell lemon
oil, so I know Sila's been there to clean in the last day or so.
I feel sad because I can imagine it as it was, with my grandparents. Some of the furniture's been taken because it was
left to some of us. There were always fresh flowers on the
entrance table. I'm sorry they're not there any longer, sorry
it's so dim. It's such a raw, gloomy day, and I wish there was
more light. I hear voices. I'm annoyed and sad and hear
voices coming from down the hall. The study, I think, but
I'm not sure. They're . . . angry or excited. I didn't realize,
but yes, raised voices. My cousin's, I think, yes, and someone else. A woman. I think a woman."

He opened his eyes again. "I think a woman was with
him. Is that helpful?"

"Yes. What did you do then?"

"I went back. I hated to be rude, but I intended to tell the
Realtor there was no point in being there, as I didn't intend
to sell. I knew Edward and I would argue, but it had to be
done. I turned into the study, and saw him. I was . . . thrown
off, you could say. Primed to argue, braced for it, and he
was in the chair, but the chair was in front of the desk, not
behind, and his face was bleeding—at the mouth. His eye—
ah . . ." His closed his own again, patted his hands in the

air. "His right eye was blackened and swollen. He looked terrified. I started to rush in, to help him, and . . ."

He lifted a hand to the back of his head. "Something hit me, and the next thing I clearly remember, I was waking up—my head throbbing—on the floor of the study. Edward was gone, and the chair was back behind the desk. I might have thought I imagined it all, but my head was bleeding, and I was on the floor."

"What did you do then?"

"I looked for him, called for him. Initially I was a little dazed, and I was confused. I went back to the kitchen, and upstairs, looking for him. When I couldn't find him, I knew something had to have happened. I contacted Charlie. Charlotte. Dr. Mira. Told her something had happened, and could she come, bring you to my grandfather's house. I looked some more, then you came."

"Why didn't you call nine-one-one? Your cousin had been injured and was missing, you'd been attacked. But you called your wife instead of the police."

"I didn't even think of it, not then. She works with the police—my Charlotte. She works with you. I probably should have called nine-one-one, as you say, but I wanted you. Something had happened to my cousin."

"I'm a murder cop, Professor Mira. Did you believe your cousin had been murdered?"

"No. No, I never thought . . . I still can't quite . . . But it's the cop that counts the most, isn't it? And you're the best I know. I knew you'd find out what happened to Edward."

"You contacted your wife," she said again, pushing a little, "and requested a police officer you have a . . . friendly relationship with."

"Yes, that's true." He measured out milk, poured it into the chocolate. And crushed some sort of bean in a little marble bowl with a little marble dowel. "But then, my wife is a renowned and respected criminal profiler, and you are a renowned and respected police lieutenant. I'd have been foolish to settle for less with such talent available."

He added the crushed bean, sugar, and stirred methodically.

He'd given good answers, she thought. Very good, simple, logical answers. But she wasn't done.

"Did you fight with your cousin, Professor Mira?"

"Oh, yes." He said it so easily, without even a hint of guile. "Over the years we fought—argued, that is—numerous times. Our worldviews had shifted away from each other's, on different orbits you might say, and we had little in common. Not like when we were boys."

"You argued about the disposition of the property on Spring, which was left to both of you equally."

"We did." No hesitation, and no animosity. "We'd promised our grandfather to keep it in the family, and Edward believed that promise had an expiration date. I didn't."

"Did you argue yesterday, at the house?"

"No. We didn't even get a chance to speak. I said his name, but then someone struck me. I never got to speak to him, or him to me. I believe we would have argued if . . ."

Though he continued to stir, he looked down at his pot as if he'd forgotten why it was there.

"Upon his death, what happens to his share of the disputed property?"

"I'm sorry? Oh, yes. Unless he changed his will—I can't be sure—it would go in equal parts to his two children."

He took the bowl out of the freezer, along with something she was pretty sure was some sort of whisk. Into the bowl he poured . . . milk, cream—something out of a small container—added some sugar. He stuck the whisk on some little hand tool.

It hummed busily in the bowl.

"What's your relationship with the children?"

"They're fine young people. We get along very well. We need to go see them. I hope they're with their mother now, but we'll go see them. They've lost their father, and will need family around them."

"Will they be more inclined to keep the property in the family, Professor Mira?"

"Yes, absolutely."

She saw he'd made whipped cream. People actually whipped cream to make whipped cream? Who knew?

He set the bowl aside, used another tool to make shavings from the remaining chocolate bar. "Eve—that is, Lieutenant Dallas, Edward, no matter how determined he was, couldn't sell our grandfather's house. There was nothing he could do to make me break my promise. I believe we would have remained at odds, but then, as I said, we haven't been close since my early college days. We were together at Yale, though he was a year ahead of me. If he'd lived, we weren't likely to ever be close again, but I would never wish him harm. And he would never have bullied me into selling."

"Sometimes people strike back at bullies."

"Yes, they do. I counseled my children to do just that. And I've done just that myself with Edward for more than forty years."

He turned, took mugs from a cupboard. "Some mistake a mild disposition for weakness. Do you?"

"No, sir, I don't."

"I can—my family will attest—be extremely stubborn when something is important."

From across the room Gillian made a little snorting sound that had a smile twitching at the corner of his lips.

"A promise to a man I loved deeply is important, even sacred. I didn't have to hurt Edward to keep it; I simply had to continue to keep it. I'm not a violent man."

He poured the rich hot chocolate into the mugs. "And while I didn't like Edward, didn't like the man he'd become, I loved him."

"Professor Mira, would you give me your whereabouts from eleven last night to three-thirty this morning?"

"Right here—or not right here, in the kitchen, that is. In the house. Charlie, my wife, insisted I go to bed early. I can be quite the night owl as a rule. But she was right, I was very tired. I believe I went to bed by ten. She doesn't think I know she was checking on me every couple hours."

He smiled, sweetly, toward the breakfast nook. "And our

daughter Gillian snuck in twice to make sure I hadn't lapsed into a coma—which is exactly what she said to her mother at about midnight. I didn't sleep very well. I did rest," he added quickly, with another glance toward the nook, as he piled whipped cream on top of two mugs of hot chocolate. "But I was worried about Edward, and didn't sleep very well."

"Okay. Okay. Thank you for your time and cooperation. Record off."

Dennis sprinkled chocolate shavings over the cream, then put the mugs in front of Peabody and Eve.

"Stand up," he said to Eve.

She got to her feet, braced.

"You need a hug." He wrapped his arms around her, and melted everything inside her. "There now. That wasn't so bad, was it?"

"It was horrible."

"Well, that's all right. It's all done."

"I'm so—"

"Hush. You sit and drink your chocolate."

"I could use a hug."

Dennis beamed at Peabody, obliged. "You're a good girl," he told her. "Gilly, Charlie, come on now. I made enough for everyone."

Mira walked over, framed his face with her hands. "I love you, Dennis."

"It's a good thing. Where would I be otherwise?"

"You sit down. I'll put the rest of these together."

As she dolloped on the whipped cream, Mira looked over at Eve. "You did exactly right. It was hard for you, hard for me to listen to. But you did exactly right."

"Sorry, but will you just say it—that you know he was here during the aforesaid hours."

"I absolutely do. He's right. I did check on him every couple hours, and Gilly went to check on him just before midnight, and again around three. We thought he was sleeping."

"You'd have started poking at me again if you'd known I was awake."

"He's right about that, too. Do you believe it was a woman?"

"There had to be at least two involved, and one of them was a woman. I'm sure of that, and Mr. Mira gave that some weight."

"He's never been a suspect," Gillian put in.

"No. There's no motive, no opportunity. I just needed it all spelled out on the record. It's going to be a feeding frenzy in the media. With this on record, Mr. Mira is firmly, unquestionably a witness."

"I just want to say something." Peabody, eyes closed, took another sip from her mug. "This is the Holy Grail of hot chocolate. Mr. Mira, you're a genius, but I don't know how I'm going to settle for the sludge at Central ever again."

"Knock it back, Peabody. We've got to get back to work."

It took a little time—Peabody wanted to savor—but even with the extra, Eve felt lighter when Gillian walked them back, got their coats.

"I'm going to apologize for wanting to smack you even though I could see it was hard for you to push at him that way."

"I want to smack people all the time. And he's your father."

"I love my husband, and one of the many reasons is he'd agree with me when I say my father is the best man I know. You're a little bit in love with him."

"Probably more than a little."

"And you're going to look out for him."

"That's a promise."

"All right then. Bright blessings on both of you, and safe travels wherever the path takes you."

As they hiked back to the car, Eve shoved her hands in her pockets, found her gloves again. Tugged them on. "Plot us a sensible route to hit the sidepieces."

"Already done, and you can cross off Allyson Byson, for now anyway. She's been in St. Lucia for the past week with her husband and several friends. It's an annual thing. Spends six weeks there every winter."

"Very tidy alibi. We'll look into her otherwise."

"We should start with Carlee MacKensie—he played with her right before he hooked up with Downing. Freelance writer."

When they got into the car, Peabody plugged the address into the in-dash. "Then we'd go to Asha Coppola, to Lauren Canford, and finish with Charity Downing, the latest."

"I want a conversation with the vic's children before the end of the day." Eve considered tactics while she negotiated traffic. "We keep it simple, get the how and when they met, how long the relationship went on, who ended it, that kind of thing. Right now, we're just fishing."

"How did he keep them straight?" Peabody wondered. "We've got five, and that's only covering around a year. So there's a lot more going back. How did he keep them all straight?"

"They were all the same to him, that's my take. Just a score. He was a predator. Spot the prey, stalk it, bag it, play with it awhile. Then, when you're bored or the prey no longer satisfies, discard it and go after fresh meat."

She noted a second-level street spot, zipped over and grabbed it.

"We could maybe have gotten closer."

"We could maybe not have."

"Loose pants, loose pants," Peabody chanted to herself as they clanged down the iron steps to the street.

"They'll be a lot looser when I kick your ass up, down, and sideways."

"I'm using the power of positive thinking. But to spare my ass the pain, what are you guys getting Bella for her birthday?"

"I don't know." Instant panic gripped her. "How the hell do I know what to get for a one-year-old kid? How does anybody? The kid can't tell you, and nobody remembers *being* a one-year-old so it's just a crapshoot."

"The party's in a couple weeks."

"Shut up, Peabody."

"Okay, but shutting up means I can't tell you what I know she'd really go for—and McNab and I can't really spring for a good one."

"What?"

Peabody clamped her lips smugly.

"I swear, I'll drop-kick you from this spot three blocks east so you splat in the middle of Fifth Avenue."

"A dollhouse. She's young for it, but we had her up for a few hours a few days ago, and I'd sent for mine. It's just a little one my dad made me, but she went nuts for it. Played with it the whole time, and really well, too, rearranging the little furniture, pretend cooking in the kitchen."

Eve wondered why—seriously why—anyone wanted to pretend cook.

"If dolls aren't alive, why do they need a house?"

"That's where *pretend* comes into it."

"Does it? Does it really? Or is it when you're sleeping or not around they start having parties in it, drinking brew, eating snacks, watching screen?"

"You're creeping me out."

"You should be creeped. What's to stop them from having doll orgies in there? Ever think of that?"

"Not until right now."

"Next thing you know, there'll be doll weapons and vehicles."

"They already have those."

"See."

Point made, Eve turned to the sturdy building that housed Carlee MacKensie's apartment. She opted for her master— Why give the woman time to prepare?—and walked into the skinny lobby.

"I have to pee. You scared the piss out of me, now I have to pee. Don't make me walk up four flights of steps."

"Seriously?"

"Seriously." To settle it, Peabody pushed the elevator button. "I can't get this image of a bunch of drunk dolls doing it all over the dollhouse. Gay dolls, straight dolls, threesomes. It's my new nightmare."

"They probably make doll strap-ons."

"Oh God, I beg you to stop." Peabody all but jumped into the elevator when it opened. "Loose pants, loose pants. Don't kick my ass, I'm trying to take my mind off having to pee. And sex-crazed dolls. I'm seeing Gracie Magill with a strap-on."

"Who?"

"My favorite doll as a kid. Loose pants, loose pants."

"You had a doll with a last name?" Eve pressed the buzzer on the MacKensie apartment. "Why do dolls need last names?"

"For their ID, to buy the brew and the strap-ons."

"I figured they just stole them when they climbed in and out of windows at night to burgle houses."

"You're just being mean now."

"I could keep this up all day."

The intercom buzzed. "Yes?" And Peabody breathed a quiet, "Thank you, Jesus."

"NYPSD," Eve announced, and held up her badge. "We'd like to speak with you, Ms. MacKensie."

"What about?"

"Edward Mira."

After a moment, locks clicked off, the door opened a couple cautious inches. Eve saw pale red hair messily bundled into a top bun and a pair of suspicious blue eyes.

"What about him?"

"Do you want to discuss your relationship with him out here, Ms. MacKensie?"

Eve saw the lips compress, the eyes dart left then right. "We don't have a relationship," she said, but opened the door.

She wore baggy sweatpants and a hoodie with thick socks. Her skin was so white it nearly glowed beneath its scatter shot of ginger-colored freckles.

"You did have," Eve said and stepped in.

"I haven't seen or talked to Edward in weeks, since the end of November."

"Excuse me. I'm sorry," Peabody interrupted. "Could I use your bathroom?"

Now Carlee bit her bottom lip, but nodded. "Ah, okay. I guess. It's . . ." She gestured, but Peabody was already on the move.

"Thanks!"

"I guess you want to sit down."

"I can stand if you'd rather," Eve told her.

"I guess we'll sit down."

She had a couch and a couple of chairs, facing an enter-tainment screen—and facing away from a workstation under the window.

Carlee chose a chair, sat with her knees together, her fingers linked in her lap. "I don't understand why you want to talk to me about Edward."

"He's dead, Ms. MacKensie."

Carlee's tightly pressed lips fell apart. "What? How? When?"

"He was murdered last night."

"Mur-murdered?"

"You say you haven't seen him since November."

"That's right. Are you talking about Senator Mira?"

"Yes. How did you meet him?"

"It was— It was a political fund-raiser. I had a media pass because I was researching an article, and . . ." She paused as Peabody came back.

"Thanks," Peabody said again, and sat beside Eve.

"That's okay. I, um, usually tend to observe rather than ask a lot of questions. I guess I was about the only one there with a media pass who wasn't asking questions, so he came over to me when I was sitting, taking notes, brought me a glass of wine. He said how if I didn't have any questions for him, he had some for me. I was a little flustered, but he was so charming."

"How soon did you begin a sexual relationship?"

Carlee flushed brightly, hotly pink, and her eyes darted away. "I know it was wrong. He was married—I knew he was married. He said he and his wife had an arrangement, but that doesn't make it right."

"We're not here to judge you, Ms. MacKensie," Peabody told her. "We need to gather information."

"I knew it was wrong," she repeated. "He said we'd go have a drink, and I thought how I could get a bigger article, or maybe a couple of stories, so we left there and went to have a drink. Then two. He had his driver take me home. Nobody's ever done that for me. And he paid such attention. I don't know how to explain it, but he made me feel pretty and sexy."

She looked down at her hands. "So when he contacted me the next day and said he was taking me out to dinner, I went. I knew where it was heading. He was married and, okay, a lot older, but I knew where it was heading. I went anyway. And I went with him to the hotel. The Palace. He has a suite there, just beautiful, like something in a vid. And dinner was waiting, and a bottle of champagne. I slept with him. We only saw each other like that for about five weeks, then he sent me flowers—white roses—with a card. It said how all good things had to end, and it had been lovely."

"That must've pissed you off."

"A little, but more it was hurtful. He could have told me in person. I'm not stupid; I knew it wasn't going to last. But he should have told me face-to-face. I thought about contacting him, but I didn't. And he never contacted me again."

She let out a breath. "It was like it never happened."

"Were you in love with him?" Peabody's tone was gauged to sympathy.

"Oh, no." MacKensie's blue eyes rounded—guileless. "No, but it was exciting, those few weeks. Maybe, at least partly, because I knew it was wrong. I felt a little . . ." She trailed off with a quick little gasp. "Am I a suspect? You think I killed Edward?"

"Did you?" Eve asked coolly.

"Oh my God, my God." She trembled all over, hunched

her shoulders, gripped her hands together under her chin. "No. No, I didn't kill him. I didn't kill anyone. You said last night?"

"That's right," Eve said, and left it there.

"I-I-I was here, working." She gestured to her workstation with a hand that shook. "I didn't go anywhere."

"Did you see or speak to anyone?"

"No. No. I was working on a piece, and I stuck with it. I had leftover Chinese and went to bed early. I think it was around ten because my brain was tired. Do I need a lawyer?"

"That's up to you. Have you ever been to his property on Spring Street?"

"Spring? I didn't know he had any. We always met at the hotel. Officer—"

"Lieutenant."

"Lieutenant, I lead a quiet life, by choice, by inclination. This was a few weeks of excitement, and, and"—she flushed again—"sex."

"Which he ended with flowers and a card."

"You don't kill somebody for ending an affair."

Eve lifted her eyebrows. "You'd be surprised."

They left MacKensie wrapped in jittery nerves, rode back down to the lobby.

"Impressions?"

"Not used to being noticed or singled out, I'd say," Peabody responded. "A little OCD. The bathroom was as clean as an operating room, and more organized. Everything matches. Same with the bedroom. I glanced in. Bed's perfectly made, no clothes or shoes tossed around. She's the type who figures she's going to get dumped, so isn't surprised when it happens. She didn't buzz for me."

"She doesn't have an alibi."

"If I planned to kill a former U.S. senator, I'd have one wrapped tight."

"Having absolutely none's not a bad strategy," Eve countered. "She asked how he was killed when we first got there. I never gave her an answer, she never asked again. How do you write articles on anything without asking questions, pushing the follow-up?"

"She seemed really flustered and embarrassed."

"Yeah. Maybe. Right now, she stays on the list. Let's talk to the next."

Chapter 7

The Brighton Group proved both efficient and unimposing. It held offices over a bustling deli in a squat building tossed up post-Urbans. The casually dressed staff worked together in a cacophony of noise that struck as cheerful. Some glass partitions separated the higher-ups.

Personal photos, plants, files, paperwork jumbled together on desks. The air smelled candy sweet—which Eve understood as they were offered birthday cake minutes after arriving.

"Asha's through there." The cake-bearer gestured to one of the glass-walled offices. "We're all just getting back to it after celebrating Sandy's birthday at lunch."

"We'll pass, but thanks."

"If you change your mind, just dig in. You can go right in—Asha's office is always open."

"Cake," Peabody mumbled as she followed Eve. "Why did it have to be cake?"

"Toughen up, Peabody."

Eve studied Asha through the glass. The woman wore a poppy-red sweater that suited her caramel-toned skin. She had snug black trousers tucked into stubby-heeled knee-high boots, and wore her hair scooped back from her sharp-boned, big-eyed face in a mass of red-tipped black curls.

She turned from the mini-friggie where she'd taken a bottle of water, put on a professional smile when Eve stepped to the doorway.

"Hi. What can I do for you?"

"NYPSD." Eve lifted her badge. "Lieutenant Dallas, Detective Peabody. We'd like a few minutes of your time."

"Of course. It's about Edward." The smile faded away. "I just heard. The media flash came over my comp. Please, sit. Do you want some coffee? It's really terrible coffee, but . . ."

She stopped, shook her head, dropped down into one of the visitor's chairs rather than behind her desk. "He was murdered. That's what the media flash said. I needed a minute."

She looked down at the unopened bottle of water in her hand. "Just a minute before I looked at the details. Are you going to give them to me?"

"The investigation's ongoing. You had a relationship with Edward Mira."

"Yes. Briefly, stupidly. Last spring. I'm married—but you must already know that. My husband and I were having some issues, and I had an affair." She paused again, pressed her fingers to her eyes. "I knew the senator through my work, and . . . I have no excuse for it."

"Who ended it?"

"I did, when I came to my senses. Trying to live two lives? It's awful, and when that initial buzz wears off—and it does—the guilt and stress are huge. I couldn't live with it."

"You ended it? What was the senator's reaction?"

"He was . . . What's a couple steps down from annoyed? Irked? He's a powerful, commanding man—that was part of the attraction—and I'd say accustomed to ending his affairs on his time clock. But it wasn't ugly."

She took a breath. "I want to say I liked him, personally. I hated his politics. That was another part of the appeal—those passionate debates. I can't believe he's gone, and this way. Murdered. The flash said he'd been hanged. Is that true?"

"Yes."

"Oh God." Asha squeezed her eyes shut. "I don't understand how anyone could . . . I don't understand."

"Was he irked enough when you ended things to pressure you, threaten you?"

"Oh, no." When she opened her eyes again, they gleamed behind a sheen of tears. "Lieutenant, it didn't mean that much to either of us, that's the really sad part. I was lashing out at my husband, and Edward was simply taking an opportunity. I hurt Jack and nearly destroyed my marriage because I was feeling angry and unappreciated."

"You told your husband about the affair."

"I couldn't live with the lie. How could we ever get things back if I tried to? I'm very lucky Jack agreed to couple's counseling instead of walking out the door. I forgot—and since it's my second time around, I shouldn't have—but I forgot marriage is work, with peaks and valleys. I won't forget it again."

"Can you tell me where you were yesterday afternoon, from about four to six?"

"I can tell you I was right here until about six."

"Can you verify that?"

"There were at least six of us here, and I wasn't the last to leave. You can ask anyone. Is that when he was killed?"

"I also need to know where you were last night/early this morning. Say from midnight to four."

"Wait." She sipped water, blinked at the tears. "Ah . . . I met Jack and some friends for dinner, about seven, then we went to a vid, polished it off with drinks after. I think Jack and I got home about twelve-thirty. I know I was tired— Jack's the social one, and late nights take a toll on me. I went to bed."

"Was it a planned evening?"

"The dinner was; the rest evolved. Like I said, Jack's social. I'd figured dinner, then home in my pj's. Marriage is work," she repeated with a shaky smile. "I guess everyone says this, but I didn't kill him. Why would I? He was a mistake, but it was my mistake."

Peabody noted down names and contacts to verify the alibis. They left Asha sitting in her visitor's chair.

"My impression is she alibied herself and her husband," Peabody said before Eve could ask.

"Yeah, she did. We're going to verify, and we're going to check out the husband, but everything she said rang the truth bell for me. Unless we feel differently after looking at the husband, my sense is if he wanted payback, he'd have killed or attempted to kill the senator way before this."

They got back in the car. "We'll take the next."

"Lauren Canford."

"Her. Run the husband on the way."

While Eve bitched about parking in the madness of downtown, and finally resigned herself to the kick-your-ass price of a slot in an underground lot, Peabody reported.

"Family law attorney, does the pro bono thing every Friday in a legal aid clinic. First marriage for him, and no criminal."

"I'm keeping them on the list." Eve hiked to the grimy elevator. "But they currently hold last place. What floor is Canford on?"

"Eighteen."

Eve debated, very briefly, then used her master to bypass the lobby.

"Woo!"

"Tired of dicking around."

They got off on eighteen to much shinier, and worked their way down to Lauren Canford's offices.

No casual dress here, Eve noted, and no cheerful noise in the small, glossy outer office.

Eve stepped up to reception and the man in his twenties with a bold blue tie precisely knotted at the base of his really long neck.

"Lauren Canford."

He didn't bother to glance up, but continued to work on his screen. "Your name?"

Eve put her badge on the counter. He glanced at it, briefly.

"I'll also need your name."

"It's on the badge, right there with NYPSD. My partner and I need to speak with Lauren Canford."

"Mrs. Canford's in meetings all day."

"Kid?"

He did look up at her now, all bored resentment. "One of those meetings is going to be with me, unless you want to be the one to inform Mrs. Canford that we'll have that meeting at Central at the end of her workday. I can arrange to have it in one of our Interview rooms."

"I don't believe you have the authority to—"

"Law school, right? You want to test my authority, Junior?" She leaned in close. "Try it."

Resentment went to sulk as he tapped his earpiece, swiveled around to give her his back. He muttered, but she caught *police, threatened, bitch*.

She found those three words very satisfying.

"Through those doors, straight back to the end of the hall. Mrs. Canford can give you ten minutes."

"Good choice, all around."

"And my name's not Kid or Junior," he called after her. "It's Mylo."

"I'll make a note of it."

Most of the office doors that lined the area stood closed. She did see a man, suit jacket off, tie loosened, sweating over his 'link.

"You want to be reasonable about this, Barry."

From the look in his eye, Eve judged the guy didn't figure Barry for reasonable.

Lauren Canford's office stood open. Pausing at the doorway, Eve saw the woman, black suit sharp as a blade, raven hair in an equally sharp wedge around a sternly attractive face.

A man—pinstripes, paisley tie—stood beside her desk.

"Your identification, please," he said.

"Who are you?"

"I'm Curtis Flack, the head of this organization. I'm also

a lawyer, and will represent Mrs. Canford's interests here. Your identification."

Eve took out her badge. "Lieutenant Dallas."

"Detective Peabody."

"And the nature of this visit?"

"You both know the nature of this visit, so let's cut the bull. Since you're using your right to an attorney, I have to figure you need one. We'll do this on the record, and I'll read you your rights."

Eve did the dance.

"You had an affair with Edward Mira," she began.

"Mrs. Canford has a prepared statement on this matter."

"Is that so?" Eve smiled, very, very pleasantly. "All prepared."

"I believe in being prepared." Canford spoke for the first time. "I asked Curtis to come in, and wrote this statement, as soon as I heard the media report."

She angled just a little, to read off her screen.

" 'Senator Mira and I have been acquainted, professionally, for approximately ten years. In the summer of 2060, for between five and six weeks, we engaged in an affair. When said affair ran its course, we agreed to end it. The decisions to begin and end this area of our relationship were mutual. Senator Mira and I continued our professional relationship and casual friendship, as we share many of the same political and world views. I'm deeply saddened to learn of his death, and must hope the authorities identify the person responsible quickly.' "

Lauren folded her hands. "Is there anything else?"

"Yeah, a few things. Senator Mira was married, as you are."

"That's correct."

"How does your spouse feel about the affair?"

"My husband and I, like the senator and his wife, have an understanding."

"Your husband understands you cheat on him?"

Before the lawyer could interrupt, Lauren held up a hand. "It's all right, Curtis. My husband and I understand a sexual affair is nothing more than that. Sex. If you feel the need to speak with my husband, he will also have counsel present."

"Noted. So you and the senator just rolled off each other one day and said, Hey, this was fun, but let's call it quits."

"If you persist in being crude," Flack put in, "this meeting is over."

"Okay. You and Ed finished up a spirited round of cards one night, and agreed to fold them."

Canford inclined her head. "Basically, yes. With the understanding that should we both wish to reconnect, the door was open."

"Did you? Reconnect?"

"No, and now we never will. If that's all—"

"I need your whereabouts yesterday, between four and six in the afternoon."

"I was here until five. My assistant can certainly verify that, as can my driver. I met Congresswoman Lowell for drinks at the Taj. I would appreciate it if you'd verify that with the lounge rather than disturb the congresswoman. My driver picked me back up and took me home. I believe I was home by six-fifteen. The house droid would have that on record, if necessary."

"How about last night between midnight and four."

"My husband and I attended a dinner party at the home of Martin and Selina Wendell. It began at eight-thirty. We left there around one, I believe, and returned home. Again the house droid can verify our return. We were in for the rest of the night."

"Okay. Thanks for your time."

"If you have any further questions for Mrs. Canford, or for her husband, please contact me." Flack offered his card.

"No problem. Record off."

Peabody held it in until the elevator, then spewed on the ride down. "She's just hateful. That's the exact word for her. Hateful. And she sent off bells all over the place. She could kill, oh yeah, she could. Then she'd go get a fricking manicure."

"You're right, and that's why she hits rock bottom on the list."

Peabody literally danced in place. "Come *on!*"

"If we could break her afternoon alibi, and if she'd been in that house, Mr. Mira would be dead. She's not the type to leave a loose end."

"Oh but . . . Damn it!" Wound up, Peabody stalked off the elevator. "What if she wasn't there for that—she sent minions. I bet she has minions. But then . . . big dinner party. But she could fudge the time. She could."

"Could. Didn't. Here's why she doesn't pop for me." Eve got behind the wheel, let her head rest back for a minute. "She doesn't give a rat's ass. Now, maybe we'll scrape the surface and find out he dumped her and she didn't want to be dumped. Bumps up motive, but then it falls apart. She wouldn't have worked with anyone, and this took at least two people. She wouldn't use a partner because a partner is a loose end."

"Hey, I'm a partner."

"In crime, Peabody." Eve started the car, wound through the garage. "More than one person does a crime, the other is always a loose end. Besides, I believe her. More truth bells rung. They decided to cheat, cheated, decided they were bored with each other, and ended it. You know why they bored each other, Peabody? Because they're so fucking much alike. Users, power freaks, and your word."

"Heartless."

"Yeah. That's a bull's-eye."

"At least I got one right."

"We'll verify her alibis, but she's going to be covered. Why do people like that bother with marriage? Her and the vic? It's just for politics, for show, for fancy dinner parties and professional advancement. So it's bullshit. Coppola had it right. It's work—it's supposed to be work."

"She cheated, too."

"Yeah, but she owned it. No excuses."

"Her husband forgave her—or they're working for that. Could you?"

"Could I what?"

"Forgive that. I mean, it's never going to happen, but hypothetically if, say, Roarke and I lost our minds for one wild night and had hot, crazed sex involving many multiple orgasms, then came to our senses and begged your forgiveness. Owned it, you know? Could you forgive us?"

Eve drove in silence a moment. "Well, it would be hard. It would be work, but marriage is work. So's partnership. I think I could. It would take time and that work, but I think I could forgive both of you. After I boiled you in big vats to make it easier to peel the skin, very slowly and carefully, off your bones while I danced to the music of your agonized screams. Then I made you watch while I fashioned people suits out of your skins for a couple of sparring droids I would then beat into rubble that I'd bury along with your quivering, skinless bodies in unmarked graves. After that," Eve said with a considering nod, "I think I could forgive you."

"That's good to know. It's good to know the conditions. Except, I don't think you can fashion people suits because you don't know how to sew."

"I'd learn. For something this important, I'd learn. Stupid parking, stupid parking. Wait!"

Peabody sucked in her breath as Eve punched it, went vertical, zipped, zoomed, and arrowed into a spot just vacated at the curb.

"Bagged it."

"I might have to pee again."

"Forget it. We're dealing with the baby slut, then heading back to Central. I want to update my board, think, and have some goddamn coffee."

"How did you know that car was going to pull out?"

"I've got a sense."

They walked a block in busy SoHo with crowds loaded with shopping bags or hustling out of the cold into restaurants where warm scents teased out into the winter air.

The gallery display window featured an elongated sculpture of a woman bowed over backward nearly into a U with an expression of either agonizing grief or mindless ecstasy.

Either way Eve found it mildly disturbing and much preferred the painting of a city scene that mirrored the bustle going on around them.

Inside, the walls and floors were a soft cream, making the gallery feel like the inside of a fancy box.

She saw a painting of what seemed to be a series of big blue dots connected by a jagged red line.

And wondered: Why?

In the hushed reverence a woman's heels clicked sharply.

Eve recognized Charity Downing from her ID shot. Young, several rungs up from pretty with a waterfall of blond hair, deeply blue eyes, a full and generous mouth.

She wore blue almost the same color as the dots in a slim, short dress.

"Good afternoon. I'm Charity. If I can . . . Oh God, I know who you are. I recognize you." She glanced quickly over her shoulder, quickly came forward, dropped her voice. "This is about Edward. I heard. Please, I don't want my boss, my coworkers to know. I can take my break. Please, can I meet you across the street? The coffee shop right across the street. I can't talk about this here."

"You're not going to try to run, are you, Charity?"

"Where would I go—and why would I? I just don't want anyone here to know I was . . . with Edward that way. It's right across the street. I just need to get Marilee to cover for me, get my coat."

"All right. Make it fast."

"You don't really think she'd rabbit?" Peabody asked as they went out again.

"No. If she killed him or if she didn't, she had to know the cops would want to talk to her sooner or later."

Eve jaywalked—it wasn't hard if you were fast and agile enough—and stepped into the coffee shop.

It didn't smell as bad as most—boy, had she gotten spoiled—so she grabbed a four-top that gave her a view of the art gallery.

Peabody studied the automated server. "Maybe I could

get another latte. I missed cake twice today. No, tea's probably a better bet, and they have jasmine. Jasmine tea's nice. Want some?"

"Not in this life or the next. She's coming out."

Charity didn't jaywalk, but hurried in her skinny heels to the corner, waited for the light. Eve watched her come in, cheeks pink from the cold and the hurry, spot them.

"Thank you. Really, thank you." Her words tumbled out in a breathless rush. "I'm still trying to get my head around what happened. Edward, dead. Murdered. I . . . I'm going to have some tea if that's okay. I need to settle down. I heard about an hour ago."

"I'm going to have the jasmine," Peabody said.

"Yes, it's nice. I'll have that, too."

"Coffee," Eve said. "You and Senator Mira were having an affair."

"Yes. It started a couple weeks before Christmas. I know he's married, I know it's wrong even though he said his wife doesn't care. Why wouldn't she care? I don't know."

Charity pressed her fingers to her eyes.

"How did you meet?"

"At the gallery. I had a small show—it was exciting. He came with . . . it wasn't his wife, she was too young, but I don't know who it was. He said he liked my work. He bought a painting. I was flying. And about a week later, he contacted me—he asked me to meet him for a drink. I thought it was about the art, but . . ."

"He hit on you," Peabody suggested.

"It was . . . classier than that, but yes. At first I was really surprised. He's old enough to be my grandfather, but he's interesting and persuasive. I ended up meeting him for drinks a second time, then he asked me to dinner, and I went. I knew what I was doing, and I knew it was wrong. But there I was in this fancy hotel suite with champagne and . . ."

She trailed off as their orders began to slide out of the automated slot.

"I knew what I was doing," she said again. "I knew he

just wanted to be with a young woman. I'm not stupid. And
I also knew he could help me. He nudged his rich friends
and associates to come to the gallery, and talked up my work.
I sold a couple more pieces. We were using each other, that's
what it was. I let him have sex with me, and in exchange, he
helped my art career."

She lifted her tea, drank. "I'm absolutely aware of what
that makes me. I'm not proud of it. And I'd do it again."

"Any trouble in your arrangement?" Eve asked.

"No. We'd generally go to the hotel once a week. Sometimes he wanted me to stay the night, sometimes he didn't.
He ran the show, and I didn't have any complaints."

"Was he rough with you?"

"What? Oh, no, no."

Composed, almost coldly so, Charity met Eve's gaze.
"Look, Lieutenant, I knew he was taking an aid to keep it
all going. And for a man his age, he was in pretty good shape.
But I wasn't attracted that way. The first time, it was curiosity
and the circumstances. After that, it was, just—it was what
it was. I didn't say that to him. I just pretended."

"You don't have a boyfriend?" Peabody asked. "Anybody?"

"No, I don't, so I figured I wasn't hurting anyone. It was
really clear he did this a lot, so I could justify it as far as his
wife went. I don't know her, so I could pretend that didn't
matter, either. I don't want anyone at work to know, that's all.
I don't want the gossip, or the looks. I don't care if I deserve
them, I don't want it."

"You seem a lot more concerned about gossip than murder. The man's dead."

Defiant, Downing jutted out her chin. "And I'm sorry.
I'm really sorry. I'm just scared. I'm scared I'll lose my job.
I'm scared somebody knew what I was doing—what we
were doing, and killed him."

"Did you feel threatened? Did you feel watched?"

"No. But, I mean, the staff at the hotel, they had to know.
I can't think why any of them would care, but . . . Hell." She

drank again. "It's not about that, about me. I didn't really matter. I'm just scaring myself."

"Do you know anyone who'd wish him harm?"

"I really don't, but he'd go on about it sometimes. How a man in his position makes enemies. A powerful man makes powerful enemies. He'd talk and talk about his political views—I stopped really listening. Just pretended to."

"You're good at pretending."

This time a hint of a flush rose in her cheeks. "I guess I am. I had an affair with an old man because he could help my career. I pretended to enjoy the sex when I was mostly thinking I hope he doesn't want me to stay tonight so I can just go home. I listened to him talk, and didn't disagree out loud. You want to say I prostituted myself, I can't say I didn't. But I've sold six paintings in the last six weeks, and I know five of them were directly because of him. I was grateful to him for that."

She knuckled a tear away. "And I'm sorry he's dead."

"Where were you yesterday between four and six?"

"I . . . I don't know exactly. It was my day off. I met a friend for lunch, and after, we got our nails done, did some shopping. Well, looking. And we had a drink somewhere. We decided to go back to my place, I had some pizza in the AutoChef. We just hung out until, I don't know, maybe nine or nine-thirty. I'm a suspect. Oh my God."

"We'll need your friend's name and contact information."

"Oh God. God. Lydia. Lydia Su—that's *S-U*. She's the only one who knows about Edward." She covered her face, then dropped her hands and gave them the contact numbers. "I wouldn't kill him. He was helping me. I figured he was starting to get a little bored, and all I had to do was wait for him to tell me it was done. Maybe he'd help me a little more if I didn't make a fuss. Why would I kill him for helping me?"

"How about between midnight and four last night?"

"I was in bed! I went to bed. I did some sketching after Lydia left, but we'd had wine, and I couldn't concentrate. I was in bed by like eleven, watched screen until I fell asleep. This can't be happening."

"Calm down, Charity," Peabody told her. "We have to ask, we have to check out the information you've given us. It's part of the routine. When did you last see or speak to him?"

"Ah, God, the day before yesterday. He kept it week to week. He contacted me, asked me to dinner. That's how it worked. We were supposed to have dinner tonight. Then I heard, on the bulletin. I only saw him once a week, as a rule. I saw him last week. Last Thursday night. What should I do now? What should I do?"

"Go back to work," Eve said.

"Here's what I think. You want to know what I think, right?"

"Peabody, I live to hear what you think in all things."

Eyes narrowed, Peabody climbed back into the car. "You're being bitchy now."

"I'm tired of talking to whiny cheaters. I'd rather grill murdering bastards."

"Well, sure, but you gotta do what you gotta. Anyway, she *was* whiny, but killing him's the whole golden goose deal. You can't get those shiny eggs if you kill the goose."

"Why would she want shiny eggs? Why would anybody want shiny eggs?"

"It's like a metaphor."

"It's a stupid one because shiny eggs are probably contaminated, then you die. But we only have her word about the eggs anyway."

"Yeah, but it's easy to check out."

"Which we will. Just like we're going to check out everything and everybody else on the list from today. And how about this? The old, horny goose is getting ready to move on, so no more eggs soon. She's not ready to give them up, so she gets pushy. You don't keep giving me eggs, I'm going to go tell everybody you've been putting that old thing in my young parts. Fight, blackmail, murder."

"When you put it that way."

"I need to think about it. I need decent coffee and think-ing time because the only one I'm pretty damn sure didn't do it is the bitch with the snotty lawyer. That just pisses me off."

"It'd be nice if she did it."

"It'd be nice if geese shat out golden eggs, too. But it's all just goose crap."

Chapter 8

Eve found Homicide full of cops and noise, and the lingering scent of someone's veggie hash—extra onions. Reineke and Jenkinson huddled together at Jenkinson's desk, Carmichael worked her 'link, Santiago scowled at his comp screen while Baxter strolled out from the break room with a jumbo mug of coffee.

Trueheart—she'd have to get used to seeing him out of uniform—earnestly worked his comp.

"Is there no crime on the streets?" she wondered.

"Hey, LT." Reineke angled toward her. "We got one in Interview A. Letting him stew awhile. Asshole cut up his boss on the loading dock. Told the arresting officer the guy fell on his knife. Three times."

"That's a relief. I was worried we'd all be looking for new jobs. Peabody, run the hateful bitch's husband, verify alibis."

Santiago answered his desk 'link, held up a finger. "Yeah, yeah. Got it. On the way. We caught one," he called to Carmichael. "Guy took flight out a window on the fourteenth floor on Sixth, went splat on a parked mini. And we remain gainfully employed."

"Earn your pay," Eve said, and started for her office. Baxter caught up with her just outside her door.

"We don't have anything hot," he began, "so I pulled a cold case, gave Trueheart the lead."

Since she'd done the same with Peabody when her partner's badge was new and sparkly, Eve nodded. "Good way to give him more experience, and maybe close a case."

"He's working it hard. Now I've got to school him in detective wardrobe."

Eve looked over at Trueheart in his dark gray jacket, quiet blue tie. "He looks okay."

Sort of clean and earnest, she thought. Like he was on his way to church.

Hmmm.

Baxter only shook his head. "I'll work on it. We get anywhere on the cold one, I'll let you know."

Eve went in, hit the coffee, then updated her board and book, wrote up her notes. She copied Mira, unofficially.

After entering the data, she ran probabilities on each woman she'd questioned. As she suspected, the computer liked the ones without alibis.

"That's the easy way," she muttered and, with another cup of coffee, put her boots on her desk, sat, and studied.

Allyson Byson—off in the tropics. Potentially could have hired someone to take care of Edward Mira, but it just didn't ring true. The kill was vicious and personal.

She made an additional note to verify Byson's travel, any possible circling back to do the murder.

But there, she and the computer agreed. Dead low probability.

Carlee MacKensie. Jittery, came off pliable, harmless, on the weak side. No alibi, so the comp liked her. And here, Eve didn't altogether disagree.

"Something a little off there, Carlee. Something not quite right. Too wide-eyed. I don't think we got the full story from you. I don't think you rang that truth bell."

On to Lauren Canford. Total bitch, no two ways about that one. And Eve could see the woman in a violent outburst.

She could see her planning a murder with care and cunning.

But . . . Eve didn't sense passion. She didn't sense the sort of attachment to or anger with the victim it took to torture and kill.

More the type to backbite—there was an expression that made sense. The type to go behind an enemy's back and smear reps, plant gossip seeds.

Asha Coppola. Came off honest—if you overlooked the adultery. But largely honest. Screwed up, owned it, working to fix it. It played all the way through for Eve.

Then Charity Downing. Something there, Eve thought again. Something not quite what it seems. Something . . .

"Cagey," Eve said out loud, studying the face on her board over the rim of her mug. "That's what I got from you, Charity. You're cagey. Your alibi's going to hold up, too, and when it does, I'm inclined to take a look at your day-off pal.

"Lydia Su. Friends lie for friends. We'll take a look because there was a lie in there somewhere. Some truth, but a lie buried in it."

She set her mug aside, rearranged the board in her preference.

Charity Downing
Carlee MacKensie
Asha Coppola (maybe her husband wasn't working on
     forgiving)
Lauren Canford

She'd have a 'link interview with Allyson Byson, but suspected that name would replace Canford's at the bottom of her list.

Artist, freelance writer, nonprofit marketing manager, lobbyist, society type.

"Didn't have a type, did you, Edward? It was more looks and availability. And age. Average age of this group is—shit, math. I don't know . . . early thirties. And that's just this group. Bound to be more. What if—"

"Sorry, Dallas." Peabody rapped knuckles on the door-jamb. "Edward Mira—that's junior—and Gwendolyn Mira Sykes are here. They want to talk to you—us."

"Saves us the trip. Set them up in an Interview room. We'll keep it strictly official."

"I think B's open. I'll take them down."

Eve nodded, looked back at her board. But her focus had shifted, so she pushed up from her desk. She'd see what the vic's children, and likely top beneficiaries, had to say.

She walked out, saw Baxter had pulled his chair over to Trueheart's desk. She didn't know if they were discussing new angles on the cold case or the cut of a suit, the weight of fabric.

Didn't, at that point, want to know.

She headed toward the Interview area, saw Peabody coming out of B.

"I'm getting her a sparkling water, him a Coke."

Eve dug in her pockets for enough to cover it. "Get me a tube of Pepsi, and whatever you want. Official, but pleasant."

"They're a little bit wrecked, Dallas. Pushing through it, but you can see it. And they're a solid unit—really tight."

"Okay."

She stepped in, and though she'd already viewed their ID shots, it still struck her that Edward Junior had Dennis Mira's dreamy green eyes.

He wore his dark hair long enough to pull back in a stub of a tail—as Roarke habitually did when in serious work mode. He had a strong, handsome face—she could see the resemblance to his father—and wore scarred work boots, jeans, and a red-and-black plaid shirt.

His sister had taken her looks from the mother—statuesque and striking despite the reddened eyes. She wore a dark suit, dark tights, and flashy red ankle boots with skyscraper heels.

They sat at the battered Interview table holding hands.

The brother gave the sister's hand a squeeze, and stood as Eve closed the door.

"Mr. Mira, Mrs. Sykes, I'm Lieutenant Dallas. I'm sorry for your loss."

"It's Ned. Ned and Gwen." His voice was rough and strained. "Thanks for talking to us, for making the time so quickly. Dennis told us you were working hard to find—to find our father's killer. We don't want to get in the way."

"You're not in the way. I intended to come to you before the end of the day."

"We've been with our mother." Gwen cleared her throat. "Their security guard contacted Ned, and he came to get me. We want to apologize first for the way she spoke to you."

"It's not on you, and it's nothing."

"It's something," Ned corrected with a grim smile. "We've been on the receiving end. But despite how she behaved, she's shattered. We know your reputation, Lieutenant, and your work with Charlotte. So."

He rubbed a hand on his sister's arm. "You know by now that our parents didn't have what most think of as a traditional marriage."

"What did they have?"

Before the question could be answered, Peabody came in with the drinks. "Hope tubes are okay."

"That's fine, thanks." Ned looked back at Eve. "They cared for each other, but the marriage was more a partnership. Political, social."

"You don't have to be delicate, Ned. They both had relationships outside the marriage," Gwen continued. "They produced us—two offspring, male, female—then they were free to pursue other interests. We knew it, growing up, knew it wasn't to be discussed. As long as we presented the accepted image, everything stayed balanced."

"You screwed that up," Ned said, making her laugh a little.

"You screwed up first." Then her eyes filled. "Oh God, Ned."

"It's okay. It's all right." He scooted his chair closer to hers, put his arm around her. "I did screw it up first. I didn't want to go to Yale. I didn't want to study law, go into politics.

So I made sure it couldn't happen. Tanked my grades, ditched school when I could get away with it. I'd have taken off the minute I hit eighteen, but—"

"He wouldn't leave me. I'm two years younger, so he toughed it out. I didn't go to Yale, but took Harvard instead. I did study law. I wanted to. But I used my degree to become a children's rights attorney."

"We were disappointments," Ned finished. "We were constantly at odds with our father, particularly. I partnered up with two friends—who weren't on the approved list—and we started our own business. We build, repair, recycle, reimagine furniture. I work with my hands, and he never forgave me. Twenty-two years we've been in business, but he still called it my rebellion."

"You're not— Are you Three Guys Furniture?"

He grinned at Peabody. "Yeah, that's us."

"I *love* your stuff. My father builds furniture, and my brother, so I know quality. I love your work. Sorry," she said to Dallas, "but you should know his business has a really exceptional rep."

"I appreciate that. Gwen's got her own solid rep in her field, but . . ."

"We didn't follow the plan," Gwen said. "We didn't maintain the assigned image. We didn't marry the sort of people they would have chosen. It didn't matter that we are both happy, that we married wonderful people we love, both have terrific kids. It wasn't the plan."

"My parents would never say we're estranged," Ned said, "because that wouldn't fit, either. But we barely speak, only see each other on holidays when we have to."

"And when you did see each other or speak?" Eve asked.

"Nine out of ten, it ended in an argument. Charlie said to be brutally honest with you about it, so here we are. Brutal. I didn't like my father."

"Oh, Ned."

"What's the point, Gwen? I didn't like or respect him. But he was my father. My mother's a pain in the ass."

"God, she is." Gwen sighed, let her head tip to her

brother's shoulder. "But she's our mother, and she's grieving. Our father's been murdered, and however strained our relationship, he didn't deserve to be killed, to be hurt the way he was hurt. We'll tell you anything you need to know, answer any questions you have to help you find who did it."

"And we'll release a statement to the media that reflects family unity. We'll maintain the image for him, and for our mother."

"Let's get this out of the way," Eve began. "Where were you yesterday, four to six, then midnight to four."

"Four to six, in the shop, working. Well, until about five-thirty," Ned corrected. "Then Grant—one of my partners—and I hung out, talking shop for a while while we closed up. I was probably home by six or a little after. We had dinner around seven. My wife, the kids, and I. By midnight? I was out for the count."

"In court until nearly five," Gwen said. "Custody case, nasty. Trewald v. Fester, Judge Harris presiding. I had to check in at the office, but I was home by six. Chaos ensued. I have a thirteen-year-old girl in the crazed clutches of puberty who was going into the tenth round with her eleven-year-old brother, whose job it is to irritate her. About midnight my husband and I were having a second glass of wine, in bed, and trembling like earthquake survivors—and wondering where our sweet, loving, happy little girl had gone."

"You'll get through it," her brother told her.

"As long as there's wine at midnight."

"Mr. Mira—Dennis Mira—indicated the two of you will inherit your father's interest in the Spring Street property. My information is it's worth eight figures."

"Sure it is." Ned nodded. "If it's coming to us, that simplifies something at least. It stays in the family. We don't need the money, Lieutenant. Both Gwen and I are solid there, and that place means a lot to Dennis."

"Let's set that aside. Do you know any of the women your father was involved with?"

"We made it a point not to," Gwen began. "A few years ago I was facing off against Leanore Bastwick in court, and during a recess she made it a point to follow me into the ladies' room and tell me she was sleeping with my father. She did it to throw me off my game."

"Yeah, I can see that."

"When I heard about what happened to her a few weeks ago, I was shocked. But—brutal honesty—I didn't lose any sleep over it."

"Down, girl." Ned squeezed her hand. "One of them came on to me."

"What!" Gwen goggled at him. "You *never* told me!"

"It was twenty years ago, easy. I don't even remember her name, but she came into the little storefront we had back then and cornered me. Said she wondered if I resembled my father in all ways. She grabbed my crotch—not something I wanted to tell my sister. Zoe saw it—my wife. Well, not my wife then, we weren't even dating yet. She is—and was—a designer, interior. We were working with her on some projects. But she saw the whole thing, and while I was trying not to scream like a girl, she marched over, kicked the crotch-grabber out, and told her if she ever came back, she'd call the cops."

"I love Zoe," Gwen said, with feeling.

"Me, too. It took me over a month to get up the courage to ask her out after that. But it all worked out. Sorry, that doesn't help you."

"You'd be surprised. You've told me that for most of your life, your parents had this sort of arrangement, but each of you only clearly remembers one incident where the woman involved at the time made herself known. That tells me as a rule, they were discreet, and not looking for trouble when the liaison ended. So, to the best of your knowledge, none of the women he had affairs with caused trouble for him, threatened him?"

"He'd have crushed them. I don't mean physically," Ned said quickly. "But in every other way. If they'd even hinted at causing trouble, he'd have let them know how he could and would ruin them. Their lives, their business or career, their family. He was my father, and I want whoever killed him

found and put away. But he was vindictive, and he was ruth-
less, and he never forgot anything he considered a betrayal."

"Is that enough? Can that be enough for now? It feels
awful to talk about him this way." Tears swirled into Gwen's
eyes again. "We want to help, but can this be enough?"

"Sure. And you have helped."

"Then I want to go home. I want my family."

"I'll take you home." Ned got to his feet.

"You don't need to."

"How about if Zoe brings the kids, we just hold together
at your house for a while?"

Gwen closed her eyes. "That would be great. That would
feel right. My aunt—our mother's sister," Gwen told Eve,
"came in. That's who our mother really wants now. The rest
of us will hold together."

They'd do just that, Eve thought when they left. They'd
hold together.

"It had to be rough, growing up that way. Being ordered
to toe a line, never seeing real love and loyalty between your
parents."

"They got out of it," Eve said. "They made their own."

She'd done the same.

She went back to her office, added to her notes. Hesitated,
then copied Mira. It might be hard to read what Ned and
Gwen had said, but she imagined Mira already knew all
of it.

She wanted home, too, she realized. She'd find her focus
again working at home.

She gathered what she needed, grabbed her coat, then
made the mistake of answering her 'link.

The media liaison informed her she needed to give a
statement on the Mira case.

Resigned—she'd known it was coming—she went out to
the bullpen and Peabody's desk.

"I have to go do the media statement, and I'm taking this
home from there. I want reports on the spouses, and the verified alibis. You can do the rest here or at home, as long as I
have everything tonight."

"I'll stick with it here until McNab's off."

"Copy Mira, but not through official channels. Got that?"

"Got that."

She might hate this part of the job, but she would get it done. And she was grateful the liaison set a strict time of ten minutes, for statement and questions.

The questions sent up an echoing bang in her head on the drive home.

Is it true Senator Mira was found naked?

Why was his abduction not reported?

Is Dr. Charlotte Mira attached to this investigation?

Is Professor Dennis Mira a suspect?

How long was Senator Mira tortured before his death?

Christ, she thought, what public had the right to know that? Which was exactly how she'd answered the question before she'd walked away.

Home, she told herself. Maybe a workout or a swim before she dug back into it. Just something to take the edge off the ugliness of the day.

A workout and a swim, she decided as she drove through the gates. Thirty minutes each. She could take an hour, then start back fresh.

Just seeing the house made her feel more centered. She didn't know why the conversation with Gwen and Ned had left her so unsettled.

They hadn't been beaten or brutalized. They'd grown up privileged. Nothing like her own experience. But she'd felt her own old dread rising up as she'd listened to them, greasy memories of fear, of helplessness.

She needed it gone.

She prepped herself as she parked. She could start getting it gone by exchanging swipes with Summerset. That should shove back the echoes.

But Summerset wasn't in the foyer, and that threw her balance off even more. He was *supposed* to be there, lurking, sneering, making some lame-ass comment.

"Early," she grumbled to herself as she went up the stairs. "Damn right I'm home early. I made a point of it so I could catch you crawling out of your coffin. That would've been a pretty good one. Now it's wasted."

She started to head for the bedroom, changed her mind, aimed for her office. She'd dump everything there, take the time to update her board. Then she could let things simmer in the back of her brain while she pounded out a few miles, swam a few laps.

She was still steps away from her office when she heard the humming. Female humming.

What the hell? One of the house droids she rarely, if ever, saw? Did they hum happy tunes?

She stepped into the doorway.

Not a droid, but a glam-type redhead with a tablet, prowling around *her* personal space humming that fucking happy tune.

And where was her board?

Who the hell was the woman in crotch-high stiletto boots walking around . . . and sitting her skinny ass on *HER* desk.

Eve flipped back her coat, laid her hand on the butt of her weapon.

"Who the hell are you?"

The redhead let out a quick squeal, bounced her skinny ass off the corner of the desk. She slapped a hand between her perky breasts and goggled at Eve.

"Oh God! You scared me."

"Yeah?" Hand on her weapon, Eve stepped into the room. "Want to get really scared? You will be if I don't have your name and how you got in here in ten seconds."

"I'm Charmaine. You must be Lieutenant Dallas. It's just lovely to meet you. I was just finishing up the measurements."

"What measurements?"

"For the . . . I'm so flustered. You really did give me a scare. I'm not really supposed to say. Roarke's just—"

And he walked in from his office. "Sorry about the interruption. If you'd . . . Eve."

He noted her stance, the position of her hand, the look in her eye. And sighed. "You're home early."

"Yeah, how about that? Who's this, what's she doing in my office?"

"Charmaine Delacroix, Lieutenant Dallas. Charmaine's an interior designer I've worked with on a number of projects. Including the dojo."

"Wonderfully minimalistic," Charmaine said, "yet far from rigid or Spartan."

Roarke subtly angled himself between her and Eve. "Do you have everything you need?"

"Absolutely. I can't wait to get started. I'll have some options for you by next week. Wonderful to meet you," she said to Eve. "I know the way out."

Eve gave her five seconds to beat feet, then rounded on Roarke. "You let somebody prowl around my office."

"I had a designer come in, get a feel for it, measure, and would have been in here with her the entire time—though she's perfectly trustworthy—but there was a call I had to take."

"Why does some designer have to get a *feel* for my office? It's *my* office, isn't it? And where's my goddamn murder board?"

"I put it away, as you wouldn't want anyone not involved to see it. And if you hadn't come home unexpectedly, it would've been back in place."

Outrage wanted to blow the top of her skull through the ceiling. "So it's okay if I don't know the difference? It's okay if I go into your office, take things and put them somewhere else, tell somebody to come right on in, as long as you don't know about it?"

"If you had a reason to, as I did."

"What possible reason did you have for moving my murder board, for letting some humming woman into my space?"

" 'Humming'?"

"She was *humming*. For Christ's sake."

"I suppose she has a cheerful disposition. The reason was to surprise you with some ideas for redoing your space."

Another round of outrage wanted to blow flames out of her ears.

"Why do I need ideas for redoing it? It's fine. It was just fine for you, too, when you put it together so I'd move in here. What, now it's not good enough? Not fancy enough?"

His eyes chilled to blue ice. "If you're going to deliberately be an ass, if you insist on raving over something this simple, we can talk about it when you're not."

"I'm an ass? You start messing with my space, and I'm an ass?"

"People change, Eve. They change their minds, their attitudes, their look, and often the look of their spaces. I thought, after this amount of time, you might be ready for a change here, in this space, to have it reflect what's now rather than the past. Obviously, you're not. But that's not why you're an ass. You're an ass for being so pathetically insecure you'd react as if you'd walked in on the two of us naked and banging each other on your precious desk.

"I still have work."

She set her teeth as he walked back toward his office. "If I'd walked in on that, you better believe I'd have used my weapon. On both of you."

"That's something, I suppose," he said, and shut his office door.

Chapter 9

Oh, she hated when he did that. Hated when she was primed for a good, bloody fight and he just iced over and walked away from it.

And he *knew* she hated it.

Her instinct was to bang right through that door and battle on, but . . . He'd probably like that, wouldn't he? She paced and prowled around her office. *Her* space! He'd just love it if she went barging in, raging on, while he sat there with his scary Roarke iced calm.

She knew how to get through the ice, oh yeah, she did. She knew which buttons to push to bring on the heat. But he'd probably like that, too. He'd just *love* being able to think he'd been *reasonable* while she barged and raged and bitched.

She wouldn't give him the fucking satisfaction.

Screw it. She'd come home to take an hour to clear her head, she'd take the damn hour.

She stalked out of her office, snarled all the way to the bedroom, where the cat's full, pudgy length was sprawled across the center of the bed.

"Don't even start on me," she warned as he opened his bicolored eyes to stare at her. "How would he like it if I had somebody come in here?" She yanked off her coat, tossed it on the bed. "If I just decided, Hey, I'm going to change everything in the bedroom. Yeah, a decorating bug crawled up my ass, so I'm going to toss this all out and haul in something else.

"How do you like *that*?"

She dragged off her weapon harness, pulled out her 'link, her communicator, her badge, tossed them and the other pocket debris on the dresser.

Galahad, who knew something about moods and timing, kept his own counsel while Eve stripped out of her street clothes, pulled on workout gear.

"You could be next," she warned Galahad as she strode onto the elevator. "He could get another bug up his ass and dye you pink and dress you in a tux."

She fumed all the way down to the gym. Definitely not the time for a holo-session with Master Wu. She considered beating the crap out of one of the sparring droids, but thought Roarke would probably enjoy *that*, so she opted for the tread, programmed it for a hard urban run, with obstacles.

A beach run would have relaxed her, but she wasn't ready to relax. Instead she pounded the city streets, kicked a little street-thief ass, climbed, leaped, rolled over barriers until she had a solid five miles in.

She switched to weights, pumped until her muscles burned, then finished up with some ab-searing crunches before she stretched it out.

Sweaty, winded, she headed to the tropical wonder of the pool house, stripped off. Dived into the cool, blue water.

Five double laps later, her body begged for a break. And her thoughts snuck back.

Her space. Hers. He didn't have any business pushing her to change her space, bringing in some fancy redhead because it wasn't all . . . fancy.

Nothing wrong with her office, she thought as she let herself coast through the water. It was serviceable. It was good enough. Maybe it was a blight, a dumpy box in the grandeur of the house.

But it was her blight, damn it.

She got good work done in there, and he had never complained about it before. He'd made it like that in the first place, completely stunning her with the replica of her apartment, right down to the crappy desk.

Damn it. Damn it. He'd turned her heart inside out with that gesture, and now he wanted to change it.

Because she didn't live in the old apartment with the crappy desk anymore, she thought.

She hissed out a breath, muttered, "Hell," and let herself sink under the water.

She had herself under better control when she came back up. The mad simmered under it all, but the control skimmed a fine veneer over the rest. She changed into cotton pants, a sweatshirt, skids, then sat down, stroked the cat.

"He wouldn't dye you pink or dress you in a tux. He likes you fine just the way you are. Sometimes I wonder about me, but you're good."

Galahad bumped his head against her arm, so she stroked him into ecstasy. It only took a couple of minutes, making her think cats were a hell of a lot easier to live with than people.

He followed her out and to her office, where Roarke's door remained shut.

She curled her lip at it.

"He could stay in there, iced over, for days. So let him. I've got work. See anything wrong in here?" she asked the cat.

Galahad looked at her, then jogged over to leap onto her sleep chair.

"See? Everything we need. Except my damn board."

She found it, neatly stowed in the storage area, hauled it back.

She updated it, got coffee, studied it, circled it, made a couple changes, then went to her desk—suitably crappy for her—and reviewed her notes.

She barely glanced up when Roarke walked in. He went to the wall panel, chose a bottle of wine.

Uncorked it.

"Wine?" he asked.

"No, and I'm not going to apologize."

"What a coincidence. Neither am I."

"I'm not the one who had some redhead poking around, humming in those boots."

He cocked a brow. "You object to the boots?"

"I object to any boots that have six-inch heels the width of my pinkie, but that's not the point. And you can go all ice storm, but I have plenty of objections to coming home after a pissy day and finding out you've decided to make changes to where I work without saying a damn thing to me about it. Without seeing how I felt about it."

"You're wrong."

"The hell I am."

"You're wrong," he repeated, "that you wouldn't have been consulted, that I would have changed a single square inch without consulting you or seeing how you felt, what you wanted. That's bollocks, Eve, and I don't deserve it."

"You're the one who had her in here. I didn't get the memo."

He looked down at his wine, drank. "I had her come in to revisit the space, to take a fresh look at it with some ideas I'd given her."

"You'd given her."

"Yes. As I'm intimate with where and how you work."

"This is where I work when I'm here. This is how. You're the one who put it together like this in the first place. Goddamn it." She shoved up from her desk, yanked out the tear-shaped diamond she wore on a chain under her sweatshirt.

"When you gave me this fat-assed diamond and said you loved me, I just thought you were crazy."

"I recall." Eyeing her over it, he took another sip of wine. "Clearly."

"But when you showed me this, what you'd done for me here, in your home. How you'd made this space for me, just like my apartment, because you understood I needed my own, I needed what I knew. You *got* that, so I started to believe you did. You loved me. Now it's not good enough."

"It's not good enough, no," he said, striking her to the core. "It's not good enough for you—for who you are and what you do every bloody day. But that's only part of it. Once, you needed that familiarity, that security, to leave your apartment and come here. I needed you. So I gave you what you needed to be here, to have your own here. I thought three years was enough time for you to let it go, really leave it behind, and to make something new, for yourself. Not in my home. In ours."

His eyes remained cool on hers, but she thought she caught something behind that blue frost. And that something was hurt.

"It's . . . troubling to realize you still need to hold on to what was before. Before us."

"That's not it." No, no, she wouldn't swallow that. "That's not fair. That's bullshit wrong. I'm not holding on to anything. Much," she amended. "I'm not insecure. Exactly."

Shit, shit, *shit.*

"I'm used to the space. It works fine. How can I have cops come up here, work here, if you go all fancy with it? It's a work space, for solving murders, closing cases, not for showing off."

Frustration eked through the ice—which was better to her mind than hurt.

"Updating and creating an efficient work area isn't showing off. Christ Jesus, for a woman with such professional arrogance, you're forever worried about your idea of showing off otherwise."

"You want to talk arrogance, pal."

"No. I want to talk about that desk."

"The—what?"

"Are you attached to that desk?"

"I . . ." Thrown off, she shoved at her hair, frowned at the desk. "There's nothing wrong with it."

"I can't count the manner of things wrong with it. But if

you're attached, it stays. It's that simple. If you're not, you might consider one of the options you'd have, such as the command center I have in mind."

"I don't . . . 'command center'?"

"A wide-curved U, controls and swipe screens built in, the main D&C at the top of the curve, auxiliary on one side, disc storage, holo controls on the other. I'll be updating some of my own in my office, and in my office with the unregistered. Technology makes leaps almost daily, and it pays to keep up with it."

"I don't get along very well with technology, so—"

"That would be taken into account."

He rolled right over her. Not so icily now, she noted. He'd heated up all on his own. Maybe there was some hurt, definitely some frustration. But mostly he was deeply pissed.

"You prefer a physical board, so that remains. You'd have the option for the screen, and the screens here, as elsewhere, would be updated. We're hardly talking about fussy window treatments and bloody divans."

"Yeah, but—"

"We have dinner in here more often than not." He rolled right over her again. "So it's time we had a more pleasant area for it—likely over there. Table, chairs, part of the space, but in a more defined area. With a table that would expand when we're invaded by half your department. Which takes us to the secondary workstations and the seating area."

" 'Seating'?"

He gestured with his wine. "You can go on about not liking visitors in your work space, but the fact is, you often have people in here. Cops, in any case."

"They'll never leave if you make it all comfortable." She rubbed at the back of her neck because, damn it, she could see some of it. And she was still hung up on the idea of a command center. "I'm used to it, that's all, and then I come in and some redhead in boots is in here humming. And you're: Here's what's going to happen."

"I say again, nothing would have been changed, been

touched without your approval. It's not just your office, Eve, bloody hell, it's your *house*."

"That's why I was pissed!" At wit's end, she yanked at her hair. "It's my house, too, and it felt like you were just taking over without telling me."

He paused a moment, poured more wine. "There's a point. I'll give you that. And it's lowered the troubling quite a bit to have you say it. I wasn't taking over, but laying the groundwork for something you could choose. Or not. Would you like to work with Charmaine?"

"Have you lost your mind?"

"I haven't. I brought her in, and would have presented you with some completed options I felt would appeal to you. If none did, she could come up with more, or, again, not. If you liked any, but wanted changes, there'd be changes. Just as we handled the dojo. I strongly suspect if I'd said to you I wanted to have a dojo designed, particularly for you, you'd have said . . ."

"Who the hell has a dojo in their house?" he demanded in a snarky American accent that surprised a laugh out of her.

"I don't sound like that."

"Close enough. And you should know now she'll be working up some fresh looks for the bedroom."

"What? What? Why? It's nice. It's—"

"It was designed for me, before I ever set eyes on you. Well before, come to that. Now it'll be designed for us."

"I'm fine with it."

"You'll have to be fine with any new design before anything's done. So if you come home unexpectedly, and there's a redhead humming in the bedroom, you'll know why, and not react as if I'm about to shag her on our bed."

Insulted, she jabbed a finger at him. "I didn't react like that. If I had, there'd be a droid wearing your skin suit. Just ask Peabody because I explained it to her just today."

"And why is that?"

"Because I spent most of today talking to adulterers. And I do want wine," she decided, taking his. "And it put me in a mood I came home early to ditch, before I dug back into the work. And Summerset wasn't even where he's supposed to be so I could insult him and start the ditching."

"I was home even earlier, and told him to go out with some of his friends."

"Corpses don't have friends, they have other corpses."

His eyebrows lifted; his head angled. "Feel better?"

"Not really."

He went to get himself a new glass of wine. "I wanted to do something for you, for the cop, and I'll circle back here and say again, this isn't good enough for you. Don't argue with me on that," he said before she could. "You're your own cop, and as brilliant a one as I've ever known. You're also mine, and this isn't what you deserve."

It touched her because she knew he meant it, just exactly that. "You're trying to seduce me with command centers."

"I am. And the other part of why is purely selfish in that I need you to let this go. I want to know you can."

"This?" She gestured. "It's not that. It's not. Mavis, Leonardo, the kid, the apartment's theirs. They've made it so theirs, there's nothing of what was mine. I don't need that—not there, not here. I swear I'm not clinging to that. I'm used to this, that's pretty big. But bigger, it's that you gave it to me. You knew me, even then, and gave it to me. That's what I don't want to let go."

She swallowed more wine, muttered, "Dumb-ass."

He came back to her, trailed a fingertip down the shallow dent in her chin. "I'll always have done that, when we both needed it. Dumb-ass. Let's try this, for both of us. And if what you need is to keep this as it is, then it stays."

"If I say okay, let's try it, the redhead's not going toward fancy."

"Not within miles of fancy, my word on that."

"Okay. But I'm not apologizing."

"Neither am I."

"I guess that works."

He leaned down, touched his lips to hers. "Did you murder a droid?"

"I wanted to, but I didn't because I knew you'd ask. I didn't want to give you the satisfaction." She smirked, then sighed. "But I kind of wish I had. It really has been a pissy day."

"You were right about the senator. About finding his body."

"Yeah, score one for me. They did a number on him—we didn't release all the details, but they've already started to leak. I had to end the day with a media conference. And I need to begin tomorrow at the morgue. I didn't get there today. No rush on that, really."

She walked back to the board, around it. "They pushed through his tox, and they didn't dose him. They wanted him to feel it, all of it. They beat him, face, genitals. Beat the shit out of him. Sodomized him and, unless Morris tells me different, the way I see it is he was alive, probably conscious when they put the noose around his neck, fastened it to the entrance hall chandelier, and used the mechanism. You know? Lowered it to hook him on, then raised it. Slow, I bet, slow so he'd feel every inch, so he'd choke, struggle. Left his hands free, because he clawed at his throat some. He died hard. They thought he deserved to die hard."

A pissy day indeed, he thought. And though he wouldn't bring it up, felt it proved his point. She should come home to a work space she deserved.

" 'They'?"

"Had to be at least two. At least one's a woman."

She needed to talk it out, Roarke thought as he leaned back on her desk. "How do you know?"

"Sex. Sodomy—and no evidence he went for men or boys. Plus Mr. Mira heard a female voice. I got that when I grilled him, in his own kitchen. While he made me hot chocolate."

The tears burned up, nearly out. "Oh shit, oh shit."

"Here now, what's this?" He set his wine aside quickly, went to her. And took the wine out of her hand before she wrapped around him.

"I had to push him, dot the *i*'s. He did great, he did fine, and he understood. They all understood I had to, but, oh

God, you could see he was grieving. He was grieving for the worthless son of a bitch, and trying to soothe *me* because he knew . . ."

"It was hard for you, but you were protecting him."

"I wanted to punch the reporter who asked me if he was a suspect. If Professor Dennis Mira was a fucking suspect. But I couldn't. I have to look out for him, Roarke, but the worthless son of a bitch is my victim, and I have to stand for him, whatever I think of him."

"You did have an all-around pissy day."

"That's not all of it." She won the war with tears, eased back.

"I tell you what we'll do. We'll have an early dinner, and you'll tell me. Then we'll work on it. Dennis matters to me as well, very much matters."

"I know he does. I don't know if I can eat."

"That means it has to be pizza, and I'll make that deal with you if there's a side salad involved."

"Okay. Let's give it a shot."

She paid a little more attention to the setup while they ate: the replica of her old table where she'd sat for a meal— occasionally. More often she'd eaten, when she'd eaten, at her desk.

It probably wouldn't kill her to consider a better table, she thought as she poked at the salad. But—

"Tell me," Roarke said.

So she did, from the early meeting at the Mira Institute to the break for Trueheart's ceremony, finding the body, notifying next of kin, and on to the Mira home. Then the interviews and her impressions of the women who'd had affairs with the senator.

"You pushed a lot into one day."

"It didn't end there. And there'll be more women, that's a given. Bagging women was like his fricking hobby. And with them? Guilt or defiance, cold calculation, self-preservation. They all had reasons for cheating, and I don't buy any of them."

"You think they're lying?"

"No—or not exactly. The two I have at the top there?" She gestured toward the board. "Something more, something a little off. But I mean I don't buy the concept. You stick or you don't—and you don't roll around with a married guy because he sticks or he doesn't."

"You see it in black-and-white."

"Damn straight."

"Fortunately for my skin, I agree with you. But there are many who see the concept as a more gray area, depending on the circumstance."

"Then why do the marriage thing? Stick or don't," she said again. "MacKensie? Needs a harder look. She comes across as the type who stays home, observes rather than participates. And is a—what is it—Plain Joan?"

"That's Jane."

"Yeah, right, because it rhymes. I'm not going to say the vic had a specific type, but every other one of the list is a looker, and comes off confident. Is she the exception, or is she putting on a show? Harder look. Same with Downing. Not the Jane bit, but something that felt off. Letting some rich, influential old guy do her for profit and advancement, okay. But there was a lie in there. MacKensie played it too Jane, and too jittery, and Downing? Way too prepared."

"More prepared than the one with the lawyer already on tap?"

"Yeah, the one with the lawyer was just a stone bitch. Downing? She's got sly in her eyes. That rhymes, too. Plain Jane and Sly Eye."

She picked up a slice. It was rare for pizza not to appeal, but she only ate it to avoid the inevitable nudge from Roarke.

"The one you dislike most is the one you suspect least."

"Right now. But here's what I started wondering. What if sleeping with the vic isn't the only connection here? All of them knew him for a dog, banged him anyway. What if they knew each other? Not just knew there were others, but more specifically."

"An I Slept with Senator Mira Club?"

"I think when you cheat with many, the odds of paths

crossing go up. I'm wondering whose paths might have crossed, and what happened then."

She shrugged. "I didn't have much time to play the angle before the vic's son and daughter showed up. And that was the second hardest part of the pissy day."

She'd eaten a baby bunny's portion of her salad, Roarke noted, and barely touched the pizza, which usually did the trick.

So whatever the second hardest part had been was still with her.

"Why is that?"

"They're tight. He's got Mr. Mira's eyes. That's irrelevant," she said.

"Not to you."

"To the investigation. They're tight," she repeated. "And when you listen to them, observe, it's clear they've always been tight, and basically they only had each other. Parents who had them primarily—maybe exclusively—to present an image. The image of an attractive, traditional, well-heeled family, because that image could further the vic's career. Lawyer to judge, judge to senator. And likely he hoped for more, but backed off it rather than lose an election."

"I see," he said, and he did.

"It's also clear they understood this, and their expected role from a young age. They understood their parents' marriage, and the family itself, was surface and show. They were expected to behave in a scripted manner, to follow the family line to Yale, to law, to an advantageous marriage. Just pawns, right from the jump, who knew their parents for cheats and liars and hypocrites."

She set the half slice of pizza down. "It's not the same, I know it's not."

"Not so very different." And because he understood, he laid his hand over hers. "Physical abuse is a tangible thing. A child beaten and raped as you were, that shows if anyone cares to look. Emotional abuse leaves marks and scars, but they're internal. You, as they, knew from a tender age you were created for a purpose. It doesn't matter that theirs was to walk a golden path, and yours was dark and brutal. You were all caged in and devalued by the very people who should have cherished and protected you."

"Same with you."

"Same with me, yes. They had each other, and that got them through. We found each other, and that changed the path for both of us. It's hardly a wonder, darling Eve, that you related to them, felt for them, and for yourself."

"It's not something that can get in the way of the job. It could if I let it, so I needed to come home, settle it all down, start fresh."

"And walked straight into the redhead in boots. Poor timing all around. I can apologize for the timing adding to the general pissiness of your day."

"You didn't know about it, so . . . They're not in this." She looked back at the board, at the ID shots. "Not just because he has Mr. Mira's eyes, or because I can relate. They made their own lives, they didn't follow the path, made their own. And they're happy. I'll look. I'll cover the ground, but this wasn't a family thing. It hinges on sex."

"You may not have done justice to the food, but I'll help you cover the ground."

"We can save it for later." Grateful, she took his hand, gave it a quick squeeze. "Once I get some work under me, I might feel more like pizza."

"All right then. Let me take the senator's children. Your instinct says they're not a part of this, so you won't waste time looking into them."

"Or relating."

"Or that."

"Okay, then I can start at the top of my list."

She looked back at the board, and Carlee MacKensie.

Chapter 10

At her desk, she brought up her incomings, found Peabody's verification of all alibis, right down the line. Considering, she decided rather than starting with MacKensie, she'd do a run on Downing's alibi.

Lydia Su.

Make that Dr. Lydia Su, Eve discovered. Biophysicist, on staff at Lotem Institute of Science and Technology, New York. Age thirty-three, single. Asian—Korean and Chinese. One sib, a sister, four years younger—a linguist, Eve noted, living in London. Parents married thirty-five years—a nice run, in Eve's opinion. Father a neurosurgeon, mother also a scientist. Nanotech.

So, Eve thought, highly motivated, highly intelligent, highly educated family.

Well-educated in Lydia Su's case, Eve read, at Yale.

"Interesting. Isn't that interesting?"

But then a lot of really smart people, rich people, motivated people went to Yale.

Still . . .

Following the line, she toggled back to check where Charity Downing had studied art. NYU, she noted, not Yale.

It nagged at her enough to have her checking the education data on every name on the list.

No other Yale connection.

Until she scraped off a few more layers.

Coincidence equals bollocks, she thought and, shoving up from her desk, strode into Roarke's office.

"I believe your instincts on your victim's children are on target," he began. Then glanced up, saw her face. "And you have something."

"Yale."

"An honorable and prestigious institution."

"The vic went there."

"Yes, I recall. It would have been nearly a half century ago."

"That's a long time, but I have two connections to Yale through my sidepiece list. Downing's alibi did her undergraduate work there—she's a biophysicist, whatever the hell that is. Mixed race Asian, from a smart, successful family."

"I have to mention that a considerable number of people from smart, successful families have attended Yale in the past half century."

"Yeah, and another one of them's Carlee MacKensie. Partial scholarship, did one semester and dropped out."

"Which also happens quite a bit, but—" He sat back. "It's interesting, isn't it, that with all the universities out there, you'd cross the same one three times in such a small group."

"A numbers geek like you could probably run the odds, but let's just say *interesting* for now. I went a little deeper."

She eased a hip onto his workstation. "All that crap about your permanent record's pretty serious. Her grades were stellar." Eve held a hand, palm down, over her head. "She'd had two short stories published in literary venues before she turned twenty. And after two months into Yale, the grades?" Eve dropped her hand. "Totally tanked it. And, yeah, that happens, too. She managed, over the next five years, to get a degree from an online college, and she's eked out a living freelancing. But no more high-class literary venues."

Considering, Roarke picked up the bottle of water on his desk, gestured with it. "Devil's advocate must point out, this also happens far too often—that early peak and fall. And she would have attended Yale, however briefly, some four decades after your victim."

"Maybe, but coincidence is bollocks, and it's more bollocks it doesn't pertain. Another big scoop of bollocks that one name on the list has another Yale attendee as her alibi. And how does an artist who works in a SoHo gallery get to be pals with a scientist who's on staff in a fancy uptown R&D center? Where's the common ground?"

He offered her the water, got a head shake, drank some himself. "Some might ask the same about you and Mavis."

"She was on the grift. I arrested her. Cop, criminal, common ground." She held up two fingers as she spoke, tapped them together. Then pointed them at him. "Just like you and me, ace."

"I feel obliged to point out you never arrested me—nor did any other cop."

"Being slick doesn't negate the common ground. Is it thin?" She swiveled to face him more directly. "I'll give you it's thin, but it's there. Add on the fact that the vic went through sidepieces like Feeney goes through candied almonds, and those odds of paths crossing. Maybe you show Su's ID shot to your people at the hotel. Maybe she's another of his affairs. I link that, not so thin."

"I can do that."

"Can't see the motive, not yet. These women chose to have sex with him. He didn't hold a stunner to their throats. Every single one stated it was consensual, and I'm betting any others I turn up will say the same. Not a single one of them showed or expressed any genuine affection for him, so thwarted passion doesn't click. And if any of them worked as partners, and that's going to slide in when I figure it all out, jealousy doesn't play.

"'Justice is served,'" she murmured. "For what? What

crime, what sin, what wrong? That's the motive. So it's back to the vic."

"The women on your list wouldn't have been born when Edward Mira was at Yale."

"Yeah, yeah, I get that. But a big-deal guy from a big-deal school? Don't they go back for stuff? For ceremonies or guest lectures, for important events. Maybe I can place him there when either Su or MacKensie were there. That would thicken things up. Thanks," she said as she rose.

"I didn't do anything."

"You were Satan's mouthpiece."

"Devil's advocate."

"That *is* the same thing."

She went back, nailed down the exact times Su and MacKensie attended Yale, then tried to wade through archived articles on alumni events, on appearances at the university by Edward Mira.

After a frustrating hour, she decided she'd need to contact whoever might be in charge of those kinds of records.

She got more coffee, a slice of cold pizza that went down just fine now, then sat to search for any connection between any of the women on the list.

Salons, banks, fitness centers, clubs, committees, doctors, churches, hobbies.

Nothing lined up, but she did uncover the fact that Carlee MacKensie had been in therapy with a Dr. Natalie Paulson from 2058 to early 2060. Su entered therapy in 2055, and stopped her sessions with Dr. Kim Ping four years later. And Downing hooked with a Felicia Fairburn for a six-week stretch in 2059. Fairburn billed herself as a body-mind-spirit therapist.

And Satan's mouthpiece would say, rightfully, that scores of people went to shrinks.

But she'd look into it.

Yale. Shrinks. Edward Mira. Three lines that crossed for a percentage of the names.

Then there were negative connections.

No violent criminal on any. No sign of addictions that

would lead to incarceration or a big dent in finances. At least no signs of *current* addictions. People went to shrinks to help them with drinking or illegals problems, with gambling problems, with sex problems (too much, not enough). Hell, people went to shrinks to help them figure out what to eat for breakfast, but still . . .

What if?

She started poking, picking at layers, tugging lines that led to another angle or dead ends.

Then she sat back, drummed her fingers on her thigh.

Interesting, wasn't it interesting that Carlee MacKensie moved back home after dropping out of Yale, moved out again within six months and into what was nothing more than a glorified flop with one Marlee Davis—who, yes, indeed had herself a very long, colorful sheet peppered with illegals busts, soliciting sex without a license, petty thievery, and assault.

Now, what was a nice, bright girl from New Rochelle doing palling around with an habitual small-time loser from Alphabet City (currently doing a nickel in the Tombs for yet another assault bust)?

Eve followed the line, found a pattern in the fabric of Carlee's life. Wrote up a theory, questions, shot them to Mira with a copy for Peabody.

Then began to pick and scratch at Lydia Su.

By the time she'd switched to Charity Downing, she'd grabbed a second slice of cold pizza and indulged a craving for Pepsi.

She glanced up when Roarke came in.

"I see you're onto something that's boosted your appetite and put a cop's smile on your face."

"Carlee MacKensie. Smart, talented—go back and dig and you'll find cheery little articles on her from a young age. Won various writing contests, some with cash prizes. Wrote her high school blog, did her stint of community service as a peer tutor, and volunteered with Teens for Literacy. Pretty much aced her way into Yale, with a partial scholarship. Solid, middle-class family, nice little house in the 'burbs. And check this. Computer, Image 1-C, on screen."

Acknowledged.

The image flashed on, a pretty blonde in a bold red dress, hip to hip with a pretty guy in a black suit, bold red tie.

"Lovely young things."

"Yeah, she's got the looks. That's her senior prom picture—the guy, according to her mother's archived We Connect feed—"

"One moment." He held up a finger. "You actually managed to access archived data from a now-defunct social media site?"

"I can do stuff. When I have to."

"I may need to sit down, as my astonishment weighs heavy."

"Bite me."

"Darling, I fully intend to at the first opportunity."

"I dug for it, and what I found was mother-type pride data on her kid. Pictures like this, which show she was a pretty young thing, with a pretty young boyfriend—also bright, went on to Harvard. And about seven months after this picture was taken, she's all but flunked out of Yale and living back home."

"All right. She's pretty, and she didn't realize her potential."

"More. A couple months after moving home, she's moving out, and into a flop on Avenue A with a skank. The word fits. Long sheet, even then, for illegals possession, for selling Bounce to an undercover, for soliciting sex—no license. Where'd they hook up? Where's the common ground?"

"The pretty young thing was using."

"Bet your fine Irish ass. No record of it, but an eighteen-year-old girl doesn't jump from New Rochelle and proud mom to Alphabet City and the skank unless the skank was her connection. A few months later, she's back home again."

"Which is likely why she's still alive or not in prison."

"Skank's in year three of five for agg assault. MacKensie lived back home for two years, and during that time did her own stint. Two three-month stints at Inner Peace. I had to dig, way down, as it's billed as a lifestyle enhancement center, not rehab. Guess who else did some time at Inner Peace?"

"My money and the look in your eyes say either Su or Downing."

"Su. Not at the same time, which is annoying, but they both went to Yale, both went to this lifestyle deal. Su took a sabbatical, three years ago, and did the lifestyle enhancement deal. Prior to that, I've got her in this program—this study on insomnia. And, what a coincidence! Charity Downing also took part in a program—again, not at the same time—on insomnia."

"That's too many connections even for a devil's advocate." Because it was the only thing there, Roarke picked up the tube of Pepsi, took a swig. "It's gone warm."

"Still does the job. Here's how I see it."

She rose, gestured to the board as she paced. "These three women had some previous encounter with the victim. Sexual. That encounter was disturbing enough or intense enough to send MacKensie into a sharp downward spiral. The probability is each of them sought help for, we'll say side effects of that encounter at some point. And through that, the three of them come together."

Eve interlinked her fingers. "Two of the three hook up with the vic again. I don't guess you had time to check with hotel security on Su."

"I did, in fact. I can tell you she doesn't show up on any feed through the hotel in the last eighteen months."

"Not surprised. Pretty sure she's gay." When he lifted his eyebrows, she shrugged. "Not because she didn't show on the feed. Because I've got some photos of her, too. Big-deal science award ceremony—her date's female. A White House dinner deal—female date. Then there's her interview in this big-deal science journal where she says she's gay, that leans me in that direction."

She circled the board again. "These three women know each other, they knew Edward Mira, and my gut says they conspired together and killed him. Considering the nature of the torture, I'd say it's serious payback. It's payback for sexual assault, molestation, or rape because three women don't come together to torture and kill because they had a fling with a married man."

Shifting, Roarke studied the photos of Edward Mira. The soberly handsome statesman—and the murder victim.

"You believe a former United States senator was a serial rapist?"

"Yeah, I do." Eve heaved out a breath. "Yeah, I fucking do. That's how it lays out for me. Proving it? That's a whole different ball of string."

"Wax, but never mind that. Eve, trying to prove it is going to take you into very dangerous waters."

"I'm a strong swimmer."

"You are that," he agreed. "But it's also going to bring you personal pain."

"I can't let that get in the way. You know that."

"I do." He set the tube aside, went to her. "I love you."

She shifted. "Yeah, same goes."

He cupped her face in his hands, kept his eyes on hers. "I love you."

Her heart stuttered, so she cupped his face in turn. "I love you, and what you're telling me is we'll get through this."

"I am."

"Even if you end up pouring a soother down my throat."

"That's exactly what I'm telling you." Firmly, he pressed his lips to her forehead. "You'll do what has to be done, and so will I."

"I could be wrong. It may turn out I'm completely out of orbit on this angle, but it's what I see."

"And the way you've gone through the steps, it's what I see. There will be more of them. If you're right, and he forced or coerced these three, there will be more."

"Yeah, there will be more. Yale students, or women who he encountered somehow through that connection when they were college age. There's a three-year span between when MacKensie was at Yale, and when Downing was at NYU.

Five between MacKensie and Su at Yale. So there will be others. But I'm not seeing those others—not yet anyway—on my list. His daughter . . ."

"I don't believe so." At least, Roarke thought, he could give her that peace of mind. "I don't think you need to go there. I looked into her, and her brother, and there's no sign of that."

"I got all the way to lieutenant of the NYPSD, and nobody saw any signs."

Now he brushed a hand over her short cap of hair. "Do you really believe Mira saw nothing, saw no signs?"

She needed to move, so she stuffed her hands in her pockets while she prowled the office. "No, you're right. She probably saw plenty way before I got to the point I could talk to her about it. Still—"

"You didn't have her when it was happening to you. You had no one. Gwendolyn Sykes did. She had her brother, she had the Miras. Everything I turned up on them reads they had a rigid, unloving childhood, leaned on and were embraced by Charlotte and Dennis as often as possible. And they've made strong and happy lives. Mira would have seen the signs, Eve."

"You're right. You're right." Though she'd have to ask, directly at some point. "That's something anyway. It's going to be rough enough on the Miras."

"We'll be there for them. Whatever they need from us. Now it's late, and you'll need to reinterview with all this in mind tomorrow. And considering how this may go, we could both use the sleep while we can get it."

"You hardly sleep anyway." She continued to prowl. "I don't want you worrying about me before there's even anything to worry about. I can deal with what was, Roarke, just like I can deal with . . ." She stopped at the desk, ran her hand over it. "What was."

She *had* dealt with it, she reminded herself. And didn't need replications of what she'd once had, not when she knew and cherished what she had now.

She sent him a speculative look. "Do you really want to get rid of this desk?"

"That will be up to you."

She shook her head, waved that off. "No, I'm asking you. Do you want to get rid of it?"

"For reasons of aesthetics, efficiency—Christ, yes. It's a bloody, miserable excuse for a workstation."

"Huh. You're seriously soft on me to leave it sitting here for nearly three years, offending your aesthetics and efficiency levels. Its days are probably numbered, so . . . we should send it off with a bang."

She boosted up to sit on it, sent him a slow smile. "Come on over here, pal, and bang the hell out of me on my bloody, miserable excuse of a workstation."

He let out a half laugh. "I never know what odd path that mind of yours might take. But it never disappoints."

It wasn't about the ridiculous desk, he thought—though knowing her, that could be part of it. But it was to show both of them she could take whatever ugliness would come her way. She'd face the nightmares, the fears, the brutal memories to do the job she'd sworn to do.

So he went to her. Though the glint in her eyes dared and demanded, he cupped her face again. And thinking of the nightmares, the fears, the memories, laid his lips gently on hers.

To cherish.

In response she took two fistfuls of his hair, yanked him to her, hard. "Uh-uh. This is desk sex. That means it might hurt a little." So saying, she bit him.

Then she shoved him back, deliberately rough, so she could pull off her sweatshirt. "Give me what you have."

"What I have?"

"Yeah. And more."

"And when you say you can't take it, remember what you asked for."

"Oh, I can take it. Let's see if you can when—"

He slid a hand between her legs, pressed, and the rest of

the words died in a gasp. Before she could draw the next breath, his free hand clamped on the back of her neck, holding her in place while his mouth ravaged hers.

Now he used his teeth, left her breathless and churning on that erotic edge just this side of pain. She wrapped her legs around him, holding him hard and tight against her, rocking, rocking against the hand driving her mad.

"Inside me. You should be inside me."

"Not yet, no. I've more than that," he reminded her and caught her nipple between his thumb and forefinger. Light pinches, relentless friction drove her straight over the edge.

Her legs tightened around him like a vise as she came, but he didn't stop. Wouldn't stop.

Even as she moaned out her release, he shot her up again.

Her own breath burned her lungs as she stumbled along that edgy, dangerous line of pleasure. She dragged at his suit jacket with hands that trembled with outrageous needs.

"Take it off, take it off."

Desperate, she tore at his shirt, sent buttons flying. Then at last her hands found skin. Hot, firm, hers. Now her arms wrapped around him, her fingers digging into flesh, her nails scraping, biting.

"Now. God. Now."

But he said, "More," and sent her flying.

Something thudded to the floor when he pushed her back on the desk. Her flailing hands sent disc files tumbling.

Then he was feasting on her breasts even as his hands drew the cotton pants over her hips. She struggled to reach his belt, to unhook it, to find him. To take him.

He left her quivering to glide his tongue down her body, to take it over her, into her.

The world was heat and glory, and needs newly incited the moment they were met, hungers keenly sharpened the instant they were sated.

She gripped his hips, said his name, only his name, saw his eyes, a wild and wicked blue with what they made each other.

And at last, at last, he plunged into her. Hard and fast,

whipping them both past all borders of control. She met him madness for madness, greed for greed until the world dropped away.

She wondered her heart didn't break through her ribs. Its crazed beat rang in her ears as aftershocks—for that had been an earthquake of sex—shook her body.

They sprawled over the desk like barely conscious survivors of a cataclysm, and she gave a passing thought to the desk.

How bad could it be if it could support all that weight?

"I might be lying on murder files. That's just not right. It's so disrespectful."

"You're not." His face was buried between her breasts. "They fell over. Maybe off. We'll sort it out. Christ Jesus, I can't find my breath."

"If you do, see if mine's with it."

He lifted his head, looked at her with eyes that managed to be wild and wicked, and a bit sleepy all at once. And she managed to lift her hand and brush the hair back from his face.

"So . . . was that all you've got?"

How, given their position and current state, he got his hand under her to pinch her ass—hard enough to make her yelp—was a wonder.

"Just asking. I may have seen God. She may have been smiling."

"Well, she made us to fit together, didn't she?"

"We do."

"So we do." He laid a kiss between her breasts, winced a little as he eased back to stand. "I believe it did hurt a little."

She laughed, then hissed as she sat up. "Yeah, maybe. We did knock over murder files," she noted. "And the coffeepot— but that was empty. Mostly. Can't you wear less clothes? I ripped the shirt—the buttons off anyway. It probably cost more than the damn desk."

"If I'd known desk sex was on tonight's agenda, I'd have worn less."

"If I go with the command center, there could be regular command center sex. Dress appropriately."

Laughing, he picked up his shirt—a soft slate gray with just a hint of blue—examined it. "Well now, it's done for, I suppose, and a small price to pay."

She took it, put it on. Subtly breathed him in. "We have to pick this stuff up. I can't pick up murder files naked."

"Apparently I can," he said, and helped her pick them up, gather up the clothes they'd discarded. "You can organize it all in the morning."

"I guess. Maybe we should put that desk in some sort of display. With a plaque."

" 'Dallas and Roarke Banged Here'?"

"No—though we could make a secret plaque for that. Just something like: 'It Served Us Well.' "

"You're oddly sentimental over a desk."

"I am now. I need my pants."

"Why? We're going straight to the bedroom."

"And Summerset could be lurking somewhere between here and there."

"I can promise you he's tucked into his own quarters by now."

"Maybe he's in his coffin, maybe he's not, but I'm not walking to the bedroom in nothing but your torn shirt."

"We'll take the elevator," Roarke said, solving the problem by calling for it. "So, what was it you asked for? All I had. And more?"

"You pulled it off."

"Not yet. That was all I had." He pulled the bundle of clothes out of her hand, dropped them. "This is more."

"You couldn't possibly—"

He just pushed her back against the elevator wall, and took her there. Fast and fierce.

When he was done, and very satisfied with himself, she started to slide bonelessly down the wall.

He plucked her up, restarted the elevator. Then carried her to the bed when the doors opened.

"You know what they say." He wrapped an arm around her. "Mind what you wish for."

"I didn't mind." But her voice was blurry as she slid toward blissful, exhausted, thoroughly used-up sleep.

Then she popped right up again. "Jesus cross-eyed Christ, the clothes! They're still in the elevator."

"They can be sorted out in the morning."

"He'll *see!* All those sex-tangled clothes. Get them back!"

"The elevator's still there if it worries you."

She leaped up, all but dived in to grab the clothes when the doors opened. Near to shuddering with relief, she dropped them in a heap on a chair.

She crawled back into bed, sighed, and slept in seconds.

Apparently, Roarke thought, sex-tangled clothes were acceptable when sorted out from a bedroom chair.

What a marvel her mind was, he decided, and slipped into sleep after her.

The dream gripped her with sharp, digging claws. Even knowing it for what it was, she couldn't break free of it. It held fast, dragged her down.

Into the study in the Spring Street brownstone.

Edward Mira sat in the desk chair dressed in one of his senatorial suits, his glossy black hair swept back from his stony face.

"I'm dead."

"I'm aware."

"Yet you make my murderers my victims."

"The way I see it, you did that. Did you rape them, Senator Mira?"

Leaning forward, he banged his fist on the desk. "I'm *dead.* Your responsibility is to me. But you'd smear my reputation, destroy my legacy? This is how you stand for the dead?"

"I'll do my job. I'll do my best to identify and apprehend the person or persons who killed you, even if doing that smears your rep."

"Your best?" He sneered at her. "Your best to paint me as a monster so those who took my life are coddled and stroked."

"My best to uncover the truth, whatever that means."

"The truth?" He banged the desk again, but this time with the gavel he held. "I know the truth. I know what you are, what you did. You're just like them."

He struck the desk again, and on the explosion of sound they stood in the room in Dallas with the ugly red light flashing.

"No. No." She backed away as panic coiled up, struck like a snake. "I'm done with this. I don't come here anymore. It's finished for me."

"It's never finished." The senator sat, wearing his black robes, at his raised judge's platform. "Murderer!"

At the next bang of his gavel she saw herself, the terrified girl she'd been, struggling with, pleading with Richard Troy. With her father as he raped her.

She heard her own high-pitched scream, felt the pain in her own arm as the bone snapped when he broke her arm.

Felt the horror and the hope when those small fingers closed around the little knife.

"Guilty!" the senator shouted when the desperate girl plunged the knife into flesh. "Guilty, guilty, guilty."

Stabbing, over and over and over. The inhuman sounds growling in her throat, and the blood, all the blood washing warm over her hands.

"Blood on your hands. Guilty. Murderer. Just like them."

"Kill the bitch." Richard Troy stared at her with glassy eyes as blood bubbled from his lips. "Give her what she deserves."

With the next strike of the gavel she was back at the crime scene, the noose around her neck. She dragged at the rope with her blood-smeared hands, but it only tightened, tightened as the mechanism hummed the chandelier higher.

"Now," the senator said, "justice is served."

"Wake up! Eve, you bloody well wake up and fucking *breathe*."

Roarke's words, his rough shakes finally got through.

She sucked in air, still dragging at the dream noose around her throat.

"It's a dream. A dream. Do you hear me? Come back now."

"I'm all right. I'm all right."

"You're not, but you will be. Look at me."

She couldn't stop the shaking, but made herself look into his eyes. Anger, yes, some anger in there, and the kind of desperation she understood too well.

"I'm okay. I'm sorry."

"Don't apologize. It'll piss me off." He grabbed the throw from the foot of the bed, wrapped it around her, rubbed her back, her arms while the cat bumped his head against her hip. "You're cold."

Then he wrapped his arms around her and rocked. "I swear, you stopped breathing for a moment. Just stopped. You'll have a soother."

"I—"

"Don't argue about it, you're having one. I'm having a bloody soother myself."

She said nothing when he got out of bed, but sat, shivering under the cashmere throw, stroking the cat. They'd have tried to wake her, she thought, her husband and her cat, but she'd been in too deep.

Roarke lit the fire first to add more light and warmth to the room, then moved to the AutoChef.

"You need the soother," he said more calmly. "You haven't had a nightmare that . . . intense in some time."

"Soothers all around." She fought to make her voice sound normal. "Maybe the cat needs one."

"He's his own soother." Roarke brought two glasses back to the bed, handed her one, gave the loyal Galahad a rub. "He's fine now, though I'll say he was nearly as shaken as I. Drink that now."

She gulped some down, sighed. "It's chocolate."

"I know my cop."

That brought the tears up, had her pressing her face to his shoulder. "I couldn't get out of it. I knew what it was, but I couldn't get out."

"You're safe now." He kissed the top of her head, dug in for tenderness. "Drink the rest, darling. Drink it up, and tell me."

She did what he asked, and when she was finished, when he'd set the empty glasses aside, he gathered her close.

"I know it's not true, what he said—what my subconscious went into. But—"

"There's no but in this. You were an innocent child defending her life against a monster. These are grown women who killed with calculation."

Yes, yes, that was the logic. That was reason. But . . . "The motives align. If I'm right, I will smear his reputation."

"If you're right, his reputation is a lie. It's truth you're after, isn't it?"

"Yeah. If I'm right . . . you'd come down on their side of it."

He kissed her cheek, then the other before drawing her down so she could curl into him, find the warmth.

"We have different views on some matters, but as you're fond of telling me, you're the one with the badge. You'll do your job, Lieutenant, as you must. And I'll help you as I can to find the truth. After that, it's not in my hands or yours, is it?"

"No."

The cat curled against the small of her back, sandwiching her in the safe. Tears stung her eyes again, so she closed them. And as the soother did its work, she drifted back to sleep.

Holding her close, Roarke lay awake, listening to her breathe.

Chapter 11

Eve's communicator buzzed, a rude, insistent sound that woke her in the dark.

Roarke said, "Bloody, buggering hell," and called for lights on at ten percent as she crawled out of bed.

"Baxter." She hissed it as she scanned the readout. "Block video," she ordered. "Dallas, and this better be damned good."

"Sorry, LT. Trueheart and I were on deck, and we caught one."

"I didn't figure you were tagging me at four-fricking-thirty in the damn morning to chat about Arena Ball."

"Nope, but how about those Metros?"

"Baxter, want to do everybody's fives for the next six months?"

"Can't say I do. We caught one," he repeated, "but I'm pretty damn sure he's yours."

"Why? Who's the DB?"

"Jonas Bartell Wymann."

"And what makes him mine when I don't know who that is?"

"DB's sixty-eight, and was the chairman of the Council of Economic Advisers about a decade ago, also was once chief economist of the Department of Labor. Big money guy with his own big money. He went to Yale, LT. Same class as Senator Mira."

"Fuck. Do you have COD?"

"Flagging him for Morris, but he's been beaten—face and genitals. Sodomized. Hanged—naked—same as the first DB. And there's a comp-generated message around his neck."

"'Justice is served'?"

"Yeah."

"Give me the address."

"He was practically your neighbor," Baxter told her, and gave an address only two blocks from her house.

"I'm on the way. Save me time, tag Peabody. Scene secured?"

"You bet. We'll hold here for you."

She clicked off, and Roarke—already up—handed her coffee. "Thanks. Shit. I'm going to grab a shower and get there."

"We'll grab one. I'm going with you. I'm hardly going back to bed," he said before she could argue. "And I knew him."

She gulped down coffee as she headed for the shower. "How?"

"Slightly. We weren't friendly, but I can say he was brilliant—when it came to economy issues." Roarke didn't bother to sigh and barely winced when she ordered jets on full at 102 degrees.

He'd asked for it, after all.

"He sure as hell knew Senator Mira. Now we have two. And if my angle is right, that's two BFDs from Yale, probable rapists. But—" She shoved her wet hair out of her eyes. "That angle may be a dead end now, and we might just have a couple of psychopaths torturing and murdering BFDs."

She jumped out of the shower, let her thoughts swirl as hot and fast as the air in the drying tube.

Then she put them aside. Better to go in cold, stop trying to bend new angles. See, observe, gather data and evidence.

They dressed, and as she sat to put on her boots, Roarke handed her an egg pocket on a small plate. "Eat. He isn't going anywhere, and we'll be there in minutes."

To save time, she bit in, then scowled at him. "There's more than eggs in here."

"Is there?" With an innocent smile, Roarke sampled his own. "I believe you're right."

She ate it anyway, gulped more coffee. "I need things from my office."

To save time, they took the elevator, then the steps from there. He'd already ordered her car remotely, so it sat out in the cold, dark night, heat already running.

She let him drive and did a quick run on the newest victim.

"Two marriages, two divorces, currently single. Three offspring, and five offspring from them. Lots of letters after his name. Graduated magna cum laude from Yale, did some postgrad work there, some at Columbia, did some more at Oxford. Guest lecturer at Yale, at Columbia. Wrote a couple of books on economics, lots of papers. Served as adviser for two administrations—and did that while Senator Mira was in Congress. They damn well knew each other."

Before she'd finished the run, Roarke pulled up at a three-story townhouse. A couple of black-and-whites sat outside, along with Baxter's snazzy vehicle.

Two uniforms stood out on the sidewalk in their heavy winter coats, gloved hands around go-cups. Eve held up her badge.

"Lieutenant," one of them said. "Detectives are inside. Said wait on the canvass until you said different."

"Hold on that until I take a look at things. Who's first on scene?"

"That's us. We were on patrol, and Dispatch sent us over, oh-three-forty-two. We arrived on scene within two. Vic's grandson called it in."

"Does the grandson live here?"

"No, sir, but he's got the passcodes, swipes. Said he stayed here now and then."

"Okay. Hang tight."

The cop on the door must've been watching for them as he opened it before they started up the short flight of steps. "Lieutenant," he said, and stepped aside.

They'd left Wymann hanging. His eyes bulged out of his swollen, bruised face as he swayed gently from the rope attached to a complex series of boldly colored swirls that served as the foyer light. Dried blood left thin ribbons down his throat, his torso, his legs.

Like Eve, Baxter stood, looking up. "He's yours."

"Yeah."

"My boon companion and fresh-faced young detective and I want in."

"Yeah. Where's the grandson?"

"Baker, Jonas Wymann. Put him back in the kitchen with a uniform. He's pretty wrecked."

"Have you talked to him?"

"Nope. First on scene got the basics. It only took one look to figure this was yours, so we just secured the scene, stowed the wit, and tagged you."

"Peabody's on her way, Lieutenant," Trueheart told her.

"Okay, seal up," she told Roarke, "and let's get him down. Where's the thing to lower the thing?" she wondered.

Roarke found it, and at her nod, brought the swirling light and its burden down.

"Detective Trueheart, verify vic's ID."

She knelt with him, took out gauges to establish time of death while Baxter and Roarke exchanged small talk.

"TOD's reading oh-three-eleven. Nine-one-one came in about thirty minutes later. Didn't miss them by much. Facial bruising, looks like a broken jaw, ligature marks on wrists, more bruising on the genitals, signs of anal rape. All injuries consistent with those on Edward Mira. Bag his hands," she ordered. "Bag the placard and the rope for the lab."

"ID's verified, sir, a Jonas Bartell Wymann, this address."

She put on microgoggles, got closer. "Busted his nose, too. It's going to be a weighted sap. Security?"

"The hard drive and discs are missing," Baxter told her. "No signs I can see of forced entry. The little bit the uniforms got out of the wit was he wasn't able to reach his grandfather all evening."

"Let's talk to him." After a glance at Baxter, she rose. "You and me, Trueheart. Baxter, go ahead, bring in the sweepers and the morgue. Let's see what Morris can tell us. Have EDD come in, go over the electronics."

"Um," Trueheart said as he started back with Eve.

"Spit it out, Detective."

"Baxter and I cleared the house. There wasn't any sign of struggle, any sign any of the beds had been slept in. There are two house droids, sir, but since we could see this would be your case, we didn't take them out of sleep mode."

"We'll get to them. Big fricking house," she commented.

"Yes, sir. Ah . . ." He cleared his throat. "There's also what appears to be a sex droid in the closet of the master bedroom."

"Is that so? How do you know it's a sex droid?"

He flushed, pink and pretty. "Well, ah, Baxter mentioned he'd seen that model before, and it was built for that particular purpose."

"Uh-huh," she said and walked through to a kitchen so shiny silver and glossy black her eyes wanted to twitch.

A man sat at a square table of glass on a silver pedestal, his head in his hands, a cup of something in front of him.

He looked up as she entered, showed her a ridiculously handsome face poet pale with shock and grief. And young, she noted as she gauged him as barely old enough to drink legally.

"Are you in charge?" He had a voice like a bell—deep, clear, resonant.

"Lieutenant Dallas. Yes, I'm in charge. This is Detective Trueheart. I'm sorry for your loss, Mr. Baker."

"I don't understand. I don't understand any of this. Granddad—someone killed him. I don't understand."

Eve flicked a glance at the uniform, dismissing her, then sat across from Baker. Another glance, this one at Trueheart, had the new detective taking a seat.

"This is hard. Why don't you start by telling me why you're here. This isn't your residence."

"No, I don't live here anymore. I did for a while, when I was just starting out. I stay sometimes. He's mostly alone here, so I stay sometimes."

"When did you get here tonight?"

"It was late—early, I mean. Three-thirty or something."

"Do you usually come over so early in the morning?"

"No. No. He didn't come to opening night, and he always . . . I thought maybe he forgot or just got busy, and I was even a little upset because it was my first . . ." He paused, pressed his fingers to his eyes, tawny gold, rimmed with red.

"*Whatever Works.*"

Baker dropped his hands at Trueheart's words. "It's been getting a lot of buzz," Trueheart continued. "I just put it together. Jonas W. Baker, you're the lead. I was going to try to take my girl to see it sometime. You opened last night?"

"Yeah. Opening night. Musical comedy," he said to Eve. "I'm the male lead. It's my first time headlining. My mother's in Australia, and my father—well, even if he was in the country, he probably wouldn't have come. But my grandparents never missed."

"Your grandparents?" Eve repeated.

"Yeah, they're not married anymore—not for years—but they do the united front for my plays. But she's stuck in Chicago. Her flight got canceled—they're snowed under good. What I mean is whenever I got a part, they'd be there opening night. Front row center, every time. And my grandfather was the one who backed me when I wanted to go into theater instead of law or medicine or politics—whatever would've been suitable for my parents. He backed me, and he helped me, and let me live here while I was getting my start."

He picked up the cup in front of him, set it down again, pushed it away.

"He never missed, so when he didn't show, I thought he was running late or something. I had to put it away, you know, and do the job, do the show. We rocked the house, too, yeah, we did."

"You must've been upset not to have him there. Big night for you," Trueheart added.

"The biggest."

"I guess you didn't have time to try to reach him. Try his 'link."

"I did, actually. I left a couple v-mails. The last one, during intermission, was pretty pissy. God. And when the show was over—six curtain calls, and a standing O—what did I do? I sulked about it."

"You wanted to share it with him," Trueheart prompted.

"I've got a girl, too, and she was there. But . . . he's the one I wanted most. I just wanted him to see all that faith and support, they weren't wasted."

"You wanted to make him proud."

"More than anything. So when he didn't come, didn't contact me, didn't even send a message, I thought, Okay, fine, and went to the after-party. I drank a shitload of champagne, basked in the glory, basked some more when the reviews started coming in. Megastar—that's me—in a megahit. I'm a freaking triple threat who owned the stage. Yeah, I basked. We're all flying, nobody wants to let go of the night, you know. We're going to go have some food somewhere, but I can't let it go, I can't let go he didn't come. So I tell everybody I'll catch up, but I have to take care of something."

He took a breath. "I know it was getting on to three o'clock by then. It just started nagging at me. My voice coach was there, my ex-girlfriend was there, my girlfriend, actors I'd worked with off Broadway, friends from Juilliard, all there. But the most important person hadn't come. And it nagged at me because why hadn't he come? I finally realized—got over myself and realized—something must've happened. Maybe he got sick or had an accident, something. So I came over, half expecting to find him sick in bed, or hurt on the floor—though he's healthy as they get and really fit. Then I opened the door, and . . . God. God, God, God."

Eve gave him a minute while he wrapped his arms tight, rocked, as tears streamed down his face.

"Mr. Baker—"

"Jonas. You could call me Jonas. I was named for him."

"Jonas, was the door secured?"

"Was the door secured? Ah, yes. Yes, I have the swipe, the codes. I came in, and saw him. I thought: That's not real. It can't be real. I called for him, I actually called for him as if he could make it stop."

His breath tore; his voice broke.

"It's okay, Jonas." Trueheart's voice was gentle as a mother's touch. "Take a minute. Take your time."

"It's just—I didn't know what to do. I feel like I just stood there forever, doing *nothing*. Telling myself it wasn't happening. Just stood there. Then, I don't know, I looked down and my 'link was in my hand. I don't remember getting it out of my pocket. Don't remember doing it. I called nine-one-one, and the guy on the other end, he kept telling me to stay calm, to breathe, help was coming. And the police came. Everything in slow motion but really fast. How can that be? I didn't know what to do for him. He always knew what to do for me."

"You did the right thing," Trueheart assured him. "You did what was best for him. You got help."

"They—someone—took his life. And they took his dignity. Why?"

"It's my job to find that out." As Trueheart played it easy, Eve played it brisk. "When was the last time you spoke with him?"

"Yesterday. Early in the afternoon. I tagged him to remind him his ticket was at the box office, and I could tell he was upset about something. His old friend Edward Mira died. He'd been murdered. Granddad didn't have a lot of the details, but . . ."

Now any hint of color drained. "Jesus God. Senator Mira,

and now Granddad. Is it the same? Is it the same person who did this?"

"Did you know Senator Mira?"

"Yeah, sure. He and my grandfather go way back—they were college buddies, and they stayed friends. Miss—"

"Lieutenant. Lieutenant Dallas."

"Lieutenant. Is it the same? Did the same person kill them both?"

"We're pursuing all leads and angles." She hesitated a moment. He wasn't in this, she thought. And if he was, he already knew. "There are enough similarities that I believe the same person or persons are involved."

"But that's . . . it's crazy."

"Nonetheless. When you spoke to your grandfather, did he express any thoughts or opinions on the senator's murder?"

"He didn't seem to have any real details. I was on a media blackout—just keeping my head in the play—so I hadn't heard. He said it seemed as if someone had abducted Senator Mira, and killed him. He was shaken up—like I said, they went back. I never thought of it, not when he didn't show for the play. I didn't think of it, or that he'd be grieving. If I'd gotten out of myself long enough to think of him, I would have. And I'd have left him be. I wouldn't have come here this morning. I don't know which is worse."

"What is, is. And the fact that you did come means we're able to start gathering information quicker. Do you know of anyone who had a grudge against your grandfather? Or against both him and the senator?"

"Not really." Jonas sat back, scrubbed his hands over his face, and some color back into it. "They were both political, and politics makes enemies. Hell, what doesn't? Not everybody liked Granddad's line on economic issues, but you don't kill somebody for that. I'd say not everybody liked Senator Mira's lines, either, and he wasn't my favorite person, but Jesus."

"You didn't like him."

"I didn't dislike him, especially. I just thought he was kind of a jerk, and pompous." He shrugged. "He was my grand-father's old college buddy so, you know, allowances. I have to tell my mother. Jesus. And Gram. God. I have to tell my grandmother."

He dropped his head into his hands again. "And my brother. My half sister, she's in Australia with Mom, but Gavin's in law school."

"Yale."

Jonas managed a shaky smile. "Yeah, family tradition. I didn't make that cut. I got into Juilliard, and never looked back. I have to tell them. And my uncle. My mother's brother. What do I tell them?"

"I can make the notifications if you'd rather."

"I would rather, I'd rather anything, but I have to do it. I have to tell them myself. They shouldn't hear it from a stranger. They won't see him like that, will they? I don't want them to see him like I did."

"No. The medical examiner will make sure he's taken care of, given that dignity back. You and your family can check with Dr. Morris at the morgue about seeing your grandfather, and when you can make arrangements for him."

"Okay. Okay." Now his ravaged eyes bored into hers. "I want to tell them, tell myself, you're going to find whoever did this, why they did it, you're going to put them away. Is that true?"

"I can tell you that finding who did this and why is my focus, it's my job. I take my job very seriously."

"That's a good answer."

"I need to ask you a few more questions, then you can contact your family."

When Eve left Jonas, she spoke quietly to Trueheart.

"You did good, smoothed him over. It takes insight and the right touch to do that."

"I knew who he was. I didn't remember last night was the opening, but the play's been getting a lot of hype, and

I've seen him on a couple billboards. He's probably a good actor, but—"

"He's bottom of the list. If that was show, he's Oscar worthy."

"It's actually a Tony for Broadway."

"Whatever works," she said, making Trueheart grin.

She found Peabody with Baxter. The morgue team was in the process of removing the bagged body, and sweepers were already scattered around the area.

"He's not in this," she said straight off. "But we verify. Trueheart, check the names on the list he gave us, who he was with up until around three this morning. And who he was with when the senator was taken, and at Senator Mira's TOD. Let's just cross him off."

"I brought McNab," Peabody told her. "He and Roarke are taking the electronics. Roarke's already gone over the front entrance. No sign of forced entry. According to the expert, whoever brought him in used the proper swipe, the code, the works."

"They'd have had Wymann's, whether or not they did him here or elsewhere."

"We've done a walk-through." Baxter took another look around. "Nothing that shows the vic was restrained and bashed around in here."

"Maybe they cleaned up." She did her own look, slipped her hands in her pockets. "More likely they took him wherever they took the senator. They've got a place set up. When they took Wymann, where they took him from. Let's find out. The why's going to be the same as the senator."

"What's that?" Baxter asked.

"Sex. It's going to come down to sex. Our killers are female. Or at least one of them is. Yale's another connection. Both vics were there, same time. Both go back for events, lectures, that sort of thing. Both were in politics, so that's another link."

"Sex and politics," Baxter said, "the most natural of bedfellows."

"And coincidence is bollocks."

"If that means bullshit, damn straight."

"Two of my suspects and one of the suspect's alibis also have connections either to Yale or each other."

Baxter's expression turned feral. "Coincidence is bollocks."

"Oh yeah, it is. Two wealthy and successful men." Eve paced as she thought it through. "Both Yale alumni, both aimed toward politics, different areas thereof, but power seekers. First vic had a sidepiece of the month, or close enough."

"Love to say the same at his age."

That earned Baxter a stony stare. "We find out if this vic had the same ambitions in that area."

"Very sexy sex droid up in his bedroom."

"So I'm told."

She glanced up as Roarke came down.

"And the sexy sex droid tells us it was last utilized thirty-two hours ago," Roarke commented. "McNab's taking in electronics, but we found nothing that pertains on his comps and 'links on a surface search. A spare pocket 'link in his home office, desk drawer. It hasn't been used, so spare is literal to my way of thinking."

"And the one he did use isn't here. So if anything on there pertains, the killers have it. Baxter, you and Trueheart take the vic's professional contacts. Get a feel, get alibis. Find me his sidepieces if he had them."

"Can and will."

"I'll send you names and pictures of the women on the first vic's list. Let's find out if they ring for anybody at the second vic's office. Peabody, tell McNab I want every byte of data on every piece of equipment here and from the first vic's office. Any- and everything that overlaps gets priority. This is payback. What did they do—together—to earn it? Tell him now. We need to get to the morgue."

"The morgue before breakfast. Pro or con?" Peabody started upstairs. "I'll let you know."

"Professional contacts," Eve repeated. "Confirmation of alibis."

"LT, it's oh-five hundred," Baxter reminded her.

"We're up. Why shouldn't potential murder suspects be up? Get gone."

"We're going to be a couple of popular guys, Trueheart."

"Any orders for me, Lieutenant?" Roarke asked as they headed out.

"You should go home, buy another chunk of the solar system."

"Just another day at the office." He watched a white-suited sweeper bag the noose. "For both of us." But he took her arm, led her a short distance away. "Do you believe these two men were partners in some sort of ugly sex game? Partners in rape?"

"I don't believe anything yet. But that's an angle I'm going to look at. The grandson said they took his life, and took his dignity. They damn well did. There's a reason for the humiliation as much as the torture and kill. I read payback. Who did these two men humiliate?"

"And what sin or crime did they commit that what was done could be considered—by any—justice?"

"Yeah. Good friends, long-term friends. What secrets did they share? There's something, yes, ugly under this. And it still reads sex. I can get you a ride home."

"I can get my own ride, thanks all the same. Tend to yourself," he murmured. "Not just my cop, but to that young girl you still carry with you."

"Don't worry about me."

He took her face in his hands, kissed her firmly before she could stop him. "Don't be a git. I'll be in touch," he added as he walked to the door.

She let out a huff of breath, turned in time to see the nearby sweeper grinning through her face shield.

"What are you grinning at?"

"Just imagining having a guy who looks like that lay lips on me. It's a smiley thought." She bagged a blood sample from the floor. "You take 'em where you find 'em."

Maybe so, Eve thought. She wouldn't find many smiley moments at the morgue.

"Peabody, with me, damn it! Keep your hands off McNab's bony ass or you're walking to the morgue."

She was already pulling the front door open when Peabody rushed down the steps. "How did you know where my hands were?"

"I'm a trained detective." She glanced back, saw the sweeper grin again. "Another smiley moment?"

"Ain't it grand?"

Chapter 12

Peabody scrambled to catch up while winding today's scarf—icy winter blue with candy-green zigzags—around her neck.

"If the two vics were pals, and sex is motive, maybe they shared some of the women on the list."

Eve slid behind the wheel. "Now you're thinking."

"I can think even with my hands on McNab's bony ass. And it was really just a friendly pat." She let out a happy sigh as she settled into the passenger seat. "Ah. The seat warmer's on. Now my not-so-bony ass is happy."

"I hereby issue a ban on any discussion of your ass or McNab's." Eve flicked a gaze in the side mirror, did a zip-switch of lanes. "Roarke's going to ask security at the hotel if Wymann used the suite, and if so, who used it with him. We connect any of the sidepieces, we have a whole other conversation."

"On the other hand, why have a sex droid in the bedroom closet—and McNab said it was programmed for the universe of sex—if you're diddling with live ones regularly?"

"The answer to that is: penis."

"Oh yeah, how could I forget?" Peabody didn't mention her ass, but snuggled it happily into the warm. "But don't you think that has to slow down some once the penis has going on seven decades under its belt? And I just got a mental picture of a penis wearing a belt. It wasn't pretty."

"Thanks for sharing that. Before the day's over, after the sweepers are done, I'm going back to go through the vic's house, and you know what I'd bet a year's salary I'm going to find? Boner drugs and other sex . . . extenders."

"Boner extenders, good one. I'm not going to take the bet because we found boner drugs in the first vic's place—really his grandfather's place, so more eeww—and it follows. Okay, here's another question."

Since the traffic was hell on Earth and the ad blimps insisted on blatting on about *Cruise Wear Specials!* (What the hell was cruise wear?), Eve resigned herself to Peabody's endless curiosity.

"Is this the last one?"

"Probably not, but it's another. Why do guys always sniff out the young ones? Dudes in their fifties, they're hunting up sex partners in their twenties. In their sixties, same deal. Into the seventies, they'd go for the twenties if they could get them, and settle for the thirties, maybe forties, if they crash on younger."

"Same answer: penis."

"How is it the same answer?"

As Eve made a turn, she watched oblivious tourists huddled at a glide-cart with their bags and wallets all but screaming "Steal Me!" to the canny-eyed street thief who sauntered their way.

She couldn't save everybody, and kept going.

"The penis needs to convince itself it's still twenty, and therefore urgently desired by sex partners of the same age. The penis refuses to accept it's attached to an old guy."

"Then the penis is self-deluding."

"It's good you've learned that while you're still in your twenties. I suspect many women find it a harder lesson once their own decades pass. Now, put the penis in the same box as the asses, and close the damn lid."

Peabody held her silence for a moment. "You know what's going to happen with a penis and two asses in the same box, right?"

Despite herself Eve laughed. "Jesus, Peabody, get your mind out of the sex box."

"It's not easy since we're figuring sex as motive."

"Okay, that's a point. Sex plays. You don't bruise and bloody a guy's genitals and sodomize him unless it's about sex, so sex plays. Second vic's got two divorces—the last one more than six years ago. We'll check out the exes, see if there's any overlap with the first vic, but it's a stretch to think Wymann's ex or exes waited this long for payback. Start digging, see if Wymann's connected to anyone romantically."

"Gossip sites, here I come!" Peabody pulled out her PPC.

Eve tapped her fingers on the wheel as another ad blimp announced: *Get your summer bikini body in January at Slimderize! Free consult!*

Maybe a summer bikini body counted as cruise wear.

"Scenario," she said, doing her best to block out the blimps. "The senator and Wymann have a little sex club. The women involved join in—either knowing about the other women or not. If not, this is a pisser. If they did know, something went wrong, got ugly. Women form their own club. Murder club."

"If they went into it knowing, it had to get really ugly."

"Rape's ugly. I think brutally sodomizing two men reflects rape. Otherwise, maybe, yeah, you kick him in the balls a couple times, but the rest . . ."

"That sounds like *rape* club, not sex club. The women on our list weren't raped."

"Not that they told us. Why tell us, why hand us a big, fat motive? It's an angle we need to look at because we've got more than one killer. Torture and murder as partners, that speaks of a bond, a shared goal, and, in these cases, a mutual rage.

"We know the senator let in his killers. So he felt no threat. A man who considers women objects, sex toys? He doesn't see them as a threat."

"We still don't know the identity of the Realtor."

And that, Eve thought, was a big hole that needed filling.

"When we find it, we'll find the killers—but . . . strong possibility there wasn't a Realtor, but a ploy. We need to know when Wymann was taken, where he was taken from. Eventually, we're going to learn where he and the senator were taken to."

"You sound really confident."

"It's fucking hard to keep secrets—they wear on you. It's fucking hard to maintain a bond that leads to murder. One of them's going to slip."

By the time she got to the morgue she was jonesing for coffee, and knew she couldn't face the sludge she'd find in Vending on their way down the white, echoing tunnel.

Barely six, she thought, and realized Morris might not be in yet. But she could take another look at both bodies, and have one of the other MEs run through the findings with her.

She stopped at the short line of machines, scowled at them. Not only would the coffee be piss-warm sludge, but the machine would give her grief. They always did.

Some sort of conspiracy, she thought bitterly.

"Get me a tube of Pepsi, and whatever you want." She dug in her pockets for credits, passed them to Peabody.

"I'm never going to be able to go back to Vending hot chocolate now, not after experiencing Mr. Mira's. Even what you've got stocked in the vehicle AutoChef doesn't hit that stupendous mark. Coffee's as crappy here as it is at Central. Tea . . . maybe."

"Would you like to see the full menu, perhaps request a sampler?" Eve's all-too-pleasant tone had Peabody risking a sidelong glance. "Or are you going to plug the damn credits in and get something before I boot your ass?"

"My ass is still in the box." Pleased with herself, Peabody ordered up the Pepsi, and opted for a Diet Cherry Fizzy.

The machine spit them out, then began to drone on about

nutritional value—zero—as Eve turned her back and kept going.

She cracked the tube, using her shoulder to push through the doors leading to autopsy.

It shouldn't have surprised her to find Morris already wearing a protective cape over a suit the color of wet stone. He'd chosen a tie of shimmery lavender, and twined his black hair into a single thick braid.

He had music on low, something . . . jazzy, she thought.

He glanced up. And though he held his scalpel, he had yet to start the Y cut on Wymann's body.

"You were quick," he said.

"Or really slow, considering we didn't make it in yesterday for Senator Mira."

For now, Morris set the scalpel down, gestured to a second steel table. "I had our earlier guest brought out of the drawer, as I expected the doubleheader would bring you by this morning."

He stepped over, brought up the lights.

"Without delving deeper into our newest arrival, and going by a visual exam only, the injuries are similar: facial and genital insults, the ligature marks on the wrists, sodomy by foreign object. In the senator's case, that foreign object was about two inches in circumference, tapering down to a rounded point on the end. It had also been heated to a degree to cause severe burning around and in the anus."

Peabody blanched, turned away.

"The proverbial hot poker," Morris added, giving Peabody a sympathetic pat on the shoulder. "The object was used multiple times, with considerable force. The pain would have been excruciating. Again, only with a visual exam, I believe the same object was used on Wymann."

"That's beyond rage," Eve stated. "Maybe we're looking for sexual sadists—a team like Ella-Loo Parsens and Darryl Roy James."

"I don't like thinking there are more like them out there," Peabody replied, back still turned.

"There are always more. But . . ." No, Eve thought, not

like the two twisted lovers they'd recently locked away. Not like that.

"These two weren't picked randomly. They were targets—and the sex, the sadism, the message left, all clearly read revenge."

"Revenge was had," Morris said. "In the biggest of ways. I agree with your insight regarding the contusions. A smooth, weighted sap. There are no indications fists were used."

"Might break a nail, ruin your manicure. It's a woman. Women," Eve added.

"No defensive wounds."

Because they didn't give him a chance to fight back, Eve concluded. "Stun marks?"

"One, barely visible even with microgoggles. In the groin."

"The groin."

"I sense a theme. A mild stun, enough, in my opinion, to debilitate—and hurt, considering that sensitive area, like a swarm of angry wasps—but not enough to render him unconscious. Which plays to them being female."

She walked it through. "Two of them could easily get him into the chair. One works on him, the other holds the stunner. Mr. Mira walks in, and they adjust."

"How is Dennis?"

"He's good. He's dealing. What else can you tell me?"

"From the ligature marks on the wrists, recent injuries to the rotator cuffs, arm and shoulder muscles, the victim was restrained with cord, arms above his head, with his full weight pulling downward. The restraints were removed an hour, no more than two, before TOD."

"He was alive when they hanged him."

"Yes, he was, and his hands free so he attempted to drag the noose from his neck. It's his own skin under his fingernails, along with fiber from the cord."

Morris shifted his attention, and Eve's, to the neck. "This wasn't a sharp drop—not the trapdoor on the gallows, or a chair kicked out that could snap the neck, but a gradual strangulation. The drag of his own weight tightened the cord, increased the pressure, choking him. He died slowly, and painfully."

"Not just an execution. Those are done quickly, efficiently. They wanted him to know, to feel, to suffer. It was torture to the end."

"Yes. A torturous death. Other than that, I can tell you there were no other injuries. He'd had regular face and body work—what you'd call tune-ups—and was in excellent health. His last meal, consumed approximately fourteen hours before his death, included lobster bisque, a field green salad, and some Pouilly-Fuissé. As there were traces of vomit in his mouth, I can only guess at the amounts consumed."

"What did he do—did they do—to earn this level of vengeance? I'm looking at rape, but this brutality? It's beyond even that."

"Kids maybe." Steadier, Peabody took a testing sip from her fizzy. "Maybe they went for kids."

"Pedophilia . . . Yeah, that could work up this sort of rage. There's not even a whiff of that around either, and the first, at least, had regular sex with adults. But we'll look. Because anyone who considered this justice believes the crime is horrific."

"If it was," Morris commented, "both men kept it well hidden. They lived public lives, where the media slides every act under the microscope. Hiding the horrific takes a great deal of skill and work, particularly if more than one person is involved. Secrets rarely hold."

"Agreed. Now that we know we're looking for secrets, and possibly the horrific, it should be easier to find. He's going to run about the same," Eve said, glancing at Wymann. "His injuries, COD, the works. But if you come up with any surprises, let me know."

"I will, of course, but that reminds me. I thought little of it at the time, but the senator has a small tattoo."

"Lots do."

"Including myself. His was barely visible, again, due to the bruising. Groin area."

"He has a tat there?" Eve said as Peabody went, "Ouch!"

"Just to the left of the root, we'll say, of the penis." He offered Eve microgoggles, took a pair for himself.

"Check the new guy," she told Morris as she put on the goggles, bent down, searched. "Yeah, yeah, I see it now. Barely. It . . . it looks Celtic, right? Like one of those Celtic symbols. Mira's not Irish or Scots, though. Is it?"

"Arabic, perhaps, or American Indian. But . . . yes, your second victim has the same. Same tat, same area."

"Can you tell me when? How long ago they got the ink?"

"I'll work on that. I'll excise the dermis, test it myself, and send it to the lab."

"What the hell does it mean? Peabody, get a picture of it. Let's run it, see if it has a specific meaning."

"You're already there, ah, with the goggles."

Eve only rolled her eyes, dragged out her 'link. She called up the camera function, took three shots. "It's going to need to be enhanced, cleaned up."

"I can do that," Peabody began, but Eve was already tagging her expert.

"Hey."

"And a hey back to you," Roarke said.

"Quick one, just in case you know. What's this symbolize or mean? Wait a sec."

She fumbled a little, but managed to send him the image.

"Can you see the tat? There's a lot of bruising and discoloration, but—"

"I see it, yes. And it happens I do know its meaning, as my mates and I nearly had the same done one memorably drunken evening. It's a Celtic symbol for brotherhood."

" 'Brotherhood.' Yeah, that fits. Why didn't you get the ink if you were drunk enough to think about it?"

Amusement sparked in his eyes. "Not quite drunk enough to forget identifying marks aren't wise for some of us in certain areas of business. I've a meeting in a moment, unless you need more."

"No, that's great. Thanks. Buy that solar system."

She clicked off, looked back at both victims. "Brotherhood," she repeated.

Back in the car, she headed for Central. "Tag Harvo at the lab. See if the Queen of Hair and Fiber found anything on the rope fibers. Odds are low, but we'll check. And whatever other hair or fibers the sweepers managed to get to her."

As Peabody contacted the lab, Eve tried Mira's personal 'link.

"Eve."

"Sorry it's so early."

"Not at all. We're up. I thought I'd come in early today in any case."

"I need some time."

"As much as you need, whenever you need it. I can come to you."

"That would save me some steps. I need to tell you Jonas B. Wymann's been murdered."

"I . . . we know him. He was a close friend of Edward's."

"He died the same way."

"Oh, dear God. Are you at Central?"

"Heading there now."

"I'll be on my way in ten minutes."

"Can you put Mr. Mira on?"

"Oh, yes, just a moment."

Eve heard murmuring, shuffling. Then Dennis Mira's gentle face came on her screen. "This is very distressing," he said. "Jonas Wymann. He was a brilliant economist."

"Yes, I heard that. Mr. Mira, do you know when your cousin got his tattoo?"

"Edward?" Those dreamy green eyes went blank. "Edward had a tattoo? That doesn't seem in character at all, does it?"

"You weren't aware he had one?"

"No. I can assure you he didn't have one when he went off to college. We spent the last weekend before he did at the beach, and there was some midnight skinny-dipping involved. I would have noticed no matter where it might have been. I do tend to forget things here and there, but I'm sure I'd remember that."

"Okay, that's helpful. One more thing: your last name? No Celtic connections?"

"Celtic? No. There's a bit on my mother's side, if that helps."

"That's all I needed." She imagined Mira had been at the bruising scrape on his temple with a healing wand regularly, as it barely showed now. "You're feeling okay?"

"Absolutely fine. And how are you?"

"Good. I'm good. If you'd tell Dr. Mira I'll be waiting for her. Thanks."

"You be careful now. Someone very, very angry doesn't want you to find them."

"You got that right. I'll be in touch."

"He's about the sweetest man on the planet," Peabody commented.

"And insightful. 'Angry,' he said. Not sick, twisted, dangerous, violent. Angry," she repeated with a slow nod. "And he's right because it's anger leading the charge. What have you got?"

"Rope's as common as they come, like you'd figure. And no hair other than the vic's on the body. No fiber."

"They had to get him back in the house. Wrapped or rolled him in plastic." She nodded again, visualizing it. "At least two of them, so they could carry him inside. After what they did to him he'd be too weak to fight even if he'd been conscious. Wait until the middle of the night, haul him in there, unroll him, and string him up."

She pulled into Central's garage, beelined for her space. Then sat a moment, thinking.

"It's a hell of a lot of trouble. A body dump's easier, but it's not enough here. Taking an injured, probably unconscious man back into an upscale neighborhood, even middle of the night, says the murder site's as important as the murder. Home. A safe place. A safe, upscale place. It has to mean something."

"Maybe the killer or killers are familiar with the safe, upscale place. If we go back to sex, maybe that's somewhere it happened. If it deals with rape—"

"It's going to."

"Okay, maybe that's where the rapes took place."

"Maybe. Just maybe. Get in touch with the housekeeper again while I'm with Mira," Eve ordered when they got out, walked to the elevator. "You gotta figure somebody who cleans your house, washes your sheets, like that, has a pretty good idea what you do in it and in them."

She got a sudden flash of Summerset—horrifying—and willed it away. Far away.

"Any signs of sexual activity in the Spring Street house other than the boner drugs since the grandfather died. And have McNab drill the house and sex droids at Wymann's, same deal."

"I know rape's about violence, power, control more than sex," Peabody began.

"It's about all of that. All of it. If sex wasn't a factor, sex wouldn't come into it."

"Still, both the vics could get, and did get, plenty of sex. They were both powerful in their field, in their lives. Prosperous, attractive older men who could have paid high-class LCs if they needed to. Why force anyone?"

Eve thought of Richard Troy—no way to avoid it. He'd raped his own child, again and again, because he'd been a predator, a brutal man, and one with a purpose. But when all that was put aside?

"Because they could. I want to hear from Baxter and Trueheart the minute they get back. Two men don't know each other for half a century, stay pals, then end up murdered the same way unless there's overlap. At least one of the women on the senator's list is going to be on Wymann's. Let's find which one."

She went straight to her office, grabbed the time she had to update her board and book. She needed to talk to both of Wymann's ex-wives, his daughter, any known associates, companions.

The overlap was there; she could already see pieces of it. And at some point, she'd find the major cross, the point of origin.

She needed to try to convince someone at Inner Peace to talk to her about Su and MacKensie. Try to get some data on those insomnia studies.

She heard the quick click of heels, pushed up from her desk so Mira could take the single decent chair.

Mira rushed in. She wore a winter-white scarf with glints of icy silver carelessly wrapped around her neck. The clicks had come from the high silver heels of gray boots. Her coat was a soft cloud of blue over the bolder pop of her blue suit.

Eve expected to find her upset. Instead, she found Mira angry.

"I could use some coffee," Mira said briskly as she tossed her coat and scarf on Eve's visitor's chair.

"Sure."

"I should tell you, right away, Jonas was always polite and pleasant to me on the occasions we'd meet. We had socialized a bit more in the past, as his first wife and I were—are—friendly."

"Yeah?"

"Vanessa's a pediatric surgeon, and an interesting woman. We're friendly enough to have the occasional lunch when it fits into our schedules—which isn't often, as she's based in Chicago. Though we aren't and weren't close enough for confidences, it was no secret she and Jonas divorced because he was unfaithful."

"Must've pissed her off."

"I imagine so, but she never spoke of it to me." She took the coffee Eve handed her, sipped, and paced. "She handled it quietly, and built a life and a career, raised her daughter. She remarried about twelve years ago—quite a gap between marriages—and appears very happy. She has grandchildren she visibly adores, and appears close and content with her second husband's children and grandchildren."

"One of her grandchildren would be Jonas Baker."

"Yes."

"That's who found Wymann."

"Oh." Mira sank onto Eve's desk chair. "I'm sorry to hear that. He's a fine young man, very talented. Whatever acrimony Vanessa might have felt for Jonas, they were absolutely united in their love and support of that boy. Their daughter and her husband had a different attitude toward his ambitions."

"Yeah, I got that much."

"I'll tell you in my personal and professional opinion, Vanessa didn't care enough about Jonas to kill him. She moved on, and more than two decades ago."

"She's alibied for at least part of the time Wymann was held. She had to know the senator."

"Of course." Settling a bit, Mira crossed her legs. "We were all young, newly married couples, so we did socialize here and there. Vanessa and I also shared an intense dislike for Mandy. But I can't think of the last time she or Edward came up in any of our conversations. They haven't been part of her circle, not in more than twenty years."

"What do you know about the second wife?"

"Not a great deal. She was considerably younger, and the grapevine reported she'd been one of his flings. Unlike Vanessa, she didn't go quietly, and the word was he had to buy her off to get her out. I don't know where she is or if she remarried, but I could easily find out."

"So can I. Don't worry about it. Would you say he and the senator shared a predilection for casual sex, for affairs, and for using younger women?"

"Absolutely."

Eve stepped onto boggy ground. "Senator Mira has a daughter."

"Gwen, yes. She—" Understanding struck, a quick shock that made her jolt. "Oh, no. I can tell you on both personal and professional levels, no. Edward would never have touched Gwen, and wouldn't have allowed Jonas to, if he'd been inclined. I would have known, Eve. Gwen would have come to me if I'd missed the signs."

"What about going younger. Kids?"

"Again, no. Both these men wanted conquests—proof of

their own virility. Children don't provide that. They sought out young, attractive women. I understand why you'd ask given the violence of the murders, but this isn't about children."

"Okay. I needed to cross it off."

"It can't be a coincidence they both regularly sought out those conquests, and were killed in the same manner. Was there a message?"

"Same one."

Mira sipped her coffee, gathered her thoughts. "So while the killers may perceive this as justice, it's retribution, and the method indicates sexual retribution. A partnership forged for that purpose, carried out swiftly and brutally. The killers are goal-oriented, and bound to each other by this mutual purpose. It's possible they're lovers, but while the killers are violent and brutal, they're also complex and calculated. This isn't piquerism, and I don't believe we're looking for sexual sadists."

"No, they're making a point, not getting off. They're focused. The second murder is almost a mirror image of the first."

"Organized, intelligent. Patient. It took time to set this up. And controlled," Mira added. "They took Dennis out of the equation, but didn't kill him. He isn't a target, and it isn't justice to kill a man who isn't involved. What's this about a tattoo?"

"Both men had a Celtic symbol inked on their groin. Pretty obvious symbolism there. It stands for brotherhood."

" 'Brotherhood,' " Mira murmured. "Sexual. Virility. A symbol of their bond, and their . . . predilection."

"Somewhere along the way, they crossed a line. From seduction or mutual gratification to rape."

"You make that leap due to the nature of the torture."

"The nature of the torture screams: You did it to me, I do it to you. Maybe they did it together, maybe they had a fricking contest," Eve continued before Mira could speak, "but they crossed that line. Put aside your personal feelings on both victims. Tell me, from what you know of them, what you can profile, were they capable of not only raping women, but also forming their own sort of partnership from doing the act?"

Mira sat back, rubbed her fingers at her temple. "It isn't easy to set aside personal feelings for a professional opinion when there's such a long history."

"If you can't—"

"Not easy," Mira interrupted. "But." She drew a breath, met Eve's eyes directly. "I believe Edward was a sociopath. A highly functional, highly intelligent, and highly successful sociopath. He believed himself above the rules when it came to . . . everything. And certainly when it came to relationships. So he married a woman who wouldn't hold him to those rules. He—What's the most dignified term?—propositioned me once."

"What? You didn't mention that before."

"It was decades ago, shortly after Dennis and I were engaged. I never told Dennis because it would have hurt him, and to what purpose? And I knew, even then, Edward only did so because I belonged to Dennis."

Mira studied her coffee, drank some, sighed.

"Dennis's memories of Edward are colored by childhood, but he'll tell a story about them as boys, and it's obvious the man was a bully even then."

"*Proposition* is sort of dignified. Was it?"

"We were at his grandparents' house—I'd nearly forgotten. I'd used the powder room, and as I came out, Edward was there. He backed me into the powder room, suggesting we should get to know each other better. He trapped me against the wall, and as he moved in, I put my knee on his groin. I told him if he ever put his hands on me again I'd break them both off at the wrist."

She set the coffee cup aside, folded her hands together. "It frightened me—you understand."

"Yeah. He was physical with you?"

"Initially, yes. Rough, I suppose, and completely sure I'd be responsive. He backed off, laughed, claimed he was just testing me for his cousin. He never touched me again. But . . ."

"Spill it," Eve demanded. "You're not helping if you hold back."

"I'm not, and I won't hold back."

She picked up the coffee again, just stared into it. "I've given this a great deal of thought, and concluded I'm being rational rather than reactionary. Eve, women like you and I, women who've suffered sexual abuse, we have a sense about predators. For us, it helps us with our work, for others it's a survival instinct. These men were predators. I recognized it in them. I assumed they simply hunted the willing, then discarded them. But, yes, I believe these men could have formed a bond, a pact that crossed the line from the willing."

Mira set the coffee aside again, pressed her fingers to her eyes. "And because I assumed, because I didn't look deeply enough, it may very well be that women who were their victims have crossed the line into murder."

"That's bullshit." Annoyed, Eve jabbed a finger into Mira's shoulder. "And bullshit doesn't help, either. Unless you're going to tell me you're all of a sudden a sensitive who can see into somebody's head or the future or the past, being a smart shrink doesn't mean you know every damn thing about every damn body. We may have a couple of victims who crossed their own line, but that's a choice they made."

"That's completely unsympathetic and oddly comforting." And comforted, Mira took the hand Eve had jabbed her with. "I can know in my head you're right. It's harder to get the rest of me there."

"Here's something that might help. The two victims?" Eve gestured toward her board and the crime scene images. "Did they have any other 'brothers,' any other close friends with similar 'predilections,' to use your fancy word?"

"I . . . Oh God."

"Yeah." Eve hooked her thumbs in her pockets, studied the board. "They may not be finished serving justice."

While Mira absorbed that, Eve tossed out the next. "These three women." She tapped a finger on MacKensie, Downing, and Su. "I'm looking hard at them. Su's Downing's alibi, Su went to Yale, Su went to one of those life enhancement centers—Inner Peace—and so did MacKensie. Different times, but they both end up there. And Su and Downing both did—separate—sessions in an insomnia study."

"That many connections . . . You can't put them together—at Inner Peace or in the studies. But—"

"Yeah, but."

"I don't know that organization. Inner Peace."

"Maybe you could find out more about it." Which would not only give Mira something tangible to do, but would save Eve the time. "Whoever's in charge there would be more likely to talk to you than to a cop. Same with the insomnia deal. I can get you the contact, the dates of each suspect's term."

"Yes. Yes, let me see what I can do on those." With a brisk nod, Mira rose, gathered up her coat and scarf. She stood a moment, studying the board. "Those three," she murmured. "What did Edward and Jonas do that could make those women—if you're right—murder so brutally?"

Chapter 13

Eve checked out Wymann's second wife, and crossed her off. The woman had married again, and again aimed for the older and the wealthy. She was now sitting pretty in a villa in the south of France.

Still, she poked a little more, and came up with an alibi, as wife number two had been cohosting a winter gala in Cannes at the time of Senator Mira's abduction. The international style and society pages were full of reports and photos—and fashion critiques.

Reading them made Eve's brain ache.

Not the wives, she thought, angling to study her board. They'd moved on. But others hadn't.

She toggled back to Charity Downing. And Downing took her to Lydia Su, who'd attended Yale and, like MacKensie, Inner Peace. Time to talk to Downing's alibi.

Before she did, there was something she could do from her desk. She contacted Edward Mira's daughter.

The woman looked pale and drawn, but fully awake. "Lieutenant Dallas."

"Sorry to disturb you this early."

"It doesn't matter. We're not getting a lot of sleep around here. Have you found my father's killer?"

"Working on it. If I ask you who are his closest friends—for now stick with his age group—who comes immediately to mind?"

"Oh, well. Jonas Wymann. They go all the way back to Yale."

"Right. Anyone else?"

"Ah, Frederick Betz. He and my father and Mr. Wymann—and Marshall Easterday—all went to Yale together. They had a group house together. And there's Senator Fordham. They became good friends when my father was a senator. Is that helpful?"

"Yeah, it is. Mrs. Sykes, the media reports are going to start hitting soon. Jonas Wymann was murdered early this morning, in the same manner as your father."

"What?" Her eyes went blank. "What? I don't . . . Why? Why is this happening?"

"I'm working on that, too. Can you think of anyone who would want to cause your father and Wymann harm? Who might link them together?"

"I don't understand any of this. I'm sorry, I don't understand this. He—Mr. Wymann—he used to sneak Ned and me little chocolates when we were kids. He's dead. Murdered. Like my father?"

"I'm sorry. If you or your brother think of anything that connects them, of anyone who might have a grudge against them, let me know."

"I need to contact Ned. I don't want him to hear about this on screen. The others, the others you asked about. You think someone might do this to them?"

"It's something we need to consider. I'll be speaking with them. If anyone else comes to mind, contact me. Anytime."

"I will. I'll ask Ned. Thank you for telling me. I need to . . . I have to go."

Eve pulled up addresses, started to push away from her desk when her 'link signaled. She might have ignored it, but she saw Baxter on the display.

"Dallas. What've you got?"

"A lot of shock from the work contacts we've pulled out of bed so far, and a handful of names we pried out. Ladies he's dated in the last year or so. For an older guy, he gets a lot of touch. We've talked to two of them so far. More shock. Shaky alibis all around for TOD as everyone we've talked to claimed to have been home in bed. Some spouses or cohabs to corroborate, but that stays shaky in my books."

"Find out if any of the sidepieces went to Yale, or has a connection to Yale. Any of them do a stint at a place called Inner Peace."

"Can do. None of the names we've got cross with the ones on the senator's list. Looks like they didn't poach each other's forest."

A man who'd poach on his cousin's fiancée would poach on a friend's skirt, Eve thought. "We'll see about that. Any Yale connection, any Realtors, anybody looking for inner fricking peace, tag me."

"Got it. One more thing. We rousted his admin out of bed, and once we'd calmed her down, we got she'd spoken to him via 'link at about three in the afternoon. He was pretty broken up about his pal, taking the day at home. And she confirmed he had plans to see his grandson's performance last night. But here's something. He had a four o'clock on the books. She asked him if he wanted her to cancel, and he decided to go ahead with it."

"What appointment?"

"A writer. Somebody doing a biography on him—or planning to. Meet was at four, his home."

"Tell me you've got a name."

"I'm telling you I've got a name. Cecily Anson, age fifty-eight, married, one offspring, female. Lives in SoHo. Ah, let me look here . . . No Yale. Went to Brown. Her wife, that's Anne C. Vine, age fifty-nine, MIT—software designer. And . . . daughter, Lillith, age twenty-six, Carnegie Mellon, architect with Bistrup and Grogan, a Midtown firm."

"I'm heading out, so I'll take them on the way to where

I'm going. First vic's admin didn't have the name of his appointment. Feels too pat to have all this with number two."

"Sometimes you get lucky."

"Mostly you don't. Keep at it until we do." She cut him off, grabbed her coat. When she hit the bullpen, she said, "Peabody," and kept going.

Peabody, puffing a bit, caught up with her at the elevator. "Did we get a break?"

"Maybe. Wymann's admin spoke with him at three, so he was still at home and under no duress. But he had an appointment at four, at home, with a biographer. Cecily Anson."

"We've got a name."

"Name, address, basic data. She's late fifties, so old for the vic's taste, and since she's got a wife probably not sexually oriented to be his sidepiece. Got a grown daughter who might be, and a place in SoHo. We'll hit that before we go talk to Lydia Su."

Peabody pulled on a hat—candy green with icy blue edging. "It doesn't feel like they'd leave us such a direct line."

"No, it doesn't. But whoever kept that four o'clock is likely the one who abducted, tortured, and killed him. Check in with Morris. Let's see if he can give us a ballpark on when Wymann incurred the injuries. And let's get some uniforms back out, canvassing neighbors with that specific time frame. It might spark something."

Within two minutes the elevator was jammed with cops, sad-eyed civilians, and a couple of shady characters Eve made as cops undercover.

But she stuck it out, telling herself the stupid elevator would be quicker than the glides.

"I got more names from Gwen Sykes—tight friends. We're going to talk to them—in person or by 'link."

"You think they'll try for three?"

"We're not going to risk it. Two go back to Yale where they and the two vics had a group house together. That may prove interesting. The other made pals with the senator when they were both in East Washington. Senator Fordham."

She muscled off the elevator at her garage level, sucked in air. In the car she plugged in the Anson-Vine address, considered her options, then contacted Whitney as she drove out.

"Sir," she began. "I had additions to the report I sent on Jonas Wymann. Peabody and I are en route to interview a person of interest. Earlier I spoke with Senator Mira's daughter and she gave me three names, close friends of her father. While we will contact them, one is Senator Fordham. I believe his security detail and staff should be informed of a possible threat."

"Agreed. I'll see to it."

"Commander, I may need to interview Fordham, and under the circumstances, I can't be overly delicate about it."

"Understood. But some delicacy will be called for. Either I or Chief Tibble will set up the interview if and when it's necessary. I'll be in touch."

"Yes, sir."

"Jeez." Peabody goggled. "You really think a sitting senator is involved in some sort of sex club? If that's what's going on. I mean . . . What am I saying?" Peabody shook her head. "Sex and politics, right?"

"I don't think the sex has anything to do with politics. It's brotherhood. It's power. Do a run on the names I've got. Frederick Betz and Marshall Easterday. Both Yale alumni, same time frame as our two vics. All four sharing a house during college. Find out if Fordham went to Yale."

She navigated traffic while Peabody worked, spied a street spot and bagged it.

"Betz," Peabody told her. "As in Betz Chemicals—everything from household cleaners to rocket fuel. He's third generation. Stands as current president. Currently on wife number three, who's younger than his youngest daughter at twenty-nine. They've been married three years. He has four kids, including a three-year-old courtesy of the current wife.

"Why would a guy cruising seventy want to procreate?"

"Must I repeat?" Eve asked. "The penis."

"Okay, the penis has no shame. Easterday, Marshall. Lawyer, and that's third generation. Senior partner of Easterday,

Easterday, and Louis. On wife number two, but that's stuck for . . . fifteen years, and she's actually fifty-two. Two kids, both from the first marriage. Daughter is the second Easterday in the firm. Son is a neurosurgeon in Philadelphia."

"Okay, we'll roll on them this morning."

"And Fordham went to Ole Miss—no Yale connection."

Eve got out of the car, studied the five-story building. The old post-Urban squat and square had been refaced, whitewashed. The double-wide entrance doors looked old in a rich, important way, but she noted on closer inspection they were reinforced steel, done up with some illusionary fancy paint.

The security was first-rate.

"Anson has the first floor." Eve considered, pressed the buzzer for the main floor unit.

It took a minute, then a sleepy female voice came through the speaker. "It's way too early for anything you're selling."

Eve held up her badge. "NYPSD," she began.

"Mike? Is it Mike? Oh God."

Before Eve could answer, the buzzer for the locks sounded. As she pushed open the door, a woman came flying out of a door at the end of a smart-looking foyer.

Heavily pregnant, barefoot, and clad in penguin-covered pajamas, she moved with astonishing speed.

"Something happened to Mike." She grabbed Eve's shoulders in a vise-grip, her big brown eyes glassy with fear. "Tell me fast."

"We're not here about Mike. Take a breath."

"You're sure? It's not Mike." She pressed a hand to her swollen belly, swayed a little.

Peabody caught her arm. "Ma'am, let's go sit down, okay?"

"You're not grief counselors? You're not making a notification?"

"Nothing like that at all." Peabody used her most soothing voice as she gently steered the woman around.

"Sorry. It's probably hormones. Everything's hormones right now. It's just Mike—my fiancé—he's on the job, so I thought . . . *whoosh*. Yeah, let's just sit down."

"You're not Cecily Anson," Eve said as Peabody supported the woman into the door of a living area as smart as the foyer.

"No, she's my mother. Oh God, did something happen to the Moms?"

"No." Eve said it firmly before hormones could kick in again. "As far as we know, everyone's fine. Lillith?"

"Yes." Lillith levered herself into a big red chair in the middle of the smart space and bold colors. She shoved a hand through a mass of curling brown hair. "Lil, mostly. And I'm sorry for the hysteria. I know better. I'm carrying a cop's kid, after all." She smiled—a dazzler—and some color came back into her face. "Mike Bennet—Detective Bennet, out of Central. Maybe you know him."

"I do." Judging the crisis had passed, Peabody sat down. "He's a good guy."

"He really is."

"How far along are you?"

"Just hit thirty-one weeks, so I've a ways to go." Lillith folded her hands on the penguin-covered mountain. "I don't know how."

Neither did Eve. Could that mountain actually get bigger? How was it possible?

"Is your mother at home?" she asked.

"No. The Moms are in Adelaide—Australia. Mike and I have the third floor, but we're having some remodeling done due to . . ." She patted the mountain. "So we're staying here while they're away. He's on nights right now. He should be home pretty soon. Sorry, can I get you something?"

"We're good. How long has Ms. Anson been out of the country?"

"Just over three weeks. They'll be back next week, plenty of time to fuss over me before the baby comes. What's this about? I should've asked that right away."

"Do you know if Ms. Anson is working on, or planning to work on, a biography of Jonas Wymann—the economist?"

Lillith frowned, absently rubbed her mountain. "I don't think so. She's working on a bio of Marcus Novack right now. That's why they're in Australia. He built schools and health centers in the Outback. She sometimes has something else in the works—or in the planning stage—but I never heard her mention that name."

"Taking a monthlong trip to Australia takes some planning, I guess." Peabody kept her voice, her smile easy. "They must've been planning it for a while."

"Since last summer, though Mike and I had to convince them to go. I had to swear I wouldn't go into labor until they got back. Look, I'm steady now, and like I said, engaged to a cop. What's this Wymann have to do with my mother?"

She looked steady now, Eve judged—considering the penguin mountain. Clear-eyed and calm.

"Mr. Wymann was murdered. He had an appointment on his books for yesterday at four P.M. with your mother."

Lillith just shook her head. "He couldn't have. Mom doesn't make mistakes like that, and honestly I've never heard her mention that name. She talks about her projects. I understand why you're here now. She'd be a suspect, but she's halfway around the world. You can contact her. I'll give you the information you need to contact her."

"I'd appreciate that, but not because she's a suspect. I believe you," Eve said. "But her name was on the victim's appointment book, so someone used it to get to him. You said she talks about her projects. I bet she talked about this trip."

"To anyone who'd listen. The Moms love to travel. And I follow you. Someone who knew she'd be gone, out of contact, used her name. God. She'll be so upset."

Lillith shoved up from the chair, belly first, when the door opened. The way she said "Mike" told Eve the seed of fear planted by the early morning visit had rooted.

"Hey, babe, what's—" He all but came to attention when he spotted Eve. "Lieutenant."

"Detective. There's no problem here. We're looking for Ms. Anson to assist in an investigation."

"CeCe?" He wrapped an arm around Lillith, his eyes on Eve.

"We believe someone used her name, may have impersonated her, to gain access to Jonas Wymann."

"Wymann. I heard about that. Hey, Peabody."

"Hey, Mike."

"Come on, Lil, sit."

"I'm just glad to see you." She rubbed a hand on his cheek, a little scruffy after his night shift. "Just glad to see that face. I want my one measly cup of coffee for the day. How about I make some all around?"

"That'd be great."

"I'll do that and the lieutenant can fill you in. I didn't even ask your name," Lillith remembered, and Mike shoved the dark watch cap off a messy thatch of sandy hair.

"Man, Lil. It's Dallas."

"It's— Oh!" Lillith held the belly and laughed. "Hormones ate my brain. Of course it is. Dallas and Peabody. We've seen the vid three times. Mike loves it. Well, I'm going to stop worrying about the Moms right now. If Mike thinks you're the best, you are. I'll get the coffee. He can help," she added as she walked away. "He's a really good cop."

"She has to say that. But I'll help any way I can." He pulled off his coat, a man with a slim build and a cop's keen eyes. "Edward Mira, Jonas Wymann. Pretty high-powered targets. I can't see how CeCe, or either of the Moms could connect. They're solid as they come."

"Lillith said they'd had this trip planned awhile."

"Yeah." He sat on the arm of the chair Lillith had vacated. "We had to give them a boost out the door because of the baby, but CeCe really wanted to go, to absorb the place, to talk to people who'd known this guy she's writing about. So we compromised. They were going for six weeks, but cut it down to four. And we talk to them every day. Sometimes a couple times a day."

"Did they book the trip—the travel, the lodging—themselves or use a service?"

"Annie handles all that. CeCe and Annie—the Moms."

"Can you give us a list of people they'd talk to, people who'd know they'd be gone?"

He puffed out his scruffy cheeks. "It'd almost be easier to give you a list of who wouldn't know." He popped up when Lillith came back in with a tray, took it from her.

"Do they belong to any clubs, any groups?" Peabody asked. "You know, women's groups?"

Eve saw the quick understanding flicker in Mike's eyes. They were looking for female killers.

"Oh Lord, yes." Obviously amused, Lillith sat while Mike passed around the coffee. "I remember how you like it, if the vid's factual. Anyway, Femme Power—that's a lesbian-based activist group. They're charter members there. They go to a book club that's pretty much all women, and help out at a couple of shelters for battered women, rape victims. C-Mom teaches writing as therapy, as an outlet for self, and A-Mom does the same with art. She does bad watercolors. I mean not horrible, just bad. But it makes her happy.

"Now the three of you are wondering what you can say in front of me. I can go in the other room, but it'll annoy the crap out of me."

"It's okay." Mike rubbed her shoulder. "You're thinking someone they know through their hobbies or volunteer work used CeCe as a ploy."

"It's possible. I'd like as many names from those areas as possible."

"They won't betray the women who they've met through the shelters or in the therapy sessions," Lillith said, and her shoulders squared under Mike's hand. "You can't expect that."

"I'm looking for names that are already on my list of suspects," Eve explained. "Someone used your mother to get close enough to kill someone. She's killed twice. I believe she'll kill again."

"Let me work on that, Lieutenant." Mike kept rubbing Lillith's shoulder. "I'll talk to them, explain. It's doubtful they have full names, not from the shelter or the sessions anyway."

"Staff," Eve added. "We might be looking for other volunteers or staff."

"They run what they call Positive Forces on Wednesday nights at Community Outreach on Canal," Mike told them. "The social worker who coordinates is Suzanne Lipski. Twenty-five-year vet, tough and sharp. And clean. I ran her."

"You did not! Mike!"

"Once I hooked you, they became my moms, too. Bet your ass I ran her. She'll protect her women, Lieutenant, but she won't protect a killer. She knows me, so maybe I can get something there if there's something to get. Or at least pave the way for you some."

"The more names, the better. And the sooner the better," Eve said as she rose. "I appreciate the time, the help, the coffee. How do you live on one cup a day?"

Lillith took a tiny sip. "I ask myself that every day when I've finished the one cup. And somehow I do."

"They look good together," Peabody commented when they walked back to the car. "Come off solid. And since he's got an in, he might be able to wrangle some names."

"Maybe. It's worth giving him a shot at it first. Clearly somebody connected to Anson knew she'd be out of the way long enough to use this ruse, and wasn't worried about cops following up."

Once in the car, Peabody unbundled herself a little. "Those groups—support groups—they're like priests in the confessional. Absolute confidentiality. So whoever tapped Anson counted on that. A lot of it's just first names, or code names."

"Everybody's got a face," Eve said and pulled away from the curb. "We show pictures, get reactions. We may not get confirmation, but we'll get reactions."

And that's what she was looking for with Lydia Su.

Eve had to settle for a crappy little parking lot and a two-block hike in wind that decided to swirl up and kick through the city canyons. Peabody rebundled, and Eve yanked the snow-flake cap on.

It made her think of Dennis Mira.

"We need to get Mr. Mira's impressions of the three names I got from the senator's daughter. We'll notify them first, talk to them, but I want his take."

"He usually has good ones."

"Yeah, he does. But Mira told me he's got a blind spot where his cousin's concerned. She taps Edward Mira as a sociopath—highly functional. Said he was always a bully, and a sexual predator."

"Harsh. But if we're following the right line, it fits."

"It's the right line." Eve stopped in front of Su's building. A slick high-rise, probably along the lines of what Nadine was after.

No doorman, she noted. An auto-scan that accepted a scan of her badge with minimal fuss.

Identification verified, Dallas, Lieutenant Eve. Please state the nature of your business and/or the party you wish to visit.

"That would be police business seeing as you scanned the badge, and we're here to speak with Lydia Su, unit 2204."

Thank you for that information. The resident of unit 2204 is being notified. You are cleared to step inside and wait.

Eve walked into a generous lobby of white and silver with some bold blue chairs, verdant potted trees, and a moving map of the building.

It boasted its own market, both a men's and women's boutique, a business and banking center on its mezzanine level (for residents and their guests only). It held a fitness center, two bars, and three restaurants. Building management and administration had offices on level three.

By the time she'd scanned the map, noted the location of

2204—corner unit, facing south and east—the computer cleared them to an elevator.

Guests cleared to twenty-second floor, the elevator announced. Have a pleasant visit.

"Why can't they ever just shut up?" Eve wondered. "Who needs a comp to wish them a pleasant visit? Su cleared us pretty quick," she added and, glancing around the silver box, noted the security cams. "Maybe expecting this follow-up to your conversation with her yesterday, verifying Downing's alibi."

"She breezed through that. Just the right amount of surprise, and all cooperation."

"I bet if we checked her 'link, she alerted Downing we're here."

Eve stepped off on twenty-two. She walked down the wide hallway carpeted in muted silver, past glossy black doors to 2204. She pressed the bell with one hand, held up her badge with the other.

The minute Lydia Su opened the door, she thought: You're in this.

It was only a flicker, there then gone, an angry awareness that lit the long, searing brown eyes before Lydia offered a polite if puzzled smile.

"Good morning. Is this about Senator Mira's murder? I spoke with a detective yesterday."

"This is a follow-up. You spoke with Detective Peabody," Eve added, gesturing to her partner.

"Oh, yes. Well, please come in. I'm a little befuddled. I was sleeping. I had to work quite late."

"Sorry to disturb you. We won't take up much of your time."

"Can I offer you some coffee or tea?"

"We're fine."

"Please, sit." She led the way into an airy living area with two curved chairs, a long, low sofa with a central pillow fashioned as a peacock, tail feathers spread. Some sort of exotic flowers speared out of a clear, square vase with shiny black pebbles layered in the base. Filmy shades flowed down the windows.

Lydia hit about five-two and crossed to the sofa on small feet clad in house skids. She wore a lounge set in creamy white with a long black cardigan.

She might have been sleeping after a long night, Eve thought, but she'd taken the time to groom her hair—straight as rain—back into a sleek tail.

She sat, graceful as a dancer. "How can I help?"

"You spent your day off with Charity Downing. Day before yesterday."

"That's right. We had lunch, did some shopping, had our nails done. We were enjoying ourselves, so we stopped for a drink, then decided to go back to Charity's, have some dinner, watch some screen. I left around nine, I think. It was a nice day with a friend."

"Sounds like it. How did you come to be friends?"

"I'm sorry?"

"You don't seem to have much in common."

Eve shrugged as she looked casually around the room. And at the fancy bronze riot bar on the door.

Fancy or not, a riot bar was overkill in a place like this.

"The struggling artist," she continued, "and the Yale alum, the scientist with the doctorate. How long have you been friends—the intimate sort of friends you must be, as Charity said you were the only one she'd told about her relationship with Edward Mira?"

"We found we have a great deal in common. An appreciation of art, we enjoy—for the most part—the same music, enjoy watching vids at home, in the quiet. We like each other's company. I like to think I was supportive and non-judgmental when it came to the choices she made with Edward Mira. As a friend should be."

"Right. How'd you meet again?"

"I went into the gallery where she worked one day, and we simply hit it off, as some do."

"Lucky chance. I figured you had that whole insomnia thing going together."

"Excuse me?"

"The studies you both volunteered for."

"I . . . Yes. But . . . We weren't in the same study, and didn't know each other until after."

"What a coincidence. So you were looking for some art?"

It came again, that flicker. But only anger this time. "I was," Lydia said coolly. "Browsing, really, and Charity was knowledgeable and personable. We ended up going for coffee on her break, and simply became friends. Is that so unusual?"

"Like I said, lucky chance—just like the insomnia. So, did you buy anything?"

"Yes. That painting." She gestured to a large study of a trio of bushes flowering in deep, deep pink, and a woman in the background, facing away, head bowed.

"Lucky chance for her, too. So you left Charity's place about nine. And then?"

"I came home, caught up on some reading, and went to bed."

"How about last night?"

"Last night? Why?"

"Jonas Wymann, a close friend of Edward Mira's, was murdered. Were you and Charity hanging out again?"

"No. I was at work until nearly ten, then came home and put another three hours in on a project. At least three. I didn't go to bed until after two."

"Did Charity ever mention Wymann to you?"

"No. I don't recall the name. I don't believe she met any friends of Edward Mira's, or she would have told me."

"Even if she'd slept with him, too."

The muscles in Lydia's jaw tightened, as did—for just an instant—the fingers of the hands she'd calmly folded in her lap. "As I wouldn't have judged her, I believe, yes, she would have told me. And if you see Charity as whorish because she was foolish enough to sleep with a powerful, married man who appears to have made it a habit to prey on foolish women, you judge far too harshly. His death is, undoubtedly, difficult for his friends and his family, but to my mind he victimized Charity and others like her."

"That's pretty judgmental, isn't it, Peabody?"

"Leans that way."

"But we all have our own scale, don't we? How about Carlee MacKensie?" Eve threw out the question on the heels of the other, and got a reaction. More than a flicker—a quick flash of shock.

"I'm sorry?"

"It's pretty simple. Carlee MacKensie. But I can refresh you. You both spent some time at Inner Peace."

Anger burned low and sharp in her eyes, but her voice remained coldly controlled. "My visit to Inner Peace is personal."

"Nothing stays personal with murder. Did you meet Carlee MacKensie there?"

"As the conditions of Inner Peace are headlined by confidentiality, we used only first names while in residence. I recall no one there named Carlee."

"I've got a photo," Peabody said helpfully, and took one out.

Lydia glanced at it, then away. "I don't recognize her."

"You know what's another coincidence?" Eve kept her eyes on Su's face. "MacKensie went to Yale, too. Just like you. Just like Senator Mira, like Jonas Wymann. School ties, insomnia, and Inner Peace. Yeah, that's a lot of . . . what's the word, Peabody?"

"Maybe *happenstance*."

"Hmm. Not the word I had in mind, but we can go with it. Happenstance."

Lydia pulled back, folded her hands in her lap again, palm to palm. "I suppose it's a necessary part of your job to be suspicious. How unfortunate for you."

"Unfortunate? Nah. It's what gets me going in the morning." Eve smiled then, deliberately predatory. "It's more unfortunate for people who think they can get away with murder."

"I can only tell you Charity and I spent the day together, as described. Now. Is there any other way I can help?"

"No, that ought to do it." Eve rose. "Thanks for your time."

She paused at the door. "Oh, you can let your good friend

know we'll be following up with her, too. Suspicions not only get me going in the morning, they keep me going all day long."

They went out to the elevator. Eve glanced back down the long, elegant hallway. "She's lying, right down the line."

"I gotta say, oh yeah on that. You got under her skin and more than once. She nearly flubbed it when you brought up MacKensie. She absolutely recognized her, and never saw it coming."

"No question about it. Interesting she said Edward Mira preyed on Charity *and* women like her. Nonjudgmental, my ass," she said as they stepped into the elevator. "That one was part judge, jury, and executioner. And she took a lot of pride in it. We're going to start peeling the layers off."

Chapter 14

Knowing Su was a liar—and by association Downing and MacKensie were liars—didn't prove them killers.

But she damn well would prove it.

Part of that process would be talking to the other men who might be part of this brotherhood.

The shortest route took her to Easterday's townhome. What had once been two three-story row houses had been converted into one expansive home on Park Avenue.

A woman in a simple black suit with a wide, homey face answered the door.

"Lieutenant Dallas, Detective Peabody, NYPSD. We'd like to speak with Mr. Easterday."

"Mr. Easterday isn't receiving today."

"We're not looking for a reception. Just tell him the cops are here."

"You can wait in the foyer—it's very cold. I'll ask Mr. Easterday if he'll see you."

White marble floors and heavy dark wood gave the generous foyer what Eve thought of as in-your-face dignity. She glanced up at the many-tiered chandelier, and thought that's where they'd hang him if they got the chance.

Belatedly she remembered the cap, pulled it off, finger-combing her hair as she stuffed it in her pocket.

Seconds later a woman started down the long sweep of stairs.

She wore a black suit, but unlike the first there was nothing simple in this one. It fit the svelte body in a way designed to show off lines and curves, and it shimmered subtly in the crystal rain of the chandelier.

The deep blond hair had been twisted back into a knot at the nape of a long neck, leaving the face unframed. Easterday's wife might have hit the half-century mark, Eve thought, but she knew how to turn back the clock.

"Lieutenant, Detective, I'm Petra Easterday." She extended a slim hand with a glinting diamond to Eve, then Peabody. "My husband is indisposed. He learned of a close friend's death this morning."

"That's why we're here. That would be his second close friend in the last two days."

"Yes, and Marshall is simply shattered. In fact, I was just upstairs trying to convince him to take a soother and lie down."

Worry naked on her face, Petra glanced toward the stairs. "I'm happy to do anything I can to help you, but my husband simply can't be disturbed at this time." Even as she spoke, they heard footsteps descending. Petra sighed. "Oh, Marshall, you need to rest."

"Petra, the police are only doing their job."

He didn't look shattered, Eve mused, but he certainly looked dented. Dark circles under his eyes, lines of strain around his mouth showed a man carrying grief.

While a tall man, he seemed to stoop as if his shoulders carried far too heavy a weight.

He also wore a black suit, with a black mourning band, and a quiet blue tie in a Double Windsor.

"Petra, dear, I could use some coffee."

When she merely cocked an eyebrow, he smiled a little. "Tea then. If you would."

"I'll see to it. I hope you'll both respect that my husband is grieving," Petra said before she left them.

"She's feeling very protective, understandably. Lieutenant Dallas, isn't it? And Detective . . ."

"Peabody."

"Yes, of course. Please, let's go in, sit down."

The front parlor continued the formality of the foyer, offset just a bit by a small, cheerful fire in a white marble hearth. The flowers here were red as blood roses; the big, boxy sofa was covered in a fussy floral print that made sitting on it feel like squatting in a garden.

Easterday took a chair with wide wings, sighed.

"It feels—it all feels impossible. I hadn't gotten my mind around Edward, and now Jonas. Do you have a suspect?"

"We can't discuss the details of the investigation. I'm sorry for the loss of your friends," Eve continued, "and understand this is a difficult time for you."

"I haven't practiced criminal law in more than two decades—I leave that to my daughter—but I know how it's done. Do you have questions for me that may help in your investigation?"

"Yes. You've lost two friends in two days, Mr. Easterday, to murder. Men you've known since college—about fifty years—and have stayed close to. Close enough so your name is on a short list."

His eyes widened. "Of suspects?"

"No, sir. Of victims."

Now he glanced quickly toward the foyer. "That sort of statement will upset my wife."

"She'll be more upset if I come back here to notify her of your murder."

He shoved out of the chair. "This is ridiculous. No one has any cause to kill me."

"But did to kill your friends?"

He sat again, spread his hands. "Edward was my friend, and has been more than half my life. As his friend I can say he could be difficult, even abrasive. No doubt he made enemies in politics, as a senator, and now through his institute."

He'd known this was coming, Eve thought. Known there would be a list and he'd be on it. Grief aside, he'd prepared.

"And Jonas Wymann?" she asked him.

"Politics again. Surely you've made that connection. Jonas was brilliant, but his views were not always popular, and he's wielded considerable influence for many, many years."

"There are other connections," Eve began.

Petra walked into the room just ahead of the housekeeper, who wheeled a large tea tray.

"Thank you, Marian. I'll pour out."

The housekeeper didn't quite curtsy, but Eve sensed it was implied.

"I can deal with this, Petra."

"I'm not leaving." She spoke pleasantly, but the steel beneath was more than implied. "Cream? Sugar?" she said to Eve.

"No thanks."

"Detective?"

"A little cream, two sugars. Thanks."

"There's no point in arguing, Marshall," she continued as she poured the tea. "I'm staying. You were saying something about connections, Lieutenant."

"The two victims have more in common with each other, and with you, Mr. Easterday, than politics."

Petra made a sound—not quite a gasp—and passed Eve tea that Eve didn't want. "You think Marshall . . . This person who killed Edward and Jonas, you think he might try to hurt Marshall?"

"Now, Petra—"

"Don't placate me, Marshall. It's something that caught me by the throat after I got over the shock of hearing about Jonas. I dismissed it, but . . ." She looked back at Eve, dead in the eye. "Is this what you think?"

"It's something we have to consider, and have to take seriously to ensure your husband's safety."

"Yes. Good. Take it seriously. We're all going to take it very seriously."

"Petra, Edward and Jonas shared political networks and leanings I haven't."

She only shook her head. "You've been friends for decades. You socialize regularly, you golf, play poker, travel together. You lived in the same house for years back in— Oh God! Fred and Ethan."

"That's Frederick Betz," Eve said quickly. "Who's Ethan?"

"Ethan MacNamee," Easterday told her. "One of our housemates back at Yale. He and Edward didn't stay particularly close, and he lives in Glasgow most of the year. I only see him myself every few months."

"And when you get together, it's like no time's passed," Petra insisted. "You're like brothers."

"A brotherhood," Eve said, watching Easterday's face.

That face went stony, and his eyes cut away, just for an instant. "Yes. We're like brothers, you could say, and I've lost two."

"Three," Petra said quietly, and took her husband's hand. "There were six of them who shared the group house at Yale. The other was William Stevenson—Billy. He died, tragically, just before Marshall and I were married."

"What happened?"

"He suffered from depression." Marshall began to rub his temple. "He'd poured considerable money into a new business venture that failed, and was going through a second, brutal divorce. His father was—and is—a hard man, and berated him. It was a terrible series of blows."

"He self-terminated?"

"He did, yes, without the legal authority, without going through the necessary counseling. He went to his family home in Connecticut, locked himself in his old bedroom, and hanged himself."

"Hanged himself."

"You can't connect that to the murders. It was clearly suicide, and more than fifteen years ago. And while we were and are good friends, Edward and Jonas were the closest to each other. They shared more interests, and again, those political and social views."

"What else did they share?" Eve asked. "Edward Mira had regular sexual relationships with a variety of women."

Easterday struck a fist to his thigh. "I'm not going to sit here while my friends are on slabs at your morgue and impugn their reputations."

The bluster was insult, but fear glinted through it.

"I have a list of names, of women Edward Mira had relationships with during just the past year. One of those women might be responsible for what was done to him. I need to know if Jonas Wymann shared any of those women, or shared the predilection for women."

"Marshall." Before he could speak, before he could release the anger Eve saw in his eyes, Petra took his hand. "They're dead, and if this is why, you owe it to them to speak out. Please."

"Edward made no secret of his enjoyment of women outside his marriage. And Mandy was aware."

Easterday bit the words off.

"Their marriage was their business. Jonas was more circumspect, but . . . His habit of enjoying women outside marriage certainly led to the dissolution of both of his. However, if they shared a woman, I'm not aware."

"And you, Mr. Easterday? Do you go outside the lines?"

"This discussion is over."

"It's not!" Now Petra gripped his arm. "Marshall and I have a relationship based on trust as much as love and respect. I'm fully aware he was unfaithful to his first wife. My first husband had affairs. I refused to marry Marshall for more than a year due to trust issues. We met not long after our mutual divorces."

"I've never had an affair—not since you and I began."

"I know it." Petra laid a hand on his cheek. "I lived with a cheat," she said to Eve. "I know the signs. Every one of them. I promised myself I'd never live with one again. I don't break promises, Lieutenant. Marshall and I have built a strong, healthy marriage—and trust, fidelity, respect—those are cornerstones."

"You'd know where to look," Marshall said to Eve. "You

can check my finances, my travel, you can speak to anyone at my firm. I haven't had a relationship with another woman since I met Petra."

"What about Betz?"

"Lieutenant, I appreciate your concern for my safety, and I respect your position, but I'm not going to gossip about my friends. Speak to him yourself."

"I intend to. Are you friendly with Senator Fordham?"

"Not really. He's Edward's friend. We've socialized, of course, but I'd consider us acquaintances."

"He's not a brother then."

"No," Easterday said flatly, and the hand holding the tea-cup trembled. He set the cup down. "I'm finished with this. I don't see how it's in any way helpful, and you put me in the position of being disloyal to dead friends. I want to rest now."

"Yes, you should. I'll be right up," Petra told him. "I'll show the officers out, and be right up."

To Eve, the weight on his shoulders seemed heavier as he left the room.

"We have good security," Petra said briskly, "and I'll make certain it's in full use. He won't go anywhere without me. I can hire private security to stay with him until this is resolved if you think I should."

"I think it wouldn't hurt. He shouldn't keep any appoint-ments alone," Eve said as she rose. "That's how both victims were lured."

"He's not like them—not the way you mean. He loved them, deeply, but he's not like them. I'm not Mandy Mira, Lieutenant. Believe me."

"I do." Eve held her gaze. "I believe you. Thanks for your time, and your cooperation."

Eve stepped outside, took a long breath. "Impressions, Peabody?"

"He knows things, things he hasn't told his wife. Things he doesn't want her to know. And he's scared shitless. But she'd know if he cheated on her, and it came off sincere when he said he'd been faithful."

"He didn't use that word," Eve pointed out. "He said he

hadn't had affairs, hadn't had other relationships. That's a distinction to my ear."

"I don't hear it."

"He doesn't cat around like his friends—and, yeah, she'd know if he did. She'd toss him out for it. But rolling in the sheets at a hotel, having drinks, maybe dinner, conversations? That's different from targeting a woman, raping her, then moving on."

"Well, Jesus."

"Yeah. Add he knows things. Add he's scared. Scared and angry, and defensive. He's part of the brotherhood, Peabody, and loyalty to them, trying to hide what he's part of from his wife, could get him or one of the others killed. Let's see if we can shake more out of Betz."

The Upper East Side home of Frederick Betz had once been a small, exclusive boutique hotel for the ridiculously rich. The ridiculously rich made it a prime target during the Urbans. It hadn't been razed, but it had been gutted with all the original marble, stone, wood, gilt, crystal, and silver leaf chipped, hacked, pried, and hauled off.

It sat, a sad, graffiti-laced shell, for nearly two decades before Betz—an enterprising soul—bought it for a song and dance right on the edge of the revitalization trend.

He spent fully ten times the cost of the shell to turn it into his personal palace. In spending his millions, Betz proved, beyond a shadow, money couldn't buy taste.

On the arching front door of glossy red lacquer, fat cherubs in what looked like G-strings cavorted with sly-eyed centaurs and winged horses. Three-headed dogs snarled; fierce-eyed dragons spat fire.

Some of the cherubs were armed with bow and arrow, and looked ready to use them.

Eve couldn't decide if it was meant to be whimsical or obscene.

"It's just creepy," Peabody stated.

"Yeah, that's the best word. *Creepy*."

Eve glanced at the palm plate, noted it attached to the wall of the building with shiny gold fingers, and decided it took all kinds.

Of what, she'd never know. But it took all kinds.

She rang the bell, centered in a tangle of gold vines.

Good morning, the computer intoned in a rich and fruity British accent. Mr. and Mrs. Betz are not currently receiving guests. Please leave your name if you wish one of their staff to contact you.

"Scan this," she ordered, and held out her badge. "Lieutenant Dallas, NYPSD. It's imperative I speak with Mr. Betz immediately."

One moment.

The red light beamed out, scanned the badge.

Your identification has been verified, Dallas, Lieutenant Eve. Regretfully, Mr. Betz is not in residence at this time. If you would like to contact his personal assistant or his administrative assistant—

"I'll take Mrs. Betz," Eve interrupted.

Regretfully, Mrs. Betz is not in residence at this time. If you would like—

"Screw this. Who is in residence? I'll speak to any damn human being in the house."

One moment.

"Contact his office," Eve told Peabody, "see if you can talk to a human. I want to know where the hell he is."

"One moment," Peabody couldn't resist saying, stepping out of range as she took out her 'link.

Before Eve decided whether to snicker or snarl, she heard locks disengaging.

"Lieutenant. Detective."

"Sila. You work here?"

"Yes, ma'am." The cleaning contractor bobbed her head, stepped back to let them in. "For about six months now. Mrs. Betz, she fired her other cleaning company, and she got our name from Senator Mira. Is something wrong?"

"There might be. I need to find Frederick Betz."

"Oh, golly, I don't know where he might be. I know Mrs. Betz said how she was going to their place in Bimini, I think it is, with the baby and the nanny, and the nanny's helper."

"The nanny has a helper?"

A little smirk escaped. "Oh, sure. And Mrs. Betz, I think she was taking her personal assistant, too, and maybe Mr. Betz was going—she didn't say. But we started upstairs, and well, the master suite's a mess—that's just usual. But I can't say if I noticed any of his things gone, like packed up for a trip."

"Who's we?"

"Oh, my mama and Dara—my daughter. It takes the three of us two full days to do this house, it's got so many curlicues and fuss, even though they have a house droid who sees to it daily. We come in twice a month, go top to bottom."

"Do me a favor, Sila. Stop the others from cleaning anything, for now."

"I . . . All right." She pulled a 'link out of her pocket, tapped out a quick text. "Can you tell me why?"

"There's been another murder, a friend of the senator's. I'm checking in with other friends."

"Oh my goodness. Oh my. What should we do? We've been working on the bedroom floor for over an hour."

"It's all right. Don't touch anything else. It would help if we could talk to the house droid."

"Oh. It's back in the kitchen, in the storage area. I don't know how to turn it on. Mrs. Betz, she said Mr. Betz would shut it down while they were gone, and would program it by remote to come back on, freshen the house when they planned to come back."

"If we can't get it on, we'll get someone from EDD. Peabody?"

"Working my way up to his admin. Lower assistants either don't know or won't say where he is."

"Keep on it. Would you show us the droid, Sila?"

"I sure will."

She started back, out of the entrance hall—with its central koi pond and massive gold chandelier with hundreds of . . .

"Curlicues," Eve repeated and made Sila smile.

"And folderols and gimcracks. I swear they must've used two tons of gold paint and a couple acres of silks and velvets. If they could put a tassel on something, they put six."

She shook her head as they walked past art—more cavorting cherubs, women in filmy, flowing white robes, men with swords or bows—and all framed in ornate gold frames.

"I took one walk through this place, and named my price as double what I usually charge. Mrs. Betz didn't so much as blink, so that's fine for both of us. Lieutenant Dallas, they got themselves his and hers bathrooms off the master. Not unusual, but he's got a full bar in his. A bar, with stools and everything, and she's got herself a long divan in pink silk, and a wine friggie. In the bathroom. I mean to say, I don't know anybody who does much entertaining in the toilet, no matter how fancy it is."

They passed archways leading to rooms packed with furniture, and with furniture so loaded with pillows (hundreds of tassels) no one could possibly fit their ass on a cushion.

She didn't know what she'd expected in the kitchen, but bright, bloody red was the signature color.

A half mile of cabinets gleamed red, as did the appliances: the two massive refrigerators, the wall ovens, the cooktop. The counters were a sea of white and the floor a spread of midnight black.

"Horrible, isn't it? I do for a lot of people, and everybody's got their own taste and style. But this one? My mama says it takes the cake and two slices of pie with it."

Sila moved around the center island, took a jog left to a door—red, of course—carved with people in various states of undress gorging themselves from bowls of fruit, from fruit hanging from trees or growing fat on bushes, from fruit clutched in other figures' hands.

"They keep the droids in here. House droid, and its backup," Sila said as she gestured. "The vac droid, the scrubber droid, and so on. But this one's the, well, head droid, you'd say."

Eve approached the dark-suited droid. Tall, slim, dignified, with some whiffs of Summerset to her eye. He'd been designed with dark hair winged with silver, thin lips, and edgy cheekbones.

Eve glanced back, saw Peabody nod, hold up a finger, continue the conversation on her 'link. So Eve stepped in, angled her head, and started searching for the manual power up.

It pleased her when she found it, under the left wing of hair.

The droid made a quiet hum, then the pale blue eyes jittered, blinked, focused.

"Good morning," it said in the same fruity Brit as the intercom comp. "I am called Stevens. I'm afraid I'm not programmed to assist you today without the authorization of Mr. or Mrs. Betz."

Eve took out her badge. "Scan and verify. I'm here on police business. I need information. You can give me that information or I'll have you taken into Central where EDD will extract said information."

"One moment."

"Yeah, yeah."

"Your identification is verified. Dallas, Lieutenant Eve. Is there a police emergency?"

"Let's hope not."

"Dallas."

Eve pointed at the droid to signal wait, turned to Peabody.

"His admin says he's expected in this morning. He plans

to join his wife, but didn't leave with her. She left yesterday morning, and as of now, his plans are to leave tomorrow or the day after."

Eve turned back to the droid. "When did Mr. Betz leave the premises?"

"I am unable to answer accurately. Mrs. Betz shut me down at ten-thirty-eight yesterday morning at her departure. Mr. Betz had already left the residence. He departed for his office at approximately nine-fifteen."

"His return?"

"I am unable to answer accurately as I have been on off mode since ten-thirty-eight yesterday morning."

"Would Betz generally put you back on when he returned?"

"Most usually, yes."

"How does Mr. Betz get to work?"

"He engages a driver. Royal Limo and Transportation Service. His most usual driver is George. I regret I have no last name."

"Peabody."

"On it."

"Do you know if Mr. Betz had any appointments scheduled yesterday, appointments here, in the residence?"

"No such appointment was programmed into my calendar."

Maybe he hadn't had one, Eve thought, and they'd taken him by surprise.

But they'd taken him.

"I'm going to need contact information for Mrs. Betz, and I need to know where the security center is in this residence. Security center first."

"Dallas, he didn't order his driver for this morning."

"Yeah, I figured."

The droid led her through a second door, and one look told her everything.

"Hard drive and disc are gone. And so's Betz. They've got him."

She turned to see Sila in the doorway, arms clutching her

middle, hands clutching her elbows. "Oh my God, Lieutenant. Oh my God. Do you think he's . . . we haven't been all through the house yet. Do you think he's . . ."

"Not yet, but we'll go through it. I want you to get your mother and . . . Dara, right? Get them downstairs, into the room at the front. I'm going to need you to tell us exactly what you touched this morning. Peabody—"

"Contacting EDD. Do you want Baxter and Trueheart?"

"Send them to the admin. Send EDD there, too. We'll probably need a warrant, but I figure we've got cause at this point. Let's have somebody sit on the Easterday house, and see about getting protection for the others. They're probably all right for the moment, but we won't risk it."

It might be too late for Betz, she thought, and that would make it three for three. But she'd be damned if she'd let them add another to their scoreboard.

Chapter 15

Eve gathered the cleaning team, and got the first buzz from the "retired" Frankie.

"We started on the master—it's big as a house on its own, especially with the two bathrooms and all the fuss. Started with the bathrooms, and the two sitting rooms. And Sila said why didn't I go ahead and work on the baby's room, so I was just about to when she came down to let you in, then you called us off."

"Okay. Anything strike you?"

"Not there, no, but when you called us off, I thought, Why, something's going on here, so I poked into the guest suite—the gold one. That's the big one, opposite end of the house from the master. And it was set up."

"Set up how?"

She curled her lip, just a little. "For what we'll call a rendezvous. There's a bottle of French champagne in a silver bucket up there—sitting in water now, as the ice melted. Got two fancy flutes, and some strawberries been dipped in chocolate. White and dark, though white's not really chocolate, is it?"

"It's okay," Eve heard herself say.

"There's a rose on the pillow on one side of the bed, and since I was poking, I looked in the drawer of the nightstand, and there's what you'd call adult play toys, and the like. I'd say the mister was expecting someone not his wife, like he has before."

"Before?"

"Twice since we've been working here I've done that room. Both times when we knew the missus was away for a day or two that room was used. The bed was used—and I've been doing beds long enough to know when somebody's had relations in that bed. There'd be that, and the bucket, the empty bottle, the glasses, and so on. The setup. Bathroom would've been used, too. Nobody used the bed or the bath in there this time, but it was set up for relations."

"Mama." Sila shook her head. "*You* take the cake and a slice of pie."

"It's a terrible thing happened to Senator Mira—and now this other man. I know because while we were waiting upstairs I had Dara look on her handheld to see if there's been another murder, and there was. A terrible thing, though I didn't like Senator Mira as far as I could spit rocks. But a man shouldn't be killed, and killed so mean, just because he's a prick."

Dara giggled, then slapped her hand over her mouth. "Sorry."

"No problem. Mrs. Trent, that's really helpful. Did you notice anything else?"

Frankie sucked air in her nose, furrowed her brow. "Well, I don't know how much help, but I think he changed out of his business suit when he came home. It was tossed in the chair in the master, and his good shoes were under the chair. Nobody in this house puts a thing away proper. I can't tell you what he put on, but it looks to me like he came home, took himself a shower in the master bath, and put on fresh clothes. Then he went about setting up for relations in that guest suite. I guess he doesn't think it counts if he doesn't take them into the bed he shares with his wife. Put your hand over your mouth in advance, Dara, because I'm going to say a man who cheats is a prick, but I hope he doesn't get killed for it."

Since Eve thought the same, she couldn't argue.

She asked a few more questions, just to see if something else popped up. Then let them go.

Peabody joined Eve in the hallway.

"I got ahold of the wife," Peabody began. "Played it light, and she's too involved in her morning massage to clue in. Plus, dumb as a brick, which I'm pretty sure is an insult to bricks. She says 'Freddy' will be joining her tomorrow or maybe the day after. She needed a little alone time first. *Alone* means a house full of staff, her personal assistant, the two nannies, and her masseur. His name is Sven."

"If her husband ends up dead, she'll have plenty of alone time. Frankie Trent says he uses a guest suite upstairs for sex when his wife's away, and it's set up for same now. Unused, but set up."

She gave a come-ahead head jerk and started up. "She said twice in the six months they've worked here, she's cleaned up that room while he's supposedly having *his* alone time."

"Jeez, why doesn't he go to a hotel for it?"

"My guess? He thinks this is more discreet, and he's lazy. Woman comes here, he wines her and bangs her, then she goes home. He just rolls himself down to his own room, sleeps in his own bed."

"How does anyone live with all this red?" Peabody scowled down at the red carpet. "And all the gold braid? Oh, and I wandered into what I guess is the formal dining room. All the walls are mirrored, and so's the ceiling. How can you eat when you're watching yourself eat? I don't know how—"

"Screaming Jesus Christ!"

At Eve's shout—nearly a shriek—Peabody drew her weapon. "What? What?"

"In there. Oh, Christ on a catapult, they're *everywhere*."

Slowly, reluctantly, Peabody turned, half expecting a

room filled with giant, hairy spiders. Hairy, red-eyed spiders.

And faced a room filled with dolls.

Baby dolls, glamour dolls, smiling dolls, crying dolls. Dolls *en pointe* in tutus and dolls in swaddling clothes. Dolls with tiaras, dolls with fur coats, dolls in native costumes of every culture and land.

Dolls as small as her hand. Dolls the size of a healthy toddler.

Peabody liked dolls fine—had played with her share and never quite understood her partner's deep phobia. But the sight of them, of *hundreds* of them, had her backing up a pace.

"I . . . think we should close the door."

"I think we should lock it. I think we should barricade it. That one." Eve pointed. Slowly. "That one over there on the horse thing. I think it blinked."

Peabody cast a leery eye toward the cowgirl doll with her smiling face and pink hat. "She did not. You're weirding me out."

"You're seeing what I'm seeing, and I'm weirding you out? Who does this? What kind of sick, twisted mind has a room full of dead-eyed little humans on display?"

"I don't want to know." Holding her breath, Peabody reached out—slowly, slowly—then pulled the door shut with a loud *snap*.

"That many of them?" Eve said. "Oh, they can get out if they want."

"Stop it. Just stop it." Peabody hustled down the hall, and kept her weapon out until she was two yards away. "Don't say anything more about them. Nothing. Sex and murder. Let's just think about sex and murder."

Eve walked into the guest suite—cast one glance over her shoulder (just in case)—then got down to business.

"Frankie isn't wrong. Betz was expecting sex company. Unopened champagne, two glasses, the strawberries, rose on the bed."

She opened the drawer of the bedside table. "Vibrators,

a variety, glides in various flavors. Condoms, also flavored. Nipple clamps—jeweled."

"Ouch."

"Some get off on the ouch. Velvet cuffs. And, some Erotica, some Stay Up, other chemical boosts. Illegal ones mixed in. But they never got up here. Took him out downstairs, easy and quick, I bet. Stun to the groin. No bashing him around here. They learned that the first time. Stun him, get him out of the house and into their transportation. He let them in. Maybe he had a double scheduled, maybe he thought he got lucky. Maybe they just caught him off guard, but he let them in, and they took him out."

"If they took him last night, they took him while they still had Wymann."

"Yeah, they're the ones who had a twofer." Eve thought of the big, gaudy chandelier in the entranceway. "They'll want to string him up tonight."

"Following pattern, they'll bring him back here."

"When and if they do, we'll be all over them. We're going silent on Betz. No chatter, no media, no alerts. Meanwhile, let's see if we can find out the name of his date for last night."

They started for the master suite, giving the doll room a wide berth. The doorbell pealed.

"I'll take it—probably EDD."

Peabody stopped dead. "You're going to leave me up here? Alone? With *them*?"

"You're armed. They probably aren't. Check his nightstand, his closet, and his bathroom. If he's hiding anything from his wife, those are likely the places they'll be."

She checked the screen downstairs, saw McNab with his long tail of blond hair under a big, wooly cap with striped earflaps. And to her surprise, her former partner and the captain of EDD. Feeney, his wiry ginger hair uncovered, and his hands deep in the pockets of the magic coat she'd given him.

She hit the locks, opened the door. "Didn't figure I'd rate the brass."

"Gotta get out in the field now and then, kid. And with you shooting for three in three days, you rate. What the hell kind of door is this?"

"Wild to the mega," McNab said, "and deep into bizarro."

"It's just the entrance into bizarro. There's a room upstairs that'd curl McNab's hair."

"S and M?" Feeney asked.

"Dolls. A zillion dolls."

Feeney hissed through his teeth. "Sick fucks." Hands still in his pockets, Feeney lifted his droopy eyes to the gold chandelier. "That's where they'd want to hang him. Right over those weird fat fish. Good security. No forced entry on the other two, right?"

"None, and unlikely here. You can clear that, but here's the rundown as I see it."

While she briefed them, McNab went over the security on the front entrance.

"Crotch tattoos and sidepieces." Feeney shrugged. "It's a stretch to sex club—more a rape club. But you got two of them done the way they were done? Somebody's really pissed off."

"They start off stunning them in the balls, Feeney, and sodomize them using the ever-popular hot poker. That's more than really pissed."

"Can't argue. It's got sex all over it, and it don't feel like any of that woman scorned crap. Me and the boy here will take the electronics. You got a club, you got a roster or rules put down somewhere."

"Nobody came through the front without the codes," McNab told them. "I'll check the other doors, the windows. She-Body upstairs?"

"Yeah—no ass-grabbing. Like I said, he was expecting company, and it wasn't the first time. We need to cross off break-in, but he let her in—or them. So he knew at least the one he was planning on sexing, but she didn't worry him. He knew about Edward Mira, had to. But he wasn't worried."

"They got him? He's worried now. He got a home office?" Feeney asked. "I'll start there."

"Third floor, according to the cleaning crew. I haven't been through yet. Let me check with Peabody, and I'll find you. I want to look at his personal spaces."

She found Peabody in Betz's closet.

"More sex stuff, both nightstands. His and hers goodie drawers," Peabody said. "Makes me think the stuff in the guest room is reserved for women other than his wife."

"Well, that's delicate of him."

"He's got a closet comp—wardrobe in categories—and I haven't finished, but I'm not finding any evidence he packed for a trip. There's a notation that he removed black silk boxers, gray twill trousers, a navy blue cashmere crew neck sweater, gray loafers, and navy blue cashmere socks. The comp says those items came out at six-sixteen P.M., yesterday. There's also a jewelry safe. It's locked."

"We'll have McNab or Feeney take a look."

"Feeney's here?"

"McNab's on doors and windows, Feeney's starting in Betz's office. If you've got this, I'm going to take the office, any place else he might claim as just his."

"I got this." Stepping back, Peabody fisted her hands on her hips, turned a circle. "I keep thinking there should be some hidey-hole. If he's into something bad, he wouldn't leave anything about it in his workplace, right? I mean, less likely to leave it where some nosy somebody might stumble on it. And here? He'd want it hidden away from his wife. She was a sidepiece before, right?"

"That's right."

"So cheat with me, cheat on me. That's my thinking. I figure she probably gets into his stuff now and then, just checking. Or even if she doesn't maybe he'd figure she might. So where's she going to look?"

"His personal spaces," Eve agreed, and frowning, studied the room-sized closet. "False wall, false drawer, hidden floor access."

"If it's here, I haven't found it yet, but I'm going through with that in mind."

"Good thinking."

"I'm not checking in that creepy doll room." Face set, Peabody swiped a hand through the air. "I draw the line."

"He doesn't strike me as a guy who plays with dolls. That's her space."

"Just so we're clear."

"I'm on the third floor. If we need more hands and eyes, I'll pull in Baxter and Trueheart."

"Maybe you could tap Roarke—if he has some free time. If there's any hidey-hole, he'd find it."

"I'll keep that in my back pocket."

If there was a secret panel, drawer, safe, hole, Eve thought as she climbed to the third floor, Roarke would find it, and quicker than any cop.

But she couldn't tap him, ask him to toss off whatever world-shaking meeting he might be in to follow her partner's hunch. A good hunch, Eve thought, but still only that.

But like Peabody, she'd look with that in mind.

Betz's office space proved as ornate as the rest. The desk must've been custom-made, as it had the frisky cherubs carved into its heavy, dark wood. The top was a marble slab with a lot of silver squiggles and flecks running through the black. Behind it sat a throne-like leather chair in bright gold. The combination put her teeth on edge.

If this decorator Roarke hired suggested anything remotely close to this scheme, Eve decided she'd deserve a boot out the window. She'd just keep that in mind, too.

Feeney sat on the throne, looking rumpled, wrinkled, and normal.

"This butt-ugly desk has two locking drawers. Neither locked now."

"Is that so?"

"It looks to me like somebody riffled through them pretty good."

She crossed to him over red carpet so thick she wondered it didn't suck the boots off her feet. Both bottom drawers were fitted with keypad locks. Feeney had them both open.

"Paper files?"

"Looks like house and personal stuff in one, work stuff

in the other. Finances, insurance, repairs, like that. Lot of people don't trust digital, keep paper backups. You're one of them."

"Yeah." She fingered through. "Either he's disorganized and messy, or someone went through these, at least superficially. Looking for what?"

"Can't say, but the desk comp was riffled with, too. Full scan and search executed at nineteen-twelve."

"He changed clothes about an hour before that—closet comp—getting ready for his date. Date comes in, with a friend because there's two of them, and likely three. Stuns him, maybe roughs him up a little. We didn't see anything like this at Wymann's, but I'm going back, looking again. What did they want here?"

She circled the office with its hard colors, elaborate space.

"Nothing to find in the Spring Street house, and they can't get into the Mira penthouse."

"Tortured him."

She turned back, nodded. "Yeah, and maybe he gave them something on Betz. Betz has this or that. Maybe, like you said, that roster, those rules, something on this brotherhood of theirs. But what's the difference if they're going to kill them anyway? It's not like they're looking for evidence. They've already tried and convicted."

She looked behind art of strange, long-bodied dogs and rearing horses.

Finding nothing, anywhere, she looked back at Feeney as he busied himself checking 'link transmissions.

"You cheated on your wife."

He kept working. "Not if I wanna live past Tuesday."

"Think like a cheat. You end up marrying one of the women you cheated with. You're still cheating—it's what you do. Do you keep anything to do with your sidepieces, and more, anything to do with something that would turn a woman murderous, where the current wife could find it?"

"Me? I'd have a separate account she didn't know about, maybe a bank box, too. And, if I'm rich like this asshole,

I've got a place she doesn't know about. If I had a place when I was cheating with her, it's gone, sold, done when I'm cheating *on* her. Anything I did cheating with her, I switch up now."

"A place. A place," she murmured. "Like Edward Mira had the hotel. His wife knew he cheated, so he didn't have to worry about it. Wymann wasn't married—I'm still waiting for Roarke to tell me if he used the hotel. We'll do the same with Betz. But, a place. A place just for sex. You can only have it here when your wife's out of town, and you really like cheating.

"He'd need a key, a swipe, codes, something. And he wouldn't keep it in a desk drawer, even a locked one, where his wife might get to it."

She opened a door, looked into a red and silver powder room, turned and studied the bar in the corner of the office.

"I bet I know where she doesn't go."

Eve walked out, jogged downstairs, back into the master.

She found Peabody and McNab beside the huge red (naturally) bed with its avalanche of pillows. They had a look in their eyes, but fortunately for them nobody's hands were on anybody's ass.

"I don't think anybody broke in a second-story window."

"Nobody broke in anywhere," McNab told her. "Two other doors on the main, and neither of them have been opened for twenty-six hours. The windows haven't been opened for weeks. I figured I'd take the 'links and comps in here."

"Is that what you figured?"

He grinned. "Abso-true. And hang with She-Body while I'm at it."

Saying nothing, she walked over, looked into the hers bathroom.

As she suspected, it was filled with frills and a carnival full of pink.

The cleaning crew had started there, so fresh pink towels and white towels with pink edging were stacked on a painted bench or hung on a standing rack. Surfaces—all pink and white—shined, and the air gave off a faint whiff of citrus. Jars of various girl products stood on the long counter between two pink vessel sinks. The faucets were silver mermaids, and that motif was repeated in the triple-glass shower.

In addition to the divan—pink-and-white stripes—there was a curvy vanity; drawers full of creams, lotions, enhancements; a closet filled with various robes and slippers; a mini AutoChef and friggie built into the wall.

The toilet rated its own little room with mermaid art and a wall screen.

She stepped back out. "Have you been in there?"

"Yeah. Any woman would kill for a bathroom that size all her own. But she showed how even that mag space can be ruined."

"Her side. Her bath, her closet/dressing room, her sitting room, her side of the bed, her dresser—the one with all the pink bottles. Right?"

"Yeah. His side." Peabody jerked a thumb. "You know they've got a toddler, but you don't see any kid stuff in here. Not even a stray teddy bear. It's a little sad."

"When your nanny has a helper, you don't spend a lot of time with the kid, and this space is adults only. With a definite line of demarcation. Anyway, you're the woman of the house."

"I'm the queen of my castle," Peabody agreed, and got a wink from McNab.

"This house, Peabody. Keep up. You've got staff and servants, and three floors to decorate into terrible death. Where's the one room you don't go into?"

"The doll room. Okay, that's just me. She must like dolls. Well, from my brief conversation with her, I'd cross off the laundry facilities. That's staff territory. And she probably doesn't go into the kitchen much."

"Try this. What's the one place he goes you don't go?"

"I . . . his bathroom!" Peabody shot her two index fingers in the air. "She's all pink and shiny in hers, and his is full of man. What woman wants to go into a bathroom after a guy?"

"We do all right," McNab said.

"Abso-true." But when his back was turned again, Peabody rolled her eyes at Eve. "You're thinking potential hidey-hole."

"Let's check it out."

If the hers bathroom was an explosion of pink and fuss, the his was a study in desperate masculinity. Black tile with red flashes covered the floors, the walls. The odd addition of a bar—red, with cherub carvings—along one wall stood before a portrait of a zaftig reclining woman eating a fat purple plum. The black counter held a large square of red sink with a wolf's head faucet that would vomit out the water.

Shelves held bottles and bowls, the manly versions of creams and lotions and oils, as they were all cased in red or black leather.

The rest of the wolf pack occupied the shower, where they'd spit out water from the showerhead and jets.

The drying tube had a padded bench, in case its occupant grew too tired and needed to rest in the two minutes it took to dry most humans.

He had a vanity of his own, fashioned to resemble a desk. Peabody started there.

"I think this may be uglier than hers, but it's neck and neck," Peabody said. "Wow, he's got as many face and body enhancements in here as she does—almost. Big on the tanners and bronzers, and hair products. This vanity's an eyesore, Dallas, but it's well-constructed. I'm not finding anything out of proportion, nothing that looks like a secret compartment."

"How about the bar?" Eve circled around it. "You've got a good eye for compartments."

It was how Peabody had first come to her notice, as a uniform finding a hidey-hole in a murderer's apartment.

"Well. Again, really good work wasted on the ugly."

Peabody swiveled on the vanity stool, studied the bar from that perspective. "All that carving—I mean it mirrors what they've got all through the house, but it's also the kind of thing that can hide a mechanism. And a cabinetmaker this good? He could hide one really well. My dad's done some totally mag hideys."

She angled her head as Eve ran her hands over cherubs. "Maybe microgoggles would help—if there's anything to see."

"Go get some from the field kits."

Eve hunkered down, putting aside how odd it was to rub her fingers all over fat, naked butts.

Wouldn't be on the front face, she decided. What if someone inadvertently hit the release? If there was one.

She straightened, moved around the back.

Glasses and mixers and liquor on shelves, and a single cabinet with the carved front. She opened it, peered in at the ice machine, the wine friggie.

Closed it again, opened it. Closed it.

"Got the goggles."

"Why have a door in front of the ice-maker thing, the wine friggie? Anytime you want ice, you have to open the door. Everything else is on open shelves. Handy."

"Could just be the design. Or he didn't want the mechanics to show."

"Maybe. But how deep are these units? They wouldn't be the depth of the bar, right?"

Now Peabody hunkered down beside her. "Dad and Zeke have made some nice bars—fully outfitted, custom. One this size . . . Seems like the ice deal wouldn't need that much depth."

Eve closed the door again, wiggled her fingers for the goggles. With them on, she began to scan inch by inch.

"This one." Eyes huge behind the goggles, Peabody gripped a cherub butt between her fingers. It turned fractionally.

"Why does it turn and not open any damn thing?"

"A code or a pattern," Peabody muttered, "like a puzzle. Yeah, yeah, I've seen this kind of thing. We have to figure out which ones to turn, in what order. It's pretty damn clever. It's really good work."

"I'm getting a hammer."

"No!" Sincerely appalled, Peabody scooted over. "I can figure it out. Give me a little room. You can't bust up this kind of work."

"It's fucking ugly."

"It's still art. Here! Here's another. I bet there's three. A combo of three. We've got this."

Eve would've preferred the hammer, but since she didn't have one handy, she let Peabody tap and twist and rub cherubs.

"Hey, Dallas?" McNab stepped to the doorway. "I've got a transmission from Marshall Easterday, unanswered. It came in today, at eight-fifty-two."

"Right after we talked to him," Eve said. "About the time he went upstairs 'to rest.'"

"He doesn't sound restful. He says it's urgent they speak, and says he's tried his personal 'link, tried the office. Guy's sweating scared, LT."

"He should be." Eve started to push up, to listen for herself, when something clicked and Peabody let out a "Woo!" When she opened the door, the shelves holding the ice machine and friggie slowly swung open.

"Frosted," McNab said, coming in to hunker down with them.

As they were hip to hip, Eve caught his scent and thought of cherry lollipops.

A small silver box sat in the hidden compartment. Eve pulled it out, stood, set it on the bar top.

"That's old," Peabody said. "Like antique old. I know it's locked, Dallas, but you can't just smash it."

"McNab, get my field kit, would you?"

"Sure." He rose, turned, grinned. "Hey, Captain, my girl found a secret compartment in the john bar, and we got ourselves an antique box."

"What kind of sick fun house is this?" Feeney wondered as he looked around. Curious, he poked at a power pad. The black tiles shimmered into mirrors. "Oh, hell no," he said and deactivated. "Dug out an e-mail from Marshall Easterday on the office comp."

"From this morning," Eve said.

"Yeah. Copied to an Ethan MacNamee. Marked urgent. 'My brothers,'" he quoted, "'beware. Contact me immediately. Seek safety. Come home.'"

"'Come home,'" Eve murmured.

"Got your field kit." McNab brought it in, set it beside the box. "We could scan that thing and work on getting it open back at Central."

"Give me a minute."

From the field kit, Eve took a small leather wallet (a gift from Roarke), opened it, and selected lock picks.

"Extra frosted," was McNab's opinion.

"We'll see about that." She went to work and, as Roarke had taught her, used her ears, her instincts as much as the feel.

"Step back." Annoyed, she rolled her shoulders. "You're crowding me. Just stop breathing all over me."

Maybe Roarke would have had it open in a finger snap, but she felt enormous satisfaction when after three struggling minutes, the lock fell.

"New skills," Peabody said.

"I've been practicing." Eve opened the lid, looked at the two large, old-fashioned keys and the two twenty-first-century key swipes resting on dark blue velvet.

"Little hidey-hole to hold the keys to bigger ones. Old doors," Eve decided. "Those are too big for anything but doors—I think. And new doors."

She used tweezers to pick up one of the swipes, turned it. "No logo, no name or code. Probably a code buried in it, right? Can you get that out, Feeney?"

"I'd have to turn in my bars if I couldn't."

McNab pulled a scanner out of one of the dozen pockets in his neon orange baggies, offered it to Feeney.

"Let's have a look."

Feeney ran it, frowned. "Got a shield, and we can break that down. This kind of code and protection? It's probably a bank box or a secured area. He's a chem guy, right? So maybe a secured area, lab deal. Let's see the other."

He repeated the process. "Shielded, but thinner—this isn't the high-security level."

He did something to McNab's scanner that made it whine, picked up and put on Eve's goggles. He scanned the first swipe again.

"Security code for the swiper. And . . . Can just make it out. LNB. FKB. Ah . . . 842."

"FKB—Frederick Kyle Betz. LNB. That's not the name of his company. Maybe a bank?"

Feeney nodded. "More likely. Too simple below the shield for a high security area. So, bank box, I'm thinking. Liberty National's my best guess. They got branches everywhere."

"And the number, that would be the box." Eve nodded, looked ahead. "We're going to need another warrant. Peabody, tag Reo. We need authorization, enough to pry out whether or not Betz has a box in the branches we're going to be contacting. And the authorization to go into said box when we locate it. What about the other one?" she asked Feeney.

"Back up once. We take this in, we maybe can ID the branch. It's too deep an embed for a handheld. Save you making half a million contacts."

"Do that," Eve agreed.

"And this one." He repeated the process. "Got his initials again, and numbers: 5206."

"Just that? But not another bank?"

"Doesn't read bank to me. Maybe a mail drop or a locker. Or an address. People lose their swipe, they cancel, get another. What you don't want is data embedded that leads somebody where it goes so they can use it before you cancel. We'll take them back to the shop, see what else we can dig out."

He looked back in the box at the keys. Studied them with his basset-hound eyes, rubbed his chin. "Those? That's a whole different kettle. Lab might be able to tell you what kind of lock, give you the age. But location's on you."

"Yeah. I've got some ideas on that."

She pulled Baxter and Trueheart in, continued to search the house while she waited for them. But her gut told her they'd already hit the mother lode.

She let them in herself. "Give me what you've got."

"It's not much. Lots of shock, and a few tears at Wymann's offices. We got the warrant and Callendar and another e-geek came in to take the electronics. The admin says she thinks the biographer approached Wymann, maybe at a party. He made the follow-up appointment himself, had the admin put it in his schedule. She herself never saw the woman or spoke with her. It seems spur-of-the-moment."

"Any sense he was dipping in the office pool?"

"Nope. But Trueheart turned his earnest young detective's face on the admin and eased a couple names out of her. No cross with your first vic's ladies. We talked to both of them, and the alibis look solid."

He looked around. "Is that a koi pond? Who has a koi pond twelve steps inside their front door? Then again, who has a fat baby orgy on their front door?"

"You haven't seen half of it. Here's where we stand."

She gave him the progress.

"I've *got* to see this bathroom."

"You'll have time. The two of you need to sit on the house in case the killers decide to bring him back and hang him over the koi pond. I need to get back in the field, check out a couple leads. Most likely is they bring him back in after dark, but you sit on it, and I'm getting backup on the off chance they come before I can get back."

She held up a finger when her 'link sounded. "Dallas," she began, pacing away.

When she paced back, she shouted, "Peabody!"

"I don't get having fish in the house." Baxter stood looking down at koi. "It's unnatural."

"I used to win a goldfish every summer at the county fair. Ringtoss," Trueheart said. "It never made it through the fall."

"See, unnatural."

"You want unnatural? There's a room full of dolls on the second floor."

"Well, don't they have a little girl?" Trueheart began.

"If a kid walked in that room, her screams would be heard from here to Queens, and she'd be traumatized for life. I'm saying hundreds of dolls. Staring dolls. Staring-at-the-door dolls. Waiting dolls."

"Jesus, Dallas." Muttering it, Baxter shuddered.

"They're up there. We're heading out," she said as Peabody came down the stairs. "Detective Bennet cleared the path to the social worker."

"Mike Bennet? Nice guy," Baxter said.

"Sit on the house. Maybe feed those fish something. Nobody's been here since yesterday. Maybe they'll start eating each other."

"Staring dolls, cannibal fish. What the hell kind of place is this?"

"Sit tight. Stay alert. We don't want to add dead guy swinging over the cannibal fish."

"Did she give Mike any names?" Peabody asked, winding her long, long scarf as they started to the car.

"No, and he doesn't think she will. But she might give us a yes or no when we show her photos."

"That's a fine line."

"What I get is she likes him—that nice-guy vibe. And she really respects his future mothers-in-law. We push on how these people used Anson to kill Wymann, and if we don't stop them, will kill Betz, we've got a decent shot at getting a nod if we show her the right face."

The minute she was in the car, Peabody ordered the seat warmer. "Reo says hey, and that she'll have a warrant for us when we get the locations on the swipes. You never said what ideas you had about the old keys."

"Old keys, old doors. These guys go back to old times. Group house. Maybe they've still got it. Or another. A place they get together, as brothers."

"If so, and Betz went to all that trouble to hide the keys, it follows they go there, as brothers, to do stuff he doesn't want his wife to know about."

"If the senator had keys, he wouldn't bother hiding them. We'll get another warrant to go through his apartment, since it's easy money his wife won't cooperate. If Wymann had keys, we didn't look in the right place, with the right eye.

We're going to need to have this Ethan MacNamee picked up, arrange a 'link or holo interview."

"Senator Fordham?"

"Not one of them, but we'll leave his security detail to watch him, in case he's just a late entry. And let's get the file on the suicide: William Stevenson."

She answered the dash 'link when she noted Roarke's display. "Hey."

"I thought you'd want to know, security did the run-through at the hotel. Wymann has never registered, and doesn't show up on any feed in the last year."

"Okay. How about Frederick Betz?"

Roarke gave her a quiet stare. "Why don't you contact Lloyd Kowalski, at the Palace, and ask him whatever you like. Your middleman on this is a bit busy today."

"Sure, thanks. Just so you know, I didn't tap you when we were after a hidey-hole, or when we had a locked box. Peabody found the hole, I picked the lock."

"I'm so proud of both of you. Don't skip lunch again, and if you need me I'll be much more free after three."

"Okay. Might need a copter and a pilot."

"Now, that's so much more fun than talking to Kowalski. Let me know. Later," he added and clicked off.

"Copter? Pilot?"

"Group house—if it's still standing, I want a look at it once we find it. Maybe those keys fit a door there, maybe they don't. But I'd like to see it either way. Once we find out where the hell it is."

"I can dig it up—it'll take some time unless one of them owned or owns it. Maybe Mr. Mira knows."

Eve let out a sigh, and once again went on the hunt for a parking space. "Yeah. He might know. We'll ask before we dig."

Suzanne Lipski had a cramped little office space in a dilapidated building that housed a rape crisis center. The center did its best, Eve imagined, with whatever funding it could scrape up, to offer support, information, medical and emotional assistance to victims. The walls of that space—one smaller than her division at Central—held soothing and uplifting posters. Calm water, misty forests, sunny beaches. And a bulletin board full of emergency numbers, counseling information, support group information.

Eve stopped, studied a flyer—a pretty summer meadow under a perfect blue sky—for Inner Peace.

"Bang," she murmured.

Lipski sat at a battered, overburdened metal desk on a squeaky swivel chair. She had no window, but a pot of greenery thrived on an ancient file cabinet under some sort of grow light.

She was a bone-thin woman of about sixty, with a messily curling mop of stone-gray hair. Her face was long, narrow, and brown as a cashew. She had dark eyes that told Eve the woman had seen it all, and was fully expecting to see it all again before she was done.

"We appreciate you seeing us," Eve began.

"Mike's persuasive. You're doing your job, and I don't fault you for it. In fact, thanks for your service, sincerely. But I have to do mine. The women who come here, to the support groups I head, to the shelters I endorse, they're my priority and my responsibility. They've been raped, beaten, abused, had their security stripped from them. And too often, the law and society strips them all over again."

Eve wasn't going to argue, as too often it held true.

"The women I'm looking for have beaten, tortured, sodomized, and murdered two men. I believe they have another, and will end him by tonight. Whatever happened to them doesn't justify these actions."

"You don't know what might have happened to them."

Eve set photographs of the two victims on the desk. "This isn't justice served."

Lipski sat back, sighed. "These men. Powerful, influential, wealthy. Does it matter to you what they might have done to engender this sort of rage?"

"It matters. And if they raped their murderers, I would

have done everything within the law to bring them to justice."

"'Within the law.'" Lipski pointed a long, bony finger. "I believe in the law, Lieutenant, Detective. I couldn't sit here if I didn't. But there are times, and too many, when I believe the law is cold and hard and blind. And still, if I knew who'd done this I would try to convince them to stop, to turn themselves in."

"The first thing I'm going to tell you, and look at me," Eve demanded. "Look at me and hear what I'm telling you. If you know, or you figure out who's doing this, you do *not* contact them, do *not* approach them. What they're doing is done with a rage so cold it would turn on you. I believe they have three more targets, and they won't stop until they're finished, they won't stop because you reason with them, sympathize with them."

With her jaw set, Lipski peered up at Eve. "And what of those targets? If you stop them, if you lock them up for what they've done, what of the men they targeted?"

"If these men raped the women I lock up? If they abused and raped them, I don't care if they're as powerful, influential, and wealthy as God, I will bring them down."

Eve set her hands on the battered desk, leaned in. "But these women will kill again, and again. Now that they've gotten a taste for retribution, what's to stop them from targeting other men? This one raped, this one tuned up his girlfriend, this one *might* have raped. Is that what you serve here? You get raped, go after the rapist and kill him?"

"No, that's not what we serve here. But I believe in violence."

"Hey. Me, too."

For the first time the faintest smile cracked the stern, thin face. "Despite what we do, you and I, seeing, dealing with, living with violence every day of our lives, we believe in using it to protect and defend."

"This isn't for protection. This isn't for defense."

"If these men raped the women who killed them, their deaths protect women they would have raped."

"Are we condemning people for crimes not yet committed? I'm not here to debate with you over what rape does to the body, to the mind, to the spirit. I'm here about murder.

"Charity Downing, Lydia Su, Carlee MacKensie, Allyson Byson, Asha Coppola, Lauren Canford. Do you know any of these women?"

Lipski's chin jutted up while her arms folded over her bony chest. "I can't and won't disclose any confidential information about any woman who has come into this center."

"The support groups. Cecily Anson and Anne Vine volunteer in some of the groups you're associated with. Ms. Anson's name was used to lure this man." Eve jabbed a finger on the crime scene photo of Wymann.

"Her time, her compassion, her generosity have been twisted into a tool for someone's revenge."

"And I'm appalled." Lipski pressed her thin lips together, and genuine anger flared in her eyes. "I'm talking to you now because using them pisses me off. CeCe and Annie are two of the kindest people I know. And still, if one of these women attended one of their groups, they're under no obligation to give their name, and even when names are used, we only use the first name. Anonymity is an essential brick in the wall, Lieutenant. Added to it, I simply don't know everyone who attends the groups. There aren't enough hours in the day to tend to all."

Eve glanced at Peabody.

"Maybe you'd recognize a face," Peabody began, and took out photos. "Um. I'm a Free-Ager."

Lipski lifted her brows, smiled more fully. "A Free-Ager cop. Rare."

"I walk a line, I guess. But one thing I know from how I was raised, and from the job. Cold-blooded revenge? It doesn't heal, Ms. Lipski. It only deepens the wound. The women who are doing this aren't going to find peace. They aren't going to erase the pain they may have endured by ending lives. If they're not stopped, they're never going to get over what was done to them. So . . ."

She held up Lauren Canford's photo, then Asha Coppola's.

Eve saw a kind of relief settle into Lipski's face, which remained when Peabody offered Allyson Byson.

"I don't believe I've seen any of those women before."

"I have a few more."

Peabody held up Lydia Su's ID shot.

Eve figured Lipski probably played a solid game of poker. But her skills weren't good enough to completely mask the quick awareness. She waited, saw something similar come with Charity Downing.

She started to speak, then saw something else when Peabody offered Carlee MacKensie. That was both an instant of puzzlement, and, Eve thought, deep sorrow.

"You recognized the last three," Eve said.

"I can't discuss this with you." But that acknowledgment remained in the dark eyes as she spoke. "Even if you get a warrant."

"I'm not going to get a warrant. I could threaten to arrest you for obstruction. I could threaten to charge you with accessory after the fact if you contact any of these women. I'm not going to do that, either. But I'm going to tell you, again, if you do contact them, they'll kill the man they have immediately, and very likely flee. You'll live with that death on your hands. What I intend to do is to bring them in, to prevent them from killing again, and to listen to their story."

"I don't and won't condone murder." Lipski stared down at the dead. "I don't and won't condone this level of retribution. But the crimes committed will carry a hard, long punishment. Victims victimized—by their own actions—yes, by their own. But also by the law."

"The law may be hard and cold—and I can be the same. It may be blind. I'm not. I need to hear them out. You know, and I know, my Free-Ager partner's right. What they're doing will only spread the wound until the wound is all they have. Let me do my job."

"I'll contact no one, my word on that—because I do know what's right. This, what was done, this isn't right. But when and if you arrest anyone, I want you to contact me. I want to be there for them. To do whatever I can for them."

"My word on that."

Eve moved fast, pulling out her 'link as they wound through the crowded space and out to the hall, down the stairwell. "Baxter, I've got three names verified. Downing, MacKensie, Su—be on the lookout for any or all of them."

"Three of them."

"It looks like. We're heading to MacKensie's now to pick her up. She's closest. I'll let you know when we have all three of them. Sit tight."

"You want BOLOs?" Peabody asked her as she jogged to keep up.

"Not yet. We need to get them into the box, start putting pressure on them. One will break. Send uniforms to pick up Su—two to her apartment, two to her workplace, just to cover it. We should be able to scoop up MacKensie, then get Downing before any of them know we're coming."

Eve went in hot, while Peabody ordered the uniforms, cutting the sirens a block from MacKensie's building. Rather than search for parking, she flipped on her On Duty light, double-parked.

The bitter resentment of other drivers and the frantic breaking of noise pollution laws slid off her back as she jogged to the sidewalk.

"Uniforms on their way, both locations. Even if Lipski breaks her word—and I don't think she will," Peabody added, "she wouldn't have time to warn all three before we move in."

"That's not what I'm worried about." Eve used her master, then charged up the stairs.

"Loose pants," she heard Peabody pant. "Loose pants."

"Get your mind off your ass."

On MacKensie's floor, Eve slowed to a walk. She pressed the buzzer, waited, then used a fist on the door.

"That's what I was worried about." She turned, pressed the buzzer on the door across the hall.

"I said I'd meet you down in the—" The woman who opened the door stopped short. "Who are you?"

"NYPSD." Eve held up her badge. "Where's Carlee MacKensie? Across the hall."

"How would I know?" The woman's forehead wrinkled under the big fuzzy black hat she wore. "Look, I'm running late. I was just heading out." To prove it she finished buttoning her coat. "Anyway, I think she's away for a while."

"Away where?"

"How should I know? I was heading out this morning at the same time she was. We rode down in the elevator together. She had a suitcase, so I asked—you know, neighborly—if she was taking a trip. And how it would be nice to get out of the city and the freaking cold. She said yeah. That's about it. I've got to go. I was supposed to work the rest of the day at home, but we got called back in. I have to go."

"One minute." Eve just shifted to block the woman's path. "What kind of suitcase?"

"Jeez, how should I know? A regular rolly. Taking a winter vacay—fixed up for traveling."

"Fixed up how?"

"Did her face and hair—and she hardly ever does, that I've seen. Had on nice boots. And perfume. I even said how I liked her perfume. You think she's done something, you're barking down the wrong alley. She hardly leaves her apartment, never has anyone over, that I've seen. Keeps to herself. Quiet, maybe stuck-up, maybe shy. I don't poke my nose in anyway."

"What time this morning?"

"Oh, jeez!" The woman looked pointedly at her wrist unit. "About eight-thirty, 'cause I was leaving for work."

"You went down together, so you went out together. Did she get in a cab?"

"Shit, like I'm supposed to keep tabs? No, now that I think about it. A car pulled up and she got in."

"A car?"

"Well, a van. The side door opened, and she got in with her rolly. I noticed because it was cold, and I thought how

I wished I had a ride instead of having to go down to the subway just to make the damn morning meeting."

"Describe the van."

"Well, for—" Her 'link signal, a blast of horns, had her digging into her handbag. "Don't give me a buncha crap, Georgie. I'm at the door, but so are the cops about Miss Mumbles across the hall. I don't know what the hell. Just wait for me."

She stuck the 'link away. "Now both me and Georgie are going to be late."

"The van," Eve pressed.

"How should I know? It was maybe white. Maybe. Not black anyway. Looked new. I had to get to the damn subway. I wasn't taking notes."

"Did you see the driver, another passenger?"

Now the woman heaved a sigh. "I don't know. Maybe. Maybe the windows were tinted, but maybe I caught a glimpse when the door opened of a woman driving. Petite, I thought she was so little to be driving that big van. Dark hair—in a pony—sunglasses. That's all I've got. Look, arrest me or let me go."

"Don't tempt me. Pictures, Peabody. Have you seen any of these women? And the more you bitch, the longer this is going to take."

"How come you can't find a cop when you need one, and when you don't they're in your face?" But she took the photos. "No, no, no, no . . . wait." She shuffled the photo of Charity Downing back to the top again. "Maybe. Yeah. Maybe. I saw her, maybe, a couple weeks ago. I was coming out of the building and she was going in. Wasn't watching where she was going, and shoulder-bumped me pretty hard. I started to give her a little what for, but she stopped and apologized. Looked like she'd been crying and was about to start up again. It was maybe about ten—I was meeting some friends, and running late. Ten at night," she qualified. "Boyfriend trouble's what I thought, since I've had some of my own. Anyway, pretty sure it was this one here. Only time I saw her around I can remember. I got a busy life, unlike Miss Mumbles."

"Why do you call her that?"

"It's what she does. If I happen to run into her in the lobby, or whatever—and that doesn't happen much—and I say the neighborly, she mumbles. Won't meet your eyes, either. Keeps her head down. Probably an axe murderer, right?"

Close enough, Eve thought. "If you remember anything else, contact us. If you see Ms. MacKensie again, contact us—and don't talk to her. Peabody, give Ms. . . ."

"Lacey. Deena Lacey."

"Give Ms. Lacey a card. Thanks for your help."

"I'll be showing my boss this card when he says he's going to dock me and Georgie for being late. You may get a tag from him."

"No problem."

Eve waited while the woman closed the door behind her and hurried to the elevator, yanking out her 'link as she went. "I'm heading down, Georgie. You won't believe this!"

"Get an update from the uniforms." Eve pulled out her own 'link. "Reo," she said without preamble. "I need a warrant."

She paced, relating the details to the APA, paced while Reo pushed for a warrant to enter and search MacKensie's apartment.

"Downing doesn't answer the door, and isn't at work—didn't work yesterday. Uniforms are talking to neighbors," Peabody reported. "Su hasn't shown up at work, doesn't answer her 'link, or her door. Looks like they've gone rabbit."

Eve shook her head. "Look at the timing. MacKensie packed up and got picked up—in a van, female driver—about an hour after we pushed on Su. But she took time to fix herself up? They're not running, not yet, because they've got Betz and they still want Easterday. They've gone to ground."

"You think we spooked them."

"I think they planned all this out, step-by-step, but it went off wrong for them right from the start, when Mr. Mira walked in on their session with his cousin."

She paced, trying to will the warrant through.

"Then the cops are on them a lot quicker than they

expected. Su's supposed to be questioned as an alibi, but we pushed there, pushed her on her connection with not just Downing but MacKensie. None of these women are idiots."

"So they panicked."

"Panicked? I don't think so. MacKensie fixed herself up, according to the neighbor. Makeup, hair, perfume. You don't take time for that if you're panicked. This is like Plan B. Things get too hot, we go to ground. She fixed up, so maybe she's the bait set to lure Easterday."

"They'd have to be crazy to go after him now."

"They've already spread the wound, Peabody. It's all there is. And they've got a place we don't know about, a place they make their plans, a place they can take these men and torture them, pay them back. Start digging now—any property under any variations of their names, mothers' names."

She yanked out her 'link. "Reo."

"Coming through now," Reo told her.

"I need two more. Lydia Su—that's *S-U*—and Charity Downing." She rattled off the addresses.

"Dallas."

"These three are working together, Reo. They've killed two and they've got number three. He's got hours at best if I don't find them."

"I'll push."

"Push fast. Warrant's coming through. I'll get back to you."

Eve checked the readout on the warrant—no mistakes now, she thought—then nodded to Peabody. "We're clear to enter."

She checked her recorder, used her master. Drew her weapon.

"Dallas, Lieutenant Eve, and Peabody, Detective Delia, entering residence of MacKensie, Carlee. We are duly warranted and authorized."

She gave the door one more good pounding. "Carlee Mac-Kensie, this is the police. We are entering the premises."

They took the door, high and low, did a quick sweep.

Eve straightened. "She's gone, and she isn't coming back."

"Furniture's still here."

"She cleared her workstation. She took the electronics. Let's clear the place, but she's gone."

The bed was tidily made, the bathroom and kitchen areas spotless. Never let it be said Carlee MacKensie didn't keep her area clean.

"It looks like some clothes are missing," Peabody said, "just by the way they're arranged, but she left plenty behind."

"Didn't matter to her. The mission matters. She took what she wanted—and didn't leave any electronics. Nothing we could use to trace her that way, nothing where she might have communicated with the others."

Eve circled the small, dull living area. "They all probably have a drop 'link. Something they use only with each other. If they use a comp, they use codes. But no chances taken: Don't leave any behind. But do you remember everything? Every little thing? Let's turn this place inside out and see."

"They didn't get the keys. Betz," Peabody said while they worked.

"Not his. Might be Wymann had the same, or the senator. We're dealing with a brotherhood there, so it's my take they all had keys. Just like we're dealing with a sisterhood on this end. United purposes, loyalties, a singularity."

Eve paused, closed a drawer, looked around. "No sign she had sex in this apartment. No toys, no enhancements, no sexwear."

"She could've taken that stuff with her."

"Why? It's not mission-oriented. She left clothes, some jewelry, photos, book discs, all the flotsam and jetsam of life. But she took the electronics, any spare discs, memo cubes, and any hard copies of business. Food in the kitchen, in the AutoChef. The neighbor claims not to poke in, but she's not blind and deaf."

Eve wandered, searched for a sense. What came to her was this was an alone place. She knew it, recognized it. She'd had one of her own once.

The apartment—the one Roarke had replicated for her.

Her alone place, because she'd had little but the mission—the job—in her life.

She knew MacKensie, she thought. She knew her under the skin.

"The neighbor? I bet she'd have remembered if MacKensie had a lover—male or female—show up regularly. There's no love in this place—just work and sleep. The neighbor remembered Downing because they bumped into each other, and Downing was crying. That stuck. She'd have remembered seeing her before, so either coming here hadn't happened before, or it was rare and they kept it on the down low."

"You think she and Downing are lovers?"

"No. I don't think she had anyone for that, not for that. They're sisters, that's what counts here. A shared experience—and one Su also shares. And a shared goal.

"What do you do when a sister comes over crying?"

"Ah. You listen, you sympathize."

"You provide alcohol and crying food. Let's check the kitchen."

They found a nearly empty bottle of white wine, a half-pint bottle of bourbon.

"Let's get the sweepers in here, do it right." Eve stepped over to the AutoChef, ran the program. "Keeps it pretty well stocked, healthy crap."

"Got ice cream—the real deal—in the freezer. Chocolate Coma, which is awesome. It's unopened, Dallas."

"Bet she got it to replace what she gave Downing. Downing comes to her, crying. How about this: Downing's the one they've got doing the senator. She's set up as his sidepiece. And she's wearing thin, doesn't see how she can keep going with it. Su doesn't strike as the have-a-drink-and-some-ice-cream type, so she comes here for sympathy. Comes here because MacKensie had played the same role earlier. MacKensie knew what she was dealing with, could empathize. And maybe because Downing's wearing thin, they decide to move on the mission."

"One of them poses as the Realtor," Peabody continued.

"Like posing as the biographer, and like—don't you think MacKensie was probably the one who got Edward Mira into Eclectia, so she could switch him off to Downing?"

"Yeah, I do. Taking turns with it, working on him."

"So the young, sexy Realtor, who isn't a Realtor, is willing to try to help the senator circumvent the deathbed promise."

"That's what plays. Unless there are four of them."

"Crap."

"Or more."

Chapter 16

They hit Downing's place next and found a much chattier neighbor. Laurel Esty lived in the apartment next to Downing's, and had already invited the uniforms inside her unit and given them coffee and cookies.

"She said she hasn't seen Downing in a couple days, but that's not unusual as she works nights. But her roommate mentioned seeing Downing leave the building with two suitcases this morning."

"Where's the roommate?"

"He'd be at work now, Lieutenant. We have his name and contact information."

"Give it to my partner, and brush the cookie crumbs off your uniform, Officer. For God's sake."

Eve moved past him to where a pert blonde sat on a little blue couch in the center of a comfortably disordered living area. She popped up like a woman on springs when Eve stepped in and nearly spilled the fizzy in her hand.

"Wow! I just tagged my roomie—Officer Tanker said it was okay if I did, and I told Reb—my roomie—how I heard Officer Tanker say to Officer Messing that Lieutenant Dallas was on the way. And Reb said, 'Bullshit, Laurie, no way.' And I said, 'True way, Reb,' but he didn't believe it. And here you are. We saw the vid. Julian is so completely iced, and Reb said when we did how he'd do you in one heart knock, and I . . . Gee, that's probably rude. Sorry. Can I tag him back and show him you're here?"

"No. You know Charity Downing?"

"Yeah, sure, she lives right next door. I don't see her much because I work nights over at the Silverado—urban cowboy bar, but we get some actual cowboys sometimes, and they—"

"When did you last see or speak with Miss Downing?"

"Oh, um, gee. A few days ago, I guess. I get home about three most nights, and she leaves about nine or sometimes ten. I'm usually out like a light by then. But we've chatted up some when we connect—days or nights off, or the laundry scene. She's really nice. Reb says she's a les but he's a guy and if a girl doesn't fall for his"—she made air quotes—"*charm*, she's a les. I don't count 'cause we've been buds since forever and don't screw around with each other like that even when we're not screwing around with anybody else. It's a pact."

"Great. Pictures, Peabody."

"I'm real sorry you died," Laurel said to Peabody. "I mean the actress who played you in the vid. She looked a lot like you. Is that weird?"

"A little. Do you know any of these women?"

"Oh." As if she just remembered she held it, Laurel put the fizzy down on a table. "You should sit down. I can get you a fizzy or some coffee, or whatev."

"That's okay. Take a look."

Laurel sat with the photos, caught her bottom lip between her teeth as she studied them. "I don't know them. Maybe it's because I work nights I never saw them come around. But I saw these two."

She held out Su's and MacKensie's photos.

"Where?" Eve demanded.

"In Charity's apartment."

"You just said you hadn't seen them come around."

"Not *them* them. But I saw them in the painting. One in Charity's place. She painted them, and herself and I think it was two other women. They all looked really sad, but really strong. I said that to Charity."

"Peabody, check it out. The other women aren't in this painting?"

"Uh-uh. One's old—I mean older. Like, I don't know, fifty? And the other looked really young, really sad. Really pretty. They were all really pretty. Anyway— Oh!"

She actually clapped her hands together, as if applauding herself.

"That was the last time. I remember now. See I got up for work, and Reb hadn't refilled the AutoChef. No coffee. Not enough anyway. And you know, it was desperate, and I went to Charity's to see if she had any to spare, and she was all, sure, I can hook you up. Then I had to pee. I went for the coffee even before I peed, so I said I need to pee, and she said I could use her bathroom. She has a two-bed unit like us, and she uses the spare for like a studio. For painting? And I saw the painting of the women, and the other one. The scary one."

"Scary?"

"I guess she'd tossed a cover over it, but it fell off, and there was this scary painting of these men—and it was like they were all screaming and falling into like a fiery pit in front of this big, spooky-looking horror vid house that was burning, too. You know, like hell. They were sort of wearing devil's masks, and nothing else. It kind of looked like they were supposed to be devils, but I only saw it for a second before Charity came out with the coffee, and walked over and closed the door."

Hunching her shoulders, Laurel flushed. "I wasn't poking in, I swear! It was just the door was open and I saw. That's not poking in. So I said I was sorry, I just glanced in. I don't think she was mad, but I could tell she didn't want me to say anything, so I didn't. I just said thanks for the coffee, and how she saved my life, and I left. That was a few days ago. Not like yesterday or the day before, but not like a week ago, either. Reb might remember because I told him about it. I texted him pretty quick because, you know, it was really scary and spooky."

"Would you be able to describe the two paintings, in more detail? The women's faces, the ones who aren't here. To a police artist."

"Oh." The bottom lip got the nibble treatment. "I don't know."

"Detective Yancy." Peabody came back in, smiling and flapping a hand over her heart.

"Really?" Laurel's lashes fluttered over eyes now sparkling with interest. "Well, maybe. Okay."

"Great. We'll arrange to have you taken down to work with Detective Yancy, and we appreciate the help," Eve added.

"Could I tag Reb? He's going to want to blow off work for this. And, honest, I'd feel better if he came with me, or met me there. He's, you know, like my brother. Like family."

"Sure, that's fine."

"Okay. I need to get dressed. Officer Tanker woke me up. Lieutenant Dallas? I don't see how Charity could've done anything really wrong, except . . ."

"Except?"

"That picture she painted. Of the devil-men? I only saw it for a second, but it gave me nightmares."

Eve walked next door with Peabody.

"No painting of women, or devil-men. Devil-men?"

"Men who looked like devils screaming as they fall into hell—with a burning house in the background."

"That is spooky. It sounds like she was painting out her issues."

They went inside. Like MacKensie's the apartment struck Eve as a place abandoned. Still furnished, flowering plants on a sunny window, but no electronics. Some painting supplies, and some canvases left behind. But none matched the ones Laurel had described. No handy sketches of any of the women.

"Fuckwear." Eve held up split crotch panties. "And a lot of it. She didn't take it because she's done with it."

"She took most of the toiletries, but left some old stuff, and I'm betting she missed this." Peabody came out with a small bottle. "Mixed in with skin creams. It's sleeping pills—the heavy-duty, put-me-out-till-morning kind."

"When we check her AutoChef, I'll bet we find regular programs for soothers and over-the-counter tranqs. She was the one in the trenches, so to speak, with Senator Mira. Wearing thin," she said again. "Sleeping pills and scary paintings. She'll break when we find them."

They repeated the process at Su's apartment. They didn't find an impatient neighbor or a gregarious one, but every indication Su had gone to ground with everything important to her.

"Hit building security," Eve told Peabody. "Get the discs for the last two days. Let's see her coming and going, and what she took when she went. It's going to be her van, so let's start checking on that."

"No vehicle registered in her name. I checked that already."

"She's got one. We'll check her parents' names. Failing that, I'm going to lean on our expert civilian consultant to find aliases. She's going to have a vehicle, and one of them owns or rents a house, a building, a place."

While Peabody hunted up security, Eve continued on the apartment. Su had lived well, she noted. A good space in a good building, what appeared to be carefully selected furnishings. Plenty of good-quality clothes left behind—because she didn't plan to come back.

She'd come from a stable family—or so it seemed, Eve thought. Got a top-drawer education, and had pursued a challenging career.

One that put her in a lab, Eve thought, probably working alone a great deal of the time. No sign or indication of romantic relationships.

Something happened at Yale, she thought again. Something that had put her on a path to ugly revenge. And on that path, she'd met Downing and MacKensie—and two other women, yet unidentified, if Downing's painting carried the weight Eve believed it did.

Most likely met them in group or the crisis center.

It cycled back to rape for her money. A brotherhood of rape.

She took another pass at the apartment, this time with an eye toward hidden drawers or secret stashes.

When Peabody came back, Eve was crawling over the floor of the bedroom closet.

"Hoping to find a hidey-hole, but I got nothing."

"I got the discs."

"Let's view them on the bedroom wall screen."

Eve pushed to her feet, stepped out of the closet into the stringently neat bedroom with its simple and elegant bed—high, dark gray padded headboard, soft gray duvet, a few pillows in shades of blue.

Eve followed the urge to poke at the headboard, peer behind it. "If she had a hole, she'd have taken what was in it anyway," she said as much to herself as Peabody.

Nodding, Peabody plugged the discs into the wall screen, cued it up.

"Full forty-eight?"

"For now, start when we came in to talk to her. We'll view the rest back at Central."

Peabody zipped through, slowed.

Eve watched the two of them step up to the door, into camera range, deal with door security. Into the lobby, and lobby cams, into the elevator, and those cams, and down the corridor to Su's door.

"Speed it up some. Split it between entrance cam and the view of her floor."

Eve watched them leave.

"I think my magic pink coat's magically slimming."

"Shut up, Peabody."

Eve watched a delivery guy hit the door carrying a big vase of red and blue flowers, and a woman in a forest-green coat and checkered scarf come out with a white dog on a leash. Another exit—a man with a briefcase who looked hurried and harried. Then . . .

"Freeze it. Look at this one. She doesn't want to have her face on the camera."

"Could be." Peabody pursed her lips. "But it was pretty damn cold. Most everybody bundles."

"She's got every strand of hair under that hat, and her face angled down. Scarf's knotted up so you wouldn't see the bottom half of her face anyway. Gloves, long coat. Start it—regular speed. Not a resident, see? She's hitting the intercom, being buzzed in. But she knows where the cameras are. This is what, about twenty minutes after we left?"

"Ah . . . twenty-three."

"Looking down or away through the lobby . . . off to the side in the elevator. Looks too tall to be MacKensie. Doesn't move like Downing. Maybe we've got one of the others. Maybe . . . And that's Su's floor—moving to Su's door. And in. She contacted someone after we left. We shook her, and she pulled in one of her partners. Keep the split screen in case she pulled in the rest. Can you speed up the corridor cam?"

"McNab could. Give me a second."

While Peabody dealt with technology, Eve paced.

"She knew we were making the connections. That's why they decided to go to ground when they did. These two, they're in there talking it out, figuring it out, contacting the others. Su's packing, you bet your ass."

"Got it! Woo, I am e-skilled. Here, here, Dallas, they're coming out again. Forty-six minutes inside."

"Su's got her suitcase, a big tote, and her friend's got a second suitcase. And the friend's still steady enough to remember not to show her face to the cameras. Not MacKensie. And I don't think Downing. One of the others. We'll have EDD go over this, do what they do. Maybe they can get enough."

"If Yancy can pull Esty's memory of the painting." Peabody nodded. "Maybe."

"Look how Su's dressed. Boots—more work than dress—casual trousers under the coat. Big black tote along with the suitcase. Hold it—look at her face. She's glancing straight up at the camera. Not at the camera," Eve corrected. "At us. She figures we'll see this sooner or later. Look at her face."

"Angry, but . . . smug."

"Yeah, that's exactly right."

"She's on her way to the others," Peabody said quietly. "On her way to pick up the others."

"And to get back to work on Betz. They have to take shifts. A woman's got to earn a living, after all. So they take shifts. But they're moving right along. Still have to try for Easterday—and in that outfit she's not the one doing the luring. That's MacKensie's job this round."

"Her vehicle, like you said."

"Yeah, most likely. Go back—go back to yesterday, start about fifteen hundred."

They watched Su exit at fifteen-ten. Dressed in full black, carrying the big black tote. Hair pulled back, sunshades masking her eyes. She pulled on gloves in the elevator, balled her hands into fists.

"Keep going," Eve murmured. "Let's see when she comes back."

They watched the life of the building—people heading out for the evening—a party, dinner, the night shift. People coming back—late night at the office, from shopping or drinks with friends. A couple who, from the body language, had fought during the evening, came home stone-faced. Another couple who, from the body language, obviously hadn't fought but had imbibed plenty, laughed and staggered their way inside.

Somebody was getting lucky, and somebody wasn't.

"There she is. Just past four hundred hours. Doesn't look smug now," Eve continued as they followed Su's progress into the building, up to her floor.

"No, she looks really tired—I'm not sympathizing, especially since we're pretty damn sure she just got finished killing Wymann, and probably spent some time working on Betz. But she looks more than tired, Dallas."

Fighting tears, Eve thought. Though Su threw one defiant

look at the camera as she fumbled with her own key swipe, the look glittered with tears.

"She's churned up, maybe even a little sick to her stomach, because the kill, this second kill, didn't give her what she needs, what she wants more than anything else."

"What does she want?"

"Peace. She wants that inner fucking peace."

It's all you want when the nightmares come, Eve thought. And the only thing you can't find.

"The justice they tag on the bodies? That's small change. She wants to be able to sleep at night. She wants it to be over. She wants, more than anything, for it to never have happened. But the killings? It's not going to give her any of that. If she didn't know it before, she's starting to know it now. When no matter how much she washes, she can still smell the blood on her hands."

"But they still have Betz."

"Yeah. Knowing it won't make her—any of them—stop. She thinks maybe, just maybe, when they finish it, she'll find what she needs. Maybe, just maybe, she'll be able to sleep. But she won't."

"I guess she looked resigned on top of the tired."

"Resigned, resolved—pretty much the same. They'll finish it. Or they'll try. There's no going back now, not for any of them. She'll go get the van after we shake her in the morning, wherever she has it, pick up the others, and they'll all gather where they're holding Betz. They won't take him back to his house. They have to be smart enough to know we'll be on the house."

Suddenly exhausted, Eve sat on the side of the bed. "We'll pull Baxter and Trueheart off that, but put another team on. Wouldn't pay to be wrong on that. The keys, Betz's keys. Maybe they're an angle. Let's go harass EDD."

"I have to say something."

Eve shoved her hair back, rose. "What?"

"This case, and what we're looking at as motive. It has to affect you. It has to make you think of what happened to you. But it's not the same, Dallas. It's not the same."

"Yeah, it does. But my kill was justified. Him or me, and I was a child. That's not the same. He was raping me, and my arm—" She brought her hand up, all but felt the bone snap again. "When the bone broke, when he broke my arm, that shock and that pain, it was *alive*. Killing him was the only way to make it stop, to make him stop, to survive. So that's not the same as this."

She let out a breath, but her stomach still clenched and roiled.

"But the rest? The fear, that pain, the violation, what takes root in you and never really goes away? That's the same. So I know they're not going to find peace, or the justice they tell themselves they're after, through blood. I sure as hell didn't."

"How did you? Find peace?"

"I'll let you know when I do."

When Peabody nodded, bent to pick up her field kit, Eve jammed her hands in her pockets.

"That's not fair, and it's not all the way true, either."

"You don't have to talk about it. I didn't mean to push on that. I just needed to say what I said."

Fuck the sick stomach, Eve thought, and the dull throb in the back of her skull.

They wouldn't win.

"I've got insight on this investigation—and I think that insight is partly why we got closer faster than they expected. You're my partner, and . . . You're my partner," she repeated, as that said it all.

"There were doctors and shrinks and counselors and cops. Child services. They could address the physical injuries, the rapes, the broken bones, the beating. But the rest? I'd locked that away where even I couldn't find it. That was survival for me, just like putting that little knife in Richard Troy."

Standing there, she felt around in her pocket, closed her hand over her badge. That tangible shape.

"I got through. I had flashes, sure, and nightmares, but I locked all that away, too. If I couldn't get to them, nobody else could. And nobody could hurt me with all that, ever again. Then there was purpose. As far as I can see, clear back from waking up in that hospital in Dallas, I had to be a cop. That got me through, all of it, the good and the bad. And when I got my badge, I felt . . . strong, directed. That was my goal, like wiping these men out of existence is theirs. The badge, the job, protect and serve, stand for the victim. I had to. Survival. Then there was Mavis and Feeney, and with them and the job, it was something like family even if I didn't know it. And every day, every fucking day, when I picked up the badge?"

She took it out of her pocket, studied it. "Every day, I had purpose. I had beaten back what I'd locked away. I stood for something. The victims mattered, Peabody, whoever they were, whatever they'd done. They were mine to stand for."

"I know that. You taught me that."

"Maybe you think I don't know what you felt the day you got your gold shield, what Trueheart felt the other day. But I do. I remember exactly what I felt. Detective Dallas. Oh yeah, I remember the thrill and the terror of that all mixed up with pride inside me. And when I made Lieutenant, Christ, all that thrill and terror again, and that pride, that purpose. The victims mattered, and the cops under me. I needed to be the best I could, for the victims, for the cops."

She tested the weight of the badge in her hand, slipped it away again.

"And I set my sight on the bars. Captain Dallas, that's got a ring. I'd beat back what I'd locked inside me until it was nothing. Until those flashes that made me sick, scared me to the bone, those nightmares that would grip me by the throat in the middle of the night were nothing. I had purpose, goddamn it, and I was never going back to being the victim. But . . .

"Let's move," she said abruptly. "We're wasting time here."

Saying nothing, Peabody grabbed up her coat, shrugging into it as Eve headed for the door. She kept a respectful, if concerned, silence all the way down to the lobby.

"Let's get a four-man team at the Betz residence. Uniform Carmichael to head it, so three more. Two from our unit, then see if Officer Shelby's available."

"Shelby?"

"She's with the Five-two. First on scene at the Catiana Dubois homicide."

"Oh yeah, I got her."

"I'm looking at her. If she holds up like I think she will, and wants it, I'm bringing her into Homicide. We need a fresh uniform."

As they walked, Eve took out her own 'link, contacted Baxter, brought him up to date.

"So when your relief gets there, go back to Central. Once EDD nails the key swipes, we'll move there. And maybe the lab will hit a miracle with the old keys. Meanwhile, we start digging deeper on the three women we know. You and Trueheart take MacKensie. I want to know what her first fucking word was, what her mother eats for breakfast, where she shops, banks, plays. Everywhere she's lived since before she was freaking born."

"Got that, LT. We'll review with the relief and we're all over it."

She grunted, clicked off. When they got in the car, it released a new blast of resentment from other drivers. Eve mentally flicked them the bird, turned off her On Duty light, pulled out.

"But," she continued as if there had been no pause in the conversation, "it wasn't going to be enough. I had to believe it would be, but it wasn't going to be enough to keep getting me through. Mira saw that, and, God, I resented the hell out of her back then because she saw what I didn't want her to see. What I didn't want to see. Just stay the fuck out of my head, I'm fine.

"There was an incident—asshole flying on Zeus, and a kid—just a baby. And I couldn't get there in time. Just too late to stop it. I don't know why that one came so close to breaking me, but it did. Maybe I'd hit some threshold, maybe it was—What do you call it?—*cumulative*, but it knocked me hard, and this was just as the DeBlass case landed on me. I'm fine, I can handle it. Handle seeing that baby cut to pieces, handle Testing because I'd had to terminate the asshole who cut the baby to pieces, handle the DeBlass case with its Code Five."

She paused at a light, scrubbed her hands over her face, wishing she could will away the fatigue and the raw feeling in her gut. "And then there was Roarke. I still remember doing the first run on him, having his face come on my screen. And thinking: Well, look at him. Rich guy—stupidly rich guy. Mr. Mystery with no first name and a face that just took your breath. I shouldn't have gotten involved with him. And I couldn't stop—it was there right from the first second, and I couldn't stop. It wasn't physical."

Then she laughed, took off at the green. "Hell yeah, it was physical, but I mean it wasn't just."

"I know what you mean. I get that."

"It was like something out there said, 'Hell, let's give these two a break. It's time they found each other.' And it broke, those first cracks on what I'd locked away. I could start facing it because I could trust him to stand for me. Trust him to let me stand for myself. There was no way to lock away what I felt for him. I couldn't make it stop or go back, and somewhere along the line I stopped wanting it to. I think, without that, I'd have lost myself. Somewhere down the line the victims would stop mattering so much, the job would just be the job. Maybe I'd have gotten the bars first, who knows, but I'd have stopped being the kind of cop I needed to be."

And that, she knew absolutely, that would have ended her.

"I'd have stopped surviving without what I let in, with him. Without what letting that in let me let in otherwise. I might have pulled you in, like maybe I'll pull in Shelby, but we wouldn't be partners. I wouldn't have had the chops for it."

She made the turn into the garage at Central.

"So I found that peace. Cases like this, they can shake it. Sometimes I can lose it, like water dripping through your fingers. But I know where to find it again, and with who. You're part of that. Part of the where and the who."

She pulled into her slot, glanced over. "Stop that!" she ordered as tears streamed silently down Peabody's cheeks. "No blubbering. We're in a cop-shop garage. There's no blubbering in a cop shop—when you're a cop."

"I'm not blubbering." But Peabody blubbered a little as she dug in her pockets for a tissue. "And I'm not giving you a really big hug right now, like I really want to do. I just want to say that anytime that peace gets shaken, you can count on me. You can count on me," she repeated and, blowing her nose, shoved out of the car.

Eve sat in the car another moment. "I know it," she murmured, and got out to get back to the job.

Chapter 17

Eve went straight to EDD, hoping the e-geeks would give her something solid.

She found the e-lab packed with them.

McNab stood—hips jiving in his neon pants, hoops sparkling around his ear—at a station peering through some sort of scope. Feeney sat in his wrinkled brown suit, his hair standing up as if he'd been electrocuted while he swiped at two screens simultaneously.

The well-endowed Callendar seemed to dance between two stations, shoulders bouncing, which made the well-endowed portion—where for some unknown reason a monkey rode a unicycle across her spangled red shirt—bounce in turn.

Yet another geek Eve only vaguely recognized sat, bopping in his stool with comp guts spread out over his station. He had hair as red as Callendar's shirt worn in long dreads with tips as bright and yellow as an exploding sun. The tips matched his bibbed baggies.

Eve vaguely wished she had sunshades as she pushed into the lab.

Spotting them, McNab wiggled his eyebrows at Peabody. "Yo, Captain, Dead Squad's here."

"We got some something and some nothing," Feeney told Eve.

"Start with the something."

"We could scan out the one swipe, and get the code and the ID. Bank was on it. Liberty National Bank of New York was on it. Did a little dance, and we got the branch for you. Whatever he stashed, he stashed it in the Bronx. I was just about to send you the address."

"Do that. I'll check it out, and thanks. What's the nothing?"

"Other swipe. We got the code, no problem. But there's no handy ID like with the bank box. We're still working, but the best we can figure is residence. It doesn't read like a company swipe, a business swipe. Still could be one, but we're leaning residential."

"It's more than I had. What about vic comps?"

"I'm giving what we got from the Mira Institute another full scan, but what I got is all business and political bullshit. Callendar's on Wymann. Juju's got Betz."

"Juju?"

"Cuz, I got it." Red Dreads grinned at Eve.

She thought it looked as if someone had splattered his round white face with specks of red paint and called them freckles.

"Getting down on the Betz," he said, tapping the toes of lightning-blue air boots laced to his knees. "Dude's flush. Be flusher he didn't ride slow ponies. Got two digs that show, one's in the Apple, other's rum and cigars. Pulls it in, doesn't put much out. Got megs game for skirts for creaky. Lists 'em, flips 'em. Likes wheels, got three, mucho slap for zipping."

"Just . . . stop." Eve held up her hand as her head was starting to throb. "Does this guy speak English?"

"Bilingual," Juju claimed with another happy grin. "American and geek. Like geek better."

He turned the grin on Callendar. "Fluid?"

"Def. Fizz me cherry."

"Check it. Black Death, Cap'n?"

"No, go with the sweet. Double Callendar."

"Yo. McNab?"

"Triple it."

He stood, showing himself to be well over six feet. An easy six-four, Eve judged, maybe helped a bit by the platform airboots with silver stars over the blue. "You up?"

"No. Whatever it is."

"Cube it, thanks," Peabody told him when he circled a finger at her.

"Covered." He bopped out.

"My head hurts."

Callendar offered Eve an easy shrug and smile. "He can go deep into e-jive, but he's got the juju. He said how this Betz has money, and plenty, but he loses at the track pretty regularly. He bets the horses, and doesn't win. He has two properties on official records—the one here in New York, and another in Cuba."

"I want that data. We'll have Cuba checked out."

"You'll get it. He also said this Betz is a—What's it?—ladies' man or whatever. Has a lot of women for being a guy his age. And he keeps a record of them handy, so he can have their names and, when he needs to, like shuffle or rotate them."

"Christ. I want all that data."

"We'll make that so. Dude has three vehicles, and a whole buncha speeding violations."

"Those, too. Let's see if we can find out where he wants to get in such a hurry. It's a good start."

"Juju's start," Callendar said. "I've got the econ dude's e's. What shows on them is he doesn't—didn't—gamble, not that shows on his e's. Unlike Betz—Juju was saying he took a lot in, financially, from the family businesses, and didn't do much work—econ dude clocked in. He put in time, worked the job. Plenty of fun time for him. Vacays, trips. Got a lot of photos on his comps, and I'm IDing family. Got a grandson he's bookmarked theater articles and reviews on, and there's mail between them, friends, family. Some work. He didn't keep a list of 'dates,' but he has a bunch of names and contacts of the female variety. Multiple properties—

some straight investment, but also a flat in London and a place in East Hampton."

"Okay, if they got their hands on keys, they could be using the place in East Hampton, or one of the other vics' second houses. But . . ."

Too easy, Eve thought. Just too straight.

"They'd have their own. Couldn't set all this up on the fly. We'll have the secondary residences, even the income properties checked out. We need to eliminate."

She checked the time. The day was streaming by, and Betz's time was dwindling. "Send me everything, and whatever else you hit. I'm going to check with Yancy on a possible, then I'm in my office for now. I need to think."

She went out as Juju bopped back with a tray of jumbo fizzies. He sent that mega-happy grin toward Peabody. "Check," he said, and pulled one out of the tray.

"Thanks."

When she started to dig out credits, he swiped a finger in the air. "Treat."

They tapped knuckles before he bopped on.

"He's good," Peabody said before she slurped some fizzy. "I've hung with him a few times."

"If Feeney put him on it, that's good enough for me. Go on down, start digging on Downing. Deep."

"Give Yancy a yo for me."

They parted ways.

Eve made her way to Yancy's division, found him at his desk, frowning at his screen. He glanced up, gave her a distracted look. "Hey."

"Hey. And a yo from Peabody. Have you been able to connect with Laurel Esty?"

"You just missed her, and her friend Reb. Connect. Yeah, you could say that. I've got a date after shift."

"With Esty?"

"It just happened." He gave a puzzled laugh to go with the distracted look. "She said how maybe I'd take her out for a drink, and I guess I said sure. Then she said, 'Mag, how about seven?' So."

Eve lifted her eyebrows. Peabody's description—the hand fanning over the heart—hit the mark. The police artist had a lot of messy dark curls around a face that slipped along an interesting line between pretty and sexy.

"So," Eve repeated. "I take it she wasn't nervous about coming in."

"Didn't seem to be. Like some, she didn't think she remembered or saw what she remembered and saw. It's just a matter of easing them along. Huh. Straight wit, right? And not even because she didn't witness a crime. Just got a glimpse at some art that pertains."

"That's right." Since it was there, Eve leaned a hip on the corner of his desk. "No ethical lines crossed, if that's what you're asking, by buying her that drink. How much did you ease along out of her?"

"Besides her 'link numbers and the fact she's not in a relationship?" He grinned now. "I think I replicated the art, as close as I can without seeing it myself. Used a regular sketch pad. I was about to transfer it to the comp and send it."

"Do that, but let's see it now."

He opened a pad, flipped up a page. "I started with the whole works, as that's how she saw it. The five women together."

"Says unity, doesn't it?" Eve studied the portrait of the women, shoulder to shoulder. "Downing—the wit knew her. But those are decent sketches of MacKensie and of Su—and she didn't know them. Makes me think we'll have some luck with facial rec on the others."

"Factoring in that this is an approximation of an artist's interpretation. The two unidentified—this one's young. Early twenties tops, to my eye. And the other more mature. Mid-forties or more."

"The youngest in the middle. It's . . . like they're supporting her."

"Might be." He frowned, studying his own work. "Might be," he repeated, "the way she's centered. I did individuals of the faces, but Laurie was clearest on Downing. Like you said, she knew that one, saw her off and on, talked to her. I can run the face rec with them."

Eve started to say she'd do it herself, then backtracked. More hands, quicker work. "Appreciate it."

"All in a day's. Now the other painting?"

He flipped through his sketches of the faces, stopped on a study of six male figures, faces masks of evil and agony, falling toward a sea of flame. More flames shot out of the house in the background.

"It's dark work," Yancy said.

Eve took the pad from him, studied it up close. He'd been able to draw more details out of Esty, she noted. The house stood three stories, and sprawled some. Flames striking out of the windows lit what looked like brick. It didn't strike her as a contemporary structure, but, despite the fire, seemed old in that rich sense. A wealthy house.

One she thought she'd know when she saw it.

Just as she recognized the men behind the demonic faces.

"Edward Mira, Jonas Wymann, William Stevenson—all dead, though Stevenson's been that way for a while. Ruled self-termination, but we'll take another look. Frederick Betz, currently missing. Marshall Easterday, trembling in his house, and Ethan MacNamee, currently alive and well in Glasgow, with the locals keeping an eye out. This is good work, Yancy."

"We do what we do. Laurie said I got it, and I don't think it was just because she was hitting on me."

Eve flipped back through, studied the individual sketches of the women, and thought they had a good shot at IDing them. Better than fifty-fifty.

"Send me everything. If you get any hits on the women, I know when you do."

"You got it."

Eve went back to Homicide, arriving in time to hear Baxter ragging Jenkinson over his choice of tie.

"How can you wear purple and gold with that shade of brown suit?"

"The tie says it all."

"It says I left my taste at home. At least you could think about color families and proper contrast."

"Gotta take some fashion risks," Jenkinson said, just to rag back. "Yo, Trueheart, I got a source on these. He'll make you a nice deal if you want to polish up your detective wardrobe."

"Thanks, Jenkinson, but I've got the one your wife gave me last night as a thank-you gift."

"Thinks he can be a smart-ass now. Hey, boss. What do you think of my tie?"

"Jenkinson, I try not to think about your new tie fetish."

"Just adding color to a dark world. Show the LT your socks, Reineke."

"I don't want to see—" She broke off when Reineke shot his foot out from behind his desk and showed off red socks shocked with blue lightning bolts.

She had a terrible flashback to Juju's airboots.

"There is no merciful God," Eve muttered.

"I gotta keep up with my partner," Reineke claimed. "Figured I'd go for the footwear, and shoes cost too much to play with."

The best cops she knew, Eve thought as she escaped to her office. Her bullpen was stocked with the best cops she knew.

But there were times.

She contacted Reo, again, for another warrant to get her into Betz's bank box.

She got coffee, updated her board and book. Then did what she'd wanted to do for hours. She put her boots up on her desk and let herself think.

Five women, with a mutual secret, a mutual goal. Downing hadn't had those two pictures in her apartment studio by chance.

Painting out her issues. Painting out her feelings.

Love and hate? Yeah, it could play like that.

Five women, Eve thought. It took deep loyalty and determination to keep a secret.

Age ranges, if the portrait held true, went from early twenties to mid-forties. A solid twenty-year gap. That gap took the older woman out of the usual range as a sexual target for the men in the morgue.

Six men. Half of them dead, and none by natural causes or accident. Six men who'd shared a house in college—and, she was convinced, a great deal more. Powerful men, wealthy men. Her two dead known adulterers with a taste for young flesh.

Something brought them together in college, she thought. Six young men, with privileged backgrounds. Ivy league young men.

What brought young men together?

Young women—the desire for them, the attaining of them.

At a university like Yale, they'd have to work, study, produce, or—money or not—they'd get the boot. A lot of stress, particularly as there'd been a war brewing. And that brew was stirred with anger and resentment against all of that privilege.

More restrictions, she concluded, for security.

What did young men want—besides women—that college provided? Freedom from the parental locks. No parents clocking their time, their activities. But now those restrictions set in, squeezing at those freedoms.

Sex, drugs, drink. Isn't that a way to celebrate breaking the parental lock? To flip the bird at rules? To prove yourself a man? An adult?

But with rebels outside the gates, shaking fists, throwing stones, the gates get locked. What do you do?

None of their records showed any bumps for illegals, for alcohol violations. Could have been covered up—war and money—but either way, that left sex.

And sex was the key.

Six young men. Had it started all the way back there?

Old keys in a hidden drawer. A rich old house symbolically—or literally—burning.

And six old men on their way to hell.

She shifted to glance at her comp when it signaled an

incoming. And dropped her boots to the floor when she noted it was from Morse.

> Analyzed tattoos on both victims. Fully scientific report to follow. Simplifying same, the tattoos are between forty and fifty years old—and I lean toward closer to fifty. Have sent samples to lab for further analysis and verification, but evidence indicates your victims were young men when inked.

Six young men, she thought again, forging a brotherhood. And five women, bound together.

She took the next incoming—Yancy's work.

"Computer, run a search for properties within twenty-five miles of Yale University that carry no less than an eighty percent match with the house in sketch two, and are no less than fifty years old. Identify same whether or not the house still exists. Copy to my home unit, all search results."

> Search parameters acknowledged. Working . . .

"You do that, and so will I."

And rubbed the tension in her neck at yet another incoming.

"Eve," Mira began. "I wish I could give you more."

"Inner Peace?"

"In more ways than one. Privacy laws, even from medical to medical, are very strict, and very clear. But, as I could already verify Su and MacKensie were guests, that eased the way a bit. While their individual therapists and group leaders couldn't give details, professional courtesy counts for some. We'll say they alluded to certain information, and/or didn't contradict my conclusions. Both women sought help for recurring nightmares. Violent ones. And both engaged in therapy to release repressed memories. These details are corroborated by the insomnia studies Su and Downing participated in."

"Okay. Every detail helps the whole."

"I can tell you this. Both of them registered for women-only areas, and sessions. My research there indicates those areas are primarily focused on physical and sexual abuse victims. Some confidence building, yes, some spiritual searching. But the main focus of that area of the center is for abuse victims. Rape victims."

"They've gone to ground."

"I'm sorry, what?"

"The three of them, and at least one more. Gone to ground."

"One more."

"There are five. Su, MacKensie, and Downing packed some things and left their apartments this morning. I have one unidentified woman—as yet—on the security feed of Su's building. And I have five sketches from a painting seen in Downing's apartment. Ages range from mid-forties to early twenties."

For a moment, Mira said nothing. "I would conclude, on the basis of known evidence, the killings are revenge for sexual abuse, rape, assaults, that have gone on for many years, involving many victims."

"We agree. I have to keep on this. Anything else you can dig out, I want it."

"Five, Eve. With that much of an age span. You have only to fill in the blanks to see the probability."

"Yeah. There are a lot more than five. I'll be in touch," Eve said, and clicked off.

She rose, grabbed her coat, headed out.

"Baxter, Trueheart, everything you get copy to my office and my home comp. I may not make it back. Peabody, the same."

"But—"

"I'm heading to the Bronx—Betz's bank box—and unless I need to, I'm not coming back into Central. Yancy's doing the face recognition on the two unknown women in Downing's painting, and I've got one going on the house in the second painting. We get hits, I'll pull you in, if necessary. Otherwise, I want you digging every byte of data there is to dig. These five women's paths crossed somewhere—and we only have three of the five for certain. I want to know where and when on all of them."

She headed for the glide—just couldn't face the elevator all the way to the garage this time. And pulled out her signaling 'link.

"Dallas. Tell me you got the warrant."

"I will have by the time you pick me up," Reo told her.

"What? Why?"

"Because banks are notoriously fussy. You can use a lawyer. Plus when you have me wrangling this many warrants in one day, I deserve a field trip."

"It's the freaking Bronx." Impatient, Eve wound through people content to just stand and ride down.

"Pick me up, courthouse. I'll be outside Justice Hall."

Before Eve could argue, Reo cut off.

Still weaving, Eve muttered. She'd intended to use the drive time as thinking time with some nagging mixed in. The lab, EDD, Yancy. Then there was the likelihood of tapping Roarke for some assistance.

By the time she got to the garage, she'd resigned herself to hauling a passenger. And, yeah, sometimes a lawyer came in handy.

At least this one was as good as her word and stood outside with a sassy red beret tipped over her blond hair. Her coat matched it, and hit mid-calf over a pair of black boots with a high-curving heel.

"How do you walk on those?" Eve demanded when APA Cher Reo hopped in.

"With grace and sex appeal." She settled her trim briefcase and enormous handbag on the floor and, like Peabody, ordered the seat warmer.

"New York winters, I wonder if I'll ever get used to them."

"They come every year."

"You're irritated because I'm coming along. How many warrants was that today?"

"Okay, okay."

"Same team, Dallas. I'm assuming Frederick Betz is still missing."

"Unless they decided to wrap it up and run—and I don't see it—he's still alive. But he'll be in a world of hurt, and he won't be breathing too much longer."

"Such cloying optimism." At its signal, Reo pulled out her 'link, scanned the readout, hit ignore.

"Don't you need to take that?"

"No. I'm all yours," Reo said cheerfully. "I've got some details. What don't I know?"

Eve ran it through. It never hurt to run it through step-by-step again, for herself as much as Reo.

"You believe these men, your two victims and the three—no, four with the suicide—others, raped these women."

"Yes. And since one of them is about two decades older than their usual taste, I think they've been raping women for at least that long. Maybe a lot longer."

"Because of the tats."

At least she didn't have to explain every damn point.

"If the woman running the crisis center recognized three of them—by your instincts," Reo added, "maybe the five of them met there."

"It's hard for me to buy five victims of the same group just happened to use the same crisis center. And none of them reported a rape. Nothing on record."

"A support group then, a therapist, something else that united them."

"Even then, all of them, independently? It's a stretch. But it's what I've got. Easterday's shaken up. If I don't find Betz, I'm pulling Easterday into Interview. I need to scare it out of him.

She shot a glance at Reo—petite, pretty. And under it, fierce.

"I could use some weight there."

"He's a lawyer, so he's going to have plenty of representation telling him to exercise his right to remain silent."

"If I make him believe his life's on the line, he'll break. It damn well is on the line. The other thing is getting into

Edward Mira's place—his things—without his wife's consent. She's going to block me however she can."

"So lawyers come in handy. When do you want to go?"

"Today's best, tomorrow latest." She scrubbed her hand over her face. "With everything else on the plate, it'll probably be tomorrow. Morning. Early. His son and daughter would cooperate. They may even help. I'd tap that if you get me the warrant. I want to confiscate his electronics. I want a search and seizure."

Now Reo took out her PPC, made some notes. "Do you think she knew? If this is what you think, and he was part of it, do you think she knew?"

"I think she's the type who can know and tell herself she doesn't. I think she's the type, when it comes out, who'd say they all asked for it, they all were willing."

"I know the type. We see it on our end as much as you do. What about Easterday's wife?"

"She doesn't know. She doesn't strike me as someone who wears blinders or doesn't give a rat's ass as long as it doesn't interfere with her social schedule. And that's a lever I'll use when I have him in the box. However I get him there."

"Do you always drive this way?"

"What way?"

"As if we're trying to outrun an earthquake."

"Time's running out. In fact." She hit the sirens, hit vertical, and punched it. "FYI? This is how you outrun an earthquake."

She made it from downtown Manhattan to the Bronx in record time, and gave Reo points for only squealing once.

But that damn Rapid Cab shouldn't have ignored the siren.

Eve squeezed into a No Parking area, flipped on her On Duty light.

Reo flipped down the vanity mirror, checked her face. "Just making sure my eyes aren't bugging out." But she fished some hot-red lip dye out of her purse. "It's power," she told Eve. "You've got the badge and the bad attitude, I've got the legal heft and Rock 'Em Red lip dye."

Reo dropped the lip dye back in her bag, curved the Rock 'Em Red lips in a feral smile. "We've got this."

Uniformed security stopped them at the door.

"Ma'am, you're under surveillance. Please surrender your weapon immediately."

"Lieutenant. NYPSD. Badge," she said, and two fingered it out.

He scanned it, gave her the hard eye. "Bank policy requires you to secure your weapon before entering to do business."

"I'm here on police business, and my weapon's secure. On me. Reo?"

"Of course. Assistant Prosecuting Attorney Cher Reo." Reo flashed a smile, opened her briefcase. "Warrant," she said, offering it. "We're duly authorized to enter the premises—and as we're conducting police business, the lieutenant is under no obligation to remove her weapon—and access the safe-deposit box clearly listed on the warrant."

"You need to wait here for the manager. Bank policy."

"While this warrant trumps your bank policy, we're happy to wait for precisely one minute." Reo checked her wrist unit. "Beginning now."

He gave her the hard eye, but hurried off.

"Nice," Eve said. "The one-minute deal. Will that hold up?"

"If we don't mind causing a scene."

The bank was quiet as a church and ornate as a museum with fake marble columns pretending to hold up the sky-view ceiling. Tellers sat on stools behind blast shields and conducted business with patrons in hushed tones.

Eve decided she wouldn't mind causing a scene.

A woman, long strides in skinny black heels, crossed the wide lobby. She had dark hair in a precise wedge and a stern expression on her face.

"What seems to be the problem, Officer?"

"Lieutenant." Eve tapped her badge. "I've got no problem as long as you recognize the warrant APA Reo is showing you, and lead the way to the deposit box listed on same."

"The privacy of our patrons, both through bank policy and federal regulations—"

"Does not supersede this duly administered warrant," Reo interrupted. "A fact you're fully aware of if you're the manager of this bank. If you choose to attempt to block the execution of this warrant, Lieutenant Dallas will arrest you for obstruction."

"*As* the manager of this bank, I'm obliged to contact Mr. Betz and inform him of the situation."

"Yeah, good luck with that." Eve rolled her shoulders. "You do that—after you take us to the box, and open it. We're going by the minute here, right, Reo? You've got one minute to decide how you want to play this. Starting now."

"It will take me longer than one minute to contact and inform Mr. Betz."

"At the end of one minute, you're going to be in restraints, and the only contact you'll want to make is to your lawyer. Make that forty-five seconds."

"I will be reporting you to your superiors. Both of you."

But she turned on her heel, used those long strides to recross the lobby with Eve and Reo following closely behind, swiped a card over a security pad, tapped in a code.

Two steel doors parted in the middle and slid open to a small warren of rooms lined with steel boxes.

"You're required to show your identification, and to sign the log. Again, both of you."

While they did, the manager took the warrant and scowled over every word.

"You've left me no choice, but I do this under protest. Our patrons' privacy—"

"Yeah, yeah." Eve moved past her, following the numbers until she came to Betz's box. "Go away."

The woman gave a long sniff and departed, yanking a smaller steel door behind her.

Eve took out the evidence bag, took out the swipe. Before she used it, she turned on her recorder, read in the data.

The box popped out from the wall so she could lift it out, take it to a table. She slid back the lid.

"Oh my," Reo murmured. "That's a whole bunch of paper money."

"It's going to be a whole bunch of unreported-to-the-tax-guys paper money."

"How much do you think?"

"About half a mil, ballpark."

"That's a very green ballpark. We're going to need a bag."

"Yeah, we'll get one." Eve lifted out stacks of hundreds, and found the collection of small, sealed bags.

"Are those—they're locks of hair."

"Yeah." Eve's stomach knotted. "Souvenirs. They're going to be DNA matches for women he—most likely they—raped."

"Christ have mercy, Dallas, there are dozens. They have names."

Eve did a quick count. "Forty-nine. Forty-nine souvenirs. A lot of fuckers can't resist taking a souvenir. And here's one marked Charity, there are a couple of Lydias, but only one Charity, only one Carlee spelled the way MacKensie does. First names only, but it's going to help."

Frowning, she uncovered a large disc in a clear plastic case.

"Look at the size of that. I've never seen one that big."

Eve turned it under the lights. "I'm guessing it's old. Maybe as much as forty-nine years old. Handwritten title."

She turned it over for Reo to read.

" 'The Brotherhood: Year One.' "

"Get that bag, will you, Reo?"

"All right."

When Reo stepped out, closed the door again, Eve tagged Roarke.

"I'm sorry, I know you've got stuff."

"The amount of which is easing up for the day. What is it?"

"I could use some help. See this?" She held up the disc so it would show on his 'link screen.

"Ah, an antique."

"Yeah, out of Betz's bank box in the Bronx."

"Say that five times fast." But Roarke didn't smile, just kept his eyes on hers.

Did it show? she wondered. Did the sickness she felt inside show on her face?

For him it would, she thought. He'd see it.

"Listen, I—"

"Do you need me to come?"

"No, no. I— Can you jury-rig something to play this thing?"

"I can, of course. Are you going home?"

"I've got a couple of stops to make, then, yeah. I think I know what's on here, and . . . I'd rather be home when I view it than asking Feeney."

"I can be home in about ninety minutes. Sooner if you need me sooner."

"Ninety's great. Thanks. I'm with Reo, and I've got a couple things. I'll fill you in when I see you."

"You take care of my cop, body and soul."

"Trying to. See you in ninety."

She clicked off and stood staring down at the little sealed bags with the locks of hair. Stood staring and fighting off waves of revulsion.

Chapter 18

"I'm not going back downtown," Eve told Reo.

"Just take me as far as you're going, and I'll get a cab." Reo made quick notes as they sped away from the bank. "Forty-nine, Dallas. Do they all have souvenirs?"

"Can't say. Not yet."

"I need to see what's on that old disc."

"When I get it transferred, I'll send it to you. Reo, I'm taking it home, the money, too. I'll count it on record, seal and log. But I'm not getting it into Evidence until tomorrow. Most likely tomorrow morning."

After finishing her notes, Reo tucked her PPC away. "Dallas, not only am I not worried about you preserving the chain of evidence, that fortress you live in is at least as secure as Central."

"Great, but I'm going to ask you to get the hair to the lab. To Harvo. That can't wait. We need to start IDing these women."

"I can do that. I'll take care of that. Are you okay?"

"Forty-nine. You always think you just can't be surprised anymore by what people do to each other. Then you are."

"If they started that long ago, the first victim is in her sixties, most likely her late sixties. Nearly fifty years. The statute of limitations . . . She's put it behind her. Or I hope she has."

She'd have put it behind her, Eve thought, but it was *always* behind you. In a corner, in the dark. Squatting there behind you and chuckling in its throat.

"I'm trying Easterday first. With what we found, I might shake more out of him." Eve set her teeth. "I'll use his wife if I have to. Then I need to speak to Mr. Mira before I go home and work on this."

"I can catch a cab from there. Do you want me to go in with you, press some prosecutor buttons before I drop the samples with Harvo?"

Eve considered. "Yeah, why not?"

She double-parked again, just didn't give a shit, and went straight to the door.

The same woman opened it. "It's Lieutenant . . . Dallas, correct?"

"That's right, and APA Reo. We need to speak with Mr. Easterday."

"Please come in. Let me get Mrs. Easterday. She's just in the sitting room. Mr. Easterday's resting upstairs. Can I offer you coffee or tea?" she asked as she led them into the front parlor.

"No, thanks."

"Beautiful home," Reo said when the woman left them. "Cheerful elegance, I guess. The fire's nice on a day like this. So . . ." Reo pulled off her gloves. "Do you want grim or consolatory?"

"Grim works. It's all fucking grim."

She turned as Petra Easterday came in. "Lieutenant, do you have news? Have you found the person who killed Edward and Jonas?"

"We're pursuing new leads. This is APA Reo."

"Of course, please sit. How can I help?"

"We need to talk to your husband."

"I know it's important. He's just so upset, as you can imagine."

Oh yeah, Eve thought. She could imagine.

"I put my foot down about him going over to help Mandy with the arrangements for Edward, and he's unhappy with me. But I took your warning to heart."

"He should thank you for that. But we need to speak to him. Now."

"All right. All right. I'll go up and tell him. Give me a few minutes, will you? As I said, he's unhappy with me, and I've left him alone to rest."

She hurried out. Eve watched her go up the sweep of stairs, worry in every step.

"When you said you didn't think she knew, I didn't really buy it." Reo took a chair. "Now I do. She's not scared, not bitter. She's worried for him."

"She loves him, and she trusts him. When she finds out what he's part of, it's going to cut her in half. She's another victim. You can make her number fifty."

Eve prowled, needed to move, move, move. She glanced toward the stairs twice, was on the point of going to them, maybe up them, when Petra ran down.

"He's gone. He's not upstairs. I tried to reach Mandy, but she doesn't answer. He left me a note."

Her hand trembled as she held it out. It said only:

Forgive me.

"I don't understand. What was he thinking? Can you look for him? If this crazy person is killing his friends—"

Slipped by the unit she had sitting on the house, Eve thought, furious with herself. She should've put them in the house, front and back.

"I want to look upstairs."

"I— You don't believe me?"

"I believe you, Mrs. Easterday. I'd like to look upstairs, have you come with me. I want you to look around, tell me if he took anything."

"All right, whatever helps. Please hurry. I asked the house computer where he was, and it said he wasn't in residence, and had left more than two hours ago. I know he wanted to help—his friends," she continued as they went upstairs. "But he should be here, safe. He should be resting."

She rushed by other rooms—guest rooms, another sort of parlor—and into a large suite.

The rich cream duvet was mussed, and the chocolate-brown throw tangled on it, as if someone had tried to rest there. A fire crackled low.

"I should have sat with him. I should have checked on him."

"Would you check now, see if he packed anything?"

"Why would he do that?"

"Would you check?" Eve repeated.

Annoyance layered over the worry as Petra marched to a closet, flung its double doors open. Eve moved behind her, watched her open a panel in the back of the space.

"He'd have no reason to . . ."

"That's where you keep the luggage." Eve moved in further. "What did he take?"

"His—his Pullman. I don't understand." Frantic now, she pulled open one of the drawers in a cabinet. "God. The sweater his granddaughter gave him for Christmas. She made it. He loved it. And— God, I'm not sure. Some shirts. I think. I think some trousers. He packed clothes and left. I don't understand."

"Does he keep cash?"

"What? Yes, yes, we both do. There's a safe . . ."

She swiveled the dresser out by a mechanism, revealed a wall safe behind it. Unlocked.

Petra pulled the door open. "It's empty. I . . . I know he kept some cash in here, as I do in mine. The jewelry's in another area."

"Did you have the combination to his safe? Did you know the contents?"

"No. It's his. I have my own. We respect each other's— Oh God, he packed and left because he was afraid they might come here, hurt *me*." Her face white with worry, she pressed fisted hands between her breasts. "You have to find him, please."

"Home office?"

"Yes, yes, this way. Please, can't you put out an alert? Whatever it is you do? Do I need to file a report, a request?"

"We'll look for him," Eve assured her. "I want your permission to bring in a search team, and your permission for our Electronic Detectives Division to take his electronics, search through them."

"Anything that will help. I'm a lawyer's wife, and I know I shouldn't, but anything that helps you get him home safe. I'm going to try Jonas's family. Maybe—"

She dashed out, left Eve and Reo alone in the office.

"He's running."

"He's going to try to."

Eve pulled out her communicator. "Dispatch. This is Dallas, Lieutenant Eve. Put out a BOLO on Easterday, Marshall," she began.

It took nearly an hour for her to set up a search team and ream out the team watching the house. She arranged for the transfer of electronics, questioned Petra, the household staff.

She watched on house security as Easterday slipped out the rear of the house with his suitcase, his face a mask of fear and guilt.

He'd been too smart to take a cab—she'd already checked. Maybe he'd caught one a few blocks away, or ordered a private car service—not his usual, as she'd checked that as well. Or maybe he'd just walked as far as he could walk and lost himself on the streets of the city.

"He doesn't have that much of a lead," Reo said as she waited for her cab. "You've got transpo stations, public and private, on alert."

"What I'd do is hire a car from New Jersey, have it take me out of the city. Maybe back to New Jersey, or upstate, or to Pennsylvania. Then I'd hire another one to take me somewhere else. Put miles on, and then with the passport I sure as hell have with me, I'd get on a shuttle to anywhere that doesn't have extradition with the U.S. I'd change my name, my hair, my face, and poof."

"You're a cop, and you could probably get away with it. He's not thinking that clear. Here's my cab. If you need me, just tag me."

Eve got into her own car, and with a heavy heart drove off to question Dennis Mira again.

She didn't expect him to open the door himself—even half expected he'd still be at the university and spare her the duty. But there he was, with his cardigan buttoned wrong and his kind green eyes smiling at her.

"Isn't this nice. Gilly just went out to spend some time with friends, and now I have company. Come in out of the cold."

"I'm sorry to disturb you, Mr. Mira."

"You aren't. I only had morning classes today, and was letting my thoughts circle around in difficult places."

He took her coat before she could stop him, then just stood holding it, as if he'd forgotten what he'd meant to do.

"I won't be long. Maybe we can just put it over the chair or something."

"Of course, like family. Now, what can I get you?"

"Nothing. Please. Mr. Mira, I'm sorry, but I'm going to have to take you into those difficult places."

"Of course," he said easily, and nudged her gently toward a chair. "It's better to go straight into them than to circle around. You've learned something."

"You know Frederick Betz."

"Is he dead?"

"I don't think so, yet. They have him, I'm sure of it. And in the course of investigating we— I found some keys. Two old standard keys and two swipes. One swipe led me to a bank box. There was a great deal of money in it."

"Yes, I can see that with Fred. He'd squirrel cash away."

"I also found forty-nine small sealed bags."

"Illegals." Now those kind eyes widened. "I would never have thought so. And being a chemist, he could simply, well, mix what he wanted when he wanted it, couldn't he?"

"Not drugs. Inside each was a lock of hair, and each bag was labeled with a different name. A woman's first name."

Something sagged in him—she saw it. And it broke her heart a little.

"You don't think they're from women who gave them willingly."

"Mr. Mira, I believe Betz, along with Wymann, your cousin, Marshall Easterday, Ethan MacNamee, and William Stevenson formed a kind of club. What they called the Brotherhood. And I believe starting back in college they selected women, and raped them."

"Edward," he murmured, and stared into the fire. "I knew these men. Not well. Not very well—and I think now not at all. William Stevenson . . . Willy? Did they call him Willy?"

"Billy."

"Yes, of course. Billy. He died, didn't he, some time ago? I can't quite recall."

"Yes."

"And Ethan—I liked him more than the others, back all those years ago. We played soccer. We played soccer for Yale, so I knew him a little better than the others. He lives in Europe, I believe."

His gaze, full of grief, came back to hers. "You want to ask me if I knew about this?"

"No. I know you didn't."

"Shouldn't I have? I knew they had secrets, and I thought . . . I honestly don't know or remember what I thought but that I was excluded. It bruised my feelings at first when Edward would brush me off. No time for me. I rarely saw him."

"They had a house, a private home."

"Yes, they lived together, a kind of fraternity of their own making. Ah," he murmured, and the sound was sorrowful. "Brotherhood."

"Do you know where? The house, do you know where it was?"

"I'm afraid I don't. Edward . . . He made it clear I wasn't part of that, and while I believe they often had gatherings, parties, I wasn't included. It was such a large campus, even then, and very strictly secured due to the Urbans, but I never visited him there."

He looked away again, into the fire. "You believe they began this there, in that house. I see. I see why he was so cruel about it now. Why he made it clear I wasn't part of that . . . fraternity. That brotherhood. I wish I could believe he'd been protecting me from it, but he was only protecting himself. I loved him, but I would have stopped him. I would've found a way."

"He'd have known that."

"How many did you say? How many names?"

"Forty-nine." She hesitated. "Some are clearly a great deal older, some are . . . not."

His gaze came back to her, horrified. "You think they were still . . . They continued, all this time?"

"Why would they stop when they got away with it?"

"Not because they were drunk or high and lost control. Not to excuse that, you see, but this is . . . calculated. What you're telling me. Planned and done as—as a pack. Like rabid animals. No. No. No. Not like animals."

He pressed his fingers to his eyes a moment, then dropped his hands in his lap. The devastation on his face cut Eve to the bone.

"Like men who thought they had the right. Worse, so much worse than animals."

In the next moment, anger burned through the devastation. "Edward had a daughter. How could he do this and not think how he would feel if someone did the same to his own child? His daughter has a daughter. Merciful God. And he died for it, for his own brutality, his own arrogance."

"I'm sorry. I'm not going to be able to save Betz, Mr. Mira. I swear to you, I've tried, but I don't think we'll find him in time. Easterday's in the wind. I'm going to do everything I can to find him, not just to see he pays for his part of this, but if they find him first, he's dead. Killing them isn't justice. What was done to your cousin wasn't just. I get you might think because of what happened to me I might see it that way, but—"

She saw his eyes change from sad and angry to shocked, then sorrowful, then so desperately sympathetic her insides trembled.

"I—I figured Dr. Mira would have told you."

"No. Oh, no, Charlotte would never betray a confidence. My sweet girl," he comforted. "I'm so sorry. What you do, every day, is so courageous, and so dangerous."

"It didn't happen on the job." She wanted to push to her feet, get out, get away from that quiet sympathy. But her legs had gone to water. "I was a kid," she heard herself say. "It was my father."

It was he who moved. He rose, came to her, took her cold hands in his. Without a word, he simply drew her to her feet and into his arms where he held her so gently she felt she would break.

"I'm okay. I'm all right," she managed even as she began to shake.

"There now. There. You're safe here. You're safe now."

"It was a long time ago. I—"

"Time doesn't heal, whatever they say. It's how we use the time that can heal." He stroked her back, as Roarke often did, and tears burned like embers in her throat.

"You sit now, sit right here, and wait. I'll only be a minute."

"I should go."

He eased her back into the chair, touched a hand briefly to her cheek. "Sit right there."

She did what he told her, struggled to find her balance again when he left the room. She *had* believed Mira would have told him. She understood the confidentiality, but they'd been married forever. Didn't that outweigh . . . ? Of course it didn't.

She closed her eyes, forced herself to take slow breaths. And both the Miras would understand and respect that. Now she'd unloaded more of a burden on a man who was already grieving. She needed to get things back on course, then get back to work.

He came back—misbuttoned sweater, house skids, and carrying two delicate cups in their delicate saucers. Tears pressed viciously at the back of her eyes just from looking at him.

"We'll have this very nice tea, with a healthy dollop of brandy. It helps."

She didn't have the heart to tell him she didn't like tea, or brandy, so took the cup.

"Drink now."

She obeyed, and discovered whatever magic he'd put into the cup was like a warm stroke on the spirit. She drank some more.

"I'm sorry, Mr. Mira. This isn't about me. I only wanted to reassure you I'll do everything I can to find the women who killed your cousin."

"I never doubted that. There's no need to explain, and you don't have to tell me anything that makes you uncomfortable. I'd like to ask, if you can answer. Where was your mother?"

"She was as bad as he was. Maybe worse. She hated me. She left. She's dead. I didn't kill her. I killed him, but I didn't kill her." She closed her eyes. "Christ."

"Do you think I'd judge you? My brave girl, I think you judge yourself far too harshly."

"No—I—I did what I had to do. I know that."

"But this investigation brings it back, and still you don't set it aside. You could."

"If I did that, he wins. If I did that, I don't deserve the badge."

"Far too harshly," Dennis said quietly. "Will you tell me how old you were?"

"They said I was eight. When they found me, after, they said I was eight. They didn't know who'd raped me or broken my arm, they didn't know I killed him. Well, Homeland did— it's complicated—but the police, the doctors, they didn't know. And I didn't—wouldn't remember. I shut it all away."

Those kind, kind eyes never left her face.

"A healthy response, I think. Just a child. A child should never have to defend herself from her father. A father should never prey on his own child. Biology, that's simply science, isn't it? There's more in the world than science, more inside the human heart than DNA and genes. He was never your father in the true sense. I hope you can understand that."

The simple heart of it all, she thought. Of course he would find the simple heart of it all.

"Been working on that for a while." Finish it, she told herself, and move on. "He always locked me up—they didn't give me a name, I was a thing. He kept me locked up whenever he went out. I don't remember the first time he raped me. They're all blurred together, except the last time. He came home—we were in Dallas, that's where Child Services got my name. And he was drunk, but not enough. He hit me, knocked me down. I fought him, and it made it worse. He broke my arm. I could see the pain, the blinding white flash of it. There was a little knife I'd dropped. I'd been sneaking something to eat while he was gone. I was so hungry. And my fingers found the knife. I used it, and I kept using it until I was covered in his blood. Until he was dead. It was just a little knife. I guess I got lucky, hit some arteries.

"Anyway." She took a breath, drank more tea. "They found me in an alley. I'd gotten out, wandered off. I didn't remember any of it."

"But you remember now?"

"It came back a few years ago. I'd have flashes, some nightmares, some memories—but I could shut them down. And a few years ago it all came back. Dr. Mira . . . she's helped me. Even when I didn't want her to."

"Of course. She's brilliant and beautiful, and cares deeply for you. And Roarke? Have you told him?"

"I guess he was the trigger, or the finger on it. Yeah, I told him everything."

"Good, that's good. He's a fine young man, and one who loves you without restrictions. Finding a mate, a true one, is a rare and precious thing."

And the heart of the heart, she thought. Yes, he'd found that, too.

"I don't even know how it happened, but even when he pisses me off, I'm grateful every day it did."

"The best possible description for a good marriage."

"I didn't intend to come here and talk about all of this, I just— You matter, Mr. Mira. I understand whatever he did, you lost family in a terrible way. I'll do everything I can to identify, find, and stop those who took his life. I swear it to you."

"You took an oath when you became a police officer. How long have you been with the police? I don't recall."

"About a dozen years now."

"And so young." He smiled at her now, that sweet, slightly dreamy smile that melted her heart. "You took an oath long before this, and from all I know, all I've seen, you've kept it. Look at the woman you've made yourself. Lieutenant Eve Dallas, strong and smart and brave. You'll forgive me if, at this moment, I feel Edward doesn't deserve you. If in my heart I can't feel he deserves you. But his children do, and so for their sake I'm grateful you'll keep your oath."

"A cop protects and serves, and everybody deserves it. But I don't think he deserved you. I've got to get back to work."

He got to his feet when she did, stepped to her again, enfolded her again. "I'm proud of you."

"Oh God, Mr. Mira." Tears flooded her throat, her eyes. At that moment it seemed her whole being was tears.

"There now." He let her go to pat the pockets of his sweater, his trousers. "I never have a handkerchief where I think I do."

"It's okay." She swiped at the tears with her hands. "Thanks. Thank you. For everything." She grabbed her coat, afraid she'd fall to pieces. "Are you going to be all right?"

"Yes. Charlie will be home soon. I'll be fine."

But when she left, he sat by the fire and mourned the death—in every way there was to die—of the man he had thought he'd known. And grieved for the little girl he'd never known, and no one had protected.

Eve got crime scene blotters out of her field kit, used them as tissues, found some sunshades in the glove box. They wouldn't fool Roarke if he'd beaten her home, but they might get her past Summerset.

She wanted to get home, stick her face in a bowl of ice water, then get to work.

She'd been honest when she'd told Dennis Mira the odds of her saving Frederick Betz were next to zero. Unless she misjudged this . . . sisterhood, they wouldn't finish him in his own house, not this time. Not when they knew she was looking for them.

She needed to ID the house in the painting, if her hunch held and it was, or had been, real. She needed to find the residence that opened with Betz's key swipe.

And she needed to watch the recording.

She shuffled that to the side for now.

Easterday, she thought as she drove. He'd be panicked, desperate, looking to both survive and escape.

Forgive me

His last message to his wife told Eve he knew what he'd done, what they'd all done, would come to light.

Where would he run?

Reo had it right—he hadn't had much of a lead. Unless he'd run straight out of the city, he'd have a hard time getting out, and with only whatever cash he'd taken from the safe. He couldn't use credit or debit or it would throw up a flag.

And he hadn't used a card to book a shuttle, a train, a car, or any other mode of transpo.

He didn't seem the type to hole up in a flop. A hotel, possibly, but that didn't ensure privacy. She had every property owned by any of the men under watch. If he had a property she didn't know about, Eve felt certain Petra would have told her.

The woman was terrified, only wanted her husband back and safe.

Would she forgive when she learned why he'd run?

Not your problem, Eve told herself and nearly wept again from the relief of driving through the gates of her home.

She ordered herself to pull it together. She had to get through Summerset and upstairs. And she didn't want to break down on Roarke.

She didn't have time to lose it again.

She got out of the car, took the bank bag out of the back—asked herself again if she should've made the trip downtown to take the hair to the lab rather than give that task to Reo.

Quicker this way, quicker was best.

She strode to the door, told herself to just keep walking.

The relief she felt when the foyer was Summerset-free dried up any threatening tears. She took the stairs two at a time, heading straight for her office.

Then slowed, stopped, when she heard Summerset's voice.

"I haven't seen one of those for thirty years or more."

"I boosted one like it when I was a boy—before you. It was old even then, but you never knew what might bring in a few punts. So I lifted it and a stack of discs with it. Turned out to be very old porn, which gave the lads and myself quite an education. I traded it off to Mick—no, no, I'm wrong, it was Brian I traded it off to, years later. He may still have it, as far as I know."

"I take it this one came without the porn."

"Sadly, it did."

"How did you come by it?"

"One of my R & R men is known for hoarding everything," Roarke told him. "He swears it will work, good as new. But the problem, as you see, is the hookup."

"You'll jury-rig it there to the comp, and then program it to screen."

"That's the plan. Bugger it. Hand me the small spanner

there. It's the wrong size plug, but I can swap it out, I'm thinking."

She considered backtracking to the bedroom, doing that bowl of ice water. But she'd taken too much time on herself already.

She squared her shoulders, strode straight in to see Roarke at her desk, hunkered over her comp and some black box thing with Summerset peering over his shoulder.

"There you are," Roarke said without looking up. "I'm just working out how to merge the antique with the contemporary. Nearly there."

"Great."

When Summerset glanced over, she realized the shades fooled no one. She saw him lay a hand on Roarke's shoulder, give it a small squeeze as he himself straightened.

"I'll leave you to it," he said as Roarke lifted his head, looked at Eve.

She supposed she owed him for leaving the room rather than mortifying her.

"What happened?" Roarke asked.

"A whole bunch of stuff."

"You've been crying."

"A little meltdown, I guess. Look, what you're doing there's really important. I'll bring you up to date, meltdown included, but I need you to keep doing whatever that is. I'll get coffee."

"What you need is sleep."

"Maybe, but it's not what I'm going to get. The ground's still a little shaky under my feet, okay? Give me a chance to steady up."

"All right."

He reached for another tool as she went to the kitchen to program a pot of black coffee.

Chapter 19

She told him all of it, from the time he'd left her that morning until she'd left Dennis Mira.

"I really did assume Mira had told him—like the Marriage Rules take over everything else after—what—three decades. I wouldn't have . . ." She shook her head. "I wanted to reassure him, I guess, that no matter what, I'd do the job. And I ended up telling him. An abbreviated version, maybe, but all the high points. Or the low ones."

"There's no kinder shoulder to lean on, to my thinking."

"I didn't go there to lean on him. But I did." The tears stung her eyes again. "And he was kind. I brought him grief, mine and more of his, and he was kind. I'm going to give him more grief, because everything I do is a step closer to bringing all this out. It's his family name."

"A man isn't a name. Who knows that better than I? It's he himself makes it. I've no worries on that count for Dennis Mira. Nor should you."

"You're right." And with that came a cool wash of relief. "You're right," she said again, taking his face in her hands.

"You're a fine young man, and you love me without restrictions."

"Well now, there's various interpretations of *fine*, and I might hit one or two. But the second part is pure truth."

"You're a fine young man," she repeated. "I have it from a good source. So . . . do you think that thing's going to work?"

Roarke glanced at the old disc player, the jury-rigged cable. "I do."

She went to the bank bag, took out the disc in its clear case. "Let's run it."

He put the disc in a little pop-out drawer that made a grinding sound that didn't inspire confidence. Then he played his fingers over the keyboard of her comp, swore under his breath.

"I just need to . . ."

He sat, keyed in something else, checked the connections, keyed in more. And this produced a series of beeps.

"There we are."

"We are?"

"We are, yes. Just give it a moment."

She frowned at the screen. The frown deepened when it turned a deep, and blank, blue.

"What—"

"It's coming," he insisted, and gave a satisfied nod when the word PLAY appeared in the top right corner.

"See, there we are." He tapped two keys simultaneously with his thumb and pinkie.

They came on screen, six young men standing in a circle in a room lit with dozens of candles. The glow flickered over their taut, naked bodies.

One of them—William Stevenson, she thought—let out a series of drunken giggles.

"Come on, Billy, cut it out." Ethan MacNamee, Eve noted, trying to look stern, but managing a glassy grin.

"Sorry, Jesus, doesn't anybody else think this is weird? Standing here naked. Plus, she's out, man." He glanced behind him. "Hot, but out."

"She'll wake up." Young Edward Mira had a glint in his eyes, and not all of it came from whatever they'd ingested. "And she'll beg for it."

"Are we really going to do this?" MacNamee swiped a hand over his mouth. "All of us? On camera?"

"Brotherhood." Betz gave MacNamee a poke in the chest. "This is how we seal our brotherhood, now and forever. We already agreed, we're all set up. We've got the girl."

"Let's get started." Easterday looked off camera, too. "Hey, she was practically humping me at the party, right? We're giving her what she wants. Is the camera on?"

"I set it up, didn't I?" Betz looked around, directly into the lens. "It's on. Let's quit fucking around and start."

"We do it right." Wymann stepped out of range. Music began to beat—something low and tribal. "We are the Brotherhood . . .

"Come on, guys, do it *right*. This is the first annual Celebration of the Brotherhood. April 12, 2011."

When he nodded, they spoke in unison.

"We are the Brotherhood. We take what we want. We take who we want. From this day forward. We are bound, we are one. What one brother needs, the brothers give. What one brother desires, all brothers desire. All men envy what we are, what we have, what we do. And none but we, the six, will know. To break the vow of silence is death. Tonight, we seal our unity, our vow, by sharing the chosen. She is ours to do with as we will. The woman is a vessel for the needs of the Brotherhood."

"Do we speak as one?" Edward Mira demanded.

"As one!" the others responded, though Stevenson ended on a giggle.

"He's stoned," Eve said. "Look at his eyes. The others, they've had some chemical enhancement, but he had more. Or he's more susceptible."

"Hardly an excuse for what they're obviously about to do."

"No, but they needed the false courage, this time anyway, to do it."

"We drew lots," the future senator announced. "I am the first to take the vessel."

"Hold on!" Betz rushed the camera. "Let me set it up."

"Make it fast."

The image tilted, shook—Eve saw parts of the room—a large area. Sofas, chairs, some game tables, a bar.

"Like a game room, a lounge. No windows I could see. Lower level? A fancy basement maybe. Good size."

Then the screen showed a woman—young, maybe eighteen or nineteen. A long sweep of blond hair, a pretty face with a rounded chin, wide-set eyes. Eyes closed now.

She, too, was naked. And bound, spread-eagle on a mattress.

"Like a convertible bed? A pullout deal. Leather straps tied to the legs. Fingernails, toenails, painted—pink. That's girlie. She's wearing earrings, glittery. Her makeup's smeared some. Caucasian female, about eighteen, looks like about five-five, maybe one-twenty."

Then Edward Mira stepped over to her, leaned over. And slapped her. One of the men off camera said, "Hey! Come on, Ed," but he ignored the protest, slapped her again.

He had big hands. Eve knew how it felt to have a big hand slap you awake.

"Wake up, bitch!"

Her eyelids fluttered. Blue eyes, Eve noted. Glazed and unfocused.

"What?" On a moan, she turned her head. "I don't feel good. What . . ." Hints of fear lit those eyes as she tried to move, found herself bound. The fear exploded as she focused.

On the six men, Eve thought. On the one standing over her.

"No, don't. Please? What is this?"

"This is the Brotherhood."

As he straddled her, she wept, begged.

"Let me give her the stuff, Edward. She'll want it when it kicks in."

"I don't care if she wants it or not. I take what I want."

"Please. Please."

She wept as Betz fumbled with a syringe, managed

to push the needle into her biceps. "Give it a couple minutes."

Ignoring Betz, he rammed himself into the girl.

She screamed.

When he was done, she turned her face away and said, "Please." Only, "Please." Again and again.

"Freddy's up."

"I'll say." Betz stroked himself. "I got a hell of a boner. Let's see how the magic juice works."

He took his turn straddling her, gave her nipple a teasing pinch. "Hey, baby."

"What? What? It's hot. It's so hot."

"Yeah, magic juice. Gonna get hotter."

She strained against the bindings, tried to rear up. But instead of fear and shock, now her eyes were glazed and wild.

"Some form, some early form of Whore or Rabbit. Chem major—family business," Eve stated.

Roarke said nothing, but his hand slipped into his pocket, and his fingers closed over the small gray button he carried there, always.

While Betz raped her Eve heard voices, laughter, the clink of glasses. Getting drunker, she thought, getting higher. Getting off on it, and waiting their turn at her.

When Betz came with a triumphant roar, they actually cheered.

"Holy *shit!* Best I ever had."

"Move your ass, Fred." Wymann shoved him aside. "My turn."

"It's enough," Roarke said and turned to the machine.

"No, it's not. All of it."

It made her sick, it made her sweat, but she watched it all. Watched as they went back for more, one by one, and again, even after the girl had passed out.

"She's done, man." Easterday sprawled beside her. She lay facedown now, limp. "No fun when she just lies there like a corpse."

"Let's clean her up and out. Douche the douche." Betz cackled at his sick joke.

"She won't remember anything?" Edward Mira demanded.

"Who're you talking to?" Betz snorted. "She'll remember the party—vaguely, but nothing after the first roofie we got in her. We clean her good—no DNA in her when we're done. We get her dressed, and we dump her back on the campus. Just like we planned. Maybe she cries rape, because that bitch is going to be sore every fucking where, but they can't put it on us. We're our own alibis."

"The Brotherhood," Wymann said.

"Bet your ass, bro."

He turned back to the camera, grinned. "And that concludes the First Annual Brotherhood Fuckfest. Thank you and good night!"

The screen went back to blue.

After a long silence, Roarke ejected the disc, put it back in its case.

"These are the men you'd work yourself to exhaustion for? These sick, spoiled, vicious animals are who you're standing for?"

"I don't get to choose." Her voice shook. She fought to steady it. "I don't get to choose," she repeated. "I have to do— God, I'm sick."

She ran out, dropped to the floor in the nearest powder room. Her stomach pitched out the vile and bitter until all that remained was the raw.

"Here now." Gently, Roarke laid a cool cloth on the back of her neck, stroked her pale, burning face with another. "I'm sorry for that. I'm sorry, darling."

She only shook her head. "No. They are animals, and the ones who live, I'll work myself to exhaustion to put in cages. I'd bury those cages so deep if I could, they'd never, never see light again. It hurts you, to see someone treated that way, and it hurts more because it makes you think of me. What happened to me."

He said nothing, only reached up to get the glass he'd set on the counter when he'd come in. "Sip this."

"I can't."

"Trust me now. Just a sip or two. It'll help settle you."

"Beating them all into bloody pulps. That would settle me."

Gently, as Dennis Mira had been gentle, Roarke cupped her cheek. "There's my Eve. Just a sip now."

She took one. "And you know I can't. I can't do that."

"And there's my cop. I'm madly in love with both of them. One more sip now."

Like Dennis Mira's brandy in her tea, whatever he'd put in the glass soothed, settled. Maybe it was love that held the magic.

"It hurts you," she said again.

He sighed, pressed his lips to her brow. Cooler now, he thought, though not a whiff of color had come back to her cheeks. "It does, yes. And yes, it makes me think of you."

"It hurts you," she said for a third time, "but you'll still help me."

"A ghrá." He urged another sip on her. "I'm with you."

She pressed her face to his shoulder, let a few tears spill when he drew her to him. "Every day," she murmured. "However we got here, however and whyever you're with me, I'm grateful. Every day."

She drew back, brushed her lips over his cheek. "I'm sorry we have to do this."

"There's no sorry, not for this, not between us. Let's find at least one of them still breathing, so we can have the satisfaction of that cage."

"All right." She pushed away tears with the heels of her hands. "Let's do that."

He slipped an arm around her waist as they walked back to her office. "You should have something—a little soup."

"I don't think I could keep it down right now. Later, okay?"

"All right. You'll watch that obscenity again."

"Yeah, I have to. But later." She stopped, studied the board. She'd update that, the book, her notes. She needed to check her incomings. Maybe Harvo—Queen of Hair and Fiber—had some hits. Maybe Yancy had some luck.

"I've got three names. There are five women, two yet unidentified. If one of the three we have has other property— I'm leaning toward private home, old building, warehouse— a place they could . . . do this work—I need to find it. And I need to find Betz's other property. All I've got is what I think is the street number. And a probability that we're look- ing at the Bronx."

"He had a bank and box there." Roarke nodded. "Why go there for that unless there was another connection. I can start on both of those, but it would go faster, this sort of wide- range search, on the unregistered. More corners can be cut without CompuGuard watching, or having to avoid that annoyance."

By agreeing to the use of the unregistered, she'd be cut- ting corners.

She thought of the girl gang-raped in a basement, and the forty-eight who'd come after her. Sometimes, she thought, corners needing cutting.

"Okay. If you could get started on that, I've got some things here I need to do. Then I'll come work in there with you."

"Fair enough." He ran a fingertip down the dent in her chin. "No coffee."

"What?" She hadn't thought anything more could appall her that day. "Did you lose your mind between here and the bathroom?"

"You lost your lunch—or whatever passed for nutrition," he reminded her. "If you need the caffeine, go with a Pepsi. Ginger ale would be better, but I suspect you won't settle for it."

"My brain can't function on the ale of ginger. I don't even know what it is!"

"Pepsi then—as if you know what the hell's in that. And a bit of broth to start when you feel more ready for it."

"Yes, Mom."

So he kissed her forehead, as a mother might. "Be a good girl, and there may be candy later. I'll get started."

"I can copy you a disc with all relevant data."

He gave her a pitying glance. "Please. As if I can't hack it out of your comp in less time."

When he strolled off, she had to admit he was probably right. Then she pressed a hand to her belly. Her brain said: Coffee, please. But he was right again—damn it—her system said: Do that, and I boot.

So she got herself a tube of Pepsi, cracking it as she sat to check her incomings.

She hissed at the number of them, opening one from Yancy first.

Dallas, we hit two high probables on the younger subject. I'm sending you both, but want to add I lean toward hit number two. Elsi Lee Adderman, age twenty—at TOD. Self-termination last year on September nine. Details in attached article. Primary on the investigation was your own Detective Reineke, with Jenkinson on board, so you can get their report, and their take. She went to Yale. Other hit did not.

Still working on the other subject. I'm going to take my pad on this date thing, see if there are any more details to work in and refine the search.

Yancy

"Good work. Damn good." She ordered the ID photo he'd attached on screen.

Young, she thought, and very, very pretty with wide green eyes and long, wavy brown hair.

Quickly, she scanned the data. Born in Crawford, Ohio, both parents living, and still married—to each other. Two younger siblings, one of each. Exemplary student, entered Yale on partial scholarship. Taking the track toward medicine— course work, extracurricular. And moving right along the track through her first year and nearly through the second.

All more than good until the previous spring, when grades took a dive.

"Like MacKensie," Eve murmured.

Dropped out, moved to Manhattan, worked as an aide at New York Hospital.

"Never reported a rape, but . . ."

Eve yanked out her communicator, tagged Reineke.

"Yo, boss."

"Last September you caught one—a suicide. Elsi Lee Adderman. Early twenties, mixed race, green and brown. East Fourth, off of Lex."

"Ah, wait a sec . . . Yeah, yeah. I got it. The Bathtub Lament. Slashed her wrists. Soaked about twenty-four, if I got it right, before one of the women she worked with—hospital work—talked the super into opening the door. Girl had missed two shifts, didn't answer her 'link or her door. We caught it. Nothing hinky about it, Dallas. Straight up self-doing."

"She leave a note?"

"Yeah. Something about not being able to face the demons—not illegals, as that came clean, and we didn't find any in her place—and how she was sorry. ME ruled it right off, so there wasn't much to do on it."

"I need the book—everything you have."

"Shit. What did we miss?"

"Nothing. I think she's tied to what I'm on. Can you get me that report?"

"Sure thing. Just having a post-shift brew with my partner and a couple others. I'll walk back to Central, send it to you."

"Appreciate it."

She continued to scan the article—more an obit, she supposed. Memorial to be held September twenty-first—vic's hometown.

"Computer, search for travel on September twenty and twenty-one, 2060, on the following names."

She reeled them off, pushed up—wanted coffee—paced, and drank Pepsi.

They did to Elsi Lee Adderman what they'd done to the woman on disc. Somewhere between the gang rape in April, like an anniversary, and September 2060, she'd remembered enough. She'd met the other women.

Support group. Just had to be.

Elsi couldn't live with it, couldn't handle it. She'd opted out.

Somewhere between September and now, the rest of them had plotted full payback.

It fit like one of the fur-lined gloves Roarke kept buying her.

But it didn't help her find Betz, find Easterday.

Task complete. On September 20, 2060, Carlee MacKensie, Lydia Su, Charity Downing traveled from LaGuardia Transportation Center to Columbus, Ohio, with a return flight on September 21, 2060.

"How far is Crawford, Ohio, from Columbus?"

Working . . . Crawford is nine-point-six miles from Columbus, and is a thriving bedroom community.

"Computer: Search manifest for that shuttle flight. Give me the names of the passengers, female, between the ages of forty and fifty. Start with passengers matching that criteria with seats behind, in front, or beside any of the three previous subjects. Coming and going."

Working . . .

Sisterhood, she thought. They went to the memorial. They went to pay their respects to one of their own to mourn her, and to cement the vow to avenge her. They *all* went.

Initial task complete.

"On screen, one at a time, name and ID shot. Go."

Working . . . Marcia Baumberg, age forty-two.

"No," Eve said when the ID shot came up. "Next."

Grace Carter Blake, age forty-four.

"Stop. There. Gotcha. Run this subject, full run. Son of a bitch. Son of a bitch."

The painting—and/or Yancy's sketch from the wit's memory—hadn't been far off. The face was leaner, the mouth maybe a little wider. But this was the fifth woman.

"Computer, pause run. Tell me when current subject attended Yale." Because she did, high probability she did. Or had some connection.

Grace Carter Blake attended Yale University from September 2035 to May 2043, including postgraduate work. Subject graduated with honors from Yale Law School.

"When did they take you to that room, Grace? That basement?"

Insufficient data.

"Yeah, for now. Continue run."

She went back, pulled up the incoming from Harvo.

Hey, Dallas! Forty-nine samples. Fun for me. I'm going to hang in the lab extra to play. I got three DNA matches for you already—easy as peasy. Data with IDs attached. Send you more as it comes. Harvo—QofH&F

Quickly, Eve opened the attached report. New names, three women, current ages fifty-two, thirty-four, and twenty-three.

She tagged Harvo.

The screen filled with what looked like an active sea of lava. Then Harvo turned toward the screen, and Eve realized that rather than an exotic natural disaster, it was Harvo's hair.

"Hey, Dallas! Click-bang on the timing. I just hit another one. I'm doing them alpha order, and figured I'd send them to you in groups."

"Harvo, you're my new best friend."

"Solid! Let's go get drunk and troll some beefcake."

"Later. You've got one there labeled Grace."

"Lemme see . . . yep, got two for Grace—a brunette, looks natural eyeballing, and a redhead that's not."

"I'm looking for one that's probably from between 2035 and 2043. But if you'd run both next, hit me back as soon as you verify. I've got a Grace Carter Blake, and I want to verify it. I'd appreciate it."

"You got it." The tiny green hoop at the center point of her left eyebrow winked as she turned her head to check some odd piece of equipment.

"And if you'd check the one marked Elsi—I'm looking for Elsi Lee Adderman."

"Sure thing, BFF."

"Those two tonight, if you can. And one more—it can be tomorrow, but if you can analyze the oldest sample?"

"It'll mean stopping some of the DNA searches, but sure. Or I can try to eyeball. That's not total, but seeing as I'm Queen of Hair and Fiber, I can do the eyeball on say the oldest group of like five or six, analyze them."

"Do what you do. When you get a name on the oldest sample, I want it. Do you need my weight to clear any of the OT on this?"

"Hell, D." Harvo circled a finger in the air, then tapped it on her chest. "Queen here. Dickhead never questions the queen. Ah, hey, I get these are rape vics, and don't want to make light. But if I think too much on that, it screws with my skill."

"Harvo, do it your way. Getting the results is what counts."

"I'll get 'em, then you'll get 'em."

"Thanks. What do you call that hair—the hair on your head?"

Harvo grinned. "My crowning glory."

"Yeah, yeah. The color."

"Lava Flow. Jiggly, huh?"

"Definitely jiggly. Stay in touch."

Updating could wait, she thought, and took what was left of her tube with her to check in with Roarke.

He'd shown her his private office and the unregistered equipment early in their relationship. A matter of trust, she thought. And had added her to the very few who could gain entrance.

She put her palm on the plate at the door.

When the door opened she saw him—hair tied back in work mode, jacket off, sleeves rolled to the elbows—behind the wide black U of the command center with all its glittery buttons.

New York glittered, too—showing her night had fallen hard—outside the wide privacy-screened windows.

He worked a swipe screen with one hand, a keyboard with the other. Paused to glance in her direction.

"Your color's come back a bit. And you've a look in your eye that tells me you've had more luck so far than I."

"I've got names. The other two women in the painting. I've got them both. The younger killed herself last fall—and a little digging shows me all four of the others traveled to a suburb of Columbus for her memorial. Harvo's working right now to verify they were in Betz's trophy case."

"You hit well. Give me the name of the one who's still alive, and I'll see what I can find."

"Grace Carter Blake. She's a lawyer, a Yale lawyer, who left her high-paying corporate law firm—where she was on track to make partner—about six years ago. And now? She has her own small firm that specializes in representing rape victims and battered spouses, and she serves as the legal counsel for three rape crisis centers."

"Well now, you have been busy."

"It's falling into my lap at this point—and still doesn't get me to Betz or Easterday, or the women who want them dead. I've got their names, I've got their addresses. I'm going to send someone to Blake's residence of record and her office, but she won't be there. She made a good living for a stretch of time, Roarke. Maybe enough she could sock some away, enough so she could buy the sort of property where you could carry out torture without worrying about security and neighbors."

"I'll look into that, but you need something in your system."

"Yeah, I do, because it's revving now, and it's telling me it's really empty. But I don't want any stinking broth. And it needs to be something I can eat while I work."

"It won't be pizza."

"That doesn't seem fair. What is this, prison? No coffee, no pizza."

"Chicken stew, with dumplings."

She wanted to bitch, but there wasn't time. Besides . . . "I like chicken and dumplings."

"I know it, and we have it on tap. Why don't you see to that for both of us while I start this next search?"

"I need to have my incomings transferred up here. I've got some coming in."

Roarke shifted, playing fingers over those jewel-like buttons. "Done. You can do whatever you need—including eat—at the auxiliary."

She programmed for two, and chose a bottle of wine—she figured he'd earned it, even if she would, for the moment, stick with water or cold caffeine. Since he was deep into it, she set the bowl and a wineglass beside him, turned to her own machine as it signaled an incoming.

Reineke's report, she noted, and began to read.

They'd been thorough, she noted, though suicide had been clear and obvious. She read through statements from neighbors, from coworkers, from family. And from the doctor who had prescribed the sleep aid.

She'd had insomnia. She'd gone to a therapist for troubling dreams, and to a support group because those dreams had awakened a fear of men, of sex, of being raped by demons.

She'd joined a church.

Eve read the copy of the suicide note.

I'm so sorry for the pain I'm causing. I'm not strong enough, I'm not brave enough. I can't face the demons anymore, can't fight what they've done to my mind, my body, my soul. I need to make it stop, and this is the only way I know how. Please forgive me for taking the coward's way. I love my family, and I know this will hurt you. I'm so grateful to my friends, my sisters of the soul, for all the support, for the understanding, for the clarity of vision they helped me find. But the vision is too hard, too dark, and I need to close my eyes, finally, close my eyes and rest. It gives me peace to know I can. I will. Don't grieve too hard or too long because I truly am going to a better place. Let that comfort you as it does me.

Elsi

She hadn't been ready to remember, Eve thought, so she hadn't been ready to survive.

In a very real sense, those six men had killed her the night they'd raped her. And those she could find would pay. She'd make it her life's work, if needed.

She sent Yancy the name of the last woman—confirmed for him he'd been on target with the younger.

She spoke to the uniforms she sent to Blake's residence, and her office, tagged Reo yet again for warrants to enter and search both.

She ate as she worked, and her stomach didn't revolt. She was done with that now. The next time she watched that obscenity of a recording, she'd handle it without breaking.

She glanced at Roarke, thought how lucky she was she hadn't remembered before she was ready, how lucky she was he'd been there—right there—when she had been. She wouldn't have chosen the Bathtub Lament—not her style. But there were other ways to end things. She might have chosen one without being fully aware she had chosen.

So she'd stand for Elsi Lee Adderson, just as she would for the murdered men who'd raped her.

She took another incoming, one of Harvo's insanely cheerful reports—and confirmed Grace Carter Blake and Elsi as rape victims.

She got up for water. Roarke—give him one more—was right. She'd do better for now with water.

"That's you, fucker," he said with such satisfaction, she stopped.

"Which fucker?"

"I had here a short list of properties in the Bronx, and I've been pulling all manner of data on this fucker—Betz. We'll give him a score as a clever fucker, but I'm better. I've got the address for a property under the name of Elis Frater."

"Where the hell did you come up with that name—it's not even close."

"Elis—a nickname for Yale, apparently based on a short-ened version of the founder's name. Frater is brother in Latin. I did a wide search for names with *brother* or *brother-hood*, any and all languages."

"No shit?" She figured she might have thought of that—eventually. "You're going to have to take the insult, ace. You're a hell of a cop."

"Not in this lifetime. He also has an offshore account in that name, with a tidy sum of three-point-four million—and change."

"I need to get there. There might be something else. More recordings, something."

"Then we'll go."

"I need the other data you're after."

"The search will continue to run without me. We can be there and back fairly quickly if we take the copter."

"The copter."

He smiled. "You did say earlier you might have need for one."

"Yeah, I did." God, she hated to fly. "Yeah, let's do it. I need any incomings here to come to my pocket 'link."

He sighed as he rose. "I just gave you Elis fucking Frater out of thin air, and you have to ask?"

He had a point.

Chapter 20

She *really* hated to fly, and zipping over Manhattan, between spears of buildings, scooting around trundling sky trams didn't help the chicken and dumplings settle in comfort.

It would be a short zip to the Bronx, she reminded herself, and she spent most of it on her 'link.

Peabody would be a little pissy—Peabody *loved* to fly. Go figure. And Eve needed to alert the local PSD she was coming in.

"Reo came through. We've got the warrant, and there's no activity as yet at the Betz residence—the other one. Glasgow cops picked up Ethan MacNamee, and are currently holding him."

"That'll keep him alive. Will you get him back here?"

"I'll damn well get him back here. I'll be copying that ugly recording to Scotland, once I touch base with the commander."

Because she felt the copter shudder, she made the mistake of glancing through the windscreen. The moving lines of cars and burning lights made her head spin. Better than her stomach, she told herself, but swallowed hard.

"If we identify the house in the painting—and I'm work-ing that by backtracking through old records, looking for an address on at least one of these bastards back in college—we may want to use this damn copter again."

"A moonlight flight over Connecticut. Ah, romance."

She hissed out a breath when he began the descent.

"Where are you going to land this thing? Why didn't I think of that before? Why is this damn thing shaking so much? Christ, I hate this! Where are you putting down?"

"Safe as houses." He said it as he fought a vicious wind shear.

"People break into houses all the time. Houses burn down. What makes them safe?" she demanded. "Where are you putting this flying tube?"

"On the very handy rooftop of the building we're going to visit." If the bloody wind didn't bash them into it first. "Can't get much closer than that."

No, but now there were a lot of buildings entirely too close to that windscreen for her comfort.

He set down on the convenient, if narrow, flat roof near what she thought must be a maintenance shed. But her breath didn't come easy until he'd switched off the copter and the engine purred into silence.

"Thank Christ." She unhooked her harness, jumped out onto reassuring concrete, and into the wild wind. "Roof access," she shouted, nodding at a steel door. "We go in like the suspects are inside. We clear, floor by floor. I know you're carrying."

"Of course I am. Do you want me to pop the locks?"

She pulled out her master, turned on her recorder. "Dal-las, Lieutenant Eve, and Roarke, expert civilian consultant, entering residence of Frederick Betz. Duly warranted."

She used her master, nodded to Roarke.

They went in fast, high and low.

"This is the NYPSD," she called out. "We're coming in, and we're armed."

They went down a short stairway to another door, repeated the procedure, and the warning.

Eve took out her flashlight, swept with it and her weapon.

"Feels empty," she said quietly, "but we clear." She gestured him one way, took the other.

There were rooms full of furniture, but more like storage areas than livable spaces. A pristinely clean bathroom, and stairs leading down.

"Clear," she called out.

"And clear here, but you should come see this."

She wanted to go down, clear the second floor, the first, but she moved in the direction of Roarke's voice.

And found a small, well-equipped lab.

"I'm going to venture I'll find another account or two," Roarke said, "as it looks as if Betz has a small illegals operation here. And I'll wager he's cooking rape drugs in his leisure time."

She stepped in toward a glass-fronted refrigerated cabinet, studied the organized crates of vials.

"He has family money, family business—though my data is he doesn't do a lot. He likes to bet on the horses. So he cooks up illegals on the side to support his habit, to have more to stow away. This is his fucking hobby," Eve said and turned away. "Let's clear the rest."

They went down to the next floor, split up again.

This time she called Roarke.

"Suitcase—guest room. Bed's mussed up like somebody stretched out there. Bottle of liquor, a glass." She spoke softly as she eased open the suitcase.

On top of a jumble of clothes—a handmade sweater she recognized from the work Peabody did—was a framed photo of Petra Easterday.

"Easterday," she told Roarke. "He came here to hide. A brother would have access to a brother's house, right?"

"He didn't unpack, or repacked hastily."

"I think didn't unpack. Brought the suitcase up, got a bottle, laid down, and drank."

"Feeling sorry for himself," Roarke concluded.

"Yeah, poor, sad serial rapist had a fucking bad day. Let's

go down. If we box him, he'll try to run. He may try to fight, but he won't be much trouble."

They turned out of the room, toward the stairs. And stopped halfway down when they saw Betz.

The first floor and its entranceway remained dark but for the beam of her flash. And that spotlighted the man hanging from the pendant light above the main floor hallway.

She'd known the chances were slim she'd find him alive, take him alive into the box and batter him into a shaking mass over what she knew. But she'd hoped. She'd hoped deeply after viewing the recording she'd have her chance at him.

"And that's four of six," she stated. "They didn't wait to deal with him, took the chance and got him in here, finished him way before their usual time frame.

"Clear first. They're not here, but Easterday might be."

She found an overturned table and broken glass on the floor leading toward the rear of the house.

Then blood—some spatter, some smears.

She stepped around it, continued to clear, saw drag marks.

"The house is clear," she told Roarke, "and they've got Easterday. It reads he was down here, probably a little drunk, when they came in. Maybe he figures his brother Betz is coming in, then he sees them, tries to run. They go after him, stun him. He goes down, takes that table with him, hits his head. They drag him back. I bet they wanted him to watch. Like he watched Betz rape them. Now he can watch while they execute Betz."

She holstered her weapon, called for the lights. "I need to let the locals know what we've got here, but it's our case. I'll pull Peabody in after all."

"If you suggest I go back home, you'll make me very angry."

"I should, but I won't. And I don't want to," she admitted. "I can handle this. I will handle it. But I want you with me. It helps having you with me."

"Always."

"It helps knowing that, too. I think, unless they're stupid—and so far, not a bit—they know they don't have much of a chance to get to the last one, to MacNamee. They might take more time with Easterday. They might because he's the last one they'll have. Otherwise, he's already dead, and they're in the wind."

Because he knew her, he brushed a hand down her hair. "If it were me, and I'd come this far, was this determined, it would be the first. I'd want to . . . do justice to the last."

She nodded, took out her 'link to tag her local contact. "This is Dallas, Lieutenant Eve, NYPSD. I've got a body."

She contacted Whitney, leaving it to him to play politics with the Bronx brass, if necessary, called in her own sweepers, and had a conversation with the two local detectives who came in on the roll.

By the time Peabody and McNab arrived—riding in hot in a black-and-white—she had the latest victim lowered to the floor, and had established TOD.

"Twenty-fifteen. We didn't miss them by a full hour. They had to get this address out of Betz—or one of the others. They went to town and back on him. Shorter time frame, bigger beating."

"He's the one who drugged them," Roarke said.

"Drugged them?"

Eve glanced up at Peabody. "It's on the recording from the bank box. We have all six of them. Gang rape, by turns—like a sporting event. This one injected the vic—their first the way it reads—with something that made her go from screaming, fighting, and begging them to stop to begging for more."

"They injected her?" Under the bright splash of his watch cap, McNab's green eyes went hard and cold. "With something like Whore?"

"Something like it, this one cooked it up himself. He's got a lab upstairs here where he's kept at it."

She saw something on McNab's face that had her speak sharply. "We're on the record here, Detective."

He simply swung away and went to work on the entrance door.

"As with previous victims," Eve continued, "the victim has a symbolic tattoo in the groin area. ME to determine if this victim was stunned in this area as well, as the damage to said area is very severe. Weighted saps again, most likely. However, further injuries are burns that may have been caused by the same heated implement used to sodomize the victim. Other evidence of burning and bruises on the torso, which was not evident on the two other victims connected to this one. The facial bruising is, again, severe. The gouges around the neck and throat were most likely caused by the victim himself in an attempt to free himself from the noose. There is skin tissue and blood under the fingernails, both hands."

She rubbed the ache in the center of her forehead, then straightened up. "Bag and tag. Morris has already been notified. McNab."

He turned back, his face still stony. "Sir."

"We'll need all electronics. The consultant has already determined the security equipment was compromised, as with the other incidents. They took the hard drive. But I want all the comps taken apart, and any communications devices you find. Send for assistance."

She turned back, blew out a breath. "Our sweepers will take the scene, and local PSD will secure. Peabody, we'll go through Easterday's belongings on the second floor. Let's see if there's anything in there that will lead us to where they took him."

When she went up, Roarke walked over to McNab.

"Don't think she doesn't feel it, that there isn't a rage in her as you feel yourself."

"I know it. It's just . . ." He shoved off his winter cap, stuffed it in one of his pockets. "I saw a lot of bad shit when I was on Vice, okay? And rape is bad enough. Gang rape's beyond. Then you add sticking Whore into her? Like it's not enough you're going to rape her, but you've got to make her part of it? And it can come back on the vic, you know? If she's dosed wrong or too much, she can have flashbacks so she wants anybody to do her, then and there. I saw a lot of it. Too much of it."

"So has she." He gave McNab's shoulder a squeeze.

McNab stood a moment as if gathering himself, with the striped tail of his cap dangling out of a pocket of his bright green coat. A crescent moon of sparkling hoops adorned his ear. The long-dead Elvis rocked on the front of his sweater.

The deep green eyes in his pretty face were all cop. "I'm not saying what they did to him was right. It's not right. But it's hard seeing it as wrong. Easier to say it's not right than to say it's wrong."

"It is, isn't it? I may not believe it as truly as Eve, or you, or Peabody, but I see the value of the belief you hold that you'd rather have him alive, alive so he could suffer the humiliation and the loss of his freedom for a lifetime, than dead on the ground like this. However much he suffered first."

"There are times it's harder to believe than others, but yeah, I do believe it. Thanks for reminding me."

"All in a day's. I'll give you a hand until your help arrives, or the lieutenant needs me elsewhere."

Roarke waited for her, busying himself with electronics. He knew worrying about her state of mind was fruitless, but couldn't stop the worry.

She wouldn't stop, he knew, no matter what it cost her.

When she came down—eyes flat as McNab's had been, the shadows dogging them only accentuating her pallor—he had to bite back a demand that she take a break, get some rest. Because together they watched the morgue team take the bagged body away.

"If Easterday brought anything relevant with him, they've got it. And the cash I know he took from his house is gone. His passport's in the suitcase, so he was prepared to get gone, too."

She shifted aside to make room for the sweepers as they began their work.

"It's clear enough, he decided to leave—his life, his wife. Better that than face what was coming."

"Because, start to end," Roarke said, "he's a sodding coward."

"Yeah. Yeah, start to end. I pushed enough buttons he knew what was coming. He came here because he figured it would be safe until he could make arrangements to get out of the country. Probably had a little pity party, like you said, with booze—poor me—maybe he came down after a while. Get more booze, maybe get some food."

She walked back to the blood, the overturned table, the broken glass.

"When they come in, he's not prepared, and maybe a little drunk. They've got Betz, carting him in. That's got to take two of them, at least, but there are four of them. Younger, faster, and plenty determined. Easy enough to run down a guy pushing seventy, one who's been drinking. He tries to get away, but they gang up on him—tit for tat, right? Whatever the hell that means. Struggle, knock the table over, and the glass vase thing on it breaks. He goes down hard. That's probably a head wound—maybe some cuts from the broken glass, too. He's dazed or knocked out, and they've got him."

She looked back to where the sweepers worked on the light, the rope. "Easy to restrain him, even wait for him to come around while they put the noose around Betz. Now they've got two—and make Easterday watch while they raise the light, while the noose tightens, while Betz claws at his own throat, legs kicking, body convulsing."

She drew a breath. "And they're thinking, You watched while your brothers raped us. They watched while you raped us. Now you'll watch your brother die, and know this is what we'll do to you."

"They could've ended it all here." Peabody hunched her shoulders as Eve's rundown brought the scene into her head too clearly. "Killed both of them, and gone into the wind."

"That's not the plan. Easterday has to suffer first. They have things to say to him, things to do to him. He has to beg, the way they begged. He has to know, the way they knew, begging won't stop what's coming.

"Hold here a second."

She moved over to where Uniform Carmichael stepped in.

"Sorry to pull you back," she began.

"It's how it goes, Lieutenant."

"It's how this is going. I want you to supervise the canvass. We need to wake up the whole fucking block, Carmichael, dig down for any information. They had transportation, most likely a van, light colored, on the new side. Make sure every uniform has copies of Yancy's sketches of the suspects. You're going to need to coordinate with and work with the local PSD."

"No problem. I've got a cousin on the job here. Already gave her a tag, let her know. She'll help smooth the way if I need it."

"Good. Let the locals secure the scene. But keep an eye. I don't know them."

She walked back to Roarke, Peabody, McNab.

"We've done a first pass on the electronics," McNab told her. "Nothing that hits on this. I've got an EDD team taking everything in. You want me on that?"

"No. We're going to hit Blake's residence and office. You and Peabody will take the office, and the civilian and I the residence. That way we've each got an e-man. Anyplace to land the damn copter near Blake's office?"

Since she would have objected, perhaps physically, to an ass pat, Roarke patted her shoulder instead. "There's always a place."

"Then you'll fly back with us, and get there from wherever that place is."

"Copter ride. Woo!" Peabody shrugged. "You had to know it was coming."

"Reo's working on the warrant for the electronics. Stickier when it's a law office, but we've got more than enough to get it now. Until we do, turn the place inside out, but don't touch the electronics or files."

"Got that."

"We're done here for now." She gave the hallway a last glance. "Let's move on."

• • •

On the short flight back to Manhattan, Eve kept in touch with Reo via 'link texts, read what she could of Baxter's and Trueheart's and Peabody's runs on MacKensie and Downing.

"You can see it now, knowing where to look. They all travel on the same shuttle to Elsi Adderman's memorial— coming and going. They all made annual contributions to a women's crisis or rape center—not the same amounts, not the same center, but every one of them put some money where their issues are. None of them are in relationships. All but Downing went to Yale, and we'll find her connection. All but Blake either dropped out or hit some skid during college. She hit hers later, that's how it reads to me."

"Lipski at the crisis center recognized Su, Downing, and MacKensie," Peabody added.

"And we now know Blake served as legal consultant there. We show Adderman's sketch to Lipski, she'll recognize it, too. They had their convergence there, or through the support group either before or after the memories came tumbling back."

She turned around as Roarke touched down on a rooftop.

"This is only a block or two from the office, and another two from the apartment."

"It'll do." Eve got out, reminding herself she only had to get back in once more.

She turned to Peabody and McNab as the wind buffeted around them, and Roarke bypassed security on the roof access door.

"Wait for the warrant before you hit the electronics. By the book. However you feel about it, these women are serial killers, and the last vic they can get to is already in their hands."

"Sorry about before," McNab began.

"Before what?" Eve said, making him smile a little as they went in and started down the stairs.

"Anything to be found, we'll find it—and send up a signal if and when."

After they parted ways, she hunched against the wind, rubbed her tired eyes. "I can't figure if they'll do him fast or draw it out. They didn't expect to come on him like they did—that's a bonus for them. Will they kill him quick, or savor it? Because if they do him fast, we're not going to have time to stop them."

"If fast was the goal, you'd have found his body with Betz."

"Yeah, I tell myself that, then I think—in their place? I'd start calculating how much time, how much risk. If they want to get away with it, they've got to get it done and blow."

"Have you considered they don't care about getting away?"

"Yeah. Yeah, I have. And that's a bigger problem."

She studied the building as they approached. Nothing fancy, but solid. No doorman, but what looked like decent security from her take on it. A Thai restaurant and a discount shoe store on street level.

Eve moved to the door of the apartments, let Roarke pop the locks. Then turned on her recorder.

"Until the amended warrant comes through, it's just straight search. Unless, of course, she's here eating soy chips and watching screen."

She ignored the skinny elevator, took the stairs. "She's on four."

"I'm aware."

"She's going to be the one with the second place—the torture chamber. Not here—this isn't set up for that—but she'll have something. We've got to dig deeper there. None of the others have enough scratch to buy or rent another property. I couldn't find anything that indicated any of them inherited a place—or enough scratch to buy or rent."

A clean, well-lighted stairwell, she thought. And a pretty quiet building. Not fully soundproofed, as she caught the mutter of voices from within an apartment on the second floor. And the backbeat of a party going on when they climbed to three.

On four, she rapped smartly on Blake's door. Gave it a minute, rapped again, added: "Grace Carter Blake, this is the police."

That resulted in the door across the hall opening a crack. "She's not home."

Eve turned, studied the slice of dark face, the suspicious dark eye. She held up her badge.

"Do you know where she is?"

"Nope, but she hasn't been home all day. Don't think she was home last night, either. Maybe took a trip."

"A trip."

"Had some suitcases yesterday—and took some stuff out a couple days ago. Maybe three. Closed down her office is what Ms. Kolo said. She's on two, and she said how the office was closed yesterday. Today, too. She in trouble?"

"I need to speak with her."

"Well, she hasn't been here much the last couple weeks."

Eve took out the sketches. "How about any of these women?"

The dark eye narrowed, and the door opened another fraction. "Saw her with that one." One bony finger poked through the crack to point at Su.

"Here?"

"Nope, down the market. Ginaro's. Couple doors down."

"When?"

"I don't know, maybe last week. Probably last week because I was doing my marketing, and I've got to do it again tomorrow. They were buying a bunch of produce and such, but they didn't bring it back here because what they did was haul it on down the street and around the corner."

"They walked south to the corner, then . . . west?"

"That's right. If she's in trouble, she keeps quiet about it. Keeps to herself. Doesn't party like that bunch downstairs. I can hear them howling and laughing right through the floor."

"Ms. . . ."

"Jackson."

"Ms. Jackson, I have a warrant to search Ms. Blake's residence. We're going to enter it now. If you want, you can verify that by contacting Dispatch at Cop Central."

"You got the badge," she said. "I know how to keep to myself, too." So saying, she shut the door.

Eve used her master, bypassed the three locks—one standard, two additional police issue.

"She needed to feel safe when she was inside," Eve murmured. "This is the police," she repeated. "We're coming in."

As a matter of course, she drew her weapon, swept it as Roarke called for lights.

Modest, was Eve's first thought. Uncluttered with a few nice pieces including a leather sofa she bet Blake bought in her corporate days.

But yeah, she'd taken a few things out.

"Took whatever art was on the wall there—you can see the variation in the tone of the paint, and the hanger's still there. I'm putting it five to one it was one of Downing's. Should be a table over there, right? Why have a chair sitting out there without a table? Nothing to put your drink on, and no light."

"Easier for a woman to carry out a table than a chair."

"Yeah, it is. No photos, good wall screen, no mess. Let's clear it."

They split up, with Eve taking the bedroom and bath off the living space.

They moved systematically: kitchen alcove, smaller room set up as an office—and now without computer or 'link.

"She took clothes," Eve said as she holstered her weapon. "You can see spaces in the closet. Pretty much cleaned out the bath—no toiletries or enhancers."

Idly, she opened the drawer in a night table. "Empty."

Roarke repeated the process on the other side of the wide bed with its simple white duvet. "The same. And the AutoChef in the kitchen is the same as well. Not even a stray bagel."

"She's had time to plan, and a place to take what she wanted over time. So when she left, she took whatever she had left that suited her. It'll be the same in her office. She'll have cleared out the electronics. No chances taken. We'll go through it, but it feels like she took her time, thought it through. When you do that, you don't make mistakes."

"If she has another place, we'll find it."

Eve nodded, began the search.

The warrant for the electronics came through, for all the good it did. When they left, they walked south, turned west at the corner.

"Parking lot over there. And not the kind that's going to keep their surveillance feed for a damn week. We'll check anyway."

Dead ends, she thought, one after another, and connected with Peabody.

No electronics in the offices. No files.

"Go home," Eve ordered. "Get some sleep. Have McNab set up a search on Su's vehicle. Use variations of all their names for it, all five women. Use variations of all her family names. Set an alarm for any hits, and tag me if you get one."

"I'm not playing mum." Roarke put an arm around her as they walked back. "But it's common sense to say you need some sleep."

"What I want is coffee, and something I can twist to bust through one of these dead ends. Maybe we got a hit on the searches while we've been in the field."

"I've checked. Nothing yet. Some take more time than others."

She didn't have time. Easterday didn't have time.

In the copter, she closed her eyes. If she could clear her mind, she thought, maybe something would slide in, something she'd missed or overlooked.

The next thing she knew, Roarke was unhooking her harness.

"Dropped off a minute."

"Because however much you want to keep at this, your system needs sleep. So will they," he reminded her as he slipped an arm around her waist.

"They can take shifts. But yeah, they need sleep, food, conversation."

It felt like walking through water, getting to the door, moving into the warm.

"They won't kill him tonight. I should've gotten to that. You were right. Fast would mean they'd have done it and left him. They've got him where they want him, and they need to sleep, to talk, to make him pay. The killing's the easy part. Making him pay takes time."

He led her to the elevator rather than the stairs, and went straight to the bedroom.

"Will you take a soother to ease my mind?"

"I haven't had coffee in hours. I'm soothed enough. I get I need sleep or I'd have to take a booster, and I don't want a booster. I'll go down until five hundred hours. Where's the cat?"

"I suspect with Summerset, as we were among the missing. Do you want him?"

She did, foolishly, but not enough to send Roarke to get him.

"Just wondered."

She undressed, still in that underwater state. How long had she been up? She couldn't figure it—didn't matter. She'd go down now and start again before dawn. It was all she could do.

She slid into bed, ready, willing to go under, but the minute she closed her eyes, even with Roarke's arm around her, the recording of the gang rape began to play in her head.

"Stevenson—Billy—couldn't live with it, so he killed himself."

"Hush now. Put it away."

"I keep seeing her eyes, the terror in them." She turned over, pressed her face to his shoulder. "And that moment when the terror's too big, so you have to go away. Go inside, go somewhere else. I know what it is when it's too big to stand. When the pain and the fear and the *knowing* you can't stop it is too much to stand. And they just . . . devoured that terror. They wanted it. They wanted it so they kept at it, and found others, so they could revisit their fucking youth. It's like that, isn't it? Like going to a reunion and remembering when you were the hotshot on the field or the king of the goddamn campus."

"There's no logic or reason to it, darling. There's no humanity in it."

He was so warm, so solid, his hand stroking her back as if to soothe the dark thoughts away. She could feel her insides begin to shake, sense the wild tears that solved nothing burn closer.

God. God. She didn't want to break again.

So she lifted her face. "Show me, will you? Remind me what it's meant to be. How it always should be."

"You're so tired," he murmured.

"Be my soother." She tipped her face up again, touched his lips with hers. "I'll be yours."

Chapter 21

She was his, and the miracle of belonging never failed to bring some light into the dark.

She knew what this physical act could mean when driven by violence, by a quest for power, when it was driven by need, by passion and lust. And she knew, from him, what it meant when driven by love.

That had saved her.

He was gentle with her and she with him, knowing gentleness was needed for both. Long, quiet kisses, like balm on a wound, all comfort to tend battered, bleeding souls.

So the swimming fatigue eased into a kind of dreamy wonder. He would give, she would give, and together they would find solace.

Patient hands on her skin, warming where the cold was buried so deep she'd never have reached it. His lips telling her wordlessly she was loved—she was cherished.

Then the words, those murmurs in Irish, like a soft caress over the unspeakable ache.

She gave them back to him, running her fingers through

that silky hair, along those strong shoulders. To touch, just to touch, the miracle in her life.

Held warm and close in the dark, she felt that dreamy wonder begin the gradual lift to dreamy arousal.

She let it go—he knew the moment she did, the instant all the dark thoughts left her. And only the two of them remained in her heart, her mind.

With her wrapped around him, offering, asking, he could let it go. Only her, only this. Only love.

Only love, with her heart beating thickly under his lips, with her long, lean body moving. And her hands, so strong, so sure, gliding over him.

A warrior she was, would always be. But even a warrior needed tending.

He slipped inside her, gently, still gently, filling her as he murmured the words beating in his own heart. They moved slowly, riding long, sweet waves.

When those waves broke, they broke in beauty and a devotion neither had known with another.

"Can you sleep now?"

She let out a long sigh. "I think. But . . . let's just hold on awhile. Okay?"

"We'll hold on, you and I."

Once again he felt her let go, this time into sleep. He lay quiet for a time, making certain she slept without the dark chasing her. Then he let himself follow her, still holding on.

She woke in the dark, heart pounding. Someone was screaming, and she feared it was her.

"It's all right. It's all right now." He gripped her, swearing all the while. "It's just the alarm."

"It's—what? It's five?"

"No, it's not yet bloody four. It's the alarm I set on the searches. Just give me a moment, let me see what the buggering hell it is."

"You got a hit. Lights on, twenty percent. You got a hit."

"Let me bloody see, will you?"

Gone was the tender lover of the night, and in his place was a very annoyed, very tired man. He grabbed the PPC he'd set on the nightstand, scowled at it.

"Get coffee," he snapped, "for both of us. I'll not deal with this without coffee first. And yes, we've a hit. Let me see it through on this bleeding thing to make certain it's worth being ripped awake."

She didn't argue. She wanted to, but she wanted coffee more. And it was so rare to see him tired and out of sorts, she'd give him that bloody minute before she pushed.

"There it is, there it is. Oh, she's clever this one, and I'll wager she had some help with it. But there it is."

"What? Say what or I dump the damn coffee."

"An address. Give me the shagging coffee." He grabbed it, downed half the mug, hot and black. "An address, if I'm not mistaken, that is no more than a couple of blocks from Central. I need this coffee and a shower—and not a bloody boiling one. The copter is still outside, and we can be there in minutes."

"I need to set it up."

"Do what you need to do. I'm having a shower, cool enough to clear my head."

"Give me that thing." She snatched the PPC from him. "Go."

She read the address—he was right. Close enough to Central that a cop with a decent arm could throw a rock through the window.

She started to tag Peabody, remembered she was naked, blocked video.

"Peabody," came the muffled, slurred answer.

"We've got an address. Get to Central. I'll be there within fifteen. Tag Baxter. I want him and Trueheart. And Uniform Carmichael. Are you getting this?"

"Yeah. I got it. I got it."

"Bring McNab if he wants in—and Carmichael needs to tap three more uniforms. Move now, Peabody."

"I'm up. I'm moving. I'll make the tags."

Eve clicked off—she'd deal with the rest on the way. But for now, she rushed into the bathroom and, bracing herself, stepped into the shower.

This time the scream she heard was her own. "Oh fucking hell, it's freezing."

"It's set at ninety degrees, precisely."

Because he sounded like himself, and amused about it, she gave him a snarl. "Get out, because it's going up to one-oh-one. I'm out in two minutes."

He left her to it, grabbed a towel, heard her heartfelt groan of relief after she called for jets at 101 degrees.

In just over two minutes, she darted back into the bedroom, dry but still naked, then dived into her closet.

By the time she dived out, dragging on trousers, he was already wearing his own, and a black sweater—and sliding a clutch piece into an ankle holster.

"I don't want to see that weapon unless somebody's pointing one at you."

She dragged on a black sweater—one she'd grabbed at random rather than by plan—shrugged into her weapon harness. She strapped on a clutch piece as well, pulled on her boots.

"I need blueprints, schematics of the building to set up this op. We need to move fast."

"I can access those or pilot the copter. Which would you like?"

"Shit. Walk me through how to access—the fast way." She snagged her coat, tossed him his. "Magic coats, pal. They're going to be armed, and they're not going to be happy."

To save time, she turned to the elevator.

"How many are you pulling in?" he asked her.

"Peabody, McNab, Baxter, Trueheart, Uniform Carmichael, and three uniforms he picks. I can tap more, but I need to see the building, get a sense of it. We'll get eyes and ears on it—you can help there. I don't want to drag Feeney in."

"He'd want you to, and be right pissed you didn't."

"Crap." She pulled out her comm as she ran out the front door. Not the 'link—the comm, more official. If Feeney slept through the signal, that wasn't her fault.

She made it fast, left the voice communication, ended it as she strapped into the godforsaken jet copter.

"This time of day we could almost drive there this fast."

"It's here, it's ready."

He lifted off at a speed that had her stomach remaining at ground level and whimpering. But she set her teeth, and contacted a duty officer to inform him she was coming in by air, and by civilian. Her comm beeped an incoming before she was done.

Feeney left his own message.

On my way.

"How do I access the blueprints?"

As he soared over buildings, Roarke gave her step-by-step directions in the simplest terms he could manage.

"That doesn't sound exactly legal."

"It's a gray area."

She grunted, followed the steps until she was looking at the floor plan of a two-story building, with full basement.

"That's where they have him," she muttered, and began to study the egress, the access, and working out the bones of her op.

He landed with some bumps on the helipad, and she jumped out into the cold, angry wind. She badged them both inside, jumped on the elevator.

"Doors front, rear, side. Corner building. Prime real estate. There's a basement, and my money says that's where they've got the torture room set up. No access to the basement from the outside, so we have to go in from above."

"They'll hear you coming."

"Maybe, but if I had a torture room— I don't, do I?"

"No. Perhaps Charmaine can design one."

"Har har. If I had a torture room, it would be fully

soundproofed." She jumped off on her level. "I'm going to confiscate a conference room. You want to be a hero?"

"Yours, darling? Every day."

"Ha. Help me transfer the board from my office. And program a vat of real coffee. I need to get the blueprints, the schematics up on screen so I can really see them. Peabody should be here pretty quick, but not quick enough."

"Doesn't your conference room have a swipe board?"

"I hate those things." She hissed out a breath. "But okay, faster."

"Ah, technology." This time he did pat her ass. "You program the vat of coffee, and I'll transfer your data. You can set it up how you please after. What room?"

She shoved open a door, saw it empty. "This one."

In her office, she hit the AutoChef while Roarke sat down at her desk. Since she didn't actually have a vat, she calculated, then programmed three large pots. It should get them going.

"Swipe board or not," she muttered, stuffing Yancy's sketches in a file.

"I'm going to start setting up. Maybe you could bring the rest of the coffee." She strode out without waiting for his answer.

In the conference room, she scowled at the computer. "Activate swipe board."

You are not registered for this room and this equipment at this time.

"Bite me. Dallas, Lieutenant Eve. Register it, goddamn it."

The use of profanity is not—

"I'll beat you to death with a hammer, then stomp what's left into dust. I'll torch the dust. Register this room and this equipment at this fucking time to Dallas, Lieutenant Eve." She slapped her badge on its pad. "Scan it. Do it. Or I swear, you'll be in the recycler in two minutes flat."

Identification scanned and verified. This room and this
equipment is registered to Dallas, Lieutenant Eve.

"Damn right. Activate the motherfucking swipe board."

Board is now activated. Profanity is against regulations,
and must be reported.

"This time you can blow me. And bring up all data currently transferred from my office comp."

Images flickered on. Ignoring the drone of the comp
informing her of the regulations, and her violations, she
began to arrange them in the way she needed.

"Activate wall screen." She frowned at her PPC, at the
comp, at the screen, and started the sticky—for her—transfer
when Roarke came in with two large pots. "Save this comp's
motherboard and transfer the blueprints to the wall screen.
I'll get you coffee."

She'd barely picked up the pot when it was done—so she
shoved the pot at him.

"I have to see this."

He poured for both of them while she stepped closer to
the screen, shoved her hands into the coat she'd yet to take
off, and fell silent.

Like a general, he thought, studying the battlefield. He
said nothing, just handed her a mug of coffee, until she
finally nodded.

"Okay," she said, turning just as she heard the clomp of
Peabody's boots, the prance of McNab's.

They both looked a little hollow-eyed, Eve noticed, but
sniffed the air like hounds on the hunt.

"Is that the smell of real coffee?" Peabody asked.

"Grab some. This is the building. It's two blocks from
here."

"Son of a bitch." McNab angled his head, currently covered in yet another watch cap of green and blue stripes.
"How'd you nail her?"

"Utility bills," Roarke said. "The property itself? Ownership's buried behind two interlocking shells, and under that, it turns out, is deeded to Grace Blake's great-grandmother—and they used the woman's maiden name. And the deed is in trust, as the woman herself is deceased. And the trust—"

"Get into that later," Eve ordered.

"Well, it's a clever ruse and worth the time, but for now, it was the payments for the heat and so on. Still not in her name, or I'd have found it sooner, but again, the great-grandmother—one Elizabeth Haversham—nee Pawter—and the utilities came to an account under Beth Pawter, so it took some doing to link it up."

He glanced at Eve, who was again studying the screen. "She has an account in that name, if you've an interest, with a brokerage firm in Iowa, where Elizabeth Pawter Haversham lived. It's well funded, that account, even with the cost of the building and its expenses coming out of it. Until a year ago, the dead Mrs. Pawter rented that building for a nice, steady income."

"Because she started to plan how she wanted to use it," Eve said, still studying the screen. "She met at least one of the others, found their mutual history, and it began."

Uniform Carmichael arrived next, with three others. Baxter and Trueheart followed.

While they made short work of the coffee, Feeney walked in.

"There better be some of that left." He stole the mug McNab had just poured in case there wasn't. "That the target?"

"That's the target, and here's how we're going to take it."

It would work, Eve thought as she went over the timing, the contingencies. And by hitting the target before first light, they'd take the women by surprise—and likely unprepared.

She frowned as she noticed Roarke step out while she went over positioning with Baxter and Trueheart. When she glanced back, he walked in carrying a stack of bakery boxes.

Every cop in the room caught the scent of yeast and sugar.

She should've known.

"Donuts may be a cliché, but they do the job, don't they?" Roarke set the boxes on the conference table. "And so will all of you."

He shot Eve a quick grin as hands darted and grabbed for jelly-filled or crullers, bear claws or honey-glazed.

"Stuff them in, and suit up. Feeney, the donut king's with you. Peabody, Baxter, Trueheart, with me. Uniform Carmichael, take your men to the pre-op location. We go in quiet."

She gave Roarke a long, flat stare when he offered her a donut.

"Bavarian cream—with sprinkles. Be happy oatmeal would have taken too long, and can't be eaten on the go."

There was that. She took the donut, and followed her own orders. She stuffed it in, and she suited up.

New York was rarely quiet, but at just past five in the morning, it hit a lull. Night-shift workers still had time on the clock, and the day shift hugged their pillows. Street LCs would have called it a night, and those higher on the food chain slept in their own beds or the client's—depending on the payment schedule.

Shops were dark, and even the 24/7s ran sleepily.

Barricading a block around a particular building could be done quickly and quietly, and barely caused a ripple on the frigid air.

And that building held dark.

She'd considered the timing, the positioning, the partnering carefully. And now, the team moved through the dark, silent as shadows.

Baxter and Trueheart on the side door, McNab and Peabody on the front. And she took the back—the closest to the basement, and her hunch—with Roarke.

She heard Feeney's voice in her earbud. "You're a go for eyes and ears."

Beside her Roarke began work with his portable, and McNab signaled he did the same. She ignored the quiet e-jargon as the three communicated, and only thought:

Show me where they are. Just show me.

"Got your heat sources coming through."

Eve narrowed her eyes, as she was damn sure Feeney had a mouthful of donut as he coordinated.

"Two on the second floor, three basement level. You got 'em?"

"I do," Roarke replied as McNab gave an affirmative.

Roarke snaked a hair-thin wire under the door, did some magic with his portable. "Quiet on this front."

"And here," McNab answered. "I'm getting movement on the basement level."

"Roger that," Feeney said. "One subject standing, now facing another. Third on that level moving east. Now stopped."

"Taking shifts." Eve nodded. "Two upstairs getting rack time. Two down working on Easterday. He's still alive. Peabody, McNab, take the stairs up on my go. Baxter, Trueheart, hit and split as planned. Carmichael?"

"In position, sir."

She gave Roarke the nod. He began to work on the locks, quickly, precisely, and the alarm that connected to them. The other teams would use battering rams—fast and noisy.

But she'd have a jump on the basement level before the suspects were alerted.

"We're clear here," he told her.

"We're moving in. Hold your positions."

When Roarke eased the door open, she went in low, swept with her weapon and flashlight.

Large kitchen, she registered. Empty and dark. And the basement door just ahead—shut.

"We're in. Feeney."

"No movement on second floor. Three in a group, basement level, center of the main room. You're standing on top of them."

She moved to the door, slowly turned the knob. When she eased the door open, she heard the screams, the sobs, the voices.

"All teams go. Move in. Move in."

She went down, leading with her weapon while Easterday's shrieks sliced through the air.

He hung by his arms from a hook and pulley in the ceiling. His body was covered with bruises, burns, sweat, blood.

Charity Downing, stripped down to a tank and gym shorts, held a weighted sap. Lydia Su, teeth bared, shouted, "Harder! Make him feel it."

"Police! Hands in the air. Now. Now!"

As Eve gave the order, the crashes came from above, and the new screams from the alarm.

Unlike above stairs, the basement lights glared on full. In them Su pivoted, using Easterday's body as a shield.

"We're not done! We're not done!"

Eve dodged the wild stun stream, firing back, a wide stream on low, as she leaped down the rest of the stairs.

"You're done. You're surrounded. It's over."

"No." Weeping, Su turned the stunner on Easterday, leaving Eve no choice.

She dropped Su, even as Downing let the sap fall with a sickening thud, her own hands shooting up.

"Please don't. Please. Don't hurt her. Lydia. Lydia." Downing went to her knees, gathered Su in her arms. "Stop, stop. Remember what Grace told us."

Eyes wheeling from the stun, Lydia shuddered. "Not done."

"We need the MTs, we need a bus! Baxter, restrain these two."

He rushed down the rest of the stairs. "I've got them, boss."

"Peabody!"

"We've got Blake and MacKensie. We're secure."

Eve turned to Easterday, who wept in harsh, racking sobs. "Help me. Help me."

"I bet that's what they said," Eve murmured, but holstered her weapon. "Roarke, help me lower him down."

"They hurt me."

"You're alive," she said, without a drop of sympathy.

He was alive, she thought as they brought him down. She'd done the job.

"Have the women taken in," she told Baxter. "Keep them separated."

Su, still reeling from the stun, shot Eve a look of tearful hate. "He deserves to die. All of them deserved to die."

"You don't get to make that call. Get them out, Baxter."

She looked down at Easterday as he lay on the floor, moaning. "Medical assistance is on the way."

"They killed Fred. They made me watch."

She said nothing when Roarke took a blanket from a sofa, tossed it over the shivering man. But she thought: You like to watch.

She hunkered down, looked him in his blackened, swollen eyes. "I'll get your full statement after you've had medical attention, but for now, Marshall Easterday, you're under arrest for multiple counts of false imprisonment, for rape, for sexual assault, for conspiracy to rape."

"You can't—you can't—"

"Just did." She stepped aside when the MTs rushed down, but took one by the arm. "This man is under arrest. When you transport him, he'll be restrained, and will remain restrained. A uniformed officer will ride in the bus with him, and remain with him at all times. Understood?"

"Got it. Better let us work on him, get him stable enough to transport. He looks in bad shape."

"Fix him up good," Eve told them, and as they went to work on Easterday, she read him his Revised Miranda rights.

"Our two are on their way to Holding," Baxter told Eve when he came back down. "The other two are about to be. They didn't give our guys any trouble. How about him?"

"He's been read his rights. I'll have Carmichael select an officer to stick with him." She handed her restraints to Baxter. "Lock him to the gurney when they get him on one. I need to check in with the rest of the team."

"I've got it. Some place," he added as she turned.

"Yeah." A replica of the room in the recording. Some

updates, some additions, but the Brotherhood had probably made the same. They'd brought the men into the nightmare, and turned it on them.

The women, Eve thought, had brought their past with them.

She went upstairs, saw Peabody with MacKensie and a woman she recognized from the sketches as Grace Carter Blake.

"You don't know what they did to us." MacKensie's voice trembled. "You don't know what they made us."

"Hush now." Blake consoled her. With the coat she'd worn on Su's security feed over simple white pajamas, she stood, shoulders straight, eyes exhausted.

"She needs to *know*. They destroyed us. They took our lives."

"You'll have the chance to tell me," Eve said. "Peabody, did you read them their rights?"

"Done. I can take them in."

"No, I need you elsewhere. Have them transported. We'll talk later," she said to both women.

"We will all be invoking our right to counsel," Blake said.

"You go right ahead."

"You don't understand," MacKensie began, but Blake cut her off.

"Carlee, not now. Lawyer." Blake stared through Eve. "We say nothing without our legal counsel. And as a lawyer, I'll stand in as same until we're able to contact other."

"No, you won't. If you're a lawyer and not an idiot, you understand you're under arrest for conspiracy to murder, among other charges, all connected to the other suspects. That conflict of interest precludes you acting as counsel, except for yourself. Get them gone, Peabody."

She rubbed her eyes, pulled out her 'link.

"Don't tell me." Curled in bed, video unblocked, Reo kept her eyes shut. "Another warrant."

"I've just busted the murder ring, and the raping brotherhood, and made five arrests."

Reo's eyes popped open.

"You're going to want to tell your boss, and meet me at St. Alban's, where I'll be questioning Marshall Easterday."

She clicked off, nearly turned into Roarke. "Don't ask," she said, anticipating him. "The answer is I'm fine. I need to finish this, and it's going to take some time. But . . . I could use you and that damn copter later. I'm not going to finish until I see the Brotherhood house. We won't have much trouble finding it now."

"None at all. The hit came through while we were taking the house—as did McNab's on the van."

"That's handy. So . . . can I tap you for the transpo later?"

"Of course. I'll clear the time, whenever you're ready."

"Don't hug me." She could anticipate that, too. "You can pretend you did, and I'll pretend you did. I'll probably really appreciate the real thing when this is done."

"I'll clear time for that as well." So he simply brushed his finger over the dent in her chin. "I'll leave you to it, Lieutenant."

"I appreciate the assist." She broke cop dignity long enough to take his hand. "All the way around."

When he left, she took a moment to settle, then got back to work.

Within the hour she stood with Peabody and Reo in Easterday's hospital suite. To Eve's mind he looked better than he had a right to.

"How can you do this?" He lifted the hand chained to the bed. "Those women murdered my friends, tortured them, and they tortured me. They—they forced me to watch while they . . . what they did to Freddy."

"They'll face those consequences. But we're here to talk about you, and your brotherhood. We're here to talk about what you and your *brothers* began forty-nine years ago."

"I don't know what you're talking about. Those women—"

"We have the recording from the first rape. Her name is Tara Daniels." God bless Harvo. "Remember her?"

"I don't know what you're talking about. I don't know anyone by that name."

"And they say you always remember your first." Her voice seethed with disgust. "Betz recorded it, and kept the old, original disc, and souvenirs from every victim since in his bank box in the Bronx."

Easterday hadn't known about the bank box, Eve thought, catching the quick leap of shock into his eyes.

"We're identifying all those victims as we speak, through DNA. You're alive, Easterday, because we got to you in time, despite the fact you chose to run rather than face what you'd done."

"You're wrong. You're just wrong. I want—"

"I have the evidence." She leaned in, close to his battered face. "I viewed the recording, I watched you rape Tara Daniels, and watch, laugh, drink while your friends raped her. I watched Frederick Betz stick a needle in her so you could all pretend she wanted you.

"Want to see it? I can arrange to have it shown right here on your view screen."

"No. No. I . . . you don't understand."

"Enlighten me."

"We were . . . we were young, and under such tremendous pressure. We needed to let off some steam—we weren't allowed outside the security perimeters without permission. And she—she—she'd been provocative, teasing. She was drunk and she'd already been with Edward. And she came on to me."

"So she asked for it?"

"He said— It was a different time."

"A different time that made it okay to tie a woman down, slap her around, gang rape her, dose her with chemicals against her will? Then what was it . . . Yeah, after you were done, after all of you took turns with her, any way you wanted, it was okay to 'douche the douche,' dump her back on campus?"

"We drank too much," he began. "All the pressure we were under. She wouldn't remember. What harm did it really do?"

"But they did remember." This time Peabody pushed close. "Elsi Lee Adderman remembered and it twisted her up so much she killed herself."

"Who? I don't know who that is."

"Just one of forty-nine," Eve said. "You disgusting excuse for a human being. What gave you the right?"

"It was tradition! It was one harmless night a year. We never hurt them. It was just sex. A kind of bond, you see? Something shared."

"I guess Billy stopped thinking of it that way. Like Elsi, he couldn't live with it anymore."

"I . . . It bound us together. It brought us luck. All of us became successful. All of us made a mark on the world, came through that terrible time and made our marks. It was just one night a year."

"You raped forty-nine women."

"It wasn't rape! It was just sex, it was tradition. It was—"

"Did you drug them?"

"It was just—"

"Did you fucking drug them?"

"Yes, yes, but only because it eased the way—for them. For them," he said quickly.

"Did you restrain them?"

"Yes, but—just to add to the excitement—for them, too."

"Did these women say stop? Say no?"

"Only at the start of the . . . It was a kind of ritual. And we selected them carefully. To be selected was a kind of honor."

She could see the panic in his eyes at his own words. "Rape is an honor?"

"It was sex."

"Keep telling yourself that. You drugged them, restrained them, you forced yourself on them when they begged you to stop. You might just find yourself in the same situation in prison, for the rest of your life. And we'll see if you think of it as just sex."

"You can't put me in prison. Do you know who I am?"

"I know exactly who you are."

"You work for me!" Incensed, he tried to shove up, and the restraints rattled. "For men like me."

"I work for the City of New York, and I put people like you in cages. I fucking love my job, and tonight, right this minute, more than ever."

"Those women are criminals. They're murderers. They're insane. They beat me. They burned me."

"Oh, we'll let the medicals fix you all up before you go in the cage. You and the last of your brothers—that's Ethan MacNamee, who's even now being extradited to New York—are going to have a long time to think about your traditions. You got enough, Reo?"

"More than. Mr. Easterday, you've confessed, on the record and after being duly Mirandized, to the charges of multiple rapes."

"No! It was *not* rape. I was only explaining." Tears spilled down his cheeks. "I don't want to talk to you anymore. I've been hurt! I have nothing more to say."

"That's your right," Reo said easily. "On the other hand, Mr. MacNamee's had a lot to say. And if he continues, once he's doing that talking to Lieutenant Dallas, he'll get the deal I was about to offer you."

"What deal?" Eve demanded, on cue, as if outraged.

"This is my job, Lieutenant. And part of my job is to save the city the time and expense of a long, ugly trial. But since Mr. Easterday has invoked his right to remain silent . . ."

"I want to know the terms."

Reo looked back at him, nodded. "All right. If you'll excuse us, Lieutenant, Detective."

"This is bullshit." But Eve stormed out, then slowed when she got out the door.

"What's the deal?" Peabody asked. "I knew you and Reo had your heads together."

"Life, no parole, but on-planet. He'd likely get that

anyway. But she'll scare him into signing off. He's done. MacNamee is done—he spilled plenty to Scotland, and we'll get the rest out of him."

She shoved a hand through her hair because she was far from done. "Let's go talk to the women."

Chapter 22

At Blake's request, Eve took her first, sat across from her and in the box.

Blake wore prison orange now.

"You have now suspended your wish for counsel or representation?"

"For the moment, yes. As you pointed out, I can represent myself. And though I would advise my client to remain silent, my client has a deep emotional need to make a statement. And in making it, hopes to help the three women you'll soon interview here.

"They're victims, Lieutenant."

"I'm listening."

"I was a student at Yale University. I worked very hard to be accepted into Yale, very hard to shine there. My ambition was law, corporate law. I wanted a high-powered job, planned to make full partner before I turned forty. I wanted a big, glamorous apartment, and glamorous friends. I accomplished all of that, and I was content. I told myself I was content, that the nightmares that recurred were stress-induced. They had no basis in reality.

"The nightmares where I was tied to a bed in a room with colored lights. Spinning lights, loud music. Male laughter. Where I wept and raged. Where I relived that shock, that pain, that humiliation. Faceless men, forcing themselves into me. Forcing me to drink something that, after each had had me once, turned me into an animal, so I begged them to take me again. And again when they could untie me, then hang me up by the wrists in the center of those spinning lights, and take me two at a time."

She paused, sipped the water Peabody had set on the table. Though her hand stayed steady, her breath shuddered out before she spoke again.

"In my ambitions I had imagined men—suitable men, entertaining men. Out of them I would select a mate and build a fine life. But in reality, after those nightmares began, whenever I tried to be with a man, a panic filled me. A terrible sickness. I thought perhaps I had some condition, and began to see a therapist."

She paused a moment, steadied herself. "I thought I might prefer women, but no matter how gentle the lover I chose, that panic would grip me. For a while, I accepted I could be with no one, could not be intimate, I'd just focus on my work, on my career. But the nightmares wouldn't relent. My work began to suffer, and the nightmares raged inside me, like the men in them raged.

"And I began to remember more, see more. Their faces. Part of me refused to believe it had actually happened. How could such a terrible thing have happened to me? How could I live and work, day after day, after that terrible thing? But it had happened. I began to understand it had. I couldn't work, couldn't sleep, couldn't eat. I thought of suicide, just to end it. And I took the medications my therapist prescribed, but it didn't relent. One day I attended a support group, one for rape victims. I met CeCe Anson, the kindest woman I've ever known, and through her Lydia Su."

"Su had the same nightmares, the same memories."

"Yes. We became friends, and I thought, with her . . . but even with her I couldn't bear to be touched. And it came out, what I remembered or dreamed. It came out she dreamed the same. We sat in the dark, holding each other as those memories fell out of us, twined together. It seemed impossible at first. But then . . ."

"There were too many details for it to be impossible."

"Yes. I quit my job at the firm, sold my fancy apartment. I bought the house where you found us, thinking that one day I might create a crisis center or a school, or . . . I wasn't clear on that. I offered my legal services to the group, to the crisis center. I continued to attend the group. It was a lifeline, and I began to do pro bono work for Inner Peace because they'd helped Lydia."

"You found Carlee MacKensie that way."

"Yes."

"And you realized she'd had the same experience."

"It was weeks, months, but we became what we'll call wounded friends. We'd have coffee after group, talk. And then, yes, we began to see all three of us had the same dreams, and what had happened, somehow, to all three of us was too similar to be chance."

Grace leaned forward. "Do you believe in fate?"

"What does fate have to do with it?"

"We met, Lydia and I, then I met Carlee, and we were three. One day I was called to assist another woman with a legal issue. Charity. She'd been in another group and had a kind of meltdown during a session. She'd gone after one of the other women—sexually. CeCe contacted me to help her with the legal issues. She told me she'd been speaking, taking her turn, and had some sort of flashback. The heat, the need—and it had happened once or twice before. She broke down in my little office, told me about her recurring nightmares."

"Then there were four."

"Yes, and no possible way this could be anything other than a pattern. I began to search through the records—and that's certainly a violation—but we were desperate to know if there were more. I found Elsi.

"All the details—I'll give you all I have. The timing, the

where and when, but I'd like to just give you the broad points now."

"Go ahead."

"Elsi was so young, and her wounds, we'll say, fresher and more intense. Maybe they'd mixed the dose. Maybe they'd experimented. I can't say. But she would have those flashes, and find herself waking up with a stranger. She'd have nightmares so violent she'd harm herself during them. She . . . she began cutting herself."

Blake paused for more water. "It had just happened, only the previous spring, so she saw the faces clearly—as they were now."

"And you had Charity to draw them."

"Yes. Edward Mira, I recognized him, and that led to the others. It led, as we'd already believed, to Yale. Only Charity hadn't attended the university, but she'd been seeing a Yale man on and off, and sometimes attended parties or events. Lectures. On one of her visits, she found herself wandering the campus before dawn, with no memory of what had happened. At first she believed she'd had too much to drink and had blacked out, or possibly been roofied and raped. But she couldn't remember. None of us remembered it all, until all of us did."

"So you planned the murders."

"Not at first. We'd meet—at the house where you found us because it became ours. A safe place, so in a way, it was a crisis center. We talked about how we could prove it, if we'd be believed if we went to the police.

"Could I have some more water?"

Peabody rose, went out to get it.

"We were five women who'd been ripped to pieces. We wanted to find proof. We needed to find justice."

"It's the job of the police to find proof. It's the courts who determine justice."

"We needed to *do* something after Elsi . . . I've left that out. It's painful."

She stopped again when Peabody returned with more water.

"Thank you. I researched the laws. I'd been a corporate lawyer, but I gave myself lessons in criminal law. And for all but Elsi and Charity, the statute of limitations had passed. We'd never reported a crime, as we hadn't known we'd been victims of a crime—until it was too late for justice. For Charity, the window was closing."

She pressed her lips together. "I can see, and I should have seen then, we put too much weight on Elsi. She and Charity were the only ones who could file charges. We would all add our own stories, and surely that would prove they'd done this, and done it, and done it. There wouldn't just be the five of us. There would be more women, and more women would remember when it came out, but . . ."

"Elsi couldn't handle it."

"She was so fragile, and she broke." Tears welled up now, spilled out. "She simply shattered, and we'll live with that guilt. They raped her, they ruined her, but we broke her trying to put all of us back together again. And then, yes then, we began to plan how to get justice for her, for all of us. At first, we told ourselves we would find proof. But we didn't. Carlee and Charity sacrificed more than I can tell you, and we didn't find proof."

"You had Carlee sleep with Edward Mira."

"She was strong, she was willing. We'd hoped she might find something to implicate him, more victims, victims who had been more recent like our Elsi. But he was careful there. And then Charity took her place. Carlee couldn't face any more, so Charity stepped in. But we found nothing. Then, yes, we began to plan how to get justice. For Elsi. For all of us."

Blake set the water down, wiped the tears away. "I posed as a Realtor, and made the appointment to meet him at the house he wanted to sell. Charity came in with me. We stunned him, we hurt him. We wanted him to know who we were, and what was coming. Then the other man came. We had a moment of panic, but we knocked him out. I knocked him out. He wasn't one of them, and we had no desire or reason to harm him. We forced Edward into Lydia's van, and brought him to the basement."

"One you'd set up to replicate where you'd been raped."

"Yes. What we did was against the law—we'll pay the price. God knows we've already paid worse. But what we did was earned, it was right, because the law protected them."

"You're wrong. You don't get to torture and execute. You don't get to decide what payment is made. And the law wouldn't have protected them."

"The statute of limitations."

"They formed a conspiracy—and that changes things, Counselor. You should've stuck with corporate. A conspiracy to drug and incapacitate, to kidnap, to hold individuals against their will, to rape and cause bodily, mental, and emotional harm to same. I would have put every one of them away, if you'd given me the chance—the way I'm going to put Marshall Easterday and Ethan MacNamee away."

"They're wealthy, powerful men, and the law is slippery, full of loopholes. They would have—"

"Look at me!" Eve slapped a fist on the table. "I would have put them away, and they'd have paid for years. Think about that. They'd have paid for years, not for one night. You decided to be judge, jury, and hangman. So now you'll pay, too. I would have stood for you, the law would have stood for you. Now I have to stand for the men who raped you. I have to stand for the men you killed."

"We couldn't take it anymore." Tears glittered in her eyes. "We couldn't bear it, not after Elsi. They're monsters. Monsters. Imagine a monster forcing his way into you. Imagine revisiting that horror night after night in your dreams. We couldn't take it anymore."

She wiped at her wet cheeks. "Each one of us will tell you the same. But they'll speak to you with counsel present. That's all I have to say until I, too, have counsel present."

Eve nodded, rose. "Subject has invoked right to counsel. Interview end. Peabody, will you take Ms. Blake back to Holding where she'll be permitted to contact her chosen representative?"

"Yes, sir. Ms. Blake."

Blake got to her feet. "Each one of us was on a path to a

life, to work, maybe to love and family. To children. Who knows? Each one of us was ripped off that path and thrown into a dark place where there would always be nightmares. They killed who we were, Lieutenant. Who we might have been. How does the law punish that?"

"The two left will never get out of a cage—it's their turn to be the animal. You have and had a choice, to make yourself into what you could be, and you made that choice."

"Elsi was a virgin. Rape was her only sexual experience. She never had a chance."

As Peabody led Blake out, Eve pressed her hands to her eyes. Her throat burned, raw and dry. Her head pounded in an ugly beat.

She dropped her hands when Mira stepped in.

"So?" Eve shrugged. "Diminished capacity? Despite the calculation?"

"It's possible they'll spend their years in a facility, get treatment, therapy. But they conspired to murder, and succeeded with three."

"But the law's slippery and full of loopholes."

"It is. But you've done your job, and more. You stood for those women, too, Eve, and you'll stand for the rest as they're identified."

"Harvo's come through with more names. Do I contact them? What if they don't remember, are living their lives? What good would it do?"

Mira laid her hands on Eve's shoulders, rubbed at the knotted muscles as she met Eve's eyes in the wide mirror.

"You needed to remember, or you couldn't live your life, not fully, not as you were meant. You could pass the notifications off, with no shame."

"It would shame me."

Turning Eve toward her, Mira cupped Eve's face. "Because you chose to take a terrible thing and make yourself who you are. You and I, we feel for Grace Blake, for all of them. But what you said to her was truth. It was truth, Eve. I'll help with the notifications. I'll offer counseling to every one you find, if they want it from me."

"You deserve each other."

"Excuse me?"

"You and Mr. Mira. You really deserve each other. Lucky when that happens. You'll tell him it's done."

"I will."

"I guess he told you I told him because I thought you'd already told him."

Understanding perfectly, Mira nodded. "Yes, we talked. He'll be your champion. He's a quiet hero, Eve, but he's steadfast, and he's true. He'll never betray your trust, and will always be there for you."

This time when Eve pressed her fingers to her eyes, tears pressed back. "Okay. I've got to finish this. I just want to go home and sleep for a couple days."

"Go home. Sleep awhile."

"No, I need to interview the rest of them."

"Then I'll observe."

"And then I have to go there. To where this all happened. I need to see it, document it, secure it. There will be other recordings. Goddamn tradition."

"Do you want me to go with you?"

"No. No. You should go home. You don't look like you've slept in a week. No offense."

"None taken, as I have a mirror. Will you do something for me?"

"Sure, if I can."

"When this is finished, and we both get some sleep, will you come to dinner? You and Roarke. Come to dinner. Dennis will make his chocolate trifle, and you haven't lived until you've tasted it."

"I'm not sure what it is."

"Amazing." She kissed Eve's cheek. Then, maybe because she needed it just as much, left her cheek pressed against Eve's. "I'm going to cook you and Roarke a lovely meal, followed by Dennis's amazing trifle. And we won't talk about any of this."

She drew back now. "Will you do that for me?"

"Yeah. Yeah, it sounds good."

"Go finish it, because you must."

Eve went to where Peabody waited discreetly outside the door. "Let's take Downing next, once her lawyer's here. She's the one closest to the edge."

"I'll have her brought up. She's contacted the lawyer. She can wait in the box. They should have trusted us. Trusted cops like us to find the proof, to work for justice."

"Yeah. But they didn't."

Hours later, what felt like days later, she sat in the cockpit of the copter, winging toward Connecticut.

"They all told basically the same story, but not so exact that it felt rehearsed. I think, yeah, they talked it all through before. If we get caught, we have to say this and that. But they're not lying."

"Easterday?"

"Took the deal. Contacted his wife. My intel is she came in, and within thirty minutes, walked out of his hospital room. She kept walking."

"And the last one?"

"MacNamee. He took Reo's deal. Both of them are smart enough to know a trial would slaughter them. The recordings—of which there are forty-eight more locked in a safe in the basement of the house—would slaughter them. They don't want the public humiliation. They don't know real humiliation. Just how to inflict it."

He laid a hand over hers. "And you?"

"I'm holding. I had to talk to Edward Mira's son and daughter. And that slaughtered them. No way around it. Same with Wymann's family."

She closed her eyes. "And Harvo's ID'd more than half of the women. I ran them. Two are dead—self-termination. Another death by misadventure. Two are street LCs. One's doing time for assault—illegals junkie. Two more have done a revolving door in and out of rehab. But a few of them seem to have reasonably stable lives. Mira says they need to know."

"Some part of them does know, as some part of you always did. Bringing it to light may help them in ways you can't see."

"Maybe. God, I hope so. That road down there? That's the one Betz racked up speeding tickets on. I wonder how many times he drove up here to watch those tapes. That's the campus?"

She looked down at it—snow-covered and elegant, spires and dignity.

"Monsters can grow anywhere," he said. "We both know it. It wasn't the place or the time. It was the men."

"Dennis Mira went here, same time, same place. That's good enough for me."

When Roarke touched down, with snow shooting up like a storm, she sat, studying the house.

Large, old, dignified, beautifully kept. Even now the walks were cleared of snow, the trees glistened with it.

She saw the Celtic symbol for brotherhood carved into the center of the main door.

It sickened her.

"Su told me they'd found it. Thought about burning it to the ground when they couldn't get through security. But they were afraid there would be some evidence in it, and didn't want to risk destroying it."

"They didn't know they were being recorded."

"No. By the time they were involved, the fucking brothers graduated from handheld or tripod to installed cams throughout the room. I got that from MacNamee."

"Are you ready?"

Was she? She sat another moment waiting for the answer. Found it.

"Yeah. I couldn't go in there without you. It would be like that room in Dallas. I'd make myself go in, but I couldn't do what I need to do, and do it right, without you."

She felt that hot wash roll over her again. "I have to get this out, get it out before we go in."

He turned to her, took her hands. "What?"

"I understand what drove those women to this, understand how they could do it, all of it. Whatever I said in the box, whatever I said on record, I understand."

"How could you not? How could anyone human not? Whatever the law, the rules, Eve, how could you not feel for them?"

"I wish I had stopped them before Edward Mira. Before they made the choice that's going to take away their freedom. But—they'll get help. They'll lose their freedom, but the law, the rules, may save their lives. I talked to them, Roarke, every one of them. And Elsi Adderman might not have been the only one in their group to kill herself to end it. I think the law they disregarded, the law they didn't believe in, will save them. That's going to help me sleep at night."

"They don't need to know how much effort you put into saving them. Because you do. You know it." He kissed her hands. "My cop."

"Your cop has to go in there, deal with this. Then she really wants to go home. With you."

"Then we will. Let's get this day over with, and take the night for us."

She could, Eve thought as she climbed out into the ankle-deep snow. She could leave the day, and all its miseries, behind—soon. And take the night, and some peace, with him.

She could let go, she realized, of the old. Of an old desk, an old chair—old pieces of an old life.

She had a new one. Reaching for his hand, she held it firmly in hers. She had a real one, built by both of them.

"We're going to get rid of that desk."

He arched a brow as they approached the door of a house where brutality had lived far too long.

"Is that so?"

"Yeah. You know why?"

"I'd love to know."

"Because we deserve each other."

Roarke laughed, brought her hand up to kiss. "We bloody well do."

And now a special excerpt from
J. D. Robb's exciting new novel

Apprentice in Death

*Available September 2016 in hardcover
from Berkley Books!*

Prologue

It would be the first kill.

The apprentice understood the years of practice, the count-less targets destroyed, the training, the discipline, the hours of study, all led to this moment.

This cold, bright afternoon in January 2061 marked the true beginning.

A clear mind and cool blood.

The apprentice knew these elements were as vital as skill, as wind direction, humiture, and speed. Under the cool blood lived an eagerness ruthlessly suppressed.

The mentor had arranged all. Efficiently, and with an attention to detail that was also vital. The room in the clean, middle-class hotel on Second Avenue faced west, had privacy screens and windows that opened. It sat, unpretentiously, on a quiet block of Sutton Place, and offered a view of Central Park—though from nearly a mile away.

The mentor had planned well, booking a room on a floor well above the trees. To the naked eye, Wollman Rink was only a blob of white catching glints from the strong sun. And those who glided over it were only dots of moving color.

They'd skated there—student and teacher—more than once, had watched the target skimming, twirling, without a care in the world.

They'd scouted other areas. The target's workplace, the home, the favored shops, restaurants, all the routines. And had decided, together, the rink in the great park offered everything they wanted.

They worked well together, smoothly, and in silence as the the mentor adjusted the bipod by the west-facing window, as the apprentice attached the long-range laser rifle, secured it.

Cold winter air eked in the window as they raised it a few inches. Breath even, hands steady, the apprentice looked through the scope, adjusted.

The ice rink jumped close, close enough to see blade marks scoring the surface.

All those people, the brightly colored hats, gloves, and scarves. A couple, holding hands, laughing as they stumbled over the ice together. A girl with golden blond hair, wearing a red skin suit and vest, was spinning, spinning, spinning until she blurred. Another couple with a little boy between them, their hands joined with his as he grinned in wonder.

The old, the young, the in-between. The novices and the show-offs, the speedsters and the creep-alongs.

And none of them knew, none of them, that they were caught in the crosshairs, seconds from death. Seconds from the choice to let them live, make them die.

The power was incredible.

"Do you have the target?"

It took another moment. So many faces. So many bodies.

Then the apprentice nodded. There, the face, the body. The target. How many times had that face, that body been in the scope? Countless. But today would be the last time.

"Have you selected the other two?"

Another nod, as cool as the first.

"In any order. You're green to go."

The apprentice checked the wind speed, made a minute adjustment. Then with a clear mind, with cool blood, began.

The girl in the red skin suit circled in back crossovers, building speed for an axel jump. She began the rotation forward, the move from right skate to left, arms lifting.

The lethal stream struck the center of her back, with her own momentum propelling her forward. Her body, already dying, struck the family with the little boy. Like a projectile, that already dying body propelled them back, down.

The screaming began.

In the chaos that followed, a man gliding along on the other side of the rink slowed, glanced over.

The stream hit him center mass. As he crumbled, two skaters coming up behind him swerved around, kept going.

The couple, holding hands, still tripping along, skated awkwardly to the rail. The man gestured toward the jumble of bodies ahead of them.

"Hey. I think they're—"

The stream punched between his eyes.

In the hotel room, in the silence, the apprentice continued to watch through the scope, imagined the sounds, the screams. It would have been easy to take out a fourth, a fifth. A dozen.

Easy, satisfying. Powerful.

But the mentor lowered his field glasses.

"Three clean hits. Target's down." A hand laid on the apprentice's shoulder signaled approval. Signaled the end of the moment.

"Well done."

Quickly, efficiently, the apprentice broke down the rifle, stored it in its case as the mentor retracted the bipod.

Though no words were exchanged, the *joy*, the pride in the act, in the approval spoke clearly. And seeing it, the mentor smiled, just a little.

"We need to secure the gear, then we'll celebrate. You earned it. We can debrief after that. Tomorrow's soon enough to move on to the next."

As they left the hotel room—wiped clean before they'd begun and after they'd finished—the apprentice thought the next couldn't come soon enough.

Chapter 1

When Lieutenant Eve Dallas strode into the bullpen of Homicide after an annoying appearance in court, she wanted coffee. But Detective Jenkinson had obviously been lying in wait. He popped up from his desk, started toward her, leading with his obnoxious tie of the day.

"Are those frogs?" she demanded. "Why would you wear a tie with piss-yellow frogs jumping around on—Christ—puke-green lily pads?"

"Frogs are good luck. It's feng shui or some shit. Anyways, the fresh meat you brought in took a pop in the eye from some chemi-head down on Avenue B. She and Uniform Carmichael hauled him and the dealer in. They're in the tank. New girl's in the break room with an ice patch. Figured you'd want to know."

Fresh meat equaled the newly transferred Officer Shelby. "How'd she handle it?"

"Like a cop. She's all right, LT."

"Good to know."

She really wanted coffee—and not crap break-room coffee, but the *real* coffee in her office AutoChef. But she'd brought Officer Shelby on board, and on her first full day she'd taken a fist in the eye.

So Eve, tall and lanky in her black leather coat, walked to the break room.

Inside, Shelby sat drinking crap coffee, squinting at her PPC while wearing a cold patch over her right eye. She started to get to her feet, but Eve gestured her down.

"How's the eye, Officer?"

"My kid sister hits harder, Lieutenant."

At Eve's finger motion, Shelby lifted the patch.

The bloodshot white, the black and purple raying out from it had Eve nodding. "That's a nice one. Stick with the patch awhile."

"Yes, sir."

"Good work."

"Thank you, sir."

On the way to her office, she stopped by Uniform Carmichael's cube. "Run it through for me."

"Detectives Carmichael and Santiago caught one down on Avenue B. We're support, just crowd control. We spot the illegals deal going down, five feet away. Can't just ignore it, but since we've got a body coming out, we're just going to move them along. Dealer? He's hands up, no problem. Chemi-head's jonesing some, and he just punched her. Sucker punch, sir. She took him down, and fast, I'll give her that. A little bit on the reckless side, maybe, but it's her eye his fist punched. We hauled them both in, with Assaulting an Officer added to the doper.

"She can take a punch," Uniform Carmichael added. "I'll give her that, too."

"Keep her tight for a few days, and let's see how she rolls."

Before somebody else wanted her for anything else, Eve cut straight through to her office. She programmed coffee, black, without bothering to take off her coat.

She stood by her skinny window drinking the coffee, her whiskey-colored cop's eyes scanning the street traffic below, the sky traffic above.

She had paperwork—there was always paperwork—and she'd get to it. But she had just closed an ugly case, and had spent the morning testifying over another ugly case. She supposed they were all ugly, but some twisted harder than others.

So she wanted a minute with her coffee and the city she'd sworn to protect and serve.

Maybe, if she was lucky, a quiet night would follow. Just her and Roarke, she thought. Some wine, some dinner, maybe a vid, some sex. When a murder cop ended up with a busy billionaire businessman, quiet nights at home were like the biggest, shiniest prize in the box.

Thank God he wanted those quiet nights, too.

Maybe sometimes they did the fancy bits—it was part of the deal, part of the Marriage Rules in her book. And more than sometimes he worked with her over pizza in her home office. The reformed criminal with the mind of a cop? A hell of a tool.

So maybe a quiet night for both of them.

She set the coffee on her desk, took off her coat and tossed it over her deliberately uncomfortable visitor's chair. Paperwork, she reminded herself, and started to rake her hand through her hair. Hit the snowflake hat she tried not to let embarrass her. After tossing that on top of the coat, she finger-combed her short, choppy cap of brown hair, sat.

"Computer," she began, and her desk 'link sounded.

"Dallas."

"Dispatch, Dallas, Lieutenant Eve."

Even before the rest, she knew the shiny prize would have to stay in the box for a while.

With her partner, Eve walked from Sixth Avenue where she'd double-parked her DLE.

With a scarf of purple-and-green zigzags wrapped around her neck, Peabody clomped along the path, shooting unhappy looks at the snow blanketing everything else.

"I figured, hey, we'd be in court, and we got temps in the

forties, I can wear my cowgirl boots no problem. If we've got to go tramping through the snow—"

"It's January. And what cop wears pink to a murder trial?"

"Reo had on red shoes," Peabody pointed out, referring to the APA. "Red's just dark pink when you think about it."

When Eve thought about it, she wondered why the hell they were talking about footwear when they had three DBs on tap. "Suck it up."

She flashed her badge when they came to the first police line, kept walking—ignored reporters who pushed against that line and shouted questions.

Somebody had their head on right, she decided, holding the media hounds back out of sight of the rink. That wouldn't last, but it kept what was bound to be complicated a little simpler for the time being.

She spotted more than a dozen uniforms coming or going and at least fifty civilians. Raised voices, a few edged with hysteria, carried clearly.

"I thought we'd have more civilians, more witnesses."

Eve kept scanning. "Bodies drop, people run. We probably lost half of them before the first-on-scene got here." She shook her head. "Media doesn't need to get within camera range. They're going to have dozens of people sending them vids."

Since nothing could be done about that, Eve set it aside, flashed through the next barricade.

As she did, a uniform peeled off, lumbered toward her. She recognized the thirty-plus-years vet, and knew the relative order established was due to his experience and no-bullshit style.

"Fericke."

He gave her a nod. He had a dark bulldog face on a broad-chested bulldog body. And eyes of bitter chocolate-brown that had seen it all, and expected to see worse at any moment.

"Hell of a mess."

"Run it through for me."

"Got the first dispatch at 'round fifteen-twenty. I'm baby-walking a rook, and had him doing some foot patrol on Sixth, so we hotfooted it. Had him start a line back aways, keep people out. But Christ on a crutch, you can't block the whole freaking park."

"You're first-on-scene."

"Yeah. Nine-one-ones started pumping in and so did cops, but people were already running from the scene when I got here. Had to work with park security to hold what we could. Had some injuries. We got MTs in to treat the minors, but we had a kid, about six, broken leg. The way the wit reports shake out—once you cut through the crap—is the first vic collided with him and the kid's parents, and the kid's leg got broke in the fall. Got their contact info, and the hospital for you."

"Peabody."

"I'll take that information, Officer."

He reeled it off without pulling out his notebook.

"Sweepers aren't going to be happy about the state of the crime scene. People all the fuck over it, and the bodies've been moved around. Had a medical on the ice, and a vet—an animal doc—and they worked on the vics, and the injured.

"First vic took it in the back. That's the female out there, in red." He turned, gestured with a lift of that bulldog chin. "Wit statements aren't clear about which got hit second, but you got two males, one gut shot, one between the fucking eyes. Looks like a laser strike to me, LT, but I don't wanna tell you your job. And you're going to hear from some of these wits about knives and suspicious individuals, and the usual crap."

You didn't make lieutenant without wading through, and learning to cut through, the usual crap.

"All right. You got the doctors on tap?"

"Yeah. Got them inside the locker room, got another couple in there, too, who claim they were the first to reach one of the male vics. And the wife of one of the male vics. She's firm he was the last hit, and I lean toward that."

"Peabody, take them, and I'll start on the bodies. I want the security discs, and I want them now."

"They got them ready for you," Fericke told her. "Ask for Spicher. He's rink security, and not altogether a dickhead."

"I'm on it." Peabody headed off, careful to avoid the snow.

"Gonna want some grippers for your boots," Fericke told Eve. "Pile of them up there. Hotshot murder cop face-planting on the ice wouldn't inspire confidence."

"Hold the line, Fericke."

"It's what we do."

She walked around to the rink's entrance, strapping on a pair of the toothy grips before opening her field kit and sealing her hands and boots.

"Hey! Hey! Are you in charge? Who's in fucking charge?"

She glanced over, locking eyes with a red-faced man of about forty who was wearing a thick white sweater and black skin pants.

"I'm in charge."

"You have no right to hold me! I have an appointment."

"Mister . . ."

"Granger. Wayne Granger, and I know my rights!"

"Mr. Granger, do you see the three people lying on the rink?"

"Of course I see them."

"Their rights trump yours."

He shouted after her as she worked her way across the ice to the female victim, something about police states and lawsuits. Looking down at the girl in red—couldn't have been more than twenty years old—Eve didn't give him another thought.

Blood pooled under her, spreading more red on the ice. She lay on her side, and Eve could clearly see bloody marks where other skaters, and the medicals, had gone through.

Her eyes, a bright, summer blue, already glazed with death, stared, and one hand laid, palm up, in her own blood.

No, she didn't give Granger and his appointment another thought.

She crouched down, opening her field kit and did her job.

She didn't rise or turn when Peabody came out.

"Vic is Ellissa Wyman, age nineteen. Still lives with her parents and younger sister, Upper West. TOD, fifteen-fifteen. ME will determine COD, but I agree with Fericke. It looks like a laser strike."

"The doctors—both of them—agree. And the vet? He was an Army corpsman, so he's seen laser strikes. They didn't do more than look at her—she was obviously gone. One tried working on the gut shot, and the other examined the head shot—but they were all gone. So they focused on the injured."

Eve rose with a nod. "Security discs."

"Right here."

Eve plugged one of the discs into her own PPC, cued it to fifteen-fourteen, and focused first on the girl in red.

"She's good," Peabody commented. "Her form, I mean. She's building up some speed there, and—"

She broke off when the girl shot through the air, form gone, and collided with the young family.

Eve rewound it, backed up another minute, and now scanned the other skaters, the onlookers.

"People are giving her room," Eve murmured, "some are watching her. I don't see any weapons."

She let it play through, watched the second victim jerk back, eyes widening, knees buckling.

Ran it back, noted the time. Ran it forward.

"Less than six seconds between strikes."

People skated to the first vic and the family. Security came rushing out. And the couple skating—poorly—along the rail—slowed. The man glanced back. And the strike.

"Just over six seconds for the third. Three shots in roughly twelve seconds, three dead—center back, gut, forehead. That's not luck. And none of those strikes came from the rink or around it. Tell Fericke, when he's got all names and contacts, that anyone who has given a statement can go. Except for the medicals and the third vic's wife.

"Get a full statement from all three of them, and contact

whoever the vic's wife wants. The female's cleared for bagging, tagging, and transpo to the morgue. And we need park security feeds."

"Which sector?"

"All of them."

Leaving Peabody gaping, Eve crossed the ice to the second victim.

When she finished with the bodies, she went inside.

The two medicals sat together on a bench in a locker area, drinking coffee out of go-cups.

Eve nodded to the uniform, dismissing her, then sat on the bench across from them. "I'm Lieutenant Dallas. You've given statements to my partner, Detective Peabody."

They both nodded, the one on the left—trim, close-shaven, mid-thirties—nodded. "Nothing we could do for the three who were killed. By the time we got to them, they were gone."

"Doctor?"

"Sorry. Dr. Lansing. I thought, I honestly thought the girl—the girl in the red suit, had just taken a bad spill. And the little boy, he was screaming. I was right there, that is, right behind them when it happened. So I tried to get to him, first. I started to move the girl, to get to the little boy, and realized she wasn't hurt or unconscious. I heard Matt shouting for everyone to get off the ice, to get clear."

"Matt."

"That's me. Matt Brolin. I saw the collision—saw that girl go into her turn for a jump, saw her propelled forward into the family. I was going to go help, then I saw the guy go down, saw him drop. Even then I didn't put it together. But I saw the third one, I saw the strike, and I knew. I was a corpsman. Twenty-six years ago, but it doesn't leave you. We were under attack, and I wanted people to get to cover."

"You two know each other."

"We do now," Brolin said. "I knew the third guy was gone—hell of a sniper strike, but I tried to do what I could for the second one. He was still alive, Lieutenant. He looked at me. I remembered that look—and it's a hard one to remember. He wasn't going to make it, but you've got to do what you can do."

"He shielded the guy with his own body," Lansing put in. "People panicked, and I swear some would've skated right over that man, but Matt shielded him."

"Jack had his hands full with the little boy, and the parents got banged around some, too. Right?"

"They didn't have time to break their own fall," Lansing explained. "The father's got a mild concussion, the mother a sprained wrist. They'll be all right. The boy, too, but he got the worst of it. Security had a first aid kit. I gave him a little something for the pain. The MTs were here inside of two minutes. You have to give them credit. I went to help Matt. And we had to try on the last one. But like Matt said, he was gone. Gone before he hit the ice."

"Nothing to do but do some basic first aid on people who'd taken falls or cut themselves on blades—skates," Matt added. He scrubbed a hand over his scruffy gray beard. "It wasn't until they put us in here that it came back to me. You've got to put it away when you're working."

"Put what away?"

"The fear. The fear you could take a strike in the back of the head any second. Whoever shot those people? They've got skills. It came from the east. The strikes."

"How can you know that?"

"I saw the third hit. Saw the angle, the way the guy was turned. From the east." His eyes narrowed on Eve's. "You already knew that."

"I reviewed the security discs. We'll reconstruct, but at this point I agree with you."

"His wife's in the office over there, with your partner. Her parents just got here." Brolin heaved out a breath. "This is why I went to veterinary school when I got out of the Army. Dogs and cats? Easier to handle than people."

"You handled people just fine. Both of you. I want to thank you for what you did here today. We have your contact information if we need to talk to you again. You can reach me at Cop Central if you need to talk to me. Lieutenant Dallas."

"We can go?" Lansing asked.

"Yes."

"How about that beer?"

Brolin managed a weak smile. "How about a couple of them?"

"First round's on me." Lansing pushed to his feet. "People come here to enjoy the park, to take their kids for a little adventure. Or like that girl, for the joy. She was a pleasure to watch. And now . . ."

He broke off, shook his head. "Yeah, first round's on me."

As they went out, a man and a woman with security badges on lanyards, stepped in.

"Lieutenant Dallas. I'm Carly Deen, rink security, and this is Paul Spicher. Is there anything else we can do. Anything?"

"Who's head of security?"

"That would be me." Carly, no more than five-two and a hundred pounds, lifted her shoulders. "People assume it's Paul. He's the muscle." She said it as a joke, struggling to smile.

"Okay. We're going to have to keep you closed down until further notice."

"We've already taken care of that. The media's bombarding the main 'link, but we've put it on record—just your standard 'The rink's closed.' One of them managed to get my personal number, but I've blocked it."

"Keep doing that. I need you to keep off the ice. You and any of your staff, until that's cleared. Crime Scene techs will come in shortly. Did you know any of the victims?"

"Ellissa. Ellissa Wyman. She's here almost daily during the season. She was going to try out for this skating troupe." Carly lifted her hands, dropped them. "She was nice. Friendly. She'd bring her kid sister sometimes."

"I knew Mr. Michaelson, a little," Paul added.

Second vic, Eve thought. Brent Michaelson—doctor— age sixty-three, divorced, one offspring.

"From here?"

"He liked to skate, would take an afternoon. Every other Tuesday. Nothing fancy, nothing like Ellissa, but he was a regular. Once in a while he'd bring his grandkids—evenings or Saturdays for that. He liked the solo in the afternoons. I never saw the other guy before."

Paul glanced toward the office.

"The one whose wife's in my office," Carly added. "Your partner's with her. She's good with her. Is there anything we can do for you, Lieutenant?"

"Give us your office for a little while more."

"As long as you need."

"I'm sure my partner asked, but so will I. Have either one of you noticed anyone coming around, either to skate or to watch, anyone who seemed too interested in Ellissa or Brent Michaelson?"

"Not like this. A lot of people hang around longer when Ellissa's skating. And there've been a couple of boys off and on who hit on her. But nothing over the top. We keep an eye out," Carly continued. "We don't have a lot of trouble. Pushy-shovies, your basic collisions."

"More trouble at night, but even then." Paul shrugged. "You get an asshole who starts a fight. Sorry about the *asshole*," he added.

"I'm rarely sorry about assholes," Eve commented. "We'll be in touch when you're clear. I'd advise your brass to coordinate with the police liaison on a statement. Timing and content."

"They're—the brass—they're going to be in a spin about lawsuits."

"The brass always is," Eve said, moving to the office.

Inside, a woman in her early thirties sat in a folding chair, flanked by a man and a woman. Each had an arm around her while Peabody crouched on the floor, talking softly.

Peabody took the woman's hand when Eve entered. "Jenny, this is Lieutenant Dallas."

Jenny looked up with devastated eyes. "We saw the vid. Alan really liked it. You look like you did in the vid. I mean like the actress did. I don't know what to do."

"I'm sorry for your loss, Mrs. Markum. I know Detective Peabody has already talked to you. If I could just have a few more minutes."

"We were skating. We're terrible skaters. And we were laughing. We were taking the whole day together, and tonight, too. It's our anniversary. Five years today."

She turned her face into the man's shoulder.

"They had their first date here." He cleared his throat, but it didn't clear the faint Irish accent that made Eve think of Roarke. "I'm Liam O'Dell, Jenny's father. This is Kate Hollis, her mother."

"It was my idea, the skating. Let's do everything we did on our first date. It was my idea to come here, like we did that day. We both took off work, and we were going to get pizza afterward, just like we did on our first date. That's when I was going to tell him why I wasn't having wine like we did then. I was going to tell him I'm pregnant."

"Oh. Oh, baby." Her mother drew her in close so they clung and shuddered together. "Oh, my baby."

"I was going to tell him, then we were going to tell you and Daddy and Alan's mom and dad. But we were going to have today, all day."

As Peabody had, Eve crouched so she was eye level. "Jenny, who else knew you'd be here today?"

"Sherry, my friend, and I think her guy—Charlie. They're our friends. I told Mom. We really just decided a couple days ago. I pushed for it when I took the test and it was positive."

"Did Alan have any enemies, anyone he had trouble with?"

"No. No. Detective Peabody asked, and just no. People like Alan. He's a teacher. We're teachers, and he helps coach soccer, and, and volunteers at the homeless shelter. Everyone likes Alan. Why would anyone hurt him? Why?"

"We're going to do everything we can to find out. You can contact me or Detective Peabody anytime."

"I don't know what to do."

"You should go with your mom." Liam leaned over, kissed her head. "Go home with your mom now."

"Daddy—"

"I'll come. I'll be there." He looked over her head to Kate, got a teary nod. "Go with your mom, darling, and I'll be coming right along."

"Peabody."

"Come with me. We'll have an officer take you home."

Liam sat where he was as Peabody led them out.

"We're divorced, you see, and Kate, she's married again. Eight years. Or is it nine?" He shook his head. "But such things don't matter a bit now, do they?" As he rose, he cleared his throat again. "He was a good man, our Alan. A good and stable man who loved my girl with his whole heart. You'll find who took him from her, from my girl and from the baby inside her."

"We'll do everything we can."

"I saw the vid, and read the book as well. That Icove business. You'll find who took the life of this good young man."

Eyes blurred with tears, he hurried out.

Eve sat, took a moment to clear away the grief that hung so thick in the air. Then pulled out her 'link.

"Lowenbaum." SWAT commander—the best she knew. "I need a consult."

"I'm getting rumors about Central Park."

"I'm confirming them. I need an expert consult."

"And to think I was going off tour. I can be at the rink in—"

"Not the rink, not yet. I've got security feed, and I need a good screen. My place isn't far from here. Can you come there?"

"The Dallas Palace?"

"Bite me, Lowenbaum."

He laughed, then just grinned at her. "Yeah, I can come there." The grin faded. "I get conflicting numbers on vics."

"Three. And it's my sense it could've been a hell of a lot worse."

"If it can get worse, it usually does."

"That's why I need the consult. I think it could get worse. I have to do the notifications. Can you be there in an hour?"

"Can do."

"Appreciate it."

She clicked off as Peabody came back.

"I need you to go to the hospital—or check and see if the kid with the broken leg and his parents are still there. Wherever they are, go there. See what they saw, write it up. I'll do the notifications."

"I'm still working on the security feeds. It's a big park."

"Have them sent to my home and office units. We can start with sectors east of the rink. Have them sent to your home and office units, too. I want you to study them—get McNab to study them. You flag anything or anyone that looks off. If this came from inside the park, we're looking for an individual with some sort of bag or case."

"If?"

Eve stepped out of the office, scanned the empty locker room. "Because I'm betting it came from outside the park. We're going to be looking at buildings with west-facing windows, starting with Sixth, working east until Lowenbaum tells me to stop."

"Lowenbaum?"

"He's coming in to consult. I want this rink feed on my screens at home, with equipment that doesn't argue with me."

"Lowenbaum. He's so cute." At Eve steely stare, Peabody hunched her shoulders. "I'm with McNab through and through, but I can see cuteness through my eyes and my Cute-O-Meter. You have to admit, he ranks high on the Cute-O-Meter."

"Cute's for kids and puppies—if you're into kids and puppies. I'll give you he's frosty enough."

"Completely. I'll push on the security feeds, and see if I can find anything new from the kid and his parents." As she spoke, Peabody began to rewind her long scarf. "We're going to be wading through piles of wit statements."

"Take the first ten. I'll start on the rest. Let's see if we can find anything that connects the three vics other than a visit to the skating rink. And let's hope we do. If this was pure random, it's already gotten worse."

As she stepped outside, Eve looked over the heads of the sweepers busy working on the scene, and stared east.

Again she thought: It could get a lot worse.

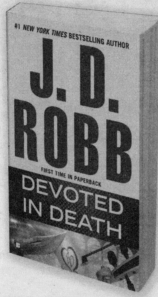

From #1 *New York Times* Bestselling Author

J. D. ROBB

THE IN DEATH SERIES

jdrobb.com
facebook.com/jdrobbauthor
penguin.com

Penguin
Random
House

BERKLEY

M1732AS1015